CRASH AL1VE

CRASH ALIVE

CHRISTOPHER KERNS

OLD BALLARD PRESS

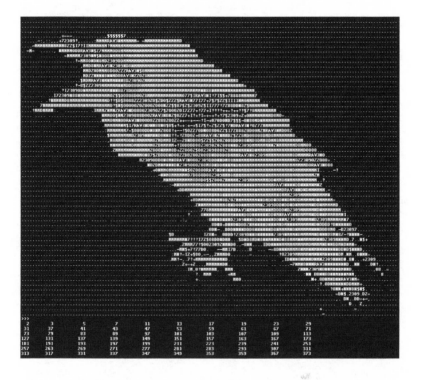

All hacks and exploits in this book are based on real technology.

PROLOGUE

The passenger in seat 5A took a deep breath, fighting to calm his heart as it pounded through his neatly-pressed oxford shirt. He had spent the past few minutes deflecting the stares of travelers filing by—*how did that teenage punk get into first class?*—but they could gawk all they wanted. He had bigger things on his mind.

The plane climbed into the night, pulling him back into his seat. He wiped the sweat from his brow and drew a long sip of ice water, resting his cup back on his armrest with a trembling hand.

He couldn't remember the last time he was this excited about something. About *anything*.

The bell signaled that the aircraft had arrived at thirty thousand feet, and passenger 5A rushed to slide his laptop from his bag. He made a quick sideways check of the person next to him; she had already fallen fast asleep, mouth agape and head flopped, spilling into the aisle like a rag doll. He logged in to his machine, connected to the Wi-Fi, and checked for any new messages, finding nothing.

He pulled the USB drive from his pocket, slowly flipping the metal rectangle end over end, again and again. As his thumb inspected the feel of raised text painted on stainless steel, he thought back to the times when he had looked forward to visiting New York; staying with his parents in modern hotels, going out for brisk family walks through Central Park. After his Dad had moved post-divorce, passenger 5A now found himself on this same boring flight every third Sunday of every month—every damn month—and the shine had worn clean off New York City. But today, that might have all changed.

When he had found the USB drive earlier that afternoon in a Starbucks at the corner of 5th and Lexington, his first reaction was to search the room for its owner. But the coffee shop was, like many in midtown Manhattan, without the luxury of extra space for anything as silly as tables or ambiance. When he had noticed the text on the drive's casing—'DEPARTMENT OF DEFENSE'—well, that had obviously piqued his interest. The device had just been sitting there like a surprise gift on Christmas morning, resting on the dark wooden rail, wedged between a stained stir stick and a flat spray of spent sugar.

This is the coolest thing that's ever happened to me. It's just like a movie.

He angled his screen towards the window and wedged himself into the far corner of his seat. After a few attempts at getting the drive into the Mac's USB slot—*why don't these things work both ways?*—he felt the click of the drive finding its mark.

He opened the drive and saw a single file inside: a PDF document. Double-clicking the icon brought up a security dialog displaying a block of official-looking text. It read:

This message has been encrypted by the Department of Defense. If you are authorized to decrypt, click Open below.

He checked on his seatmate—still fast asleep—opened his eyes wide, and clicked. *This is so awesome.* He inhaled a deep breath as the PDF window filled his screen.

"Excuse me, young man?"

His head bolted up, swiveling towards the aisle as he slammed his laptop's lid shut with one quick motion. The flight attendant jumped back. Her cherub face studied his every move as she stood in the aisle, holding a cup of assorted nuts close to her chest. She took a few breaths and forced a polite, airline-mandated smile.

"My goodness, darling, you scared me half to death. Can I get you anything?"

"I'm fine," he said, catching his breath. "I'm good with the water—thanks."

The attendant shrugged and made her way back to the front of the plane. After checking to make sure the coast was clear, passenger 5A cracked the computer's lid back open and leaned in.

His mind raced, wondering if he would find government secrets, launch codes, or lists of foreign agents. *Could I sell this stuff if it's good enough? Not that I would do that, but ... never say never, you know?*

As his eyes met the screen, his expression fell with confusion. All he saw on the first page was an empty slate of white. *There has to be something here—maybe it starts on page two.*

He clicked through the PDF and scrolled down, page after page. Fifteen pages later he had reached the end of the document and hadn't found a thing.

It was blank. It was *all* blank. He backtracked, checking the document a second time. A third time. No dice.

Nice job, super-spy. Great work today.

He chuckled softly to himself, stretched his arms above his head for a moment, and hit COMMAND-Q. He leaned back in his seat, stretched his legs forward, and stared through the thick window pane into the blackness. He watched as the tiny, white lights flew by below—just like they had on every flight home, every month before.

He thought back to the littered Starbucks counter on 5th and Lexington, exhaled, and closed the lid of his laptop.

Maybe something exciting would happen tomorrow.

Maybe tomorrow.

> > > > >

Seconds after being plugged in, the 'DEPARTMENT OF DEFENSE' drive began building its own proxy server on the root directory of passenger 5A's laptop. After testing the airplane's Wi-Fi connection and speed, the script began to ping a handful of Tor servers—a network of untraceable machines—and activated secondary scripts pinging thousands of other IP addresses. One of those pings sent a twenty-four-digit ID to a server in Southeast Asia.

That server quickly compromised the networks of all fifteen hydroelectric and six geothermal power plants in Iceland, gaining full access to each plant's internal systems.

Seconds later, the script began quietly shutting down the backup generator systems in those plants by toggling power breakers on and off in a pattern that was designed to disrupt the timing of the rotating parts in each machine, silently confusing and crippling each system without triggering a warning. The script then went to work on the primary generators, shutting them down as well, starting in the north and working its way south.

The script continued, attacking every major Internet data center and server bank in Iceland, rendering all Internet traffic silent and bringing down the IP-based landline phone networks throughout the country.

Iceland's two mobile service providers were then hit with a distributed denial-of-service attack, using an IP-based SIM-card emulator to mimic millions of simultaneous phone calls all within the same three second window. Both cellular networks, now already running on local backup power, were inaccessible within twenty seconds.

The script was designed to wipe clean the USB drive, still sticking out of the side of the machine, after completing its final steps. It could have easily formatted the laptop's hard drive to destroy all traces of the attack, but that might alert the FBI to the source. A normal-looking machine could buy a few extra days of questioning, and that time would be invaluable for the next stage of The Project.

Within three minutes, the script was one step away from running its course. All internet, landline, and mobile phone service on Iceland was completely shut down. Everything—homes, hospitals, banks, restaurants, schools—were all without power. For the first time in hundreds of years, the entire island was completely dark.

As its final step, the script sent a message to a burner email address. The message read:

Iceland test complete, status: SUCCESS.
We are GREEN for phase 2.

CHAPTER ONE

Bowie High, AP Calculus Class
Austin, TX
March 6th, 2:15PM

"Laptops shut, please."

As Mrs. Chen's commanding voice sounded through the classroom, the last rings of the sixth period bell echoed down the hallway. Haylie Black watched as Mrs. Chen pushed the door shut, watching the room for compliance.

Haylie pulled her shoulder-length, chestnut hair back behind her neck and felt an anxious air fill the room. She plucked her glasses—only good for seeing at a distance—off her desk and slid them onto her face, pushing them carefully up onto her nose. Her fingers drummed nervously across the top of her MacBook as she eyed the thick stack of papers in Mrs. Chen's hand.

Haylie's least-favorite teacher silently surveyed the class. Mrs. Chen was legendary for her enjoyment of tense moments, especially when papers were about to be handed back. You could hear a pin drop as she leaned back against her desk and savored every second.

"As you have probably figured out, I finished grading your tests. The midpoint score ended up at eighty-two. As a reminder, anyone who scored above the midpoint will make the Math Team roster and hopefully help us get back to nationals this year. Anyone below the curve sits out," Mrs. Chen said with a confident smirk. "I already know the test was fair, so please don't bother with any complaints."

Haylie saw a few nodding heads in the room mixed with a smattering of nervous smiles. As she thought back through her answers, she could feel the weight of her parents' expectations sitting firmly on her shoulders.

Pacing slowly and purposefully, Mrs. Chen moved through the room handing back tests alphabetically by first name, as always. The class watched for a reaction as the first student received her score. As the nervous girl's eyes searched for the red number circled at the top of her paper, she sighed a gasp of relief, closed her eyes and mouthed a few silent words to herself. Whispers cascaded across the class.

Haylie watched on, quietly calculating how long it would take for Mrs. Chen to reach her test in the stack. *Do your worst, Chen. I dare you.*

The next boy received his test and oh-so-subtly pumped his fists into the air, receiving a light round of laughter from the room.

Mrs. Chen continued to work her way through the classroom as all eyes watched the drama play out. A mixture of bowed heads and high fives accompanied paper after paper. Another classmate received his test and hung his head low, and Haylie suddenly realized that her name was up next.

She tugged at the lapels of her favorite coat—a drab olive green field jacket that was just plain enough, but still counted as some sort of fashion statement—trying her best to remain calm as she felt Mrs. Chen's slow, methodical footsteps approaching her from behind. Over her shoulder, a few pieces of stapled paper flopped down on her desk. Haylie continued staring straight ahead, refusing to make eye contact with reality for a few short seconds.

You better not have screwed this one up, Einstein. Haylie slowly looked down to the red ink at the top of the page.

It read: '80.'

As Haylie exhaled, placing her head in her hands, she was greeted with a tap on the shoulder. A classmate sitting at the desk next to her gave Haylie a reassuring pat.

"I'm sorry, Haylie. I was hoping you'd make it this year," she said with full eyes that were still searching for the right thing to say. "I'm sure everyone was."

Haylie sighed and stared off into the distance, fighting to hide the emotion trying to push its way out. She was already working on a plan for how she'd break the news to her parents. She could feel a growing collection of stares from across the room, watching her like a zoo animal.

"All right everyone," Mrs. Chen said, standing with folded arms back at the front of the class. "Now that you know where you stand, we'll be kicking off Math Team preparations for the rest of the period. Anyone that didn't make the cut this year—and I'm sorry if you didn't—please head down to the library to complete your daily assignment there. We'll just need you to try a little harder next year, yes?"

A walk of shame—how degrading.

Haylie quickly gathered her things, placed her laptop into her backpack and gave a timid wave to the girl next to her. She tried her best not to make eye contact with any other students as she shuffled down the long aisle. Looking back, she could see others packing up. All around them, the members of the newly formed Bowie High Math Team scattered around the room to congratulate their new teammates.

Haylie was the first one out of the classroom, letting the door shut behind her. She paced down the empty hallway, throwing her backpack onto her shoulders. Finally alone, the tidal wave building up inside of her crested.

A wide, unforgiving smile crept slowly across her face.

Haylie had spent the past week carefully gathering test score data for her AP Calculus class. Mrs. Chen's admin account had been easy enough to hack with a simple dictionary attack—a script that guesses combinations of words, numbers, and other characters until it finds the right match. *Easy stuff—not exactly NSA-level security around here.* Once inside the system, Haylie had grabbed data on each student's performance for each test, quiz, and homework assignment for the year and then left the system without a trace.

By mapping the scoring data across topic categories in a database, Haylie had created a working predictive model for the distribution of scores on the Math Team qualifying test. She had guessed the midpoint of the grades would be eighty-four, so as it turned out, her model still needed a little bit of work.

After calculating the predicted midpoint of the test scores, the rest was easy. Haylie knew the answer to any math question Ms. Chen could ever throw at her, so after completing a first pass with one hundred percent of the answers correct, she backtracked and added a combination of errors that would land her score directly under the dividing line.

It was important for her to balance her strategy—she wanted to score well enough that her parents wouldn't worry about her, but at the same time poorly enough to stay off the goddamned Math Team this year.

As she walked the long, echoing hallway towards the library, she could hear the clicks and thumps of footsteps behind her. Focusing her hearing, she thought she could even make out a few sniffles from the poor students following her down the hall.

Get it together. Good lord, it's only math.

CHAPTER TWO

Bowie High Library
Austin, TX
March 6th, 2:42PM

Haylie pushed her way through the double doors, pulling her hands back into the pockets of her jacket and turning the corner towards the study area. The library was crowded today—more crowded than usual—and she stopped to lean her shoulder on a bookshelf marking the corner of the study area. She peeked her head around the edge to survey the crowd.

Small groups of students were huddled around their tables, all with computers open and screens glowing, leaving only a few empty spaces remaining. Haylie quickly evaluated her options as she pushed her glasses up the bridge of her nose.

The first table featured a collection of guys—lacrosse players, as far as she could tell. T-shirts and mesh athletic shorts, large bottles of water and snacks scattered across the table top; none of them paying any attention to their work. *Pass.*

The second table included six of what had to be the most popular girls in Haylie's senior class, assuming they were still in the lead this week. They sat in tight pairs, flashing smirks across their faces and exchanging sideways sneers past heavy coatings of mascara as they texted back and forth, giggling with each volley. Telling secrets, spreading gossip. *No thanks.*

The third table was a mix of girls and guys that Haylie recognized, students she could give a passing smile to in the hallway and not feel like an idiot. Haylie had played on the JV field hockey team with a few of the girls freshman year. She had loved field hockey practice—and she was damn good at it, too—but had always hated the games. The build up, the travel, the crowds, the screaming parents; it just wasn't for her.

She spied one open seat at the table, tucked in close to the center of the group. Clutching the straps of her backpack with both hands, she sucked in a deep breath.

Just walk over. It's that easy. Don't think about it.

Her heart pounded as the pit of her stomach began to ache. Staring down the empty seat, she swayed back and forth, finding her bearing against the bookshelf with one extended hand. *Don't think about it.*

She began to think about it. She couldn't help it.

Her mind began to run through scenarios. What-ifs. Walking up, having them tell her that the seat was already taken. Laughing at her as she walked away. Or worse: inviting her to sit, and then giving her the silent treatment, like those kids did a few years back at lunch.

She began breathing heavier and heavier as she imagined being denied. Being mocked. In front of everyone.

Turning away, she paced quickly across the room to the windows lining the far wall of the library, stopping at the row of multi-colored bean bags. She faced the shelves, focusing on just breathing for a few seconds.

She released her bag to the floor with a plop, took off her jacket, and sunk into her seat, now with a full view of the room. She felt a burning ache in her gut—twisting and churning—as her eyes moved from table to table, like flipping channels to observe each group. Some chatted in low tones. Others kept their heads down, working in parallel, exchanging chuckles as they pointed at screens and leaned in close.

Haylie squirmed to find a better position in the quicksand of her chair as she thought back to the Calculus classroom, picturing the members of the Math Team hard at work selecting a clever, geeky, slightly ironic, and totally lame name to put on their inevitable t-shirts and bumper stickers. The fact that she was here, and not there, made her feel a bit better—she knew that despite the awkward nature of study hall, she had made the right call to dodge the math nerds.

Haylie had a long history of playing the same game set forth by every new teacher, year after year. A few weeks after each school year started, a familiar pattern would go into motion; as teachers discovered her "gifted" abilities, they'd rush to take her under their wing. She would quickly be awarded with heaps of extra homework or an invitation to join the Physics Club, something to "make the most of her potential." Haylie had turned avoiding this extra work into a sport, bobbing and weaving, trying to stay one step ahead. A few months back, she had made the mistake of getting a perfect score on a national German language test, which awarded her an all-expense paid trip to Berlin for five days to study the geo-political advances since the Cold War. It had taken weeks to wiggle her way out of that one.

It's not that Haylie wasn't up for a challenge, quite the opposite. She became a bit obsessed when she saw something on the other side of the fence—a website, a system, anything—and was told "you're not allowed to go over there." When she was problem-solving, she often found herself getting lost in the question, working through step after step, only to look up at the clock hours later to realize she had just lost a whole night. She knew she'd wasted countless hours figuring out how things worked, but it was a point of pride that she had never failed to get into a system when she had put her mind to it. Never.

Haylie pulled her laptop from her backpack and cracked the lid open, blindly typing in her password and opening up her to-do list. *Ok, focus. Get your work done so tonight you can–*

Suddenly, there was a loud ping that rang out of her computer's speakers and echoed down into each corner of the library, shattering the hushed silence. Haylie scrambled to hit the mute button on her machine.

Her grimace morphed into relief as she saw the author's name— it was Vector, the big idiot, who she hadn't chatted with in almost three waking hours. That might be a new record.

> **VECTOR:>** yo Crash. i'm organizing my media files again. should i go alphabetically or by sub-genre? i think the categories should change with my mood, tho.

After thinking for a moment, her eyes looking up and to the left, a slow smile crept across her lips. She dove back into the screen, her fingers clicking methodically across the keyboard, chuckling under her breath.

CRASH:> Good question. I feel like
you're one of those unrecognized
geniuses but in your case, no one calls
you a genius because you're not actually
all that smart. How does that feel? Does
it feel bad?

Vector, of course, wasn't his real name. His online handle just became second nature to her over the years, just like the screen name she had chosen long ago on a whim: Crash.

The chat window popped back onto the screen.

VECTOR:> you're hilarious. I'm two
months younger than you, remember? I'm
sure I'll be on your heels in the next
few weeks.

VECTOR:> hey - btw, remember that
'sparkstar' python package you were
going on about for network penetration
testing? I can't get it to install.

VECTOR:> you said you got it working,
ya?

CRASH:> yeah. but you'll probably need
to upgrade virtualenv to the latest
version. that worked for me.

VECTOR:> ugh, that's a pain in the arse.
how'd you get so smart?

CRASH:> I'm a girl, remember?

VECTOR:> of course.

VECTOR:> right, getting late, better
crack on to my new gig. i'm done with
the city of london work for now... but i
landed that new project for the
department of transport.

CRASH:> Oh, sweet. What kind of stuff?

VECTOR:> some logistics around air
travel, rail, traffic, etc. can't go on
about it much past that yet.

```
VECTOR:> cool data to play with. lots of
python and SQL work. Should be a nice
one.
```

Haylie gazed off across the library with the glint of hope in her eye. *That sounds so awesome—I can't wait to get out of this place.* With just a few months left, she was ready to run out the door as soon as it cracked open. At her parents' request, she had applied early—and been accepted—to the University of Texas in Austin, one of the best computer science schools in the country. She was due to start in the fall, but hadn't broken the news to her family that she had no intention of going. Haylie's head was filled with too many things she wanted to do and plus, college felt like it was going to be just more of ... this.

```
VECTOR:> oh, sending you a link to a
torrent of that old film, the one I was
talking about that you have to see.
Summer School, from the 80s.
VECTOR:> i can't stop watching it, it's
a whole thing.
```

Smiling, Haylie sent him back a thumbs up. She couldn't remember a time that she hadn't known Vector. She knew his favorite cereal, the bands he listened to, and that he had graduated from school the previous year. He had skipped college—they call it "university" over in the UK, apparently—and dove right into starting his own consulting company in London. To Haylie, it all sounded like a dream come true.

```
VECTOR:> so why did you bail on me last
night? we were due to watch WarGames
together. you left me hanging, mate.
CRASH:> sorry. My mom had a dinner thing
at our house for some local 'leaders of
industry'. I was asked to make an
appearance.
VECTOR:> ugh. your favorite.
```

When it came to family, Haylie had been dealt a royal flush, at least from the outside looking in. Her parents were great, but just not around a lot. Her dad was some sort of business consultant—always on the road, always on the phone. Haylie loved the time she got to spend with him, but that time seemed to drift away more and more every year. Her mother was supportive and brilliant but increasingly distracted by work. A few years back, she had accepted an offer to become the CEO of a small firm and promised Haylie that the job wouldn't change their lifestyle. But after the company grew to become one of the fastest growing startups in Austin, things just changed.

It wasn't uncommon for Haylie to walk into her house to find a networking event in progress, with suits everywhere and catered dinners being served from her kitchen. That scenario, year after year, was a great way to make a seventeen-year old feel like a stranger in her own home.

Even worse, she was often paraded around the party, counting the minutes in her head as each local dignitary asked if Haylie wanted to follow in her mother's footsteps. All the conversations, all the people, all the names—it was just too much for her. She never felt as alone as when she was surrounded by a group of people.

VECTOR: so what was your plan this time around to sneak out early? another night hiding in the bathroom?

CRASH: Nah. Faked a sprained ankle.

VECTOR: brilliant.

Haylie cracked her MacBook's lid and reached into her bag, fumbling past a collection of assorted gadgets, loose wires, and tools, searching for her headphones. Over the past few years, she had built up a collection of devices that would make any hacker jealous. Her bedroom was a graveyard of circuit boards, soldering irons and cords—so many cords, everywhere.

Haylie finally found the headphones, untangling the jack from the knotted mess of everything with a silent curse under her breath. The cord pulled a folded piece of paper out of her bag behind it. *What the hell is this?* She held the note up for a moment, unfolding and stretching it out with both hands. She furrowed her brow as she recognized her mother's handwriting.

TRY TO MAKE FRIENDS TODAY!

LOVE, MOM

Haylie crumpled the paper into a ball as she felt the heat of embarrassment climb up her neck, quickly checking the room to make sure she didn't need to do any damage control.

Placing the cups of her headphones over her ears, she gave the volume button a few taps and cranked up a classic Daft Punk mix. She opened her chat application to find no new messages, but clicked over to a recent thread that had gone cold for the past eight days—a three-year-old, twisting and turning chat conversation with her brother, Caesar.

If there was one saving grace for a close connection in her family, it was her older brother. They had grown up together just a few years apart, and definitely operated as a pair of "inside-the-house" kids. Together, they worked on writing computer programs, hacking hardware, and trying their best to stay out of trouble. In most families, the day that a radio or video game controller stopped working was one filled with frustration, but not in the Black household. When something broke, that meant Caesar and Haylie got to crack it open, take it apart and see what was inside. Sometimes they'd even be able to fix it. Not always, but sometimes.

Haylie clicked into the chat thread and scrolled down through the history—scanning messages from the past few years, ever since Caesar had left for New York City to become a hotshot programmer and darling of the tech scene. She missed having him around, but they had racked up enough chat messages back and forth that sometimes she forgot that he had even left home. They pinged each other with a frequency that ebbed and flowed with the activity in their lives—sometimes the messages flew back and forth in volleys of hundreds per day. Other times they would go a few days without any word. The current stretch of silence was the longest Haylie could remember, but she also knew that was her fault—he was waiting on her response.

She slid her finger across the trackpad, clicking on Caesar's last message. She removed her glasses, leaning in closer to the screen, hands pressed against her temples, thinking. It read:

Shelf 3. Take out book 2.

01117322051235612813311

Beyond just chatting about Caesar's job, what it's like to live in New York City, and news from the tech world, Caesar also enjoyed sending over cryptic messages for Haylie to solve from time to time. She didn't remember how or when it started, but now it had become a whole thing. Two or three times every month, Haylie would open a new chat message from Caesar to find only a puzzle; a few lines of cryptic ... something. There was one rule that Caesar always stuck by: until she solved the puzzle, there would be no other messages from him.

You're such a weirdo, Caesar.

Over the years, the clues from her brother had led her into a mix of annoying and fascinating subjects. Some had been eye-opening, introducing her to entire fields of study like cryptography, network hacking, and geolocation. Others—obscure references to Zen Buddhism, magic square math, and super-boring binary code translation—were just, like, *c'mon, dude.* Over the past week, Haylie had been too busy with her math exam hack to give any time to the latest puzzle.

She switched her music over to a new channel and stared at the message. *Ok, let's see what this is all about. Shelf 3 ... I have no idea what that means. And that long number at the end, it must be coded, but where would I start with–*

A loud noise overpowered her music and broke Haylie's concentration. She pulled the headphones down around her neck to hear a round of laughter coming from the table she had almost joined a few minutes earlier. She smiled as she watched the group make faces at each other, whispering with mischievous eyes. It looked like a blast, much better than her self-imposed beanbag solitary confinement, that was for sure.

The laughter was cut by a long, extended "Shhhhhh" from the librarian's desk. The group covered their mouths, hunched over and giggling.

I wonder what they're talking about.

Haylie angled an ear forward, straining to hear the details of the whispers, but they had moved their conversation online, now pointing to chat windows on each other's screens, frantically typing as she sat in her corner, alone. Haylie's eyes narrowed and flicked down to her bag, then back to the group.

Wait - I can find out what they're talking about. That's easy.

Haylie reached deep into the main section of her backpack and searched for one of her favorite new toys. She finally found the battery-powered router she was looking for—a small black box about the size of a deck of cards. As her thumb located the raised switch and slid it into the 'ON' position, the device came to life with a subtle click and a single blinking green light.

Earlier in the year, Haylie had realized that not only was the library's router administration panel accessible through a web interface, they had also left the default password of "admin" intact when installing it. That meant she could get full access to the router any time she wanted.

Sorry about this, everybody. I just need to reboot the Wi-Fi real quick.

As the library's Internet access went dark, she looked up to watch students across the room spin, flailing to figure out what was going on. Whispers filled the room as everyone tried in vain to refresh browser tabs, watching with mild panic as their chat messages and web searches went dark.

"Shhhhhhh!" the librarian repeated, standing from her desk for a moment, and then returning back to her work.

The small black device, now active in Haylie's bag, was a Grapefr00t Wi-Fi router she'd picked up recently. It had a very specific purpose; to conduct a "man-in-the-middle" network attack, which was a simple, but very effective, form of network hacking.

Because the school's network wasn't encrypted—and they were dumb enough to not change the admin password—Haylie had been able to reset all connections to the library's Wi-Fi. As the students came back online, each was now routing all their network traffic through Haylie's device. She could see every web site they visited, every chat message; anything they typed. And no one had a clue that it was happening.

Haylie brought up the Grapefr00t web interface and quickly found device names that had a high probability of matching the kids at the table—she had six out of the seven identified for sure with names like 'AllisonMac' and 'SteveIsAwesome.' She sat and watched the activity flow between the devices.

MARC:> Woah, that was a close one.

17

> RACH:> I know, we almost had to, like, talk to each other.
>
> STEVE-O:> no way, I just would have left the room.

The table chuckled as Haylie smiled, sneaking in closer to her screen. She pulled her headphones back over her ears, leaned in to rest her chin on her palm, and soaked it in. The group's chat flowed with three different subjects at a time: stories from lunch, plans for the weekend, and how boring the library was. As the minutes went by, Haylie found herself getting sucked in to the conversation.

> ALLIE:> so who has the Algebra answers? Rach- I'm guessing you got it done already
>
> RACH:> no way you get those again, cheater. Get your own 100s.
>
> STEVE-O:> I've got it done over here
>
> ALLIE:> no thanks, Stevie. You suck at… everything

Haylie looked up to see everyone at the table holding in their laughter. She shifted in her beanbag, realizing her stomach pains had all but disappeared. *C'mon, Steve. Don't let her walk all over you–*

> STEVE-O:> um, no I don't.

Shaking her head, Haylie held back her laughter. *That's not going to do it, Steve.* She waited, watching the Grapefr00t log to see who would respond first.

> RACH:> great comeback, Steve. Nailed it.

Oh my God, that was classic. She brought her laptop closer to her chest, waiting for the pile-on to begin, as her hand covered her smile. *This is going to be brutal!* She wiggled in her seat, watching the blinking cursor, waiting for them to let him have it. Out of her peripherals, Haylie suddenly saw the heads at the table whip around at her.

Oh no.

With her eyes wide, she pulled her headphones off, realizing what she had just done. She couldn't hear her own stupid giggling through her headphones. She had laughed, out loud, along with the rest of the table as the rest of the library sat in silence. Her eyes jumped between each member of the group, seeing a collection of shocked faces staring back at her.

Just then, the library filled with the harsh, metallic ringing of the bell, marking the end of study hall and the completion of the school day. *That was fun—gotta go.* Haylie shoved her headphones back into her bag, snapped her laptop shut, and jumped up from her chair. She gave the table a quick wave as she made her way towards the exit, feeling her face grow redder with each step.

Haylie pushed the double doors open and let them fall closed behind her.

CHAPTER THR33

Houndstooth Coffee House
Austin, TX
March 6th, 4:55PM

Haylie rolled to a stop under a rare patch of shade and tucked her car into the back corner of the parking lot. Her heart was still pounding as flashbacks to the library sparked through her head. She gripped the worn steering wheel with both hands, twisting her fingers around the cheap, cracked plastic as she breathed in and out, in and out.

She felt a warm rush of comfort as she looked up to the coffee shop, sitting right where she found it every afternoon: across the gravel lot and up a short set of cement stairs. Houndstooth Coffee House was her after-school home base, a place where she knew the name of one—no, wait, *two*—of the baristas behind the counter and could grab her familiar table almost every afternoon. Leaning back into the driver's seat, taking off her glasses and rubbing the bridge of her nose, her pulse found its way back towards its normal rhythm.

Cracking the car door open, Haylie felt the warm Texas air flood over her. She grabbed her bag from the passenger seat and made her way across the lot, crunching gravel with each step.

Haylie pulled the door open and the thick scents of chocolate and dark roasted coffee hit her like a wave. She forced a weak smile at the barista behind the bar—it was a new guy—and ordered a plain, drip coffee. She was quickly handed a warm, white porcelain mug and slinked over to the table in the back-right corner of the building.

Pulling her headphones over her ears, she queued up an electronica streaming station and wiped a few smears off her glasses with the bottom edge of her shirt. She opened her daily checklist and ran down her assignments for the day, seeing only one item left for that week: an English class essay, due in two days.

The assignment was one in a series of shorter essays that her English teacher had slipped in between larger reports—write-ups on personal experiences to "keep the brain juices flowing," whatever that meant. Each month they were also assigned long, boring book reports, but at least they had the freedom to choose what they would read, which was a pretty cool move. That meant that instead of reading boring, stuffy Victorian novels, Haylie was able to choose geeky sci-fi—*Dune, Brave New World, Neuromancer*—and that made the class not completely awful.

She brought up her online agenda and checked the details for this week's essay.

```
Write 1,000 words on how you met your
best friend.
```

The question hit her right in the stomach, harder than it should have hit any seventeen-year old high school senior. *How the hell am I going to pull this one off?* She thought through different scenarios, searching for an approach that was somewhat truthful, but also wouldn't set off any alarm bells for the school counselor. She typed something, anything, just to fill space on the blank page.

```
Miss Hiefield-

I feel that I am exempt from this
assignment due to the fact that I do
not, in a material sense, have a best
friend that I have actually met (in
person).

In addition, my lack of a best friend
grants me "protected class" status in
the state of Texas, allowing me to sue
you and the entire Austin Independent
School District for even mentioning such
a concept.

The next communication you will receive
will be from my lawyer.

Good day.

Haylie Black
```

She chuckled to herself, twisting the laughter into a long, exhausted breath as she stared down at the words on the screen. Balancing on her elbows, she looked past her computer to the growing stream of newcomers entering the coffee shop. *Who do we have here today?* She gazed dully into the crowd, taking deep sips of coffee, making up stories as she went.

At 5:04PM, a woman walked in, sunglasses still fixed on her face, clutching three different handbags. She mouthed each word as she read from the chalkboard menu; she seemed harmless.

At 5:07PM, three frat boys looking like wannabe start-up entrepreneurs stumbled in with blue oxfords and khakis. They were pacing around the room, nervous—probably pitching a local venture capital firm on their early-stage idea.

You need to get this assignment done. C'mon, dummy, focus.

Haylie turned back to her screen, cranked up her music and subtly bobbed her head to the beat as she typed the first few sentences about Vector, her best friend that she had never met.

Stay-at-home-moms, students, and lots of people in startup t-shirts floated through the door as Haylie grew the outline from single points to full paragraphs, walking through her history with Vector; how they had first met on a tech message board. That night they learned that they had a lot in common, despite living on other sides of the world. They were roughly the same age and were both fascinated by how stuff works— code, hardware, systems. That was three years ago, and she couldn't remember a day since where they hadn't chatted about side projects, the latest big company to get hacked, or a new code package that one of them had discovered.

Right on cue, a chat notification rang over the music's beat, accompanied with a new chat window.

VECTOR:> bored. entertain me.

Haylie minimized the window with a shake of her head. *Ok... last paragraph, you can do this. Finish big.* Hovering over her keyboard, she went in for the kill, crafting a concluding statement that would wrap all her thoughts together and–

Haylie's concentration broke as she noticed something out of the corner of her eye. She looked up to see a man standing by the door with a phone pressed to his ear, looking in her direction. His dark charcoal suit and serious expression gave him the air of someone that was there to arrest someone—or to sue them. As their eyes met, he pushed back against the glass door and slipped outside.

What's that guy's story?

She shook her head and sunk back into her laptop, bringing up Vector's chat window. He'd get a kick out of this.

CRASH:> total rando just crept into the coffee shop. weird looking dude in a suit. it's not you, is it?

Giggling, she watched the cursor blink as he typed a reply.

VECTOR:> nah, you're not that lucky. going to need a pic of him so we can make fun of him together.

CRASH:> not now. ttyl.

Bringing her essay back up to the foreground, Haylie pushed herself back into her work. The rest of the room faded out as she focused. She leaned in, as the perfect final line formed in her mind.

"Excuse me," a voice said from across the table. "Is this seat taken?"

Haylie jumped as her eyes shot up to see two young men standing before her. As she fought to regain her breath, she looked back and forth between them, not believing her eyes. She thought she was seeing double—both men were the same height, wore expensive-looking hoodies in different shades of gray, and had identical boyish dimples framed by relaxed smiles.

They're ... twins?

"Is it all right if we sit down?" said the man on the left, pulling out a chair but not yet taking a seat.

The man on the right moved in lockstep, keeping his eyes on Haylie's as he slid out a second chair. "I'm sorry if we scared you."

Haylie quickly realized that she had never seen two adult twins together. You see twin kids all the time, but never as a pair when they're older, when they've grown into their own lives. They looked the same but

… different. The guy on the left had longer, swept-back hair while his brother had opted for a close buzz-cut. Both were well dressed, but with slightly different styles. A reflection of each other, but a fuzzy one.

Glancing around the room at the sea of empty tables, stools, and booths, Haylie looked back with question marks in her eyes. After a few moments of awkward silence, she pulled her computer towards her and gestured at the chairs across the table.

"Be my guest," she said with a careful tone.

"Great!" the man on the left said, sharply pulling the chair out from the table, the wooden legs signaling a piercing squeak across the polished cement floor. He folded his hands together on the table as he sat, staring her right in the eyes with a slight, innocent smile across his face. The man on the right followed suit, moving a bit slower to make his way into his seat.

Looking down at the men's hands, Haylie quickly realized that they hadn't ordered any coffee. She pushed back from the table with a subtle nudge, her hand falling down to her bag to blindly fumble for her phone. *This is super weird—what the hell is going on here?*

"Listen," she said, shifting in her seat, "my boyfriend is going to be here, like, any minute, so–"

The man on the right smiled and let out a laugh. "Haylie, I think all three of us know that you don't have a boyfriend."

She froze, raising her hands to close the lid of her laptop. Her eyes flicked back and forth between the men, the barista across the room, and the exit.

"How you do you know my name, creep?"

The man on the left shuffled in his seat, fidgeting with his shirt collar as he craned his neck around the room. "Do they have drinks here? Like beer or anything?" He grabbed a flyer from the middle of the table, flipping it, end-over-end. "Do they have food? Do you want food? I'm starving. I'm going to get us some food." He slipped his phone out of his pocket, giving the screen a quick check before placing it on the table. "Marco! Marco, can you get us something to eat?"

Haylie looked back to the door and saw the man from before—the man in the suit—standing watch by the glass. He flew into action, jogging over to the barista, as soon as he heard the words.

Haylie studied the men's faces for a few seconds. Something looked familiar. Something looked....

No way.

"Wait a minute," she stuttered, pointing across the table with a few finger jabs of excitement. "Wait a minute. You guys ... you're the Sterling brothers. Right? The *actual* Sterling brothers? In *my* coffee shop?"

The man on the right nodded. "Yes. I'm Walter," he pointed to his brother, who was still more interested in getting a drink than the conversation. "And this is Benjamin."

"Of course you are. You guys...." Haylie stumbled over her words, sitting up straight in her chair, tucking her hair back behind her ear. "You guys are the coolest, ever."

Well that came out weird.

"Thank you!" Benjamin said, rejoining the conversation with a wide smile. "That's very nice of you to say."

Haylie gazed back, dumbfounded. Over the past few years, the Sterling brothers had become one of the most talked about topics in the start-up and technology world. After their father, a wealthy oilman, had been killed in an automobile crash, they had taken his fortune and created their own little empire—a startup named Brux that was now worth around $40 billion; not bad for a pair of twenty-one year olds.

"I mean," Haylie continued as she tried to stop herself from going full-on fangirl. "I'm a coder, and I know that's not what you guys are into. But I'm a big fan of the tech you're helping to build." She stared back at the brothers with a big, fat smile on her face. "It's just really cool, you know?"

The brothers looked like they had heard all of this before. While Walter and Benjamin weren't coders, they were known for making big bets on the most cutting edge technology in the industry. They were also famous for hiring the best engineers out there, including her brother,

Caesar. And those bets—whether it was on ride sharing, virtual reality, or advertising technology—had always paid off for them.

"Well if you know who we are," Walter said, giving a subtle look back to Benjamin to draw his eyes back to the table, "then you know that your brother started working for us about eight months ago at our New York office. He's been a big help."

"Right," Haylie said, not able to wipe the smile off her face. "He loves working for you guys. He doesn't tell me all the details, but I've never seen him this into his work before, you know?"

"Caesar. Love that guy," Benjamin said. "He's a badass. I mean, all you have to do is look at the press he gets. Any time he writes a blog post, it turns the industry on its heels."

"Yeah," Haylie said, "he's a smart guy."

"Not just a smart guy," Walter added. "A *good* guy. You don't find many of those out there in the startup world right now. Trust me, we've seen the whole spectrum—the good, the bad, and the downright unbelievable."

"When you find a guy like Caesar," Benjamin said, "you have to keep him challenged, that's the only way to keep him around. And you try your best to hang on to guys like that as long as you can."

Nodding, Haylie looked back and forth between the brothers. Silence covered the table as she waited for the next beat, raising her eyebrow with an "and...?" look on her face.

"Ok, ok, I'm sure you're wondering why we're...." Benjamin paused and started over. "So the last meeting I had with Caesar, he told me all about you, Haylie. I don't even remember how we got on the subject, but we ended up spending most of the hour talking about his little sister in Austin. Smart and honest and curious about any tech she could get her hands on. Seems like you're following right in his footsteps."

Haylie's eyes fell to the table as she tried her best not to blush. She began plotting any way to change the subject away from ... her.

A tray of muffins and croissants was placed on the table. Haylie looked back over her right shoulder to see Marco, now handing out napkins with a forced smile.

I'm going to need to get a selfie of this whole circus at some point.

"There's something I'd like to discuss before we talk more," Walter said. "When we meet with people there's a vetting process. Our advance man, Marco right here, checks our time table and locations to make sure our calendars are optimized. But we also have a security team doing background checks on everyone we meet. It's a standard practice."

Uh oh.

Haylie made an audible gulp of her coffee as she placed the cup slowly down on the table. The base of the porcelain teetered on its edge across two of the table's worn, wooden boards.

"Some ... *interesting* details came up with your profile," Walter said. "Despite warnings from our team, we decided to take the risk of meeting with you, but you should know that some of your talents might put you on the radars of a few government agencies at some point."

"Really?" Haylie asked, feigning innocence.

"Now, the FBI hasn't connected the dots on any of this," Walter said, now getting Benjamin's full attention as well. "It's hard for them to ... let's just say that they don't have the funding we have. Anyway, we traced some IP activity for some pretty big hacks back to a machine in Austin, to a user going by the name Crash. That's the screen name you use, right?"

Haylie's pulse beat faster as she gripped her mug, taking a heavy breath. "Huh," Haylie said, her voice beginning to shake. "That's really weird."

"Let me ask you," Walter said, "Do you know anything about July of last year, when the Russian missile command workstations were infiltrated and programmed to play 'The Star Spangled Banner' at full volume, on repeat?"

Shaking her head, Haylie tried her best not to freak out. *The Fourth of July. That was the Whitney Houston version of the song—it was the best one I could find.*

"The blackout at the Super Bowl a few years back?" Walter continued, keeping a close eye on her reaction.

Stone faced, Haylie folded her hands over each other. "I remember my Dad saying something about that, but I don't really watch football."

"Hacking into the CIA Director's personal email?" Walter asked.

That one was easy. Just a quick call to the help desk for US Online, repeat his birthday and mother's maiden name, and the password was reset.

Her eyes flicked to the door, then back to the brothers. Her hands wrapped around the edge of her laptop as she breathed heavier, deeper. Ready to run.

Walter broke the tension. "Don't worry, Haylie," he said with a smile. "We're not here to bust you. Not even close."

"Between us," Benjamin added, "we think that kind of stuff is freaking awesome."

Oh thank God. Haylie exhaled as a relieved round of laughter circled the table. Sitting back and unclutching her laptop, she took a sip of coffee, willing her hand to stop shaking.

"Listen, we're always on the lookout for good people," Benjamin said. "And the best ones aren't always satisfied with ... coloring within the lines. You know?"

"We have a program," Walter said, "where we identify young talent and bring them into the Brux environment up in NYC. Challenge them, teach them—but also understand what they are capable of."

Her heart still pounding, Haylie reached out for a muffin. She didn't even want to eat it, she just wanted something to do with her hands.

"I'd guess if you're like some of the other interns we've brought in," Benjamin added, "you're a bit out of place in school. Some don't feel challenged ... others just have trouble finding the right group that gets them."

Taking a careful bite of the muffin, Haylie rocked forwards and backwards with a slight nod as she chewed. "So, you guys went through the same thing?"

"Well, not really," Walter said. "But we hear stories from our engineers of that exact experience. Benjamin and I aren't that technical, we're better at the business side of the equation. Finding big tech trends to jump on, that sort of thing."

"So, how do people get these internships?" Haylie asked, peeling off another piece of her muffin.

"You talk to the guys that run the company," Benjamin said, laughing. He slunk back as Walter threw him a look.

"We're here to talk to you about your future, Haylie," Walter said.

"You guys just fly around the country handing out internships to high school students?" she asked. "Don't you have better things to do?"

"Normally, yes, but this is a special situation," Walter said. "We were in Austin for a venture capital meeting and, knowing that you were down here and come so highly recommended, we thought we'd stop by personally."

She wringed her hands, one on top of the other. *I can't believe Caesar is hooking me up with an internship in New York City—this is amazing.*

"But, something has come up that changes things a bit," Benjamin said. "Nothing big, just something we need to do first. Do you guys want more coffee? I think I need more coffee."

"Just wait a minute for the coffee," Walter said, turning towards his brother. "We're in the middle of something."

Benjamin nodded at Marco as he ran off to the barista. Pulling out his phone, Benjamin began to scroll, disregarding his brother.

"There's something we need to know, Haylie," Walter said, leaning in closer and lowering his voice. "When's the last time you spoke to your brother?"

Her face went blank as she twisted her fingers, one over another. *Why would they be asking me that? They work with him—they should see him every day.*

"I don't know," she stammered back, "it's been a few days. Sometimes we go awhile without chatting, but not usually this long."

"Now, there's no reason to be alarmed," Walter said, still hushed, "but we haven't seen him in over a week."

Over a week? No no no. This can't be happening.

29

She reached down to her bag and retrieved her phone, pulling it up in front of her with both hands, and unlocking the screen.

"Haylie," Benjamin said, sliding his chair around the side of table in her direction. "Please don't text your parents ... or anyone ... about this. Not yet. We can handle this—we're sure he's fine."

Her mind raced as the questions began to pile up, building on top of each other as her imagination went to work. She gripped her phone, tighter and tighter, as she fought for the right question to start with.

"But why...." Haylie stuttered, cradling her phone back towards her chest. "Why can't I just tell my mom? She can help, I'm sure she and my dad can–"

"It's only going to worry them," Walter said. "We think we know where he is, or at least where he was trying to go. Your parents can't help find him."

"But we think *you* can," Benjamin added.

CHAPTER FOUR

Houndstooth Coffee House
Austin, TX
March 6th, 5:27PM

The jingle of porcelain mugs against saucers broke the silence as the barista placed a fresh round of coffee on the table. All three sat quietly until the server made his way back behind the front counter.

"He does this sometimes, you know?" Haylie said as she cupped her mug in the curve of her hand, feeling the warmth run through her fingers. "He calls it 'rat-holing'—where he'll start looking into a problem and just lose track of the rest of the world for awhile."

Walter chuckled. "Absolutely. He does the same thing at Brux all the time, a day here or there. Other engineers try to keep up with him during his sprints, but they all give up eventually. They all say it's best to just leave him alone, let him finish his process. But he's never done it for this long before."

"I do the same thing sometimes," Haylie said, her eyes squinting as she adjusted her glasses. "Just a few months ago, I was working on getting access to a system—getting past a firewall. I was sitting in that booth right over there. One minute you put your head down and start working through the steps and the next thing you know, hours have gone by," Haylie stopped, staring blankly over at the booth for a few moments. "It's a funny feeling, you know, when you come back out of it. When you realize the whole world has been turning, and you've been in a different place."

"And we're sure that's all this is," Benjamin added. "We have some systems in place that will help. We've been diving into his communication patterns, looking at the past few months."

"Wait," Haylie said, pushing back from the table. "You monitor his communications? His messaging, his email—that sort of thing? He would never agree to that."

"He did," Walter said. "Everyone that works for us does. It's part of the Brux employee contract to grant access to hardware and personal accounts, only in the case of emergency. For big lawsuits or corporate spying, that sort of extreme event. Even Benjamin and I have signed those agreements. To be honest, we've never actually had to use them before now."

"But you said you weren't worried," Haylie said. She stared down at her coffee as the wheels turned in her head. *This doesn't make sense ... these guys aren't telling me something.*

"We're not worried, we're just being careful," Walter said. "We want him to be safe, which again, we're sure is the case. But we also have some pressure—"

"We have a business to run," Benjamin blurted out. Walter crossed him arms, staring him down, but it bounced right off of his brother. "Caesar's a friend, but we have a big product launch coming up, and it won't happen without him. Plain and simple—we need him back within the next five days. We need to stay on the good side of our investors and if he's not back leading the effort, we'll risk missing our next milestone."

"As you might have read, we've never had a failure in any of our lines of business," Benjamin continued. "We're trying to make sure it stays that way. The press has been very vocal about that fact, which is great when things are working. But the first time we make a mistake, the tech press will have a field day."

"Well, I'd hate for my brother's disappearance to make you any less of a billionaire," Haylie said, shaking her head.

"Caesar's safety is the priority here, obviously," Walter interjected. "There are business impacts as well, but we all just want to find him, right?"

Haylie took another sip of coffee, followed by a long breath. "You said you guys went into his computer. What did you find?"

Walter nudged Benjamin to respond.

"Sure," Benjamin said. "Two things, really. First, our security team pieced together all recent browsing history across his devices. It looks like he was trying to solve an Internet puzzle. Something called Raven 2309."

Haylie's eyes grew wide as she sat up straight in her chair.

Raven? Caesar was trying to solve Raven? No wonder he got sucked into a rat hole—no one has solved that thing. I'm not even sure it CAN be solved. But why the hell would he–

"Do you know anything about it?" Walter asked.

"Of course," Haylie said. "I mean, everyone's heard of Raven. It's been around for years." Staring back at two blank faces, she took a few moments to put together a description that would make sense to civilians.

"It's a puzzle—an Internet puzzle, like you said," Haylie said. "It appeared one day, a few years ago. Some anonymous account posted the first clue on a message board. People have solved a few steps using code breaking techniques, file analysis, all different types of stuff. But no one's made it to the end, not even close."

"So who made it?" Benjamin said. "It sounds weird—just some random puzzle that came out of nowhere. It must be there for a reason."

"Well, sure," Haylie said. "That's why hackers and code-breakers have been trying to solve it … to figure out why it's there in the first place, you know? The rumors are wild—that it might have been created by the NSA or CIA or a big company trying to recruit hotshot programmers. You guys really haven't heard of it?"

Shaking heads welcomed her from the other side of the table. "Like I said," Walter replied, "we tend to focus on the business side of things."

"It's been all over the press," Haylie said, bringing up the results of a news search on her laptop. "*Rolling Stone*, the *Washington Post*. It goes on and on. They call it 'The Most Mysterious Puzzle on the Internet.'" She did another search and brought up the front page of an online forum called "Raven's Keepers," with posts on everything about Raven 2309.

"There are tons of message boards like this one dedicated to Raven," she said. "They have all sorts of discussions about the puzzle and theories about where it might have come from. There are teams of people that are working together to try and solve it. The steps they've solved so far—only, like, four or five—have involved code-breaking and hacking into systems, but also some crazier stuff. Literature, art, history. Rumors that at some point, the puzzle moves from online to finding clues in physical locations. It's pretty weird."

"So what step is everyone stuck on right now?" Benjamin asked, craning his neck to see the screen.

"It's a message, but written in Anglo-Saxon runes," Haylie said as she scrolled and read the latest from the group. "See—that's what I'm talking about. The puzzle isn't just coding challenges, it's all sorts of stuff. Problem solving." She pulled the computer back in front of her and clicked into a few of the message threads, checking the post headlines.

I can't believe this. Caesar got himself caught up in trying to solve Raven. He's probably in a library somewhere, looking up everything he can find on runes. I bet he hasn't showered in, like, a week.

Haylie looked up to see Benjamin and Walter exchanging whispers across the table.

"What's up over there, guys?" she asked over her laptop's lid.

The brothers looked back and forth, as if each was hinting, "no, *you* say it" to the other.

"Here's what we're thinking," Benjamin finally said. "Caesar is somewhere out there, trying to solve this puzzle. If we walk through the same steps as he has, we should find him wherever he might be stuck. It just makes sense, right?"

Haylie broke into laughter. "You guys are out of your minds. You're not going to just jump in and solve Raven." She pointed down to her screen. "Teams of really smart people have been working on this thing for months. Hackers, professors, all sorts of people. They're all stuck."

"Well," Walter said, "I don't think we have to solve the whole thing. If what you're saying is true, I doubt Caesar has found the end. He's probably just caught on a step. Once we find that step, we'll know where to find him."

"This is your idea?" Haylie said. "My brother is missing, and you want to solve an unsolvable Internet puzzle? Maybe he'll be sitting there at the end waiting for you?" She snatched her phone off the table, unlocking the screen. "We need to call the cops. Or my parents. They'll know what to do."

"Stop—please stop, Haylie," Benjamin said with an outstretched arm. "We have a private security team that is ten times more capable than the police. They are investigating all the traditional channels, that's happening as we speak. This idea—it's a wildcard, but it might work."

Haylie rested her head in her hands, as she thought. *I hope he's okay. I just want him to be okay. He has to be, right? He has to be. But what if he's not? What if this is something else?* She cleared her throat, sniffing and fighting back the building tears. She wiped her eyes with her shirt sleeve, keeping her head hung low and her view away from the brothers.

"What's the second thing?" Haylie said, working the words around a series of sniffles. "You said when you went into Caesar's files, you found two things. What else was in there?"

"Let me ask you, Haylie," Walter said. "The last message that Caesar sent you, it wasn't just any message, was it?"

"No," she replied, thinking back to his last chat message.

The code. That stupid code. I should have just figured it out and sent him the solution—then maybe I could have caught him before he ran off.

"It was one of the puzzles he sends sometimes," she said. "But I'm not sure what it says, I haven't had time to solve it."

"Well, we think," Walter paused before continuing. "We think the message might hold a clue to the puzzle. There's a chance he's gotten farther than anyone else, and this clue may help us catch up with his progress."

Haylie looked up, her eyes filling with hope. "What makes you say that?"

"It was sent from a different device," Benjamin said, checking over his right shoulder to make sure that no one was eavesdropping. "It wasn't from his laptop or phone. We think he might have sent it to you from out in the field, as he was solving the puzzle. It could be—it could totally be the clue we need to get ahead here; to find your brother."

"So go solve it," she said. "Why haven't you just decoded the message yourselves?"

"We tried," Walter said. "We threw it over to our team. They did everything they think of to break the code and got nothing. To be honest, they had a hard time even trying to figure out where to start. 'Shelf 3, take out book 2'—they tried the library, bookstores near Caesar's house, his apartment—and found nothing."

"But he sent the note to *you*," Benjamin said. "So you must know how to solve it, right? And once you do, the three of us can just jump into the puzzle, solve the next few clues, and find him."

"Wait a minute," Haylie said, standing and backing away from the table. "I thought you guys were nuts for wanting to try and solve Raven, but that's not why you're here. You want *me* to solve it?"

She pointed a shaking finger over at Benjamin. "I knew it ... I totally knew it. You're the *crazy* kind of rich people, aren't you?"

"We can't do this on our own," Walter said, gesturing for Haylie to sit back down. "But *you*, you and Caesar trade puzzles like this all the time, plus nobody knows him like you do, it's almost like you two share a brain. If the three of us work together—"

"No, no, no way," she said, shaking her head and crossing her arms firmly across her chest. "I can't solve this thing. I'm just a teenager. I wouldn't even know where to start."

"Sure you can," Walter said. "And plus, Benjamin and I will get to watch you work along the way. I can't think of a better job interview than working on a puzzle like this together"

Haylie stood solid, her mind racing, as she pushed her hair back behind each ear, trying to figure out if this was really happening. *There's no way this is happening—the Sterling brothers, Caesar, Raven. An hour ago I was just sitting down for coffee, finishing up my homework. This is nuts.*

"Haylie," Walter said, standing and walking over to her side of the table. "Caesar's fine. We know it, you know it. Once we find him, we're all going to laugh about it and make fun of him for getting ... I don't know ... locked in some back room of a library without a phone charger. We might as well do this, the three of us, together. What do you say?"

"I ... I'd need to skip school," Haylie said, thinking through what would need to be done.

"Yeah, do you need like a note or something?" Benjamin asked. "We can do that."

Haylie shot him an annoyed look. "You're like four years older than me; you don't get to write notes to high schools yet."

"We'll figure out the school thing," Walter said. "The tricky part will be your parents."

Haylie quickly checked the calendar on her phone. She scrolled all entries for the next week, day after day. "Dad's in Boston all week at some conference; he left this morning," she said. "And Mom heads to Singapore tomorrow for some meetings ... I'll be alone at home for the next five days."

Benjamin looked over at Walter with relief, turning back to Haylie. "Well that was easy."

Walter slid a business card onto the table, spinning it towards Haylie. "Think about it and text me tonight with your answer," he said. "We've built a temporary office at a hangar at the airport. We can meet there in the morning if you're up for it."

Haylie grabbed her bag in one hand and Walter's business card in the other. She folded the thick paper between her fingers, flexing and bowing its shape. She nodded, walking out the door without looking back. She shuffled her feet across the gravel and into the darkness as she crossed the parking lot.

Her mind was already churning, working to solve Caesar's puzzle.

CHAPTER F1V3

10 Downing Street - London
March 6th, 11:47PM

The black iron gates opened as the armored Jaguar XJ glided into the private driveway. Flanked by four motorcycles, the car rolled slowly past the checkpoint and out of the public's reach.

Prime Minister John Crowne could see two guards' faces—one staring past the top of the car, the other keeping his view beyond the gate—through the rain-painted back windows. They stood at attention, searching the fog for anything that looked out of the ordinary. As the vehicle veered slightly to the right and safely in front of 10 Downing Street, he heard the gates squeaking closed behind them. They were home, at least until the next trip. *Thank God.*

Over the past two years, the Prime Minister had grown tired of these pointless excursions. Today was a day trip—a few hours west to Bristol, then north to Derby, a quick jot over to Newark, and then back home. He traveled in a surprisingly light entourage for one of the most powerful leaders in the world. You could count on one hand the number of handlers and aides that flanked him for the trip.

Years ago, he would have embraced the opportunity to have a drive out into the country, but things were different now. Every minute of every trip, especially the time spent in the back of the car, was carefully coordinated. One and a half hours to Bristol meant one and a half hours of policy decisions, political planning, and phone calls. It was all kept to a tight schedule by his Chief Secretary, changing and morphing to chase any breaking news. All the time, it seemed, playing defense. Putting out fires as opportunity flew by.

At each stop, Crowne endured a series of pre-planned moments to gain political favor. He slugged through factory tours, radio interviews, and meetings with local groups and officials. With every conversation, he struggled to remember which candidate or issue he was supposed to name-check to keep special-interest groups from issuing angry statements.

But it was the unplanned events, or more accurately "planned unplanned" events, that really got under his skin. These outings, designed to resemble daily life, were completely out of his control. Walking across the threshold of every shop was no longer a personal moment. It was a moment that belonged to everyone else. A story each person would tell for years.

Every bite of every meal was now an Instagram moment. *Have you ever tried to look photogenic while you eat? It's impossible.* Every preference he showed, especially with food for some reason, was analyzed by patrons and newspapers. Did he stop for an Indian lunch because he was actually in support of the legislative reform being discussed over at the UN?

No, I just wanted some curry.

But Crowne knew the reality of what politicians—no, *leaders*—had been reduced to in our modern times. Poster boys. Spokesmodels. Politics had morphed into sound bites to justify prior-held beliefs and top-ten lists to convince mothers that they shouldn't vaccinate their children, all based on celebrity opinion. In the past, someone standing at a podium had, at least in some way, earned the authority to have their voice heard. Today, anyone with a smartphone could tell you that was no longer the case.

The Internet and social media promised a great, open debate of ideas on an even playing field, but instead this age of technology had created a society more divided than any time in human history.

Crowne stepped from the car, pacing slowly towards the front entrance. As he approached the iconic doorway to 10 Downing, he thought of all the leaders that had walked through its door. Back during the war, Churchill had made a point of being seen right here on this spot a few times a week. He had wanted to remind the country—*Churchill's country*—that the Nazis didn't scare him.

This was the spot where countless foreign dignitaries had stopped and posed to show their strong partnerships with Britain over the years. And all for what? To watch their countries argue back and forth without action? To go to bed each night knowing that progress was impossible? To let extremist groups outmaneuver and outwit these once-powerful nations?

Crowne would declare his current position worthless if it were only that simple. But the reality was that modern leadership wasn't just fruitless, it was worse. It was a great promise, unfulfilled.

It was a *shame*.

He gazed at the open door, the number hanging slightly crooked, just as it had been on the original frame. The knocker, in the form of a great lion's head, stood proud and steadfast. He chuckled. "That must be nice," he said under his breath, turning back for another look at the foggy, slick street.

"Sir?" the closest guard quickly inquired. The PM just forced a smile and walked inside.

Crowne passed the length of blood-red carpet laying across the checkered marble and paused at the base of the grand staircase. Most nights, he would have headed back to his office for a nightcap; but tonight, he was just done. Done with all of it. This house—this damn house. Built without logic, composed of hundreds of small rooms and hallways. There were two or three walls in any direction you faced, a sea of corners everywhere. It was a house that was past its prime. *They should burn the whole thing down, just start over.*

He leaned on the thick wood banister, pushing down with his hand to aid his movement up each stair, one at a time. On his left hung portraits of heroes from times past. Black frames, gold engravings. As he trudged on, his knees growing tired, the faces haunted him as his eyes marched from frame to frame. The ghosts of Downing Street watched him push his way towards his bed—some smiling, some judging. Walpole. Thatcher. Major. Lord Gray. Spencer Perceval, the only PM to be assassinated, shot dead right in the lobby of the House of Commons.

As he reached the third floor landing, he looked over to the small bust of Churchill that sat at the top of the stairs, guarding the entrance to the private residence. He slowly walked towards the statue and palmed the head, rubbing it for good luck. Over the next few days, he was going to need it.

He turned towards the master bedroom and his foot hit something soft, sounding off a tiny squeak. His eyes fell to the floor to find his son's toy giraffe, a favorite over the past few years.

The giraffe was something of a family heirloom, having belonged to his daughter years ago. To anyone else, the toy would have appeared too faded and ragged for a Prime Minister's son, but that's exactly why they had kept it; the toy reminded them that they were a family, not just a picture on the wall. But the toy was something they kept private, as silly as that sounded; it was nobody's business what his son played with, especially if it was made by a French brand that manufactured its products in China. Crowne didn't feel like getting wrapped up in tariff discussions over a child's plaything. Sometimes, it was better for people not to know.

Sometimes, not knowing just made things easier.

He moved inside, strolling past the guest bedrooms that littered the hallway. He walked into the master bedroom and stopped next to Lucy as she slept without a sound. Her eye mask couldn't hide how she glowed with beauty, even in her clumsy sleep. She slept on her side, facing the window and safely out of the hall light's reach, a light she left on for him each and every night.

As he changed out of his suit, he took his Blackberry from his pocket to do a final check of his priority mailbox. One new message from Martin Bell, Priority Red. He inspected the details—a few action items from the Iceland test, but everything else was a go. None of the other four recipients had replied, but that was expected. That was the protocol. Crowne knew that the absence of other messages meant only one thing: the others agreed.

The Prime Minister walked back into the bedroom and stood over his sleeping wife. He looked at the curtains covering the bulletproof window, glowing ever so slightly from the streetlights standing at attention outside. As his eyes rested on Lucy, he smiled.

Soon, I'll be the change that everyone has been waiting for.

He was finally going to have the chance to lead, to break the world out of this political trench-warfare that had crippled its progress. They'd call him crazy if they knew what he was going to do; they'd say his plan was too severe. They'd lock him up. But that's only because *they* didn't understand what had to be done.

Crowne knew that a brief flash of pain across the planet would soon lead to a new direction for the world. There will be suffering, yes—but great steps forward require great sacrifice.

No one knew what was coming, but sometimes that was for the best.

Sometimes, not knowing just makes things easier.

CHAPTER SIX

The Suburbs of Austin, TX
March 6th, 9:48PM

Haylie sat perched above her laptop, getting lost in the depths of her favorite tech forum, CodeOverflow. She caught herself drifting off as she mindlessly clicked through link after link, thinking about her brother.

Maybe he just quit his job, had enough of the Sterling brothers for one lifetime. Maybe he solved the whole damn puzzle and found a pot of gold and a leprechaun at the end.

She blinked her eyes a few times, bringing her brain back online, and rubbed her temples with her index fingers. *Focus, Haylie. Focus.*

Turning back to the forum, she dove into the Raven 2309 discussion area. Haylie sifted through posts from newbies begging for clues, seasoned Raven veterans posting full-on conspiracy theories, and a few fresh requests to assemble new teams.

This feels less like a puzzle and more like a treasure hunt.

She tilted back in her desk chair and checked the thread for the current year's puzzle. Over four-hundred posts and counting, all discussing different aspects of Raven. She quickly learned that only four steps in the puzzle had been solved to date, with teams posting the solutions for others to study. The first two steps seemed pretty easy— basic substitution ciphers and messages hidden in metadata—while solving the third and fourth steps required more advanced techniques. *It's only going to get harder from here.*

Haylie clicked on a section titled "Mainstream Press About Raven 2309." The top post linked to an article about a college student in North Carolina claiming to have solved last year's Raven. Two weeks after proclaiming he had reached the end of the puzzle, strange things had started happening to him. The man's bank account, driving record, credit score, and college transcripts had all been mysteriously erased by a series of system breaches. Only then did the student admit that it was all a lie; he had tried his best to solve Raven, and failed.

A chat window popped up on the bottom right side of her screen.

VECTOR:> yo Crash - you there?

Haylie smiled, resting her chin on her palm and typing back with one lazy hand.

CRASH:> yeah, just working out some stuff.

VECTOR:> well, that's really vague. good talk.

She laughed, pulling her hair back behind her ear and sticking her tongue out at the screen.

CRASH:> whatevs. ping you later.

Flipping back to the message board, she scanned the most popular threads for the current year's puzzle. There were hundreds of topics ranging from Raven FAQs, threads on runes and numerology, and grand theories on how Raven would change the world.

As she lazily surfed the forum, one post caught her eye. It was titled "Why I finally decided to give up my Raven quest." Clicking the link, she was taken to a blog post authored by a user named Samasito55. He identified himself as a top Norwegian cryptographer and network security analyst, and claimed to have spent months solving steps from Raven over nights and weekends. Haylie's focus narrowed as she read.

> The codes I broke weren't any kind of joke, they were industrial-grade stuff. If the puzzles were designed to filter out individuals with certain skill sets, I can see why it would work. But the code breaking wasn't the reason that I stopped.

I decided to stop for two reasons.

First, the puzzle's steps became more
difficult. I'm not talking about the
math or code breaking techniques—the
puzzle was changing. Twisting into
riddles, ancient numerology, and
breaking into physical locations. Stuff
I wasn't ready, or qualified, to do.

And then there were the messages. After
about the fourth or fifth step, someone—
I'm guessing the designers of Raven—
began to send me messages. Not just
hiding things in the framework of the
puzzle like the first few steps, but
actual notes directly to me. Texts,
phone calls, chat windows within clues.
Somehow they knew my name, and they were
watching me as I tried to solve their
puzzle.

I'll be honest—I gave up on Raven
because I was scared. During the early
stages, I thought it would be a fun
distraction, but that's not where the
puzzle took me. I started fearing for
what the next step was going to mean for
my life and my family. So I stopped, I
closed the book on my Raven adventure.

And I haven't heard from them since,
thank God.

The desk lamp flickered for a second as Haylie stared into the screen.
She pulled her glasses from her face and laid them carefully on the desk,
rubbing her tired eyes.

Haylie's mind raced as a phrase from the blog post resonated and
echoed in her head. *Closed the book on my Raven adventure.* She flipped
back over to her chat window, minimizing Vector's message and bringing
up Caesar's last note.

Shelf 3. Take out book 2.
01117322051235612813

The Sterling brothers said they looked everywhere. They tried Caesar's apartment's bookshelves, his local bookstore, the library. But Caesar wouldn't have been talking about a book near HIM. He'd be talking about a book near ME.

She rose to her feet and quietly made her way down the hall to Caesar's room, the last door on the right. She turned the knob as a wave of musty, cold air hit her face. She flicked on the light and saw his room come to life, still arranged just like the day he had left.

Caesar's bookcase took up most of the wall on the right-hand side of the room. She counted the shelves up—one-two-three—and then moved left to right—one-two—pulling the book under her hand from its place.

"Alice in Wonderland?" She flipped through the pages to look for any messages. "Maybe there's a code hidden somewhere in here." She searched the front and back cover for any kind of clue. There was nothing.

Her eyes fell down to the shelf, seeing volumes of computer science books—programming, data mining, and database design. Suddenly, she lowered the book in her hand and placed it back on the shelf.

I bet he's counting like a programmer. Like a machine. Machines start counting at zero.

She looked down to the bottom shelf and counted again. One-two-three-four—and then went down the line of books—one-two-three—pulling out the resulting book. Checking the title, her eyes lit up.

"'Understanding Fibonacci,'" she whispered. Thinking back to the message, she jumped up with a quick burst of excitement. "Of course!" She hurried back to her room, gripping the volume with both hands.

Caesar had taught Haylie all about the Fibonacci sequence when they were younger. She remembered that each number in the sequence was calculated by adding up the two previous numbers. Caesar and Haylie had used the patterns to build cool, spiral Lego structures back in the day, but she knew there were lots of uses for the math—everywhere from computer science to biology.

"I should have noticed this when I first saw the code. Stupid, stupid, stupid." She typed out the first ten numbers from the Fibonacci sequence in a TextEdit window.

0 1 1 2 3 5 8 13 21 34 55 89

Haylie then pasted the number from Caesar's message directly below.

0111732205123561281 33

"Take out Book 2." I'll just remove each Fibonacci number from Caesar's code.

Working left to right, she deleted the digits from the first group of numbers out of the second group, one by one, and sat back to check the result.

173205126123

What is this? It's too long for a phone number. It can't be a–

She leaned in and typed three sharp keystrokes with her index finger.

173.205.126.123

I got you, Caesar. It's an IP address. She copied the numbers into a browser window and hit enter. As the website loaded, she studied the image staring back at her and a grin grew across her lips.

She turned to her bag, pulling out her phone and placing it on the desk with a firm click. She fished Walter's crumpled business card out of her pocket and bent it back into shape, holding it up to eye level and squinting to make out the number printed on the thick paper stock.

I can't believe I'm actually going to do this.

She picked up her phone and began to type.

CHAPTER SEV3N

Champion Drive - Austin, TX
March 7th, 6:45AM

As the cab rolled slowly down the twisting web of country roads, both Haylie and the driver searched for any hint of their destination. The cab's GPS pointed to a small airport just up the way, but Haylie couldn't see any trace of one. All she could see were fields and mailboxes and dirt tracks with makeshift, wooden signs reading "No Trespassing," sometimes even spelled correctly. They were only fifteen minutes from downtown Austin, but Haylie still felt plopped down in the middle of nowhere.

Haylie yawned as she checked Google Maps on her phone. "It should be right up here," she said, rolling down her steam-caked window for a better view. The morning air flooded the car, along with the sound of crunching tires rolling over damp gravel, as the cab pulled over to the side of the road.

"Wait a minute, lady. I see something here," said the cab driver through his thick accent. He cycled the wipers on and off to clear the condensation from the windshield, revealing a few distant lights past an upcoming bend of the road. "I think it's up this way."

The cab glided in around the bend as a collection of buildings and private planes came into view. An airstrip, locked securely behind a long razor-wire fence, stretched out as far as she could see.

Haylie's phone buzzed in her pocket. She looked down to see a message from her mom, who was just about to take off on her flight to Singapore. She shot a quick note back, then slid the phone back into her pocket.

She paid the driver and stepped out onto the side of the road. The cool morning mist fell across the back of her neck. Zipping her field jacket all the way up with a shrug, she walked towards the airstrip, her backpack across her shoulders and a small duffle bag clutched in her left hand.

She followed the curved cement road leading to a group of four buildings, each in the shape of a perfect square. Outside of the farthest building, Haylie could see two men dressed in black with their hands folded across their chests. They stood on either side of a single door. *This must be the place.* Haylie did her best to appear calm, like she had done this before.

The guards weren't just men; they were beasts. Huge, bald, thick, and stone-faced. As Haylie stepped towards the building, the guard on the right extended a hand keeping her a few feet away. As she came to a complete stop, he scanned the horizon, speaking lightly into his sleeve. The guard on the left knocked three times and, without saying a word, opened the door wide for Haylie to walk through.

She entered and looked up to take in a full view of the hangar's interior. The main room had the feel of a warehouse—plain white walls with a closed, unmarked door on the far side. A sleek private jet commanded the middle of the room, its nose facing a large sliding door that took up the entire wall. A single spotlight hung down from the center of the ceiling, highlighting the subtle curves of the wings and fuselage. The corners of the hangar were stacked with aviation equipment—hoses, gas tanks, tools, and other machinery.

As she gazed in awe at the jet, she heard a familiar voice from behind her.

"There she is!"

Haylie turned to find a strangely comfortable set-up in the corner where Benjamin and Walter stood, sipping their morning coffee. The sitting area included two cream-white couches arranged with a table in the middle and a checkered green rug beneath. The scene would have looked like a Pottery Barn catalog if it weren't for the long table against one of the walls covered in a full assortment of breakfast foods, coffee, orange juice on ice, and energy drinks.

Walter stood with his back to Haylie, speaking with Marco and gesturing to the other side of the hangar. Marco's wrinkled shirt and stressed expression hinted that he had already enjoyed a full day of work.

"I like her already, Walter," Benjamin said. "She goes home and says 'I'll think about it,' and comes back the next morning already having solved the first step. Love it."

"Morning," Haylie said.

"What can we get for you?" Benjamin asked. "We have an assortment of all the finest–"

"Coffee."

"You got it," Benjamin said.

Haylie clutched the straps of her backpack, continuing to spin around the room. She had never seen anything like this before, and she knew she might not get the chance ever again. She took a few steps towards the jet's wing, looking above and below, reaching a hand out to touch its smooth, polished surface, but then looked over at Benjamin for permission.

"Yes of course you can touch it," he said, walking to the other side of the wing, admiring the lines. "It's a beautiful thing, isn't it?"

"This plane," she reached out and ran her hand across the back flap. "This is yours?"

"Well, sure," Benjamin said. "It's how we get around. So much easier than doing the whole public airport thing. Cramming onto a plane with a few hundred strangers, sitting around waiting for connections—I don't miss any of that. Now we just hop on and go."

"That's ... that's amazing," Haylie said. "You guys are so lucky. You can go anywhere, do anything, any time you want. That's so cool ... I never thought I'd see one of these up close."

Walter, walking towards them, laughed from across the room. "You were coming to an airport and didn't expect to see a plane?"

"Well," Haylie said, "yesterday I thought I was going to get a cup of coffee and then two billionaires walked in and asked me to solve an unsolvable puzzle. My world's full of surprises this week."

The brothers laughed. Benjamin made his way back towards the sitting area and guided Haylie in the same direction with a sweep of his arm.

"Please tell me you've heard some good news about Caesar," Haylie said. "Anything?"

"No," Walter said, flicking through his phone. "There was an update from our security team this morning, but no new leads, and no messages back from him. Unless you've heard anything?"

Shaking her head, Haylie dropped her bag onto the leather couch and took a deep breath.

"He's fine, Haylie," Benjamin said. "We're going to find him. And you're going to be a huge help. I bet he'll reach out to us before we even get too far into this whole thing, you know?"

"You're doing the right thing," Walter said as he took a seat, sinking deep into the couch cushion. "We're all going to look back on this one day and laugh."

She nodded and accepted a cup of coffee from Marco, who smiled and walked back to continue arranging the table of refreshments.

"So, should we get started?" Walter asked. "I'd love to see what you found from Caesar's puzzle solution. Benjamin and I did some research on Raven last night and wow, there's a lot going on in those forums."

"Lots of crazy people," Benjamin added, taking a deep sip of coffee. "Super weird stuff."

"They're just—enthusiastic—about this sort of thing, that's all," Haylie said. "Puzzles like Raven are designed to drive that sort of chatter."

"What do you mean?" Walter asked.

"The mystery," she replied. "The references to banned books and shady organizations. It's all by design. It's all meant to boost interest, to get more people talking about it. There's a reason this puzzle is making headlines across the world. People love a good treasure hunt, especially if there's supposedly some secretive organization behind the whole thing."

"It's just so unbelievable," Benjamin said. "It doesn't seem like something that should actually exist, you know?"

"I'm pretty sure it's going to turn out to be fluff," Haylie said. "Just two or three guys that wanted to see if they could get some attention. If I had to bet, I'd say there's nothing at the end of the rainbow."

With a sudden clap of his hands, Walter sprung to his feet. "Let's get started! I've got a surprise for you," he said. "Your war room is set up over here. Come on, I can't wait for you to see it."

Haylie stared him down, puzzled, and slung her backpack over her shoulder.

What the hell is a war room?

The three walked across the hangar towards the door on the far wall. Haylie stumbled, almost tripping over a twisted braid of thick extension cords running across the cement floor and under the door in front of them. Walter pulled at the handle with a little too much effort for a guy his size, and slid to the side.

Haylie squinted as she tried her best to see inside. The room was dark, but with faint traces of light reflecting off the concrete floor. She followed the line of cords across the room to the most unbelievable computer setup she had ever seen—a desk arranged with a collection of monitors perched above its tabletop like a huge electronic peacock.

This is insane.

Featuring six screens—three monitors side-by-side with two flanking LCDs to the right and left, all capped off with a giant forty-two inch plasma hovering over the other five—the workstation was perched on a table with keyboard, mouse, a stack of paper notebooks, and two cans of Red Bull. The collection of panels towered over the desk, looking down from every angle. The room was illuminated only by the glow of the orange screensaver, igniting the walls an almost magical tint fashioned in starburst patterns.

"We've got the latest CPU, water cooling, a series of hard drives adding up to over 50 terabytes of storage, and a fiber Internet connection hard lined into the machine. It's all state of the art," Walter said, beaming and bouncing on his toes with excitement. "I hope you like it."

Haylie stared into the flat panels, the orange glow reflecting back off her glasses. She looked back at Walter with a thick air of confusion.

"This is your base camp," Walter said, filling in the awkward silence. "Your workstation for this project. We wanted you to have the best tools for your craft. We've had a team working all night to gather and assemble the components."

Haylie took a few steps forward, inspecting each individual screen, running her hand across the display edges. She reached down to click the spacebar on the keyboard. The screens immediately burst to life, showering the room with a bright blue light as Haylie jumped back, startled.

"Do you like it?" Walter asked with a proud grin.

She turned to face him with a scowl, pointing over to the machine. "What the hell do you want me to do with this thing?"

Walter's smile morphed to disappointment as he took a step back. "We want you to, you know, hack. Do your hacking thing."

Haylie shook her head and pointed back to the workstation. "With *that*? C'mon."

Benjamin began to chuckle under his breath as Walter looked on with quiet despair.

"You've got to be kidding me," Haylie said. "First of all, it looks absolutely ridiculous. Second, I don't even know what I'd do with all that stuff. Six screens? Water cooling? This thing would take me all day to set up, I don't even know where I'd start with all the packages I'd need to install. We're in a hurry here, right guys?"

Benjamin watched Walter's face drop as quiet laughter grew audible, filling the room. "You had *one job*, Walter," Benjamin laughed, enjoying every ounce of the moment.

"You guys run a tech company, right?" Haylie asked. "Have you ever seen anyone in your office with something like this?"

Benjamin looked over to Walter. "Well, Walter, have you?"

Walter just stared back at his machine, deflated.

"Guys," Haylie said, "Stop. We need to be portable to solve Raven. We may get through the first few steps here in the hangar, but before long we'll need to be mobile. Our best piece of hardware to help solve this puzzle is going to be *that*." Haylie pointed through the doorway to the jet.

"All right," Walter said, composing himself. "What do you need to get started?"

Haylie pulled her MacBook out of her backpack. "What's the Wi-Fi password?"

CHAPTER EIGHT

Capital of Texas Airpark - Austin, TX
March 7th, 11:32AM

Haylie's eyes narrowed as she stared mindlessly up at the wall, pushing back deep into the couch cushions. She let her mind work the problem as she sat motionless. There wasn't a computer system she had ever encountered that could keep her out, but she had never seen anything like this. This was new.

It was a bunny rabbit.

Well, it was a *photo* of a bunny rabbit. Or more specifically, a 37KB JPG image file of a rabbit named, quite appropriately, 'rabbit.jpg.' It was sized at 500 by 375 pixels, encoded with Baseline DCT Huffman coding, and it was staring her right back in the face.

And it was beginning to piss her off.

The image appeared to be a generic piece of stock photography—a three-quarters view of a brown, fluffy bunny. But what was confusing to Haylie wasn't just the animal, it was the printed block of text that had been added to the top right corner of the image.

The text read:

YIIIKES
Looks like you eight the wrong carrot.
Bet you can't figure out how
to get the message.

She frowned as she sipped on her cooled cup of coffee, scanning the message again and again; searching for anything she hadn't noticed over the past thirty minutes. Haylie dragged the file to her metadata extraction tool and checked the results one more time.

```
>> Camera: data not found
>> Author and Copyright: data not found
>> Location: GPS coordinates not found
>> EXIF: data not found
>> XMP: data not found
>> Maker notes: data not found
>> ICC Profile: data not found
```

She tabbed over to Google to perform a similar-images search, scouring their servers in an attempt to find pictures with the same patterns, outlines, and colors as the JPG file. But the results came back pretty much empty, only pointing back to the original stock111photo.com image site where the rabbit picture must have been purchased by Raven's author.

Turning back to the text in the image, she transcribed the first letter of each word to check for patterns. She scrawled 'YLLYETWCBYCFOHTGTM' onto a scrap of paper before staring at it for a moment, crumpling it up into a jagged ball, and tossing it into the corner. The nonsensical mishmash of text could very well be a cipher, but with such a short string it would be almost impossible to attempt a frequency analysis to find anything useful.

C'mon, Haylie. Think. You're better than this.

Standing and stretching her hands above her head, Haylie walked the length of the hangar, head down, hoping for inspiration as the ticks and pops of a fresh pot of percolating coffee echoed off the corners of the gray concrete floor.

"The message doesn't make any sense," Walter said, leaning over the couch and reading off of Haylie's laptop. "'Eight the wrong carrot?' Does that mean we went the wrong way? We couldn't have, unless Caesar pointed you to the wrong place. They must be trying to throw us off."

Haylie's face scrunched as she repeated the words from the clue in her head. From what she had read on the Raven boards, the puzzle had never signaled a "wrong way" message before, even when steps were solved incorrectly. She was sure they were in the right place.

Caesar's puzzle pointed me to a website, but websites can change. Maybe they updated the image after he–

"Let's think about this one more time," Benjamin said in a raised voice from across the hangar, breaking her concentration. "It says 'eight the wrong carrot,' what does that even mean? Is that some sort of hacker terminology?"

Haylie shook her head, trying to refocus. She was used to taking on puzzles and hacks as a solo mission, getting lost in her own mind for hours on end. She usually had to get completely immersed in the problem to find its solution—but that zone wasn't attainable with a festival crowd surrounding you, throwing ideas in the air every few seconds like verbal grenades.

What do you know about rabbits? What if the solution is actually about–

"We're approaching this wrong," Benjamin said. "We must be. It has to be easier than this."

Haylie glared at Benjamin, turning back towards the hangar's whitewashed wall, fighting once again to regain her train of thought. She strolled over to her position on the couch and sat back down.

"No one on the forums has made it this far," she said with a defensive tone. "I haven't seen any posts about the rabbit image. Everyone else is still stuck on the runes. I've checked the metadata for the file, did a similar-image search, checked for anything weird going on with the hosting location, and read up way too many things about bunnies. I've still got nothing."

She took off her glasses and rubbed her eyes. "Don't worry, I'll figure it out."

"You're just going to figure it out? *Figure it out?* How does that work?" Benjamin's voice echoed off the hangar walls as he stood tall, arms crossed and looking down on her as she huddled in closer to her machine.

"I don't know how it works," she shot back. "But it always does."

Haylie darted her eyes around the screen as she worked the problem. For some reason, she couldn't get Benjamin's words out of her mind. They began swirling and repeating, over and over.

Figure out. Figure out. Figure ... figure. Why does that sound–

"Calm down, dude," Walter said. "You heard what she said; just give her some time." He motioned at Benjamin to head outside with him. "Haylie, we'll give you some space to think it over."

Haylie tried her best to block out the chatter. She closed her eyes, concentrating on the problem. She forced everything out of her mind that she didn't need: the hangar, Caesar, the brothers. Everything.

What do I know? What do I have to work with?

A clue.

It was a file.

An image with text.

Why was it an image?

Figure out.

A picture of a rabbit.

Rabbits live in holes in the ground.

Figure out.

Why was YIIIKES spelled with three Is and in all-caps?

None of the other text was in all-caps.

Rabbits eat carrots.

Eight the wrong carrot.

No. Focus.

Focus on the problem.

Figure out figure out figure out ...

"Time? We need *time*?" Benjamin shouted, ignoring Walter's invitation to leave the building. He plopped down on the opposite side of the couch, pulling out his phone. "By all means, let's waste the whole morning just staring at a screen. Great idea."

"Can you two shut the hell up, please?" Haylie snapped. "I don't usually do this by committee."

Raising his hands with an "I give up" motion, Benjamin tapped out of the conversation. Walter paced the room, stopping to admire their jet, just trying to fill the time, somehow.

It was useless. Haylie couldn't focus. Not with the brothers counting the seconds as she worked. "I can hear you guys judging me," she said. "From inside your brains. I can hear it."

"No you can't," Benjamin replied. "You can't hear anything. You said be quiet, now we're quiet. You're welcome."

"Can we get back to the puzzle?" Haylie cut him off, pointing back to her computer. "I still don't know where Caesar is, and I'd like to figure that out."

Figure out. Figure out. Figure out.

Haylie stopped dead in her tracks as a sense of calm came over her.

Figure out. Eight the wrong carrot. Of course, dummy.

Suddenly, her mind flew into motion as she moved on to a new task. Her fingers flew, bringing up her application window.

"Hey, did we lose you there?" Walter said. "Are you still with us, Haylie?"

"Quiet," she said. "I just got it—what we need to do. Steganography. It's a program called FigureEight. Hold on, I'll explain in a minute."

"See?" Walter said, looking over to his brother, "She just needed a little bit of time to–"

"Quiet," she repeated, leaning in.

CHAPTER N1N3

The Grove Hotel - Watford, England
March 7th, 6:47PM

The Prime Minister stood firm, his eyes rolling across the curves and edges of the sculpture sprawled out before him. The crisp evening air had just made the turn from pleasant to chilled, and he knew his time was running out; he was needed inside, but didn't want to pull himself away quite yet.

The twilight's shine, reflecting off the sculpture's twisted body, had locked him in a daze. Its giant, stainless steel torso was frozen mid-crawl, emerging from the water, half-formed in its design: part flesh, part skeletal.

The exposed glimmering silver bones rose from the dead center of the calm pool, looking quite out of place in the quaint English garden. But it wasn't the brutal nature of intertwined structure and chromed flesh that captivated Crowne; it was the struggle of the piece. On all fours, half submerged, struggling to reach out of the water with one extended hand, taking its last earthly breath.

He's done for, but he hasn't given up.

The PM tilted his head, but still couldn't tell if the form was crawling towards salvation or away from certain death. *Was there a difference?*

In the distance, Crowne heard muffled, garbled shouting and the continued beat of drums echoing off the hillsides. The guards were holding the protesters back by the road, roughly a kilometer from the hotel grounds, but sound traveled far in this valley. *Such wasted energy. These people—they just need to understand how to follow and get on with it all.*

He checked his watch and sighed, dreading the formality and pomp of what awaited him inside. The morning had started nice enough, one of the best he could remember. A quiet, innocent breakfast with his daughter. A mix of hugs and "eat up, darling" nudges as he flew threw a stack of newspapers and cups of coffee. But he had been pulled away by a call from the German Chancellor. She was having second thoughts.

He had tried to subtly guide the Chancellor towards the light, but it was no use. Her cancer had returned, and her priorities had changed. She wanted out of The Project before tonight's meeting. She had asked Crowne to consider the same: to shut it all down. To go back to the way things had always worked.

She's a fool. How much more time will we waste on this earth, spinning in circles? Pretending this system works? The enemy isn't on the other side of the globe, anymore. The enemy isn't in tanks or trenches.

Staring deep into the contours of the sculpture, his hands turned to tight, balled fists as he thought of all the wasted effort, all the wasted time. A world, spinning in place, without an end in sight.

The enemy is all around us. The enemy has broken into our ranks. It's the every-man. The every-man that is dragging us down. Not with bombs or wars, but with a slow drip of constant debate. The great experiment of democracy will be the end of us.

I want the world to be great. I want the world to meet its potential. And I can't wait any more.

The English countryside lost its color, fading into gray as the sun snuck behind the horizon. Crowne thought back to the Chancellor's call, and what he had done next. He knew that most men would have felt regret or remorse for those actions, but he felt none of it. His lack of sympathy was the only thing that worried him.

I'm supposed to feel ... something ... about this, but I don't. Does that make me a monster, or does it just make me better than other people? Does it just make me the right person—the only person—that can get this job done?

After his call with the Chancellor, Crowne had called in his aide and made the first of many steps to becoming part of the solution. The Chancellor's cancer was unfortunate, but it made things easier for The

Project. Just a few phone calls to the right people inside the German system and her mid-morning medication was switched out with something a bit more potent.

She was dead within hours. The phone calls and headlines and urgent meetings by his unknowing staff filled the rest of his afternoon, until he had made his way to the Bilderberg meeting here in the countryside. Here with like-minded people, to take the first big step the world needed them to take.

It had been quite a day, indeed.

"Sir, it's time."

Crowne nodded silently to the aide that was waiting on him and turned on his heels. He fastened the top button on his jacket as he walked into the back side of the hotel lobby, past the silk-lined halls of The Grove Hotel. He quickly found himself flanked on all sides by clipboards, earpieces, and iPads holding schedules and lists that would dictate his fate for the rest of the evening.

"The first guests have arrived. We've set up an informal receiving line over to the left, which will include you and Princess Saskia of the Netherlands," the aide said, catching his breath as he skipped faster to keep up with Crowne.

"Ah, the formal-informal receiving line. My favorite kind."

"Very good, sir."

The Bilderberg group had met annually for the past sixty-two years, assembling one hundred and forty of the world's most powerful leaders. The official sessions would begin in the morning; most of the delegates were due to arrive this evening under the cover of darkness, with a few exceptions.

The Secretary General of NATO would be late due to an uprising in the Crimean Peninsula. The CEO of AlumCo was stuck in union negotiations. The head of the world's largest financial services company, who also happened to be a former Director of the CIA, was having mechanical issues with his jet. But, God willing, all the other members would arrive tonight, hidden from the prying cameras of the growing crowd.

Bilderberg attendees were greeted at the main road juncture by four armed, private security guards and a bright red 'ROAD CLOSED, USE A41' marker. Once the proper documentation had been checked and approved by a second detail via radio, the cars travelled through a double ring of ten-foot-tall security fencing topped with razor wire. They then carved up the one-lane private road towards the hotel. The road led them along a black picket fence framing acres of wide-open pastureland, finally proceeding over a white-railed bridge and to the hotel's main entrance.

The hotel itself resembled a small medieval castle stacking more than two hundred rooms into three stories of luxury suites. Its original construction dated back to the 1700s and, despite its many owners over the years, had managed to retain its largest asset—over three hundred acres of privacy and solitude. Gardens, pools, volleyball and croquet courts scattered across the grounds where wealthy Londoners enjoyed long weekends away from the bustle of the city. But for the next three days, tourists would be replaced with scores of delegates, world leaders, and hundreds of security personnel with short-cropped hair, sunglasses, and loose-fitting suits covering firearms hidden safely beneath.

Crowne followed his entourage into the main receiving hall, where clusters of men and the occasional woman huddled in each dimly-lit corner, the swells of their conversations growing into a buzz that filled the room. Simple crème-colored curtains had been pulled closed across the windows, and the reserved tone of the room was matched by the conservative nature of the crowd.

He saw a haphazard line of attendees lined against the south wall, standing at attention as he entered. At the front of the line he recognized a familiar smile.

"Your Royal Highness, so wonderful to see you." The Prime Minister extended his hand to Princess Saskia of the Netherlands, an informal greeting for royalty, but that was no matter for an old friend.

"Mr. Prime Minister," she replied. "Thank you so much for your hospitality, as always. My father would be proud to see how well you're carrying the torch for his cause."

Crowne grinned as he surveyed the crowd. Princess Saskia's father, King William, had created the conference years before. Its original purpose was to address the Communist influence spreading across the globe, but as the years went by, the topics and attendees changed along with the times. The Bilderberg meeting had grown to become an essential element of the global system—connecting powerful people on the issues that would help steer the world over the next year. The meeting's agenda items were always kept close, and remained a mystery to anyone unfortunate enough to find themselves outside the walls.

"And my God, what a shame about Adele," she said.

"Yes, yes, when I heard the news this morning from my staff, I couldn't ... I still can't believe it."

"I knew about the cancer, but something as random as the wrong prescription being filled, it's just ... such a tragedy." Princess Saskia kept close eye contact with the Prime Minister as she spoke the last few words without emotion.

"Unthinkable," Crowne replied.

The Princess took a quick check around the room, snatching two champagne flutes from a passing waiter's gleaming silver tray. She took a long sip from one. "They are angry about Adele, John. The others. No one likes surprises at a time like this."

"This is news to me," Crowne said. He checked around the room, now noticing a few icy stares back in his direction. "I'll take care of it."

"I would hope so. We're so close. Don't drive this thing off a cliff at the last turn."

"It's under control."

"It *was* under control, but now there are questions. Questions about your leadership. Go do your job, or we'll find someone else who will."

The Princess looked up, realizing that a growing collection of eyes had begun to drift in their direction. Forcing a faint smile, she raised her glass to toast with Crowne and the room filled with the sharp clink of fine crystal.

"We'll move ahead, as we always do, I suppose," she said. "Pushing forward. Isn't that right, John?"

"We always do, Your Highness. Keep calm and carry on, and all that."

"Good boy. I knew we could count on you. Chin up, this is a big day for us. Don't screw it up." The Princess turned and floated off towards her staff, handing the champagne flute off into the air, where it was quickly retrieved by a young aide.

Crowne checked his watch and exhaled. Scanning the room, he walked in the direction of the receiving line, wiping a bead of sweat from his brow.

CHAPTER T3N

Capital of Texas Airpark - Austin, TX
March 7th, 12:01PM

"Ok, tell me about this FigureEight thing. What is it?" Walter asked as he sunk back into the couch.

"I can't believe I didn't think of this before," Haylie said, doing a quick search for the tool's download location. "Here it is. It's one of the better-known open-source steganography tools out there. Let me just install it here real quick." She typed away at the keyboard as she spoke.

Walter watched on, nervously wringing his hands. "Can I help out with anything?"

"More coffee," Haylie said. "That would be a big help. Please."

Walter nodded over to Marco, who flew into motion.

Benjamin perked back up, watching as Haylie's fingers flew. "So what is stegla–"

"Steganography," Haylie corrected him. "It's when someone hides a message inside of something else. Images, documents, whatever. Back in the day, people used invisible ink for secret messages, you know? Steganography is the same thing, but with computer files. The message gets embedded in the file, and nobody can tell unless they have this tool. If they don't know any better, they just see a rabbit."

She flipped back to her Terminal window, the black command line box she knew all too well, and typed out a command:

```
HayBase$ FigureEight -r 2309.jpg
2309.txt
```

"This program checks for any hidden messages and spits the result out into a text file on my desktop," Haylie said. She hit the RETURN key with enthusiasm, the click echoing off the hangar walls.

The script paused for a few moments and then displayed the output:

```
Reading 2309.jpg....
Extracting usable bits:    29049 bits
Steg retrieve: seed: 228, len: 358
```

"All done," Haylie said.

"That's it?" Benjamin asked.

"Yeah, pretty simple," Haylie said, minimizing the command line window and searching around her cluttered desktop for the resulting file. "Let's see if we found anything good."

A TextEdit window popped up as Haylie checked the printed text in the file. It began with a greeting:

```
Welcome back.
To travel to your next clue, break this
riddle:
A text written early
And meant for the end;
From the banks of Rhodesia
His will wouldn't bend.
I:1:10 I:1:14 I:1:24 I:1:25 I:2:4
I:3:35 I:4:44 I:6:6 I:5:5 I:19:1
I:12:2 I:11:23 I:15:18 I:19:8 I:3:10
I:16:1 I:14:9 I:5:19 I:7:5 I:2:5
I:19:33 I:5:5 I:14:3 I:6:14 I:17:13
I:2:32 I:20:6
```

```
Good luck.
/2309
```

The three shouted a quick cheer as they hovered over the laptop, reading the message a few times over.

"This bottom part—it looks like a book cipher," Haylie said.

Her mind raced as she scrolled up and down through the stack of digits, squinting to make out each line.

"What's a book cipher?" Benjamin asked.

"Each number represents a letter that makes up a larger message. So we need to find the letter located at Chapter One, line one, tenth character," she said. "Then on to Chapter One, line one, fourteenth character. But that's not the hard part."

"What do you mean?" Walter asked.

"The hard part is figuring out which book," she said.

> > > > >

Walter sat on the back of the sofa, extending his arms out to the side and yawning as he stretched. He peeled off his hoodie to reveal a bright blue 'Brux' t-shirt, tossing the sweatshirt onto the other side of the couch. The hangar was beginning to warm with the rising Texas sun, and the tiny AC unit sticking out of the wall wasn't exactly up to par with the seventy-one degree, humidity-controlled office the brothers were accustomed to in their New York headquarters.

"So if we find the book, we break the code. That's the way this works?" Walter asked, staring up at the hangar's vaulted ceiling for any sort of inspiration.

"For the tenth time, yes." Haylie ran her fingers through her hair, trying to reset her brain to attack the puzzle from a different angle.

"So there's no program we can use to just figure this out?" Benjamin asked. "No FigureEight or whatever?"

"Theoretically, it's possible," Haylie said. "But that tool would need to grab the text of every book in the history of the world, and then write a script to index each individual character from each block of copy based on the book code. Then it would need to use natural language processing to check if the output matched dictionaries from a bunch of different languages, and do it all at a massive scale that no one has ever attempted before."

The brothers just stared back at her with a pair of perfectly matched annoyed looks.

"In other words, no," Haylie scrolled back to the top of the text file and zoomed the view. "Our best bet is to focus on the riddle. Let's go through it, line by line."

"How could we even begin to guess what book this is?" Benjamin said. "It's impossible."

"It's not impossible," Haylie said. "It's *difficult*. Difficult and impossible are two different things. Besides, Caesar figured it out somehow. We can, too."

How did you solve this, Caesar?

Her eyes blurred as thoughts of her brother filled her mind. She drifted back to the nights when she was young, falling asleep to the clicking sounds of his keyboard floating down the hall each and every night. Caesar had always stayed up late writing code. Building things. He had spent his nights tapping away, each key finding its place, washing into a mix of white noise that you could hear throughout their house. It was those nights that put the big question in Haylie's mind: what was he making?

And so she had peppered him with questions, trying to understand his world. At first she was too shy, or maybe too proud, to ask him to teach her how to code; she just wanted to know enough to learn what might be possible. He gave her enough hints to start her on her way and without as much as an "Introduction to Computer Science" class, Haylie had started building.

If she wanted hourly data on headlines from a news site, she'd write a screen scraper to grab the information. If she needed to study a new dataset, security wrapper, or website widget, she wouldn't buy a book to read up on the technical details, she'd just learn by building something with the tech. Learn while doing: that's what worked for her.

Haylie rubbed her eyes, trying to get back on track. "'A text written early and meant for the end.' What does that mean?" she asked, rising to her feet to try to get her mind moving again.

"It could be something that's old and meant for modern times," Benjamin said.

"Well, *The Bible* would be the obvious choice," Haylie said. "But I don't want to go down that path."

"Why not?" said Benjamin.

"We haven't seen any religious references in the Raven puzzles so far," she said. "If this was a church thing, we would have seen hints already. Hackers tend to be atheists. Or agnostic."

"What about the second line: 'From the banks of Rhodesia, his will wouldn't bend,'" Benjamin recited as he read from the screen.

"So that's Rhodesia, in Africa?" Walter asked.

Haylie stared back at him with amazement. "Were you guys, like, homeschooled or something? Of course, Africa. Rhodesia was in Africa. What other Rhodesia would it be?"

"I'm just asking the question," Walter said. "Like we say at Brux, 'there are no stupid questions.'"

"Well, congratulations," Haylie said. "You just found one."

"Can we just keep moving here?" Benjamin said, jumping in to break up the round.

"Something on the Rhodesian shores," she repeated, eyes back on Walter. "Rhodesia—in *Africa*. But here's the weird thing...." Haylie pointed to the search results in her browser. "Rhodesia, or what used to be called Rhodesia, doesn't have any big lakes or rivers. No riverbanks that would be big enough to mention. I mean, just look at the map, it's completely landlocked."

"'His will wouldn't bend.' Let's figure out who they're talking about," Walter said. "Who's an important guy from Rhodesia? Maybe we can start there."

Haylie clicked over to Wikipedia. "Rhodesia was a British Colony; let's check out the Prime Ministers. Alec Douglas-Home was in charge in the early sixties, helped define terms for independence, but I can't find any books that he wrote."

Benjamin pointed at a headshot farther down the page. "What about that guy?"

Haylie clicked the link and read the details out loud. "Ian Smith," she said. "He was the PM for fifteen years, but wasn't an author. He died in 2007." As her eyes searched the page, they rested on a black and white portrait. It was a man staring directly back into the camera, expressionless in his three-piece-suit. She read the paragraph of text beneath him and sat back into the sofa cushions, beaming.

"What is it?" Walter asked.

"Rhodesia was named for Cecil Rhodes," she replied. "The British businessman who built his fortune off of mining. He started the African diamond trade."

"Cecil Rhodes. I remember reading about him back in college," Walter said, checking the text on the page. "He was the diamond guy— made tons of money doing it. His estate still funds the Rhodes Scholar Program."

"Oh yeah," Benjamin said. "We tried to get Rhodes Scholarships back in college but … it didn't work out."

"You guys needed scholarships?" Haylie said with a cocked eyebrow.

"No, it's a status thing," Benjamin said, leaning back out of her direct line of sight. "Never mind."

"Anyway, the banks of Rhodesia," Haylie said. "A rich dude that has an entire country named after him. Maybe the riddle isn't referring to riverbanks, maybe it's the other kind of banks. The type that Cecil Rhodes would know something about." She was already Googling his name and checking the results for any books that he had written. "Damnit, he didn't publish anything. This is a book code; we need a book."

"Rich guy. Written early, meant for the end. His will wouldn't bend," Benjamin said. After a few moments, all three looked up at the same time.

Of course.

"His will wouldn't bend. Cecil Rhodes is the author of the text," Walter added, excitement growing in his voice, "but we're not looking for a book."

Haylie began a new search, her fingers flying across the keyboard. "We need to find the last will and testament of Cecil Rhodes."

CHAPTER ELE73N

Capital of Texas Airpark - Austin, TX
March 7th, 2:32 PM

Haylie massaged her temples with her index fingers, trying not to think for a minute. She had searched all the corners of the Internet over the past few hours—archive sites, museum write-ups, message boards—and found exactly what she was looking for. The problem was she had found too much of a good thing: six different versions of Cecil Rhodes's will, to be exact. The man had apparently commissioned new versions every ten years or so, each rewritten from scratch.

My brain hurts. This is the worst.

The group had decided that the best route was to start from the most recent document and work backwards, so Haylie was now beginning to transcribe the book code for the sixth time. Her mind was jelly at this point, and she knew there was a good chance she might be screwing up the code translation as her mind wandered.

So far, each transcription had only resulted in a mishmash of letters and numbers. Haylie knew that the book code's solution could very well be another code to break, so the weird results didn't necessarily mean she was on the wrong track. But it wasn't going to make this step of the puzzle any easier.

The Sterling brothers paced the hangar as she worked, stopping every now and then for brief chats with each other, staring blankly at their phones. Haylie could tell they were getting anxious, that they weren't used to the grind and boredom of trial and error. But the grind was where things happened—hacking wasn't some magical power, it was just never giving up. Good hackers just have the patience to do boring, mundane tasks over and over with slight variations until they finally see daylight on the other side, somehow.

"Finally, the *first* Will and Testament of Cecil John Rhodes, dated September 19th, 1877. This is the last one I have to transcribe."

"Thank God." Benjamin walked over from the other side of the hangar, running his hand across the leading edge of the jet's wing as he moved. "What does this one say?"

"Don't care what it says," Haylie said, the fatigue growing as she blinked her heavy eyes. "I just need the characters that match the book code." Haylie selected the full length of text and pasted it into TextEdit. Turning back to the book code, she found the tenth character on the first line and typed an 'H.'

"Well, I'll read the will while you do the math stuff." Benjamin walked over to Haylie to check the web address, typed it into his phone, and sank onto the couch next to her. "I've got nothing else to do. I'm starting to go a little crazy."

"By the way," Walter said from the other side of the room, "after you're done with school you should consider coming to work for us."

"I'll think about it," Haylie replied with a robotic tone.

"No, really," Walter said. "It would be great. You could work with Caesar, do this kind of stuff every day. You'd love it."

Looking up from her laptop with a dull sheen in her eyes, Haylie stared at Walter for a few seconds. "I could do *this* type of stuff for a living? This isn't programming, this is treasure maps and trinkets." She sunk back into her work. "I can't believe you guys run a software company and you have no idea what happens inside of it."

"We're good at what we do," Benjamin said, scrolling through the first Rhodes will on his phone. "And this is actually pretty fun. I love helping out, getting in the weeds."

"Just keep quiet and let me finish this thing," Haylie said. "You're going to screw up the result if you keep *helping* me."

After a few moments of reading, Benjamin jumped up from his seat, pointing at his phone. "Have you been reading this? Like, the stuff he's saying in here? It's crazy."

"Quiet, please," Haylie pleaded.

"No, really, it's insane." Benjamin continued scrolling. "It says here that Rhodes devoted a portion of his fortune, here's the quote: 'To and for the establishment, promotion and development of a Secret Society, the true aim and object whereof shall be for the extension of British rule all over the world.' Are you sure this is the right document?"

"I'm about ready for some lunch. We need to eat." Walter tucked his shirt back into his belt, patting his stomach and glancing around the room. "I'll call in an order. Marco, can you pick it up for us, please? What's good around here?"

"Pizza," Haylie said, eyes still fixed on her screen as she counted character positions, typing in one slow, methodical result at a time with a single finger.

"I don't want pizza. I'd like a nice salmon filet. Or maybe a smoothie?" Benjamin said, continuing to read. "Something with protein."

"I'll get something good," Walter said, walking to the other side of the hangar to talk to Marco.

"Pizza," Haylie repeated, her head turning back and forth between the book code and the text as she transcribed.

Benjamin rubbed his chin as he continued to read. "Ok, this gets weirder. The will includes a line talking about building a 'foundation of so great a Power as to render wars impossible and promote the best interests of humanity.' He was talking about creating a one-world government," Benjamin said.

"Well, the book code is working," Haylie said, raising her head out of the decoding results. "The first four letters were H, T, T, and P. The code is spelling out another URL, another link to a website. This is the will we were supposed to find."

She opened a new browser window and did a quick search. "Looks like he had some weird ideas about politics ... this article says he created Rhodes scholarships to bring more smart people to the UK from Europe, the U.S., everywhere, hoping they would stick around after school and help build the second British Empire."

"This is crazy," Benjamin said. "I had no idea."

"Lots of people think a one-world government is a good idea," Haylie said as she went back to decoding, squinting her eyes, trying to make out the next line. "There's a funny thing about that, though."

"What's that?" Benjamin asked.

"They only think it's a good idea if *they* are in charge." Haylie typed out a few more keystrokes as she located the correct letters. "What's wrong with people? You give someone money or power and they think they should run the world. Drives me crazy."

Benjamin edged back in his seat and away from Haylie, keeping his distance.

"Chill out, I'm not talking about you," Haylie said. "You guys are fine. Just give me a few minutes to finish this up. I'm almost there."

> > > > >

After fifteen more minutes of transcribing, Haylie raised her head to face the brothers in a daze. "I think I'm done," she said with an exhausted breath. The brothers quickly assembled, each hovering over a different shoulder from behind the couch.

With two more keystrokes, she had the full message decoded. Pasting the text into the browser address bar, she hit the RETURN key and they leaned in to check the result.

"Ok," Haylie said, "here it is."

"This is so cool," Walter said, leaning in closer.

A page from a popular file-sharing site filled the screen. It displayed a single icon at the center with a label directly below. The three of them watched the page, waiting for anything else to happen. Nothing did.

"It just says '2309,'" Benjamin said. "What is this?"

"It's a file," Haylie said. "Posted by an anonymous account. There's no other info about it listed in the description. We'll have to download it."

Benjamin checked his Rolex and rolled his neck left, then right. "So, download it. Let's get moving," he said. "Let's see what's inside this thing."

"Are you out of your mind?" she said. "I'm not downloading some random file. It could be a Trojan horse; it could be a keystroke monitor. It could wipe my machine clean. Let's not start making stupid mistakes."

Walter's phone let out a ping as he checked the message. "Marco's back with lunch. I'm going to go help him out; be right back." He jogged to the front door and slipped out.

"So, what do we do?" Benjamin asked.

Haylie's eyes drifted over to the far side of the hanger where, through the open war room door, Walter's ridiculous computer workstation sat, idling with a constant metallic hum.

"Walter wanted me to use that big, fancy machine, right?" Haylie said. "Well, today's his lucky day."

Benjamin smirked as the two rose, walking across the hangar in lockstep and into the war room. The world's most cutting edge hacking machine was finally going to be put to use—as a toxic waste dump.

Haylie slid into the ergonomic roller chair and all screens blinked to life with a click of the mouse. She rested her laptop to the side of the keyboard, squinting at the book code results and typing them into the browser window on the larger machine. After the page loaded, Haylie clicked the DOWNLOAD button next to the file. The machine sucked down the 130MB file in the blink of an eye. Haylie dragged it to the desktop and checked the file's details to find out what she was working with.

"Lunchtime, everyone," Walter's voice cried, loud enough for Haylie to hear through the open war room door. Benjamin stuck his head out into the main hangar and waved his brother down. Haylie could hear Walter trotting over, finally appearing with overstuffed brown bags in each hand. "What are you guys doing in here?"

"We're about to destroy your machine," Benjamin said.

"You're ... what?" Walter stuttered.

"Don't worry about it," Haylie said, scanning the details of the file. "What'd you get for lunch?"

"Oh, right," Walter said, gesturing with the bags in his hands. "I read on Yelp that the BBQ down here is amazing. So I called up the top rated place in the area and asked them for their best vegetarian stuff."

"Vegetarian?" Haylie asked, "Are you serious?"

"Sure," Walter said. "Benjamin and I try to eat healthy when we can."

Laughing, Haylie looked curiously at the bags in his hands. "Have you ever tried Texas BBQ before? There's nothing vegetarian about it."

Walter frowned and peeled open the mouth of the bag. Out came three containers of beans, a loaf of bread, and a plate full of pickles wrapped in cellophane. That was it.

"I said to give me everything vegetarian, enough for three people. They were laughing on the other end of the phone, but I figured...." Walter's eyes fell to his feet. "I don't know what I thought."

"You had *one job*, Walter," Haylie said.

"Stop saying that," Walter said, unwrapping the plate of pickles.

Turning back to the machine, Haylie pointed up to the main monitor that hung above their heads. "It's an ISO file, which means we'll need to boot up the system using the file as the OS. I'll need a USB drive." She searched the top of the desk, pushing away pens and stacks of Post-It notes to find a drive behind the stack of paper notebooks.

"Ok guys," Haylie said, grabbing the drive. "Buckle your seatbelts."

CHAPTER TW3LV3

Capital of Texas Airpark - Austin, TX
March 7th, 2:50PM

"The drive is ready," Haylie said. "If you were planning to take any photos of your shiny new computer as a souvenir, now would be a good time." She pushed the drive into the machine's chassis and rebooted.

As the computer sparked back to life, Haylie held the ALT/OPTION key down tight, forcing the machine to restart using the USB key instead of its normal OS.

boot:
Loading /boot/vmlinuz...............
Loading /boot/2309.img.............
Decompressing Linux… Parsing ELF… done.
Booting the kernel.

"What's it doing?" Benjamin stood a few feet behind the desk, crunching on a pickle. "This looks weird. I don't think it's working."

"It's just loading, doing its thing. Give it a minute," Haylie said, her eyes fixed on the main screen.

Booting Core 4.7.2
Running Linux Kernel 3.0.21-tinycore.
Checking boot options...Done.

Suddenly, after a few more commands executed, the screen came to life with a giant blurred green image constructed out of console text. It spanned the entire width of all six screens, lighting the dim room with an eerie, ghost-like glow.

Its form was unmistakable.

"It's a raven," Walter said, pointing at the screen on the left.

Haylie nodded. "It sure looks that way." She turned around to face Benjamin. "Do you think it's working *now*?"

The boot sequence paused for a few moments, displaying only a blinking lime green cursor in a field of black. A few seconds later, numbers began to appear, one by one.

```
  2   3   5   7  11  13  17  19  23  29
 31  37  41  43  47  53  59  61  67  71
 73  79  83  89  97 101 103 107 109 113
127 131 137 139 149 151 157 163 167 173
181 191 193 197 199 211 223 239 241 251
257 263 269 271 277 281 283 293 307 311
313 317 331 337 347 349 353 359 367 373
379 383 389 397 401 409 419 421 431 433
439 443 449 457 461 463 467 479 487 491
```

The numbers filled the giant screen—ten numbers, left to right, then down to the next line—until the script hit the number '1039.' The program paused printing for a few seconds, and then got back to work.

"I don't get it. It's just a bunch of numbers," Walter said.

"Not just any numbers," Haylie muttered as she scanned the readout. "Prime numbers. All of them. It's a list of every prime number, in order. 2309 is prime, too—I'm guessing this is building up to that."

"So what does it mean?" Benjamin asked.

"Maybe it's a clue—or maybe whoever created these puzzles is trying to make some kind of point. Who knows, they could just be messing with us." Haylie watched as the script resumed printing, continuing its progression with the same pattern. The readout began to scroll faster and faster as more and more rows of prime numbers were added—one at a time, ten in a row.

"We're almost to 2309," Walter said, slowly taking a few steps away from the computer. Benjamin, noticing his movement, followed with silent, backward footsteps on the concrete.

"It's not going to blow up. Get back over here you idiots." Haylie shook her head and took a bite out of the two pieces of white bread she had found at the bottom of the lunch bag. "Here we go."

The program hit 2309 and the screen froze. The cursor began to blink as the three watched and waited. With a flash, the screen went dark, and another message appeared.

> 38.466555, -122.999732
>
> now it's time to enter the real world.
>
> deep in the woods, Weaving Spiders Come Not Here.
>
> find the next step behind the founding father.
>
> good luck.
>
> /2309

"Weaving spiders?" Benjamin asked. "What the hell?"

"These first two numbers," Haylie said. "They look like coordinates: latitude and longitude." She looked down to her laptop, typing the two digits into Google Maps. As the location loaded, she saw an overhead view of miles and miles of deep green forest cover.

"What are we looking at?" Walter asked.

Haylie zoomed out, toggling between street map and satellite views; there wasn't much to see. A few, small roads that curved around the bend of a winding river. A group of small cabins, nestled together, partially hidden under the foliage.

"California," she said, leaning back into the chair. "It's just north of San Francisco, deep in the redwoods. A bunch of cabins all clustered together in the middle of nowhere. Some sort of camp."

She stood, turning to face the jet. It gleamed under the spotlight at the center of the hangar. Her heart began to pound.

This is about to get interesting.

> > > > >

The Grove Hotel - Watford, England
March 7th, 9:05PM

The Kent Room, nestled deep in the basement of the Grove's patchwork of ancient hallways, was brimming over with activity. Charcoal-suited men huddled, whispering in each corner with worn expressions showing worry and growing fear. Suddenly, a single voice shouted from the center of the room.

"This has gone too far!"

The leadership of the Bilderberg group met regularly, and even more so in the weeks and days leading up to The Project's zero hour. As the start date grew closer, the tone of the group had slid from optimistic to brittle. Earlier in the evening, Gregory Stein, the US Secretary of State, had stealthily tapped each of the twelve men and two women that made up The Project's core team, informing them that a meeting was needed in urgent fashion; each, that is, save one.

"Crowne needs to learn that we are all in this together," Stein said, spinning to catch the eyes of the room. "The foundation for this group—and the enormous risk that we have all taken on—is based on trust. This cannot be the way we operate going...."

"Forward?" Crowne entered the room as the door closed shut behind him, locking from the inside. He watched the room and paced slowly to the middle, stopping next to the Secretary. "Is this your doing, Greg? A secret meeting with everyone but me? Who is breaking the trust of the group, now?"

Stein shook his head as he pointed his finger in the PM's face. "The difference is this: I didn't kill anyone today."

"No, no. But you will. Yes? In the next few days, in fact. Isn't that what this is all about, really? The guilt of what we're about to do? Second thoughts, perhaps? Cold feet?"

"Why weren't we told about the German Chancellor?" Stein demanded. "And what else don't we know about?"

"There's no grand conspiracy here," Crowne crossed his arms, surveying the room. "I had to act on the Chancellor within minutes. I didn't have time to inform the group, and I wouldn't change my decision. I know it feels strange. Things are going to be different when The Project begins, and we should all get used to it. It's going to take a little faith, but faith grows over time. Please, sit. Everyone, sit. Let's talk about the problems we face. If we're not open with each other, we can't be successful."

Stein's face grew red. "We should have taken a vote."

"No more voting," Crowne shot back. "Voting, debating, arguing, spinning in circles with no forward motion, that's all just muscle memory. Running back to the old, forgetting to embrace the new path. The *better* path."

"We must delay. The organization is not ready," said the Japanese liaison from the back of the room. "I have submitted three different technology leaders for your approval, none of which have made it past the first round."

"I'm working on getting a leader in place," Crowne replied.

"Technology is the cornerstone of the next few months," Secretary Stein said, surveying the room for agreement. "If we don't have–"

"Understood," Crowne cut him off. Pausing to think for a moment, he grimaced and looked back up to Stein. "I'll bring in my top man, Martin Bell, to help get that process moving along. We have a candidate in the loop, but we've had some delays getting him on board. I'll make sure that gets resolved. Anything else?"

"You talk about our path and about trust," said the South African minister. "How can we have faith in *you* when you're sneaking behind our backs, assassinating members of our own group? That isn't the type of decision you get to make alone."

Crowne removed his jacket and rolled his shirt sleeves up his forearms, slowly.

"Let's all calm down and remember why we're here," Crowne said. "In fact, let me remind you. Just recently I was building a proposal to rekindle our space research program here in Britain. We'd been working over the past few years on a new push to detect intelligent life in the Universe. Fascinating stuff, yes? The chance to change the course of humanity, for sure."

Crowne continued to pace the room as he spoke. "But of course, as soon as we began testing it through the normal channels, the plans just ended up being shredded, pushed aside. We received warnings from all sides: one claimed the budget could be better used for schools, the next wanted to throw the whole lot out the window. You all know the drill. The proposal will never see the light of day, even if I think it's the right thing to do."

He paused, staring off past the walls as his mind churned.

"Even if *I know* it's the right thing to do."

Heads around the room began to nod knowingly as a few members abandoned their forward stances. Others uncrossed their arms, resting back into their chairs.

"You want to know something funny?" Crowne continued. "In one of the footnotes of the plan, there was a mention of something I'd never heard of before. Something called the Fermi Paradox. Has anyone heard of it?"

The leaders each checked around the room. Baris Ansari, the Minister from Turkey raised his hand subtly from his seat. Crowne had always liked Baris—a man that came from science and wasn't interested in the power and prestige of politics. A man that just wanted to help people. A rare man.

"Fermi was an interesting man," Ansari said. "He knew, with the vast size and age of the universe, that civilizations have absolutely existed elsewhere—species that are far more advanced than our own. But he wondered why none of these species have ever reached out to Earth to say 'hello.'"

Crowne walked towards the front of the chamber, pacing his steps to the cadence of Ansari's words, stopping to face the painting at the head of the room. The scene depicted a fox hunting party, complete with horses, hounds, and servants carrying weapons and a collection of fresh kills. The deep greens of the foliage mixed with the blended dusk sky of dark blues and oranges, making it hard to tell where one began and the other ended. Half the hunting party was pointed in the direction of the dense forest, the other half turning back.

"And what was Fermi's conclusion as to why this has never happened ... why other civilizations haven't tried to contact us?" Crowne asked.

Ansari cleared his throat and sat back. "Fermi believed that all intelligent civilizations self-destruct at some point. Whether through war, or pollution, or overpopulation—that intelligent life always has a blind spot. If his theory is correct, we can assume that other advanced species aren't contacting Earth simply because they no longer exist."

Crowne examined the painting closer, squinting for a better view. The group on the left wasn't turning back at all, they had rifles in their hands. The group moving forward was just there to drive the foxes from the brush. *Well, look at that.*

"It's a shame about Adele. We are all agreed on that point," Crowne said. "But I think we all know that we aren't here to destroy each other; so let's not get dramatic. We're here to save this place, this planet that we love. Our human race. We're here to stop our civilization from destroying itself. I don't believe it's too late for our world, but we're not going to change things by handing out flyers and having more debates. A democratic approach will bring us right back where we started. It's too late for that."

Crowne turned back around to face the group and traced his path around the head table.

"If you won't do it, I'll do it myself," he said slowly. Leaning in towards the group, balanced on his fists, the veins in his forearms popped past his crisp, rolled sleeves. "But I'd rather do it with you, my friends."

The room stirred. The assembled leaders shifted in their seats. A few whispered, and others looked to the floor with questions still lingering in their eyes.

"Genocide, famine, global warming, rising tensions from old battles already fought," Crowne continued. "What will it take? The problem is with democracy. Discussion doesn't change people's minds, and I don't know that it ever did. We are lifeguards, not leaders. None of us can say that elected officials have given us a better government, or a better way of life. Don't you all realize *we* are those leaders? That we are the ones who have been sent to solve this problem? We know that democracy is a failure. We know that a small, smart group of people can fix this. And as of next week, this group will no longer spend its energy in wasted, circular motion. From this point on, we finally *lead*."

Suddenly, the room erupted in applause. Only one member, King Raul of Saudi Arabia, held his hands at his sides.

"But can't we do this another way, my friends?" the King interjected, as the applause died out. "Can we course correct without killing millions of people and having their blood on our hands? Adele didn't have to die, and neither does anyone else."

Crowne smiled, approaching the King and sliding his hand on his shoulder.

"We're not going to kill anyone, Raul. We're just going to turn everything off."

CHAPTER TH1RT33N

A giant, glowing rectangle of white light framed the silhouette of the jet as the pilot ascended up the stairs, his freshly-shined black shoes thudding up each step, one by one. A flight attendant followed closely behind, checking final details on an iPad as she glided onto the plane.

Haylie glanced down, tracing the path of her worn, chocolate-brown leather boots as they shuffled across the concrete floor. Looking over to Walter, who was just finishing up a phone call, Haylie pulled her hair behind her head, letting it fall right back down on her shoulders.

This is all happening too fast. I barely even know these clowns and I'm about to jump on a jet with them?

The approaching sound of footsteps snapped her out of her thoughts. Her eyes rose to see Walter in front of her. She faked a weak smile.

"We're about to get going, Benjamin's already on board," Walter said, pointing over to the stairs. "Let's get your stuff ready and head out."

She watched him make his way towards the plane as Haylie turned back to face the open hangar door, the wind blowing across her face. Her mind raced, her legs stood still, frozen.

"Hey," Walter said from mid-way up the stairs, "don't worry. This will be a piece of cake. And besides, we've got your back. It's going to be fun—just think of it as an adventure."

Haylie nodded.

"Let me ask you something," Walter said. "That stuff you've done in the past: breaking into networks, sneaking past security. Can you still do that?"

"Sure," she said with a shrug. "I mean, I can find my way in when I need to."

"Good," he said with a relieved smile. "I have a feeling we're going to need some of that."

Haylie exhaled loudly and picked up her bags.

Ok, Crash. Time to get to work.

CHAPTER FOURT33N

Somewhere Over Nevada
March 7th, 5:57PM

As Haylie stared out the jet's window, she drifted off into her mind. She remembered circling her feet in unison, toes extended as they rested on the cushy ottoman, rotating around and around at the ankle. She found herself back in her living room, years ago, staring at the television set....

She was trying to enjoy her favorite show, but this episode was taking awhile to get to the good stuff. As she cranked up the volume, the *thump thump thump* of a helicopter filled the speakers, and Desmond began explaining something called a 'temporal paradox.'

Ugh. 'Lost' was so much better before they let people off the island.

Caesar walked into the living room, looking quickly over to the kitchen to make sure they were alone. "Hey, pause that for a second, would you?"

"Umm, no. I think something's actually about to happen here," Haylie said. Summer vacations were all about compromise, and he'd had his chance to watch 'Dr. Who' earlier. This was her slot.

Caesar snatched the remote from the ottoman and clicked the pause button, resulting in two smeared, frozen snapshots of the otherwise-handsome Desmond and Faraday.

"Hey, gimme that back," Haylie said, reaching for the remote.

"This will just take a second."

Pushing back into the couch, arms folded, Haylie pouted back at him.

Caesar sat down close to Haylie. "Listen. I've been hearing some rumors and I wanted to give you a heads up. A guy I talk to a lot—a guy that knows his stuff—he warned me that there has been some weird activity around the Sceptre message boards."

The Sceptre site was a rare place of refuge for Haylie in her young years. Not only did the forum host message boards with every sort of technical discussion you could think of, but also a few super-geeky text-based adventure games where she could blindly navigate through mazes and towns, bumping into other users along the way. It was addictive.

"What kind of stuff?" she asked.

"Bad stuff," he said. "A bunch of kids posting credit card numbers. Trading them, using them. You know anything about that?"

Her eyes focused on Caesar, and without blinking, replied "Nope."

Caesar shook his head. "Ok, idiot. I'm here to help you, not get you busted."

Haylie stood firm.

He whispered, continuing. "Here's the deal. This guy told me that there's a crackdown coming. Sounds like one of these cards belonged to a Senator, charged some embarrassing stuff to his account. Now he's pissed. He's ordering a task force—we're talking Federal-level stuff. Handcuffs and prison time, things you don't want any part of."

Her folded arms fell as she tried, without success, to hide her face growing flush.

"You're a minor, but they'll still bust you. You could get years of probation, fines, and they'll take everything electronic away. You won't even be able to use this DVR to watch this dumb show. You need to stop, *now*."

Haylie quickly grabbed around Caesar for the remote control, but he blocked her way with a right chop, like a hockey goalie making a quick save.

"I said I haven't done anything like that. I'm not stupid," she said.

"I know you're not stupid, and that's why it would suck for you to get caught *doing* something stupid. Sometimes we get ourselves into things without seeing the big picture." Caesar tossed Haylie the remote.

"And you don't need anything, anyway. If you haven't noticed, we're not exactly hurting for money around here."

Silence filled the living room as Haylie's heart pounded. She laid the remote down on the cushion, tears welling up in her eyes. "I figured the credit cards were bogus. I couldn't believe it when they actually worked. I just bought a couple of computer magazines, nothing big."

Caesar stood and moved a few steps away, his head hung low. Seeing him disappointed stopped her in her tracks.

"You're good at this stuff, Haylie. I know you're good. You're better than other people. It's a gift. But the bad news is: you don't get to do whatever you want with it. Don't waste it on a few stolen magazines. If you want to be special, do it the right way. Be *better* than other people."

The frozen faces from the television stared Haylie down as she sat up, nodding.

Caesar walked to the door and turned back to face Haylie. "Just remember, this isn't always going to be black and white, it's mostly shades of gray. Remember that."

"What do you mean," Haylie asked. "Shades of gray?"

"Sometimes you'll find yourself doing bad stuff for good reasons. But you always need that good reason. It's confusing, but you'll know it when you see it."

Haylie watched as Caesar left the room, her eyes floating back to the TV. She tossed the remote aside and stared down at the floor. Flushed with frustration, heart beating fast. She inhaled a deep, long breath.

Shades of gray.

> > > > >

Benjamin snapped his fingers twice in the air. "Haylie. You still with us?"

Wedged in the corner of her huge leather chair, Haylie watched the scenes outside the plane's window, getting lost in the orange of the building sunset. The patchwork clouds flowed below, like river water at the crest of oncoming rapids. The setting sun shot a line of orange across the horizon, reflecting off the window pane, spitting flecks of fire.

"Sure, I'm here," she said.

When Haylie had boarded the jet an hour earlier, she felt like she was entering a whole new world. She had slowly made her way up the stairs—ten perfectly balanced steps with delicate lights illuminating every other platform—and could smell the mixed bouquet of leather and fresh flowers before she even walked on board. Inside, she found a cabin appointed with dark wood, light leather chairs and spacious couches. Most of the chairs sat facing each other, while a few bench seats ran along the opposite side of the cabin. This was not the way she, or most people in the world, normally travelled.

It had been the quickest takeoff Haylie had ever experienced; no safety overview or long taxi down three different runways. They just closed the door and went. As the plane rose to cruising altitude, Haylie drifted back and forth between daydreams and a quick nap as the brothers caught up on email, industry news, and missed phone calls.

Benjamin sat across from her, clicking his phone down on the rich, polished wood table. "The pilot tells me we should be there in about three hours. What's the game plan?"

Haylie stretched her arms above her head and reached back down, deep into her backpack's main pocket. She retrieved her laptop and cracked the shell, quickly typing in her password.

"I did some research while the crew was prepping the plane," she said. "This is about to get a little weird."

"Weirder than rabbit pictures and Rhodesia?" Benjamin asked.

"Yeah, weirder," Haylie said. "This isn't just code breaking anymore. I'll show you—I'm assuming with the amount of money you guys spent on this plane, it has Wi-Fi? I hope?"

Walter smiled. "Sure. The password is 'indigo,' but with a '1' for each 'i.'"

"That's a terrible password." Haylie joined the network and opened the document that held her research. "You're not going to believe some of this stuff."

Benjamin, half-paying attention, as he read his email, chuckled. "Try us," he said.

"Let's look at a few different pieces of the clue," Haylie said. "First, the coordinates. They identify a camp outside of Santa Rosa, about seventy-five miles north of San Francisco. It's right by the Russian River, surrounded by a few hundred acres of woods. The Google Maps view shows a few clearings, a couple of buildings here and there, and one road that dead ends in the middle. But that's it. Anything else hiding in there is covered by forest."

"So, what's the big deal? It's just some random camp?" Walter asked, sitting down next to Haylie to get a better view of the map.

"That's where it gets interesting," she said. "When you search the geolocation of the camp with another part of the clue, the phrase 'Weaving Spiders Come Not Here,' some crazy results come up," Haylie rested her chin on the palm of her hand as she flipped over to the search results. "It makes me think this could be tricky."

"Why?" Benjamin asked. "What does it say?"

"It's the motto of some group called the Bohemian Club," she said, pointing at the top search result. "It looks like they are some sort of real-life secret society. They own a camp called the Bohemian Grove—according to this article, it's located right around the area we're looking at."

"So this Bohemian Grove, that's where we need to go?" Benjamin asked.

Walter paused for a moment. "This sounds familiar. Benjamin, do you remember … Dad used to talk about meetings out in the woods in California. He would always come back with stories. Meeting famous people, politicians, businessmen. It seemed to get bigger and bigger each year."

"Your father was a part of this group?" Haylie said.

"Maybe," Walter said. "At least for a while."

"Well, then, welcome to the one percent," Haylie said. "The Google results for this stuff start getting pretty crazy. There's like a hundred conspiracy theory websites and a ton of YouTube videos about this place. The only thing that's for sure is that it's legit, and it's very, very secretive."

Hovering over across the keyboard, Walter clicked on the top link and began to read out loud. "'Founded in 1872 as a regular meeting of journalists, artists, and musicians.' There's a headquarters in downtown San Francisco and a campground in the woods. Some of the past members include Ronald Reagan ... Nixon ... Mark Twain ... Henry Kissinger ... all of the Bushes. Alan Greenspan. Henry Morgan, son of JP Morgan. Secretaries of State, foreign heads of state ... good lord, this list is crazy."

"Sounds like Burning Man for old, rich people," Benjamin said.

"Old rich *men*. Women aren't allowed," Haylie said with a scowl as she continued reading. "For real."

"No one will go on the record about what goes on in there, except for this one guy," Walter said, still scrolling. "He bragged that the first concepts for the Manhattan Project and the United Nations both came out of the Grove. He's no longer a member, for obvious reasons." He looked up from the screen. "I can't believe this place actually exists."

"I can't believe that we actually have to get in there, somehow." Haylie's pulse quickened as she planned the next step. "The riddle says we need to find the next clue behind the founding father. I'd guess that means either a statue or picture of the guy that started this place, located somewhere in the camp."

"So," Walter asked, "you need to walk into the middle of the camp? Won't there be security?"

She thought for a few moments. A nervous wave had been sweeping over her body for the past minute or so, but now it was beginning to crest. Her stomach turned, she felt a bit light-headed. *We're not actually going to do this, right? And how did Caesar get away with this?* She took control of her breathing and refocused.

"It's just a system, like any other," she said. "All we have to do is find the faults. We'll need to gain an understanding of their physical security capabilities and then work around them. According to one of these conspiracy sites, the next big meeting isn't scheduled for a few more months. That means security should be a bit more relaxed now, right?"

"You would think," Walter said.

"So if the camp is empty," Haylie continued, "we can coordinate a good plan between the three of us, pull the security teams away from the main camp. We'll just need to work together."

Walter and Benjamin exchanged looks.

"Haylie, there's something we should have been clear about from the start," Benjamin said. "We … there's this thing."

Haylie stopped in her tracks. She leaned back from her screen, crossing her arms tight across her chest. "Oh, really?" she asked. "There's a *thing*?"

"We're here to help your progress," Benjamin continued, "but we're—Walter and I—we obviously can't do anything illegal. We're going to need you to go in there alone. We just can't…." His voice trailed off as he watched her face turn.

Haylie had stopped dead in her tracks. She shut the lid to her laptop with a firm, precise click. She spoke, slowly. "Can you say that again?"

Benjamin thought long before continuing. "You have to understand. This type of activity, if we're talking about sneaking into a high-security facility, it's a felony. Walter and I have thousands of people that depend on us for their jobs. We can't be found sneaking around in places we don't belong." He gestured around at the interior of the private jet. "We can't risk all this."

Haylie's curious stare began to flash over to anger. "But it's okay for *me*? It's fine If I get arrested by some backwater security team in God-knows-where California? There's nothing wrong with *that* plan?"

Benjamin turned to look out the window with a wave of his hand.

"You," she pointed a finger in Walter's face. "*You* said that you had my back before I got on this stupid…."

She pushed past the brothers and sprinted down the aisle, stopping at the back galley. *I need to get off this plane. I don't believe this. I need to get back to Austin.* She paced, running her hands through her hair, her mind darting from scenario to scenario, none of them good.

Walter jumped in. "Haylie, we *are* in this together. I said we have your back, and I meant it. We're here to support you—we just need to do it from a distance. And let's think about the big picture here, we all want the same thing; we all want to find Caesar. I'm sorry that this is a surprise to you, but you have to understand what Benjamin and I are risking here."

Her icy stare worked its way down the narrow aisle and back towards the brothers.

"Well, I'm not doing it," she said. "Turn the plane back around. Caesar will come back online eventually. He always does. I don't need to go on some flipping field trip through the woods. There's not going to be anything in there, anyway. I'm done with this."

Walter rose to his feet, rocking on his heels with his head down. He looked up at Haylie, but said nothing.

"Tell her," Benjamin said. "Tell her, Walter."

"Tell me *what*?" she said.

"Right before we took off ... our security team in New York," Walter stammered. "They got access to Caesar's apartment. The entire place had been overturned, his stuff was everywhere. Someone was there before us, and they were trying to find something."

"It looks like he might actually be in trouble," Benjamin said.

Haylie fell into the nearest seat, crumpled over into a twisted fetal position. Her mind raced violently, her teeth gritting together as she felt the anger rise in her cheeks.

"Who is it?" she asked. "Who has him?"

"We don't know, but we're going to find out," Benjamin said. "But this next step in the Bohemian Grove ... it's our best move to make progress. Walter and I, we'll do anything we can do, other than walking in there with you. We're here to help, absolutely. We have resources that can ... we are–"

Haylie extended her hand up to Benjamin, indicating he should shut up. She leaned over to the side of the plane, looking out at the passing clouds. The blue of the sky soaked right into amber as she could see the faint light of the night's first stars beginning to make their way through the daylight.

"Don't worry about helping," Haylie said. She walked briskly back to her seat. "I'm glad we're all clear on the rules. But if you're going to sit in your limo while I do the hard work, it's going to cost you. I need to go shopping."

Benjamin and Walter both looked relieved. Haylie cracked her laptop open and began typing. She extended her hand out to Benjamin while she scrolled with the other hand.

"Credit card," she said without making eye contact.

Benjamin nervously patted his wallet in his pocket with his right hand. "Now I don't...."

"CREDIT CARD," Haylie repeated.

Benjamin removed his wallet and handed over an American Express Black Card, eying Walter. Benjamin opened his mouth to speak.

"Don't," she shot back.

CHAPTER F1FT33N

Monte Rio, CA
March 8th, 4:25PM

Pockets of thick, wet forest air rolled over mountains of ferns as the soil gave way. Haylie marched forward, feeling the soft crunch of twigs trapped between her boot and the spongy forest floor. The sweet, earthy scents of soil filled her nostrils as she scanned the area ahead, carefully treading boot over boot.

She turned to check behind her but saw only a never-ending splatter of green and brown; tall ferns and bright moss covered every spare inch of ground. A crisscross pattern of fallen, rotting trees blocked certain paths and opened up others. It felt like a lifetime since she had stepped up the stairs of that jet, but it had only been about twenty-four hours. Still, she had to get moving.

And she was not making good time.

Haylie had been walking for over an hour and felt herself slipping farther and farther away from any trace of civilization with each step. She could hear only the dull faded buzz of the forest all around—short sprints of chirps broken by an occasional rapid-fire pattern of cackling, echoing off the damp tree trunks. She looked to the forest canopy above, seeing only a few lucky slices of daylight fighting past the twisted branches and blackness that hung above, all swaying from the building wind.

I won't be able to see anything once the sun goes down ... but that's what the drone is for.

When Haylie and the Sterling brothers had landed at SFO last night, a driver had been waiting for them on the tarmac. It only took a few hours to make their way north to Monte Rio. They had found an out-of-the-way

Motel 6, and each crashed in their own room, with Benjamin paying for the lot with a few crisp hundred-dollar bills. Haylie was able to break the weak WEP encryption on the wireless network with a quick packet injection attack to get online. Sure, Internet access only cost a few bucks but, in Haylie's mind, the real crime was asking people to pay for Wi-Fi in the first place. Not cool.

Earlier that morning, Haylie's online shopping orders had arrived at the motel front desk. *Thank God for Amazon's one-day shipping.* What she needed was pretty simple: components to piece together a custom drone capable of giving her the advantage against any security systems the Bohemian Grove would have in place.

There were plenty of models to choose from—including a bunch of plug-and-play drones that were aimed at kids—but to build out the advanced capabilities she needed, Haylie had to do some extra work. A few good hobbyist forums had helped her piece together the plans for a solid surveillance drone by choosing the best hardware and a mishmash of open source software; all it took was a few simple modifications to bring everything together.

As it turned out, multi-rotor drones were the best choice for short distances, and luckily there were a few that could be shipped to Monte Rio within a few hours' time.

The battery she chose would normally provide around forty-five minutes worth of flight, but Haylie's modifications would bring that number down. How far down was the real question. She figured the drone would need three cameras to find all security measures scattered across the camp, and each camera would add considerable weight. One camera would provide a forward-facing view for her to pilot the vehicle; another downward-facing high-definition camera would show a live feed of the ground below; and the final infrared camera would cut through the thick forest canopy, providing Haylie perspective on any heat signatures inside the camp.

Haylie's last modification to the drone was to add an onboard Raspberry Pi—a tiny, stripped-down computer that could be used for all sorts of different stuff. The Raspberry Pi was running a code package named Loopy, which would survey the forest below for anything with a Wi-Fi or Bluetooth signal, and send the information back to Haylie's phone. With this setup, she'd have a real-time aerial map of every phone, computer, or camera in the Bohemian Grove, hopefully steering her far away from security guards that would be on patrol as she explored the camp.

That was the plan, anyway.

She'd spent the night studying up on schematics and writing custom code that would allow her to operate the drone as a one-woman show, based off some flight controller code that was available on the web. Once the packages had arrived, it didn't take long to assemble the hardware and load the firmware; after a few hours of toying and testing, Haylie was happy with the result.

To stay on schedule, Haylie had time for just one test flight before she needed to enter the woods. She had snuck out into a pasture tucked in right behind their motel, waiting ten minutes to make sure the coast was clear. With a press of the ACTIVATE button, the drone, which she had affectionately named BusyBee, lifted from the ground. Her flight plan sent the device to hover over the Bohemian Grove's coordinates, instructing the machine to send back reports of any heat signatures and device signals it could find.

After a ten-minute flight at an altitude of roughly one thousand feet, BusyBee sent back its first round of data. What she found was encouraging; a series of buildings clustered together, surrounded by a loose patchwork of what must be Wi-Fi enabled security cameras fixed throughout the perimeter. The drone had also detected a handful of heat signatures slowly moving between buildings, but none on patrol in the surrounding woods. She took a screenshot of the view and saved it to her phone; that image would serve as a good map for an approach towards the camp. Once she got close enough, she'd switch over to a live feed for a real-time view of the guard positions.

After charging BusyBee back up to full power, Haylie hiked down the road and past twin reservoirs located directly south of the Bohemian Grove's outer fence line. She easily scaled the barrier, picking a section without any security cameras or guard outposts, and headed north. Checking her saved map to steer clear of the sixteen Wi-Fi-powered security stations laid out around the camp, she began her journey on a course to find the center of the Grove. She figured it would be best to arrive at the camp close to dusk, but the terrain had proven to be more difficult than planned.

Haylie, now deep in the forest, stopped to listen for any signs of civilization, but all she could hear was the patterned chatter of birds and the occasional rustle from a fern.

What the hell am I doing here?

She sat for a moment at the base of a colossal redwood, sliding down the mossy trunk to rest on the forest floor. She reached down to the earth, taking a handful into her fist and watching the dark fibers of mulch fall from between her fingers. Breathing in and out, in and out.

> > > > >

"Getting dark, getting dark, getting dark," Haylie whispered to herself as she squinted for a better view. She pulled off her glasses, wiping a thin layer of condensation from the lenses, and slid her sleeve across her forehead to clear off the sweat. She zipped her field jacket, shoving her hands in the side pockets as a chill filled the forest air.

Haylie pushed north, and the remaining daylight faded with each step. The sunbeams lighting her way had all but died off, leaving only a dark, soupy view of the path ahead. Haylie's confidence in making it to the Grove by nightfall was fading fast, but at least she had been able to avoid the web of security cameras littered throughout the woods. She had yet to see any sign of buildings or other forms of civilization, and she wasn't about to send in BusyBee before absolutely necessary, wasting precious battery power. She stopped for a pause, emptying the last of her plastic water bottle into her parched mouth.

"This sucks," she said under her breath, pulling her hair back into a tight ponytail. She took out her phone to check the map once again.

It's been a few hours ... the guards could have moved anywhere by now. Where the hell am I?

A few minutes earlier, Haylie had to curve around a stream, crawling over a downed log to find her way across the rushing water. She resumed her trek in the same general direction as before, but found it was very easy to get turned around in these woods. Even with her phone's compass, she could easily be hundreds of yards off course.

Haylie heard a sudden rustle of leaves and darted behind a redwood, pinning her back tightly to the bark. Trying not to breathe, Haylie froze in place. After a few seconds she heard the crunch again, this time getting closer. Human footsteps. *Damnit.*

She snaked her head as far around the tree as she could without showing herself, but still couldn't see a thing through the darkness. That's when she heard it: a loud exhale and sudden cough, followed by the sound of liquid hitting dirt, slowly dripping down the leaves of a neighboring bush with a pat-pat-pat rhythm.

What is that? Is someone ... taking a leak?

An audible groan filled the air from the other side of the huge redwood, followed by a steady stream of liquid wrapping its way around the trunk. The stream headed downhill and formed a small pool at her feet. *Well, this is charming.* Haylie controlled her breathing, pinning herself closer to the tree trunk and remaining as still as her racing pulse would allow. A strange, slurring voice filled the air, causing her heart to beat even faster.

"I say, I say ... there's no excuse for not getting away once in awhile. Feeds the soul, it does." The man on the other side of the tree let out a loud belch as he finished relieving himself.

"And I appear, yes, I appear to be out of wine." There was a brief break of silence and then the unmistakable sound of a zipper heading north. "They shall make more, I believe. As they always do."

Suddenly, a wine bottle flew past the tree trunk, inches from Haylie's shoulder, hitting another tree directly across from her. The projectile exploded into a spray of dark glass and fell to the forest floor, disappearing into the black.

"And I shall find some more of that wine, now. Very good."

Haylie heard the visitor's heavy, slurred steps marching into the brush, directly north and away from her position. She hadn't been expecting visitors, but as she thought back to her research on the plane, the man's presence made more and more sense. She quickly remembered a few mentions of local Bohemian Club members that would visit the Grove for smaller, private trips now and then.

That's when she smelled it. Not the smell of piss, but the unmistakable smoky whiff of a campfire, riding a quick turn of the wind and blowing light flecks of ash up into the air.

She had reached the edge of the Bohemian Grove.

Haylie shuffled to hide behind a neighboring tree, one without urine pooling at the roots, and crouched against the base of the trunk, knees bent and her back straight against the bark. She removed her phone from her pocket, clutching the screen close to her chest to keep the light from traveling, and brought up the drone controller app. She tapped the button labeled 'activate flight plan 1.'

Haylie sat firm, huddled in the darkness. Waiting.

C'mon BusyBee. Fly fast.

> > > > >

The wind whipped the curtain of Walter's dimly lit motel room as the Sterling brothers sat side-by-side on the lumpy mattress, peering out through the screen and into the California dusk. Walter looked back across his shoulder, checking the door for any surprises. All he saw was what the room had to offer: dated furniture, carbon-copy artwork in dented brass frames, and a bedspread that held more secrets than he cared to think about.

They had a front row seat to the twisting two-lane road that cut the small town of Monte Rio in half. The darkness was taking over, but Walter could still make out the lines of a rickety white picket fence that lined the opposite side of the road; power lines perched above, slicing the sky. The tree line began about fifty feet behind a gravel parking lot littered with a few odd vehicles.

"We need to tell Haylie what's going on," Walter whispered, his eyes following the headlights as they ran right to left across the window. "This isn't good."

"You really think that's a good idea?" Benjamin asked, stepping back away from the window.

For the past twenty minutes, the brothers had seen a constant flow of headlights heading in the direction of the Bohemian Grove. Most were black town cars, all with tinted windows; many of them were flanked at the front and back by larger SUVs, presumably holding security. One after another, every thirty seconds. A parade of vehicles heading right towards the camp.

This wasn't part of the plan.

"We must have seen a hundred cars heading to the Grove just in the past hour," Walter said, his eyes following each approaching pair of headlights. "There's something going on in there. We need to let Haylie know what she's walking into—this is bad. Let's text her."

"Text her. *Text her?* Great idea, Walter. I love this idea." Benjamin glared at his brother. "Let's see ... when she's caught tonight while performing surveillance on some of the most powerful people in the world, I'm sure they won't check her phone, right? Why would they? It's only the *first* thing they'll do."

Walter backed away from the window and moved to the other side of the bed as Benjamin continued to lecture him. "And whose number will be the first one they find on that phone?" Benjamin said. "Oh good, it's the Sterlings. Now we've got a *conspiracy*. Now we've got a story that press around the world will run with."

"There has to be a way," Walter said. "We can't just leave her out there on her own. She's heading right into trouble. This is no good for any of us. If she gets caught, we don't solve Raven. We *need* to solve Raven, and we can't do it on our own. The clock is ticking. If Haylie gets caught, it's all for nothing."

"There's nothing we can do here, Walter. It's up to her now."

Walter walked back to the window, pulling the curtain to the side, catching the scents of mildew and cigarettes that would live in this room long after they left. Three more pairs of headlights flew by, right to left.

Night had fallen, and as the beams of light crossed the picket fence along the road, they carried moving, living, breathing crisscross patterns along with them.

Teeth clenched, all Walter could do was stare out the window and wait.

CHAPTER SIXTEEN

Monte Rio, CA
March 8th, 8:10PM

Hands trembling, eyes darting back and forth across the shadows of the landscape, Haylie tried her best to focus. She hadn't been able to make out anything in the darkness for at least ten minutes now. She concentrated on her breathing—deep, slow breaths—a futile attempt to bring calm to her racing pulse. *Where is that stupid drone?* Fixed in her crouched position, she patted her pocket gently to make sure her phone was where she had left it.

She looked to the sky, trying to catch a glimpse of BusyBee through the trees and darkness overhead, but there was only black, gray, and green. The drone was programmed to text her "I'm watching u now" when it arrived at its assigned position, whenever that happened. Haylie's phone was on mute, so she'd have to trust that she'd feel the vibration; the last thing she wanted to do was unlock the screen and unleash a wave of LED light into the darkness, giving away her position to anyone in the area. She leaned back against the thick trunk and exhaled, scanning the woods.

I seriously have zero idea what I'm doing right now. And I hate the woods.

She reached to her backpack's side pocket for water, stopping as she felt the empty crinkle of the bottle and remembering that it was bone dry.

From her left side came a noise—a twig or a branch, something snapped—and Haylie twisted her head. Her eyes searched for something, anything in the darkness.

I need to get moving.

Haylie walked carefully away from the noise, roughly following the path her drunken visitor had taken. She concentrated on her steps—*light feet, light feet, light feet*—creeping deeper into the forest, nice and slow. Her thighs began to burn from her crouched position. Branches, leaves, and colossal ferns flowed across her shins and shoulders; vegetation of all sorts pushed into her face and hair as she slogged forward into the darkness.

The smell of the campfire grew thick as she crept closer. After fifty more feet of slow, grinding progress, she peered up to see a halo of flickering light in the clearing ahead.

Approaching from the left side, Haylie fell to the ground, lying flat and crawling towards the orange glow. Moving close to the ground was surprisingly effective in this terrain, but forced her to spit soil from her mouth every few feet and occasionally scrape spiders, or God-knows-what, off her neck. The leaves and twigs slid off her glasses as she pushed forward.

She felt a ping in her pocket as her eyes reflexively looked to the sky for any sign of the drone. She reached for her phone, drawing it close to her eyes to see a message.

VECTOR:> oi Crash, what's up.

She shook her head and crept up to the edge of the clearing, close enough to hear the cracking of the fire and to see a storm of sparks flying into the air. She squinted to make out a structure off to the left of the fire pit; it was a large, solid wooden cabin, its face illuminated by the campfire. Haylie edged closer on her elbows to get a better look.

The entire scene looked like something out of an old mining camp. Tinted in sepia, the one-windowed cabin was hand-crafted and sturdy, directly facing the center of the clearing. Strong beams framed a chunky door that swung open into the dark interior. The lines running across the cabin's façade led her eyes up to the pediment holding a curved arch over the doorway. Carved inside the arch was a peculiar wooden owl, its face was fat and bulbous, with huge eyes looking equal parts all-seeing and surprised. The eyes of the owl looked down on the fire, its mouth frozen open and ready to squawk. Under the owl and across one of the beams rested a poorly-hung, hand-burned sign that read 'UTUKURU.'

Surrounding the cabin were a collection of wooden chairs, unlit oil lamps nailed to trees, and a hand-carved table. The tabletop was a thick four-foot-wide cross-section of what must have been a massive redwood at one time, supported by stocky wooden legs. The feet pushed deep into the dirt, presumably from decades of use. Haylie brushed aside a fern to check the perimeter, but could see nothing more.

Nobody's here.

As the fire continued to burn, Haylie stood and walked slowly into the camp. Her pocket buzzed again, freezing her in the light of the campfire. She reached down to check the screen, hoping for a ping from BusyBee, telling her the drone was ready to go.

> **MOM:>** Hey honey, I just landed in Singapore. What are you doing? Did you get some dinner?

Rolling her eyes, Haylie stood frozen at the middle of the camp, typing out a text back to her mom, shaking her head.

> **HAYLIE:>** I'm good, I'm good. Talk to you in a bit.

Mom would completely freak out if she could see me right now.

Haylie made her way into the cabin, inching slowly through the doorway and activating the flashlight app on her phone. Other than two cots nestled flush to each side, a small wood-burning stove in the corner, and a few rugs and trinkets, the cabin was empty. *Find the next step behind the founding father.* She quickly checked the walls of the cabin for pictures of old members or anything else that might hold a clue inside. There was nothing.

Walking out and turning off her flashlight, she could make out the beginnings of a worn path heading down a slope and out of the clearing. She left the camp behind, entering the forest directly parallel to the path. As she stepped foot over foot, the light from the campfire dimmed with each push of progress, pulling her back into the darkness.

From what she had uncovered in her research, the Bohemian Grove consisted of a series of camps and cabins all loosely connected to a central meeting location, complete with larger buildings meant for group activities. She figured that she must have stumbled on one of the smaller camps—a spoke on the outside of a large wheel. If she could find the main path, it might lead her to the center of the Grove.

She saw a faint light twinkling off the leaves in front of her, this one brighter than the campfire. Haylie followed the glow, still taking care and effort to creep as silently as the brush would allow. The light was growing in intensity, now bright enough to make out small details of the terrain around her; the backlit silhouettes of crisscrossed trees and mossy stumps now helped to guide her way. She stopped to listen as distant sounds began to grow in the night. *What the hell is that?*

Haylie's pocket buzzed, surprising her, causing her to lose her footing, falling to one side. *Could everyone just stop texting me right now, please?* She took a knee on the soft earth, one hand hitting the dirt to keep her balance. With a quick curse, she scrambled in her pocket to retrieve the vibrating phone. She unlocked the screen, shielding the light with her free hand; it was BusyBee.

She flipped over to her drone app and could see that her drone was now obediently perched overhead in a holding pattern.

Finally.

The main screen in the app was the Dashboard; it displayed the drone's current location, system status, and a quick count of the devices within BusyBee's current range of sight. As the app loaded onto her screen, Haylie's face turned from anticipation to scowl. She was expecting a device count of around fifteen. The Dashboard read: '**132.**'

This stupid thing is broken.

Quickly toggling over to the live infrared camera, Haylie squinted as her face was bathed in the screen's light. It showed hundreds of white, blue and red dots, each representing a different contact. If the drone's view was correct, there was a huge collection of something assembled about two hundred feet in front of her. Some of the blobs stayed in place; others moved towards the larger group from surrounding structures. Haylie stared down at the screen in disbelief.

"I've only seen one other person in here," she whispered to herself. "I must have screwed up the code. Nice work, Haylie."

She walked slowly to the west, aiming her path towards the light, as the thumping beat grew louder and louder. She froze as her feet found a sudden slope in the ground. She crouched down into a squatting position, staying low.

She was on the edge of a cliff, perched above a huge clearing, about the same size as a Texas high school football stadium. The entire rim of the small canyon was illuminated with the pulsing light of torches and bonfires, with the sound of drums echoing off the rocky canyon walls.

What Haylie saw before her she still couldn't believe—a tall, looming oval-shaped structure of some sort. It was massive; it must have been forty feet tall and looked to be chipped out of solid rock. After craning her neck to either side a few times, Haylie still couldn't make out the shape. She crept along the rim of the cliff, angling to get a better view. Fighting her way past a family of vines, she found the edge once again and pulled back the vegetation to get a better view.

At the center of the clearing stood a serene mountain lake, lit by a mix of hand-held and fixed torches. A collection of men clad in light gray robes lined the edge of the shore. There were hundreds of them, and the crowd continued to grow, flowing in from the surrounding structures. A handful of boats rested at a dock, lit with torches and draped in white cloth, adorned with gold symbols.

From her new angle, Haylie could now see the large structure that stood over the lake, facing the ceremony and lit on either side with enormous fire pits; it was a gigantic freestanding stone owl with one shoulder covered by thick green moss. With strong shoulders and a knowing, downward glance, the owl dwarfed the men standing at its base, lined in formation on a row of gray stone stairs. The men stood at attention, wrapped around the statue all the way down to the lake's shore.

The drums, beating louder now, were joined by a low, growing chorus of human voices. Singing, chanting.

"Behold, the effigy of this, our enemy, is carried hither for our ancient rites."

Haylie clutched her phone, pulling back away from the edge of the cliff. She looked to the dome of forest cover hundreds of feet above her but could see no stars, no sky.

I am so screwed.

CHAPTER SE7ENT33N

Monte Rio, CA
March 8th, 9:15PM

The hiss of the gurgling river mixed with a chorus of crickets and frogs, creeping through the motel's window. Cool air swept in from the west, pushing the faded curtains back towards the bed in ripples and waves. The sounds of nature were washed out every few seconds by the rush of tires on asphalt flying through the window, headed north. Walter pulled back the curtain and saw an unbroken line of black SUVs speeding past the window.

"We must have seen a hundred so far," Walter said, peering back out to the road. "At least we haven't see any police … but still, this can't be good." He sighed and checked his watch, swiveling back towards Benjamin with a worried brow. "Where could they all be going?"

"It's pretty obvious, don't you think?" Benjamin replied.

"I think she'll be all right," Walter said, nodding to himself. "She should know how to stay out of sight."

Benjamin, sitting with his legs crossed at the middle of the queen-sized bed, laughed. With each chuckle, he sunk lower into the mushy center of the worn mattress.

"There's a pretty good chance she's toast," Benjamin snorted. He flipped channels on the plastic, square-tube television, not even watching as he clicked. "We shouldn't even be here right now. We should just head back to the jet and meet up with our team back in New York. Regroup. Think about plan B."

"We're not leaving her out there," Walter snapped, turning back to the window. He drummed his fingers on the cold, aluminum window frame, feeling a coating of grit and dust with each touch.

"This was a dumb idea. We're wasting time," Benjamin said. "She's in the forest surrounded by guards, cameras, and what looks like hundreds of Bohemian Grove members. Listen, she's great with a laptop, but she's not cut out for anything like this. She's a teenager for chrissakes."

"A *teenager*?" Walter shot back. "Really, Benjamin? She's not that much younger than we are."

"Let's get out of here," Benjamin said. "We'll figure out another way."

"And leave her in the forest? In the middle of nowhere, a few thousand miles from home?"

"Don't be so dramatic." Benjamin waved off Walter's retort with a slight flutter of his fingers. "We'll send her an airline ticket or something."

"Where? To prison? I don't think so," Walter muttered.

Benjamin clicked off the TV. He sat for a few seconds and watched as the light from the old tube faded to black. He cracked a smile. "Oh my ... I see the problem, now. Why didn't I see it before?"

"What are you talking about?"

"You don't have a solution here, either. You *agree* with me. You think I'm right—one hundred percent." Benjamin chuckled as he tossed the remote onto the foot of the bed. He turned to face his brother. "You just can't admit it."

Walter shook his head, stomping towards the door and out into the night. After a few steps across the porch his boots found soft earth, sloping downwards towards the river bank. The sound of rushing water grew louder as he approached the shore. A gust of wind pushed him back as he shifted, taking a breath. Sparkles of moonlight flashed off the small rapids flowing with gravity and time, flowing to the sea.

> > > > >

Haylie made a quick check of the drone's summary stats. The battery level was down to around 65%; it was time to get moving. She switched over to BusyBee's infrared camera and searched for her best path.

I need to get to the center of the camp.

She toggled off the heat signatures in the app, leaving only Wi-Fi and Bluetooth device locations peppered across the screen. She saw a number of contact points showing slight movement, probably phones belonging to the group of robed weirdos below her. It was the stationary points—and there were around twenty-five of those—that were her priority right now. Those points represented laptops or other hardware in buildings around the compound.

She quickly surveyed the pattern and clicked on a stationary Wi-Fi signal towards the center of the camp. The resulting pop-up showed details for the selected node—it was a router named 'BG-ArtStudio.' *That's not what I want.*

Looking again, she clicked on another node. 'BG-maintenanceStaffOnly.' *Nope.*

She checked to the right of the clusters' center and tried again. This pop-up read: 'BG-MainLodge.'

Bingo.

Peering over the side of the cliff, Haylie could see the outline of a utility path running along the lake; if she stayed low enough while making occasional checks of her phone, she should be able to have a straight shot over to the Main Lodge. There was one problem, though: the Main Lodge sat less than a hundred feet away from the torches on the lake's shore and hundreds of Bohemians. *Of course it did.*

She made her way back to the path, hiking slowly down into the valley, sneaking into the enormous shadow cast by the imposing owl statue. Another quick check of the drone's feed showed the coast was clear, and she took a sharp left at the base of the hill. She quickly found the utility path, moving as fast as her hunched-over posture would allow.

The drums grew louder as the crowd continued its chanting, the Master of Ceremonies' voice booming across the water's surface. Haylie could now smell strong waves of incense and fresh, green burning wood. The flickering torches lit her path as her feet moved quickly across the dirt, closer and closer to the center of the camp.

> > > > >

A thousand feet above, BusyBee hovered in a circular pattern, illuminated only by a small blue diode from its onboard computer. As the motors sent a dull, whining buzz into night sky, the blue light flicked off the blades as their edges rotated and pivoted slightly here and there to maintain a steady position.

BusyBee battery level: 56%

The wind shifted, pulling the drone across the night's sky like a floating tin can catching a wave towards the shore. BusyBee crested up and was dragged through the air, shooting east.

The flight controller got to work, struggling to push the vehicle back to its assigned coordinates, fighting against the building wind. The onboard computer increased the battery power to the rear rotors, forcing the craft to push even harder against the oncoming gusts.

If BusyBee's front-facing camera had been live, it would have shown Haylie a view of the oncoming wave of storm clouds heading in from the coast, with steady winds approaching twenty knots. The drone continued to increase power to the rotors, pushing back against the wind, bobbing up and down.

The motors reported a high-pitched whine as the drone fought the face of the oncoming storm. BusyBee's flight controller was finding the edge of its maximum rotor capacity to simply remain hovering above the Bohemian Grove, eating away at its most precious resource.

BusyBee battery level: 45%

It took two minutes at full power to get back to the assigned position, and even then, the motors ran hot, trying their best to keep the craft on-task.

> > > > >

Haylie kept a steady pace down the worn path, sneaking an occasional glance at the crowd to her right. The flickering orange light of the torches painted faint outlines of a few buildings directly ahead as she crept to the edge of the clearing and pulled out her phone. No heat signatures in her immediate area; she was free to explore, for now.

She walked a few steps into the foliage to her right, pushing aside branches for a partial view of the lake. The robed, hooded men now all stood faithfully facing the owl, giving their undivided attention to the Master of Ceremonies who was perched atop the steps, ascending to the owl's massive feet.

"Hail, Bohemians! With the ripple of waters, the song of birds. Such music as inspires the sinking soul; do we invite you into Midsummer's joy."

There was a burst of booming laughter that rumbled across the lake as the crowd joined in. A forced, hollow cackling echoed off the trees, the valley, and the night.

Haylie scanned the crowd as she crouched low, picking a few stray twigs from her hair and wiping her glasses clear of dirt. Her pulse raced as she checked back into the main camp, her eyes flicking between the paths and silhouettes.

That stupid school trip to Germany sounds pretty good right now, doesn't it?

She stood upright and crept towards the compound. The lake's activities lit up the worn paths and corners of the camp like a distant sunset. The wooden buildings each varied in their size, construction, and craftsmanship. It seemed that the camp had been built over the course of many decades, adding a building here and there as needed. Each structure had a door facing the main road, with hand-carved signs—'CRAFT SHED,' 'CIVIC CENTER,' 'FIRE HOUSE'—resting to the side of, or in some cases above, a small front porch.

Working her way deeper into the camp, Haylie peered down two dirt pathways snaking into cul-de-sacs of buildings on either side.

The lodge will be by the lake. I'll need to stay close to the–

From behind her, Haylie suddenly heard the muffled tones of two people approaching. She scrambled, searching for a place to hide.

There was only a single, small cabin wedged between her and the lake. As the approaching voices grew louder, she sprinted across the path and stepped onto the porch. She quietly slid her feet across the hardwood, turned the worn brass knob to enter, and clicked the door shut behind her.

Leaning back, she listened for any trace of approaching visitors. She heard nothing. Checking her phone, the view from above showed two blobs of heat walking past her location, meandering in a circular pattern around the camp's main road. They were gone, for now.

She looked up into the pitch-black nothing of the cabin, fighting to make out any shapes. The smells of mildew and wood shavings hung still in the dead air. Pointing her phone screen into the darkness, she saw a few scattered desks in the middle of the room, and a collection of file cabinets littered across the back walls of the structure. The sign hanging from the ceiling read: 'ARCHIVES.'

Turning to her left, she saw a large, sepia-toned photo of a wooden statue. Haylie recognized the photo's location: it must have been taken on the lakeshore, with the huge owl looming in the distance. The figure looked like a saint, draped in robes and wisdom, with a single finger pressed to its lips. Haylie could almost hear the saint hissing *"Shhhhhh"* as she stared into its eyes.

She tiptoed forward towards the file cabinets, sliding open a random drawer to take a peek. The steel tray rang out a metallic squeak as she lifted and pulled, revealing a deep row of multi-colored folders. Her fingers ticked across the tops of the files, hunting for anything that might be helpful.

The folders were organized by peculiar names, with labels like 'HILLBILLY,' 'THE LOST BOYS,' and 'DOOM.' Haylie kept searching until a familiar name caught her eye: 'UTUKURU.'

These are organized by camp name.

She kept thumbing through and stopped her hand on a thick folder. 'MANDALAY' was scribbled across the tab in pencil. She shrugged, pulling the file and titling her phone for better light as she opened the manila folder. Flipping through the pages, her eyes grew wider as she turned each yellowed sheet.

The folder held meeting notes that went back for decades, all with the same format: hand-written records of the date, members present, agenda, and a list of discussion topics. The names she read were almost too good to be true: Calvin Coolidge, Herbert Hoover, William Randolph Hearst, Teddy Roosevelt. Some notes she could decipher; others she couldn't make any sense of.

Opening a drawer marked 'R-S-T,' she searched over each label scrawled across the faded manila folder tabs. 'ROLLINS,' 'ROOSEVELT,' 'SHULTZ.' Haylie figured these must be member files, with labels and names that spanned over a hundred years; some were typed, some written in faint pencil or pen. A few new folders shone bright in the sea of older documents. As she scanned the labels, her eyes lit up as she saw a familiar name: 'STERLING.'

She pulled the file and placed it on top of the others, cracking the folder open with a gentle flip of the cover. Inside, she studied the top sheet: a detailed view of Andrew Sterling and his time at the Grove, with a few more loose documents nestled behind. *The brothers will get a kick out of this.* She folded the stack of papers into fours and slid it into her back pocket, returning the folder to its place.

She slid the drawer shut with a slight squeak. Haylie made her way back towards the cabin's door, checking BusyBee's view to make sure there was no one outside.

She gave a sideways look to the photograph of the shushing saint, still standing tall above her, begging her to keep the camp's secrets quiet. Haylie flashed a quick middle finger as she passed. *Good luck with that, buddy.*

Haylie snuck back into the chilled night, carving a semicircle down the main path. As she rounded the corner, she could see a huge lodge in the distance. The structure was poised above the lake with a long front porch adorned with rocking chairs, tables, and benches, complete with steps leading down to the lakeshore. A white, wooden sign read: 'BOHEMIA,' flanked by markers on either side indicating 'TO SAN FRANCISCO: 77.54 MILES' and 'ELEVATION: 41 FEET.'

This has to be it.

Glancing down at the drone's view, Haylie saw no heat signatures inside the outline of the lodge. Her eyes darted back and forth between the well-lit front porch and the crowd to her right, standing less than fifty feet from the steps.

Creeping around behind the building, she spotted a rear entrance perched above a small, wooden porch. Haylie swung open the screen door with a slight squeak, propping it open with her shoulder to turn the knob of the main door and push into the lodge. She stepped in, feeling the hollow thump of her boot on the ancient hardwood floor, and walked inside.

> > > > >

As the storm continued its push towards the coast, BusyBee struggled, fighting to remain airborne above the camp. The problem wasn't the gusts of wind hitting the craft from time to time, it was the steady wall of air forcing the drone to keep its engine levels at a constant sprint.

With the increased workload, the four motors were approaching the point of overheating. The flight controller toggled the power to each blade in a pattern that would minimize the chance of overload, but one motor had already come close to its failure point.

BusyBee battery level: 13%

As the dark clouds enveloped the drone, BusyBee fought to push against the current, struggling back towards its ordered post. Huffing and puffing.

CHAPTER E1G4T33N

Monte Rio, CA
March 8th, 9:48PM

A musty smell—the mix of burnt tobacco, old smoke, and soil—filled Haylie's nose as her eyes adjusted to the darkness. Luckily, the dark room was highlighted with shades of silver from the row of windows facing the lake's shore. To the left, Haylie could see a hallway leading to a large kitchen. To the right, chunky tables and chairs cut from thick tree trunks were fastened together at right angles and arranged in a semi-circle. On the far right wall stood a large stone fireplace, formed by a mosaic of smooth river rocks.

Squinting, she could see the outlines of hundreds of picture frames lining the walls, filling every square inch with a mix of sizes and shapes; like a giant jigsaw puzzle.

Ok founding father ... where are you?

Haylie worked her way across the wall, leaning in close to make out the figures in each photo. Her eyes flew across the tiny, faded brass plaques underneath each frame, not even sure which name she should be searching for.

She paused to examine a photo dated '1915,' picturing a collection of men proudly posing and surrounded by burning candles and hand-drawn banners fastened to a tree trunk. *These people are so weird.* Haylie moved along, dusting off another photo labeled 'SONS OF TOIL, 1910.' The scene showed six men, adorned in tuxedos, sitting in a v-formation across the front steps of an unmarked building. They had the nervous appearance of men halfway between childhood and responsibility.

How am I going to find this guy? I may not even be in the right building. This is ridiculous.

Shuffling her feet, she moved down the wall and struggled to make out the subject of the next image; it had no brass plaque, but had a faded, handwritten label across the bottom reading 'WINGS, 1925.' The photo was of thirty club members, all adorned in white and posed on the shore of the lake, each with one hand pointed towards the sky. They were arranged on all sides of the Owl statue, the massive structure looming high above them, covered in gray moss and staring down on the scene with its fixed, stone eyes.

It would have to be an older photo, something from the early times of the camp.

She breezed past a color shot of Ronald Reagan addressing a small crowd. The next frame held a photo of men sitting around a tent, beers raised high in a toast, with white banners and flags adorning the trees around them. Scenes of campfires, men in robes, and grand speeches by the shore. One of a man that resembled Richard Nixon, but Haylie didn't have time to double check.

Haylie came to the end of the wall and cursed under her breath. *Where the hell is this guy?* As she turned to face the south side of the lodge, she could see the fires still burning bright outside. She narrowed her eyes to look across the center of the dark lodge, focusing on the stone fireplace and the collection of frames perched above the mantle.

Her eyes locked on the large painting hung high on the rock. It depicted a man sitting back confidently in a wooden chair. His three-piece suit wouldn't have been out of place, except for the fact that he was sitting in the middle of a redwood forest flanked by six assistants on either side. Beneath him there was a large, brass plaque simply reading 'OUR FOUNDER, OUR BOHEMIAN BROTHER.'

There you are.

Grabbing the closest thing she could stand on—an old wooden rocking chair that rested in the corner—Haylie headed towards the fireplace. She dragged the chair across the floor with a slight squeak and steadied it in front of the painting. She placed a boot on the sloped seat, and then the other, pushing her weight with each foot, back and forth, as the chair rocked with each shift. Leaning over against the mantle, she pulled the painting up and out to unlatch the hook on the back. As she pulled, the frame tugged back, remaining confidently attached to the wall.

She angled her weight in the direction of the fireplace, lifting the frame as high as it would go. Haylie pushed it up against the back wall with the tips of her fingers to free the wire from its hook. Edging up on her tiptoes, balancing and shifting, straining to push higher.

With one last push upward, the frame released, taking Haylie with it. She fell back off the chair and onto her back, sounding off a series of echoing booms as each body part—her back, her elbow, her knee— slammed into the lodge's dusty floor. She quickly lifted her arms off the ground to catch the falling frame, but with no luck. The rip of the canvas echoed through the lodge as she pierced the center of the painting with the crown of her head.

She pushed the painting back, revealing a huge hole directly at its center. *Whatever, it was ugly anyway.* She stood, snatching her glasses from off the floor, and spun the painting on its corner. The back was empty.

Seriously?

Her fingers brushed over the canvas, searching for the next clue. An envelope, a carving … anything. She flipped the frame onto its back, catching the torch light shining through the front windows, but saw nothing. Haylie yanked at the canvas around each side of the frame, feeling with her fingers.

"There's got to be something here," she whispered, her eyes looking back up to the empty fireplace. As she scanned the river rocks above the mantle, she found what she had been missing.

A second, smaller picture frame hung in the dusty outline left by the painting, still fixed to the wall above the mantle. The frame held a simple white piece of paper with no glass. On the paper were two figures: the familiar raven image she had seen back at the hangar, and a black and white square, filled with small patterns like a crazy game of Tetris. It was a QR code.

Just as Haylie caught her breath and cracked a smile, she heard a man's voice at the back side of the lodge, moving from window to window, left to right.

Someone was heading towards the back porch.

In one move, she jumped up and grabbed the top of the paper, feeling a pop as the glue released from the back of the frame. She landed on the wooden floor with a thump, folding the paper into her pocket. She picked up the large painting and stretched up to the wall, propping the frame up on the mantle to cover the missing clue.

Haylie ran for the front porch, dragging the rocking chair back to its original location along the way. She crept outside, falling to her hands and knees and crawling below the front porch's wooden wall.

As she lay still, she heard the back door slam and felt the bumps of footsteps vibrating through the floorboards. Haylie took a few deep breaths, tasting incense and ash from the breeze rushing in off the lake. She checked to make sure the clue was still safe in her front pocket and looked across the camp to plan her escape route. She crawled down the south side of the porch steps, staying low, slithering down to the edge of the beaten path.

She rose to her feet, finding herself a stone's throw away from the backs of the hooded Bohemian Club members. Haylie stared at the crowd, drawn to their silhouettes.

In the distance, a thirty-foot boat with a small ornamental tent now stood front and center before the Owl statue, piloted by a hooded man and illuminated by six torches. A rectangular-shaped object—*was that a coffin?*—rested under the boat's cloth roof. The boat's captain chanted as he rowed, throwing his paddle up with dramatic gestures, commanding the attention of the crowd.

The scene was mesmerizing. The torchlight, the spices in the air, the cool mountain breeze, and the slow, rhythmic humming from hundreds of robed followers.

Good lord, Caesar, what have you gotten yourself into?

Haylie's train of thought was broken by a noise from above as a high-pitched whine buzzed through the air. She watched the crowd tilt their heads back towards the sky, the sound now beginning to warp and twist. The chanting and drums stopped cold as the foreign noise filled the canyon, buzzing like a mosquito on fire, left to right around the lake.

Haylie's eyes were drawn to the sky to see what could be creating such a commotion.

Oh no. It's BusyBee.

The drone whizzed over the heads of the crowd, circling with lower and lower spirals, emitting screams from the rotors as it missed the crowd by inches on its last pass. It made a flyby past the watching face of the owl statue and the crowd gasped, pointing and holding their torches up for a better view. The craft righted its direction for a slight moment, but then picked up speed. It was headed straight for the lake on a dive-bomb course.

No, no, no.

Haylie grabbed her phone from her pocket, activating the screen to take control back. It was too late. The status screen read the dreaded words: 'Battery at 0%. Craft offline.'

The drone accelerated straight across the water at a downward angle, gaining speed in a last blaze of glory. Haylie's heart raced as BusyBee found its final mark: the boat at the center of the lake.

The drone cut right through the cloth roof, spinning sideways with its final remaining rotor power and knocking over two of the torches lighting the boat. The vessel lit up like a roman candle, with fire shooting across the stern as the lake glowed red. The boat's captain jumped from the bow with a great splash, dog paddling furiously against the weight of his waterlogged robes, headed for the nearby shore. The crowd of onlookers scattered, pointing, yelling, turning in every direction.

Haylie slid her phone back in her pocket while already sprinting back towards her entry point. *Well, this was fun.* Not even bothering to stay low, she ran at full speed into the heart of the Grove, around the back of the owl, and up the beaten path to the top of the ridge. There was no time to go off-road, if someone had already returned to the cabin, she'd just have to try and get by them.

The Utukuru camp lay deserted as Haylie darted right past the cabin, jumping back into the thick gray darkness behind the campfire's light. With a quick check of her phone's compass, she headed due south into the twisted maze of the woods. Branches smacked her face and limbs as she pushed to distance herself from the growing chorus of shouts coming from behind her, blind to anything in her path.

She ran, breathing deep gulps of air as her shirt grew wet and heavy with sweat and mud, stained with moss and earth. She kept her eyes up, her feet moving. Tree after tree. Stream after stream. Ravines mixed with fallen logs, ferns and branches.

Just keep moving.

CHAPTER N1NE733N

Heathrow Airport - London
March 9th, 8:26AM

Martin Bell walked briskly through the terminal, engulfed in a churning mishmash of jet-lagged tourists and the thousand-yard stares of men with blue blazers and overnight bags. Voices boomed over the public address system with polite English accents, calling travelers to their departing gates.

Martin's flight had arrived on time, which was simply infuriating. It was a well-known fact that when flights, especially British Airways flights, were on time, they were in fact late. Airlines always padded their expected arrival by five percent of flight time in order to make their on-time numbers look better, and by sandbagging the timetable a bit, the entire industry played with the expectations and travel plans of millions of passengers every year.

If they knew they were going to be late, they should just tell the passengers that. Idiots.

He approached the customs area, veering quickly into the Premium Access lane with only a lone security officer standing guard at a podium. Martin made his way through customs in under thirty seconds and hustled his way past the mass of people waiting their turns, all standing there with dull eyes like a herd of cattle. But not Martin, there would be no waiting for him today. He glided by with a big, fat smile on his face.

You see, having privilege wasn't enough on its own. The true rush came from seeing everyone else still stuck on the other side of the fence.

As Martin navigated the final hallway out of the main terminal, he saw a woman between him and baggage claim moving slowly and fitfully. She held a wailing child dangling from her left hand, half-wrapped in a swaddle that had just twisted open, the blanket now dragging along across the cement floor. The baby's knitted blue hat twisted and pulled down across his right eye, blocking tiny tears from running down his cheeks.

In the mother's right hand, she had pinned an overflowing bag to her side while grasping the handle of a large carry-on suitcase, dragging it behind her like a circus act. She was more limping than walking, shuffling her feet towards the exit.

As Martin marched ahead, he saw her twisting against gravity, her bag sliding off her shoulder and hitting her at the elbow; dragging her down, finally succumbing to its weight and falling to the floor. She landed on her right side, her young child suspended above her, now crying with a repeated, shrill wail.

Martin moved slightly to his left and slid right around the whole ugly mess.

As he walked into the wide expanse of the baggage claim area, he searched for his driver. With a squint, he saw a man across the room with the printed name 'M. BELL' on an electronic sign. Martin quickened his step. He gave the driver a nod, handing over his suitcase without a word. Martin drank in the moment, knowing that the rest of the baggage claim area must have been watching, all wondering the same thing. *Who is that, a celebrity? A leader of industry? A movie star?* The slick smile crept back to his face as he followed the driver outside.

They stepped out of the terminal and into a wash of cool air, swirling and twisting with moisture and exhaust. Martin stood in the doorway for a moment to drink in the oxygen with a few deep breaths. On the curb stood a black BMW 750i with tinted windows, door wide open.

This will do nicely.

As the driver sped towards central London, Martin crossed his legs and enjoyed the view, not of the surrounding landscape, but of the backseat. Two bottles of slightly chilled water sat in the center console for him to enjoy or disregard; in the seat pocket were folded copies of this morning's *Financial Times* and the *Daily Mail*. Martin watched as drivers swiveled their heads to catch a glimpse of what had just passed them. He smirked, knowing they could only see their own pitiful reflections in the black tint of the windows.

As the gray nothingness of brick-fenced small towns, awkward freeway exits, and trash-lined grass flew by, he thought through the past few years. All the decisions—decisions that others were too weak to make—had finally paid off.

He'd relocated to a city with opportunity while others had stayed away from the traffic and bustle. He had stayed single, which had resulted in an optimization of his personal time and finances. Saving the trouble of finding a companion was one thing, which even with today's streamlined process of digital dating algorithms still had far too much trial and error for his tastes, but there was also the relationship itself. Every night, spending his time with another human being. Spending every weekend sharing meals and opinions and picking out paint colors. Even the thought of it seemed so exhausting, so all-consuming. Martin had much better things to do with his time. He knew that was why he had made it here, and the others had not.

He had been waiting for the moment that he knew would come, and then, yesterday, the phone rang. He heard the words he had been waiting for: "We need you at Headquarters." Someone had finally reached out and touched him, like the finger of God breaking through the clouds and down from the heavens, to be a critical piece of a plan that few people on Earth even knew about.

He wasn't lucky, this was all part of the plan. Prime Minister Crowne had asked for him, and only him, because of all the sacrifices he had made.

He had been *chosen*.

As the car worked its way deeper into the city, he leaned closer to the window and observed the people passing by. They stood on street corners, waiting for permission to cross.

What are they all doing out here in the middle of the afternoon? Don't they have jobs? Don't they have someplace to be?

The driver pulled a sharp left into a private driveway, a solid gate blocking their path. Martin squinted through the windshield to see a pair of wide-eyed owl sculptures on either side of the gate embedded into the thick red brick wall. Rolling down his window, the driver flashed a badge over the RFID reader on the gate's intercom box. A series of lights followed.

Yellow. Yellow. Yellow. Green.

A loud mechanical clunk started the gate's opening sequence, which split the barrier down the middle and opened inward, revealing a gray cobblestone road with three-foot flagstone barriers on either side. The road twisted up and to the right, revealing rich green elm trees and bright emerald grass behind the exterior walls. Two guards stood on either side of the gate, holding MP-5 machine guns at the ready. The guards wore olive shirts, military-style pants, and combat boots. They kept their guns roughly aimed in the direction of the BMW's driver-side window. The vehicle rolled down the road, crunching gravel as it approached the main structure.

As the car pulled into the forward receiving area, three porters dressed all in black with earpieces and automatic weapons made their way down the steps and towards the vehicle. As the driver came to a firm stop, the door opened.

"Good afternoon, Mr. Bell," said an attendant, dressed in a well-fitted suit with slicked hair and a stern, polite smile. "We'll handle the luggage. Please, right this way."

As they proceeded up the stairs and towards the entrance, Martin turned to take in the view over his right shoulder. The landscape was breathtaking, as if Central Park had been transplanted into North London and plunked down right in front of the driveway. Green grasses, tall shrubs, and three fountains that he could count from his vantage point: a view fit for a king.

Martin walked into the mansion to find a secretary, a thin pale man seated at a small desk and surrounded by three closed doors, one on each wall.

"Mr. Bell, sir," said the secretary, rising to greet his guest. "It's wonderful to see you. A pleasant trip, I presume?" Martin was thrown off by his accent—French, not English—but he fought the urge to telegraph any sense of surprise.

"Of course," replied Martin as he tightened his tie around his neck. "I'd like to get right to business if you don't mind. We're on a schedule, as I'm sure you already know."

"Yes, of course," the man at the desk replied. "Please, head to the east wing. You'll find your next meeting in room seventy-six. A few more appointments have been set for tonight; we'll get you a full schedule."

"Has the Prime Minister...." Martin paused as he carefully chose his next words. "Has he mentioned anything about me?"

The man at the desk stared back without reaction. "As I said, we'll get you a full schedule."

Martin gave a polite, frustrated smile. His heels clicked across the gray marble as he made his way down the long, dimly lit hallway. Every ten feet or so there was a door to the left, each with a paired picture hanging on the wall to the right.

Room 70: a sketch of elephants.

Room 72: a painting of a tiger devouring an antelope.

Room 74: a charcoal drawing of snakes coiled around a basket full of eggs.

Room 76.

Martin stopped and straightened his tie a second time. He fastened the top button on his jacket and gave a light double-knock on the door while turning the knob and walking in. He stopped after two steps across the threshold and spoke.

"Good morning, Caesar," Martin said with a smile.

CHAPTER TWƎNTY

Interstate 101
near Santa Rosa, CA
March 9th, 12:58AM

Haylie squirmed across the polished leather of the car's seat, facing backwards and sitting directly across from the brothers. She was trying her best to ignore the impatient stares coming from their direction. Walter and Benjamin were actively craning their necks to the side to catch a glimpse of her screen, but with no luck.

"How are we doing?" Benjamin asked.

"Hold on. I'm just getting set up here." Haylie opened a few more applications—an iPython browser window, a few tabs for searches—and then bent the laptop's lid towards her, giving her a full view of the brothers. "I'm assuming there's no Wi-Fi in this car. Does either of you have a hotspot on your phone?"

Walter nodded, sliding his phone from his pocket, opening an app, and extending the screen in Haylie's direction to show the login information. She typed it in and gave a thumbs up once she had connected.

Placing her computer down on the bench seat, Haylie scraped a few remaining pieces of mud from her fingertips, wiping them across her jeans. She reached for the tattered piece of paper laying on the seat next to her. She held it up to the passing headlights, stretching its wrinkled edges and searching for anything other than the QR code that she might have missed.

"You guys missed all the good stuff," she said with a yawn. "There was some crazy-lazy happenings going on in there."

Walter and Benjamin laughed.

Her phone signaled a sharp beep as she scanned the QR code. Waiting for a few moments as the app went to work, Haylie's face scrunched as she read the result.

This doesn't seem right.

She typed the address into her browser and hit RETURN.

> `http://www.ThompsonScreenDoors.com/`
> `dontPanic/2309.html`

The browser rendered the page as Haylie shook her head, not believing the results. She hit COMMAND-R to reload, and leaned her chin on her palm, staring into the screen. The page held no images, no banners, no header, no colored background. Only a single element in the center: an audio player. Haylie gulped and hit PLAY button on the controls.

As sound began to trickle from her laptop's speakers, Haylie tapped her keyboard to increase the volume. The sounds of an orchestra filled the back of the car, with the string section performing a series of violent strokes.

"I've heard this before. What is it?" Haylie asked.

"It's Mozart," Benjamin replied. The driver craned his head towards the back seat as the volume grew. Benjamin flipped a switch, closing the privacy window with a shake of his head. "It's an opera ... 'The Marriage of Figaro.'"

"One of his most famous pieces," Walter added.

Haylie shot them both a look—*trust fund babies*—and turned back to the audio controls. "The track is four minutes and fifty seconds long. Let's listen to it, see if there's a message in here."

The three sat without a word as the swoops and chords of Mozart filled the car. She cranked the volume even higher, bending her ear closer to the speakers to try and make out any faint signals or masked sounds, but heard nothing out of the ordinary. As three prominent chords signaled the completion of the track, the car filled once again with the ring of silence.

"I didn't hear anything," Benjamin said.

"Me either," Walter added. "And what does any of this have to do with Raven? It's weird, I don't get it."

"Well, 'The Marriage of Figaro' *is* about class warfare," Haylie said, reading the Wikipedia entry. "It's all about servants tricking their masters, how the people in charge are fools behind the curtain. It was banned in the time leading up to the French Revolution; I guess King Louis and his buddies were afraid the crowd would figure it out."

"So?" Walter asked.

"Think about it," Haylie said. "The clues so far: Cecil Rhodes, the Bohemian Grove. Whoever built Raven is obviously trying to point fingers at people in power."

"But that still doesn't get us closer to the next clue," Benjamin said.

"I'm checking the Internet registry for more information on where this page is hosted," Haylie said as she typed.

"What does that tell us?" Walter asked.

"It tells us who owns ThompsonScreenDoors.com," Haylie said, reading the results on the page. "There's nothing here. It looks like a legit company in Missouri; they sell screen doors, obviously, but it would be a strange shadow company for something like Raven 2309. I'm guessing they got hacked and probably have no idea this file is even on their server."

"So where does that leave us?" Benjamin asked.

"Nowhere," replied Haylie crossing her arms and staring at the screen. "I have no idea what to do next."

> > > > >

Typing away at her keyboard, Haylie had turned to her side to shield herself from the constant stare of the impatient Sterling brothers. Even in their silence, she could feel their disappointment. It was pretty obvious that the two had been texting back and forth for roughly the past twenty minutes, exchanging glances and gestures after each message notification buzzed in the other's hand.

Benjamin cleared his throat to get her attention, but she wasn't biting. He nudged Walter as he typed on his phone with his thumbs, pointing over to Haylie. Walter, typing back a reply to Benjamin, opened his mouth to speak.

"I can see you guys, you know," Haylie said above the noise of clicking keys, stopping for a moment to push her glasses back up on her nose. "I'm sitting right here. I'm like three feet away from you."

"You're obviously working on something over there," Walter said. "Are you getting closer? Anything you can share?"

"I'm not working on anything. I'm just clearing my head; I'm going to try attacking the problem again in a few minutes."

"So," Walter said, trying to get a view of her laptop's screen, "what are you typing?"

"I'm finishing up a school report on people that won't mind their own goddamned business," Haylie said with a petulant smirk. "Almost done with it. I think I'm going to get an 'A.'"

A vibration in her pocket shook her as she reached down to retrieve her phone. She checked the screen to see a 'what's going on?' text from Vector.

"Listen, Haylie," Benjamin said as he shifted in his seat. "There's something I ... we ... have been wanting to tell you."

This should be good.

"I'm not great at this type of stuff, so sorry if it comes off as strange," Benjamin continued. "But we just wanted to apologize for leaving you out in the Grove on your own. You did some pretty amazing stuff back there—things I'm not sure either of us could have done."

Benjamin looked around the rear cabin of the car in every direction but hers, avoiding even the hint of eye contact.

"That last step ... getting in that lodge, grabbing the QR code. I know it wasn't easy. This thing is starting to get pretty real," Benjamin said. "What I'm trying to say is that I'm impressed; I think you're very good at what you do. I just wanted to let you know that."

Haylie stared back, surprised and relieved. She hadn't expected an apology, at least not this soon.

"It's fine," she said. "And thank you. We'll solve this thing if we work together. Your resources and my...."

"Big brain?" Walter said, smiling. "Benjamin and I talked and agreed on one thing: we won't be waving to you from the sidelines anymore."

Waving?

"We're in it together from this point on," Walter continued, proud of himself.

One of Walter's words pinged in her head. *Waving. Waving. Waving.* Haylie nodded and turned back to her screen. She pieced together the connection after a few seconds.

Waving—that's it. Haylie searched her Applications folder, trying to remember the name of the program she was after.

"Of course," she whispered. "I'm so stupid. Stupid. Stupid. What is it called ... what is it called?" Her eyes darted around the screen as she stammered. "Sound files are made of patterns ... waves. All sound can be represented as mathematical values. It's called the sound spectrum."

"I don't get it," Benjamin said, checking with his brother. Walter shook his head back.

Haylie kept searching. "There's a type of program called a spectrogram ... it visualizes the sound spectrum from any audio file, drawing pictures from the patterns in any track. You end up with a visual look at what makes up the sound. But some spectrogram programs let you start with a picture, any picture you want. A cat or a piano...."

"Or a message?" Walter asked.

"Or a message," she said. "The spectrogram carves the message in the sound, and if there's enough going on in the music, the additional noise from the hidden image won't be noticed. A few musicians have played around with it by mixing in pictures of screaming faces or whatever into the background of their tracks. I downloaded a spectrogram to play around with this stuff last year, I just can't remember what it was called." She scrolled down and down until she found the icon she was looking for.

NanoSteno. That's the one.

As she opened the application and loaded the audio file from the Raven page, Haylie made a mental note of its filename: '1907.MP3.' She toggled a few settings to display both the waveform and spectrogram views during playback, and hit the play button. The brothers slid over to her side, now half sitting and half standing in the cramped back seat, hovering above the screen to see the results.

A spectrogram is a thing of beauty when at work, cranking out a flowing stream of multi-colored data. The output resembles a head-on collision between a Doppler radar and the smoothed, sweeping flow of a sand painting. Haylie and the Sterling brothers watched as ripples of yellow, green, and blue wavelength layers squashed on top of each other, like a cutaway view of a limestone cliff. As the Mozart piece exclaimed a violent chorus around the thirteen second mark, the pattern turned a sharp yellow, the progress bar sweeping slowly across the spectrum landscape, left to right.

"It looks like the sonar readout from our yacht," Walter said, watching with curiosity. "But I don't see any pictures in here."

"Not yet. It may be towards the end of the track," Haylie replied, her eyes scanning right to left for anything man-made as the landscape scrolled.

"Or it may not be in here at all," Benjamin added.

As 'The Marriage of Figaro' played on, the spectrogram followed; mapping bursts of energy and slower, quieter moments into a jagged electronic painting, rising and falling in peaks and valleys. The violins and cellos filled the car's cabin with its lively staccato as the three continued to search for a pattern. As they reached the final thirty seconds of the track, Haylie's pulse began to rise.

Where is it? It has to be in here.

Suddenly, the right side of the screen scrolled to reveal a stark pattern of blurred, white edges etched into the multi-colored waves.

"There it is!" Walter yelled over the music, building to its finish. "We found it!" All three leaned in closer to try and make out the shapes.

"O, D, F, M." Walter spelled out the first line of letters, stacked on top of each other. "What does that mean?"

"It's four lines of text; those are just the first letters of each line," Haylie said. "Let it keep playing for a few more seconds."

As the spectrogram scrolled on, more and more letters of the message appeared. The track came to a full stop and the NanoSteno application halted with it, displaying the final few bars of the spectrum now frozen on the screen.

> **our secrets are our power, but**
> **don't Panic.**
> **find Brother Libra's last**
> **meal, we'll see you there.**

Walter shot a blank expression over to Haylie. "What ... what the hell does that mean?"

"I don't know," Haylie replied. "Let's find out."

CHAPTER TW3NTY ON3

Titanhurst Estate - London
March 9th, 9:23AM

"It's so nice to put a face to the name," Caesar said, relieved to have another soul to talk to.

"Yes, I feel the same way." Martin crossed his right leg over his left. "I hope the accommodations have been comfortable."

"Are you kidding?" Caesar said. "From what I can tell, this place is ridiculously cool. I've never seen anything like it, and I've seen quite a lot."

Caesar's eyes flicked around the apartment. Without much else to keep him occupied over the past few days, he had learned every detail of every corner in the room—dark chocolate floors leading to the wooden plank staircase, curving up to a small loft space above. The apartment was a modern oasis, with the browns and whites of the interior offset by lush, green trees visible through the window. Bright white couches and lamps, tastefully arranged. All clean and sharp.

Caesar looked Martin up and down trying to mask his suspicion. He didn't usually trust people that were buttoned-up, and Martin certainly fit that mold. Gray suit, pressed shirt, shined shoes.

"Yes, it's quite unique here," Martin said. "We've allocated a material amount of resources to make this a very special place."

"Where are we? I haven't been able to get Internet access to figure out the location. It's driving me a little nuts." Caesar walked over to the desk and cracked the lid of the laptop. "I mean, even Starbucks has free Wi-Fi."

"Yes, I apologize for the lack of access to the outside world. I did ask the staff to hold your credentials until we had a chance to speak. That's why I'm here. I'm hoping that we can get you back online as soon as this afternoon, but first there are a few things I'd like to discuss. It won't take long–"

Martin was interrupted by a light, polite knock at the door.

"That must be the tea."

As the tea service entered the room, the two men walked over to the sitting area, directly in front of the sweeping view of the grounds. The service tray clinked and clacked as the butler placed it on the chunky wood coffee table, resting firmly but still slightly off balance.

"So where are we? What's this all about?" Caesar watched with a suspicious eye as the butler placed the items in front of them: tea cups, a stark black kettle, and a carefully arranged plate of biscuits.

"Ah, yes," Martin said. "This is the Titanhurst mansion; the complex dates back to the mid-1700s. The building we're in now was constructed in the 1920s by Sir Arnold Mayfield. He was a soap magnate, even knighted in 1938."

"The house that soap built?"

"Yes, very good, that would seem to be the case. It's the largest private residence in London, only behind Buckingham Palace. Our holding company acquired the grounds about six years ago, and we've been doing extensive renovations ever since."

Caesar walked to the window. Over the past few days, he had noticed the construction debris and fresh landscaping littering the grounds; it seemed as if the work was close to completion.

"This house has over sixty-five rooms," Martin continued, "but our build-out has concentrated primarily below ground. I won't get into all the details of what lies beneath us, but it's roughly the size of an American shopping mall."

"So you guys bought the biggest house in one of the most expensive real-estate markets in the world, and decided to make it even bigger? I figured that kind of thinking was just limited to America."

"Resources aren't an issue for our group. We're more focused on pushing ahead and meeting our goals, no matter the short-term cost. The long-term is always where our focus should be, wouldn't you agree? Keeping your eyes on the horizon?"

A ping rang out from Martin's inner jacket pocket. "That's odd." He removed his phone, checking his notifications. As he read the message, his eyes narrowed.

"What is it?" Caesar asked.

"It's Raven." Martin said. "After the first few steps, I added notification triggers. The puzzle sends a ping whenever someone makes it past a step. I haven't been pinged since back when you were solving it, but it seems that someone just cracked the audio code."

Caesar nodded, thinking back to the steps. "They're in the thick of it now."

"Indeed." Martin put the phone back in his pocket. "I'm interested in talking about your future, Caesar. But I'm sure you have a lot on your mind. What questions can I answer for you?"

Caesar's eyes lit up. "Everything—I want to know *everything*. I'm completely in the dark here. I solved your puzzle, which wasn't that hard, by the way. What do I get for my trouble?"

"An excellent question." Martin smiled, standing and heading over to the apartment's kitchen. "But if we're going to start talking business, I'm going to need some coffee, not this terrible tea. Would you like some?"

"Sure," Caesar said, shrugging his shoulders. "Whatever."

"The tea, you see, is a formality," Martin said as he poured two cups of dark, rich coffee into porcelain mugs. "A British custom, at least so I've heard."

Walking the coffee back to the table, Martin beamed as he took a long sip. Caesar watched Martin's posture, his pose, his expression. *It's obvious this guy is in no hurry to get to the point here.* Caesar leaned forward and stared his guest in the eyes.

"Martin, I've been here for what, four days now, cooped up in this apartment? I don't know why I'm here, and I'm starting to think that you don't know what to do with me. But I think I may have just figured it out."

Martin sipped his coffee, listening.

"You didn't expect anyone to solve Raven," Caesar continued. "You built a game without a payoff. You never figured that anyone would actually solve your puzzle, and then I knocked on your door. You couldn't imagine that anyone out there was smarter than you. That's it, isn't it?"

Martin said nothing.

"Well it seems I've figured out the answer. The answer is *me*. *I'm* smarter than you. I solved your little riddle and I'm standing here, waiting for my prize. And the truth is, there is none. Am I right?"

Martin chuckled to himself, taking another sip of his drink, the steam rising across his face.

"So, I'll make this easy," Caesar said. "I need to leave. *Now.* I need to get back to New York. I have things to do—I'm an important guy. Let's just get on with it."

There was a crisp stillness in the room as the two men stared across the table. After a few moments, Martin broke the silence.

"This coffee, it's wonderful. Don't you think?" Martin said, with a sparkle in his eye.

"It's ... sure. It's fine."

"Colombian. The best in the world, at least with this year's crop. You see, I have a confession: I love coffee. I love everything about it. When I go to bed at night, I dream—I dream, isn't that crazy?—I dream about what my first cup of coffee will be like when I wake the next morning. Almost every single night. The taste, the scent. The black of the texture against a white porcelain cup. It's just a little world of perfection, don't you think?"

A chill entered the room as Caesar heard a crack at the window. He snapped his head to look but saw nothing, just the sunlight flooding in from the courtyard. The sky was growing into a deep blue.

"When Europeans first discovered coffee in the seventh century, they found it so rich and wonderful that they named it 'Arabic wine.' Arabic wine! Isn't that a delight?" Martin said, with a grin stretched across his face.

"Ok, can we stop talking about the coffee? I want some answers. Are you going to tell me why I'm here? Is today the lucky day when I find out what the hell is going on?"

"It is, Caesar," Martin said with a gleam in his eye. "Today *is* that lucky day. And I think you're going to like what I have to tell you. You're going to like it very, very much. But you're going to need time. This I know."

"Time? What are you talking about?"

Martin pointed a single, thin finger at Caesar. "Because I know that you're a smart man. A very, very smart man. One who doesn't jump to conclusions. A man that understands that new ideas need to be *experienced* to truly be understood."

Sitting back in his chair, Caesar shook his head with exhaustion. "You're talking nonsense. I'm just completely lost."

"Yes, of course you are ... of course. Let me give you an example. A *perfect* example. That coffee you're drinking ... when it was first brought to Europe, it was strange and new and not like anything people had ever seen before. In fact, many factions decided that it was not natural, not right. And as humans often do, they believed that this new thing that they had never seen before—this thing that they didn't understand—must be poisonous to the soul. They believed the physical rush from coffee was, in fact, the work of the devil."

"Ok."

"Can you believe it? I, myself, cannot. To make up such tales about something so wonderful, it's unthinkable. But it's true, and what did they do when they didn't understand this beautiful thing? They tried to *destroy* it. They went to the Pope—all the way to the Vatican, can you imagine?—asking him to declare this new, amazing thing outlawed across all his lands. And do you know what happened?"

"I don't," Caesar said. "I really don't."

Martin smiled. "Pope Clement VIII, with all his wisdom, decreed that he must first take a sip before making any decisions on the matter. He had to try this new thing, this new idea, that he was about to judge.

How can you judge something that you've never experienced? Such wisdom! Such genius! And when he did, oh my goodness, Caesar, when he did, can you guess what happened then?"

Carefully watching as Caesar shifted in his seat, Martin held his cup tightly with both hands. Martin stared with dead eyes, over and past Caesar's right shoulder, out through the window and up at the blue, bright sky.

"He took a sip!" Martin said. "*Of course* he took a sip! He drank the coffee and turned to these men, these men that had told him these *lies* and declared that this drink—this drink we now hold in our hands—was so wonderful that only sinners would declare it a sin. That it shouldn't be banned, but *blessed*, because it was truly so wonderful. And instead of banning coffee from the land, do you know what he did?" Martin's tone grew from excitement to anger as he clutched his cup tighter and tighter.

Caesar sat, his heart beating faster, as he watched Martin's shaking hands.

"I'll tell you what he did. He banished those men that had attempted to cloud his judgment with their lies, these men that were themselves *poison* for not believing in this power of a new idea. He sent them away to the deepest corners of the Vatican prisons, and they were never heard from again."

Martin gazed down from the window and into Caesar's eyes, tossing his cup on the table with a crash of porcelain and a dark pool of liquid flying across the tabletop. Martin wiped the corners of his mouth, tucking in the sides of his crisp, white shirt.

"So my question for you is simple, Caesar: are you ready to take your first sip?"

Caesar began to feel the sweat form on his temple. He stared down at his coffee, now cold, sitting still and dark.

"Because today is the day, Caesar. Today is your *lucky* day."

CHAPTER TW3NTY TWO

Interstate 101
near Petaluma, CA
March 9th, 1:32AM

Haylie sparked up a fresh browser tab and typed "Brother Libra" into the search field. She hit ENTER and hovered over her keyboard.

No way it will be this easy, right?

All she saw was page after page of nonsense: search results for a failed alt-rock band from the early nineties, a contestant from a recent reality show that hadn't made it to the finals, a Hindu book of astrology. All dead ends. Looking back to the spectrogram readout, she performed a series of COMMAND+ keystrokes; zooming in.

"This is weird," she said. "The word 'Panic' is capitalized in the message." She tilted her head, thinking.

Walter jumped into the seat next to Haylie and pointed to the text. "There are line breaks that don't make any sense as well, but they could just be random. Trying to make the message fit into a tight space."

"What about that file name, '1907?'" Benjamin said from his corner.

"I was wondering about that, too," Haylie said, opening a new browser tab and searching for any hints about the number's significance. "It's prime, just like 2309 and all the other numbers from the puzzle so far, but that doesn't really tell us anything."

"Try the year. See if anything big happened in 1907," Walter said.

"Already checking that," Haylie said. "I'm seeing the Romanian Peasant's Revolt. The Japan-Korea Treaty of 1907. The Quebec Bridge collapsed. I don't see anything that would help us here."

She kept searching, but nothing jumped out. Elections in the Finnish Parliament, which was the first in the world to include women. The RMS Lusitania made its maiden voyage. The Knickerbocker Crisis also known as....

"Wait," Haylie said, pulling her hair back behind her ear, eyes filling with hope. "I think I found it."

> > > > >

Titanhurst - London
March 9th, 9:45AM

Martin pulled a folder from his black leather bag, dragging the zipper closed with a long, precise stroke. He laid the manila folder on the table, sliding his chair back across the floorboards and rising to his feet.

He walked with purpose, eying a tall, dark bookcase appointed with a collection of leather-bound books, stainless-steel electronics, and old vinyl records. His fingers traced the edge of the hi-fi system as he turned his attention to the albums stacked neatly above the speakers. He thumbed across the faces of old, faded paper bindings, slowly inhaling. He turned his attention down to the stereo and hit a single button with a firm click. Country music—*was that Willie Nelson?*—began to play from the speakers with a slow, steady beat.

"Streaming radio. A wonderful thing. Technology makes things so much better, you don't have to deal with all the fuss," Martin said, walking back towards Caesar. "But, of course, you know that already. Being so smart and all."

"What's in the folder?"

"Ah, yes. It's something we've been working on for quite some time now. Some new concepts for an outsider like you but don't worry, I think you'll see that there's nothing here you don't already know."

Caesar reached across the table and pulled the folder back, spinning it to face him. Eying Martin, he peeled back the cover. The paper inside was brittle and worn, barely holding itself together. The pages appeared as if they had been carefully ripped from an old magazine, complete with the article's title "*Who Are We? Where Will We Go? 1970*" in the bottom left corner.

The top of the page displayed a triangular diagram with the labels 'GOVERNMENT,' 'NATURE,' and 'MAN' at the tips of each corner. Dotted lines had been drawn from all three corners into the very center of the diagram, into a space labeled 'TECHNOLOGY.'

Caesar began to read.

Mankind has taken the upper hand, given its unique position on the earth, with the very vessel that created his life. Each day, he is knowingly taking more and more from nature and yet at the same time, is creating more of himself at a fearful rate. Technology—the advanced fulfillment of man's knowledge—allows him to distance himself from what is nature, and through government create a separate functioning ecosystem that is not of this world. The triangle was formed not by us, but by the beginning of time, but we now see irrefutable evidence that technology, after building exponential speed and power, has become the most powerful force in our world.

Given the growing influence of man in today's triangular force, the prominence of technology has already created destabilization. This shift will result in an imbalance that is unsustainable at its current levels of scale, and requires a reset and careful planning to keep the system as a whole functioning at its core.

"Are you serious with this?" Caesar asked, looking up to Martin and pushing the papers back towards him.

"Keep reading, there's plenty more," Martin said. His excitement grew as Caesar turned back to the faded pages.

Caesar continued on. He paused on a write-up with a large, pill-shaped diagram at the top featuring a pattern of colored circles, arcs, and thick, twisting lines. It was titled 'CRYPTOGRAM DESCRIBING THE COMPLEXITIES OF OUR WORLD.'

Moving on to the next page, a huge, slate blue graph took up three fourths of the layout, showing a sharp increase in population growth over the past few decades. Caesar focused on a large diagram with the title 'THE GROWING PROBLEM SET' with haphazardly intertwined lines representing concepts labeled as 'LARGE SCALE POVERTY,' 'INADEQUATE EDUCATION,' 'SPOILAGE OF NATURE,' 'DECAY IN INNER CITIES,' and on and on.

He met a page title that stopped him in his tracks: 'IN SEARCH OF NEW APPROACHES.' Caesar gripped the sheet of paper in his hands as he raised it towards his eyes.

We cannot deny that our balance has been offset in every manner by this growing problem of Man. Our Nature has been pillaged. Our Government has been thrown into a mode of recovery at all times. And our Technology has been confined to the corner of fixing problems we've created in lieu of the greater adventure: to build.

In a world so harshly transformed, it's not possible to tackle such a growing imbalance with the methods and mentality of the past.

Throughout history, our attempts to bridge the world have failed; democracy has reigned, and free will has splintered humanity. 'One man one vote' has not brought into account the larger picture—the knowledge that all men are not equal.

Mankind does not find balance when left to its own devices; this has been shown. But a fixed group of men, self-appointed and directed with cause, can fix

what has been wronged and ensure the long-term survival of the species, placing man back in control of his direction.

Caesar placed the paper back on the table. He looked to the window and saw that the morning was in full bloom, complete with chirping birds perched across bare tree limbs and scattered white, bulbous clouds pushing across the sky. He took a deep breath, turning back to Martin and staring into his eyes, checking for signs of life.

"Your thoughts?" Martin said, smiling with anticipation and straightening his jacket. "I must know."

"This is what Raven's been all about? *This?*" Caesar gestured down at the manifesto with an open palm, quickly reaching for the folder and flicking it back across the table. Sheets of paper flew into the air, scattering all around Martin, a few landing haphazardly across the tabletop. "Well, I think you're out of your mind."

Smiling and slowly picking the papers off his lap, Martin took his time in replying. "Why … why would you say that?"

"This stuff is all fluff, it's pseudoscience. Perfect triangles representing humanity? The complexities of the world can't just be drawn up in one, neat little diagram."

"It's a simplification of a larger set of–"

"It's childish, that's what I think. Like the work of a fifth-grader that has checked out too many conspiracy-theory books from the school library."

Martin paused, pointing a trembling finger towards Caesar, but then drawing back and composing himself. "You're a logical man. You must know the world is out of balance. Why do you lash out at someone … someone trying to finally fix the problem?"

"Because the world is a complex system, just like it says on those pages," Caesar said. "It's a complex system that requires delicate solutions, not simple ones. Easy solutions seem great on paper, but tend to have a lot of collateral damage."

Martin shook his head.

"And the Raven puzzle," Caesar said. "What does it have to do with any of this? I don't get it."

Martin stood firm. "Oh, please Caesar. You didn't see the clues along the way? Secret societies are all around us, they are the only way we can elevate our level of conversation. Progress doesn't happen in democracies; it happens behind closed doors. I am trying to give you a view behind those doors. To show you the wonders that can occur when men are allowed to *leave other men out*. If you didn't understand that, then I must have failed with my design. But I'm confident that's not the case."

"You? You created Raven?"

"I designed it," Martin said. "I don't have the technical skills to build out something that complex, but the logic was mine. I'm its father and its keeper."

"I don't believe this is happening," Caesar said.

"This world view is not new; it originates from decades of work by an inner circle of our group. Their plans are well thought out and comprehensive."

"Plans? What kind of plans?"

"The papers you didn't read, the ones you so rudely threw in my direction, those tell of the solution to our problem. We'll need a new way forward, so to speak. And while technology in the hands of the many has helped to put us in this mess in the first place, the findings from the group believe that high-powered technology in the hands of a few can help to correct it. This next generation of man will have science as its ally. Raven was built to help find men just like you. Men that can help lead this next wave of humanity. To use technology to power us forward once The Project begins."

Caesar wrung his hands through his hair, no longer trying to hide his utter disbelief. "The Project? There's a *project*? Stopping population growth, a small group of people running the entire world ... you guys are actually acting on this?"

"The world is destroying itself, and we're going to fix it. I'm here today asking if you'd like to join us."

Caesar stared with dead eyes past the apartment's kitchen at the locked front door. He looked down to the pile of papers littered across the table.

"Caesar, please. Help us save the world."

> > > > >

Interstate 101
near Novato, California
March 9th, 1:52AM

"What did you find?" Benjamin asked.

Haylie gripped the sides of her laptop as the car bounced over a rough spot in the road, fighting to keep her eyes open. She had only managed to sneak a few hours of sleep on the jet last night and the fatigue, compounded with hours trekking across the California forest, was taking a toll on her. Her head spun as she focused on the car's floor to recalibrate.

"The Knickerbocker Crisis," she said. "It says here that in October of 1907, the New York Stock Exchange fell almost fifty percent in a single day of trading. J.P. Morgan jumped in ... he called all his banker friends together to pledge huge sums of money. They effectively saved the U.S. economy."

"What's the connection to the clue?" Walter asked.

Haylie continued. "The other name for the Knickerbocker Crisis is the important piece here: The Panic of 1907."

"Ok. So the 'don't Panic' line from the message makes sense now," Benjamin said. "But how does that help us?"

"Here." Haylie pointed to a new search result. "As soon as we add J.P. Morgan's name to the Brother Libra search, the results light up. There's a bunch of them." She clicked across the top tabs of her browser, checking for anything that would help. "Looks like J.P. Morgan formed a secretive group back around that time called The Zodiac Club. They would hold monthly meetings—dinners—in his personal library."

Benjamin laughed. "Let me guess ... another conspiracy website?"

"No," Haylie replied, flipping the laptop screen back towards him. "This is from the *New York Times*."

"Huh." Walter leaned in, gently reaching for the computer. Haylie passed it to him, wringing her fingers together as he read out loud. "'The Zodiac Club is known only to its members and others that live in the world behind closed doors. The rotating collection of twelve members has met every year since 1868.'"

"Your invites must have been lost in the mail," Haylie said, clinking a few ice cubes into a glass she had plucked from the backseat bar and filling it halfway full with water.

"You joke, but it's strange we've never heard of it. This kind of stuff usually gets around in our circles," Walter said. "'The Zodiac dinners are held without public knowledge of attendance or agenda. All notes from the meetings are kept in Morgan's private library for safekeeping.'"

"Unbelievable," Haylie said, taking a long drink of water. "Raven is turning into a 'Who's Who' of rich white dudes that are drunk with power, holding secret meetings in their backyard tree forts."

"Here it is!" Walter yelled, pointing at the screen with one hand, and slamming his fist on the car seat with the other.

"Hey," Haylie said, looking down at her laptop. "Careful with the hardware."

"Listen to this," Walter said. "'Each member choses a sign of the zodiac as his codename. J.P. Morgan, the group's founder, led the charge with his moniker: Brother Libra.'" He handed the laptop back to Haylie. "This is awesome."

"'Find Brother Libra's last meal, we'll see you there,'" Benjamin repeated from the clue. "We need to find the last meal he had with the group. The meeting notes—it should be listed in the meeting notes from his last Zodiac dinner."

"So we have to break into J.P. Morgan's library?" Walter asked.

Haylie shook her head as she scrolled. "It might be easier than that. His former home is now the Morgan Library, a public museum located a few blocks from the Empire State Building. It's at the corner of Madison and 36th."

Walter pulled out his phone and dialed. He spoke to someone on the other side of the line, asking them to prep the plane for takeoff.

"Yes, that's right," Walter said. "We're heading home."

CHAPTER TW3NTY T4R33

Somewhere over Colorado
March 9th, 3:37AM

Haylie recognized the familiar feeling of panic as it crept up her spine; the rush to scatter, to be safe, to be anywhere but here. But it had never felt like this.

She swallowed her heartbeat into her throat as she hunted for sanctuary. She needed a place to hide, but there was simply nowhere to go.

The room went on for what seemed liked forever, with a grid of square tiles surrounded her on all sides, pulsing out like an inflating balloon. Every direction she tried to run, she just ended up right back in the middle, again and again; her movement pulling her back across the floor like the snap of a rubber band.

Haylie felt the presence of someone else, but she didn't know his name or face. Whoever was in pursuit—*and he was there, she knew it*—was good at this game. Crouching down, she ran her hand across the surface of the white tile at her feet. Expecting a slick, cold sheen, she jerked back her hand after feeling the scrape of sandpaper.

She had never wanted a shovel more in her life. If she had a shovel, she told herself, she'd dig for hours. Dig for days. She'd be safe down there, where no one else could see her, where no one else would even think to go. Scurry down, hide in a corner and watch the entrance above, shovel in hand, ready to strike anyone peaking over the edge.

She shouted out, calling for her hunter; to reason with him. To talk him down. To talk her way out. But the attempt met with a rush of air from her throat but little else. No sound, just dry straining and fatigue. Trying again and again, the words never came—not even stuck on her lips or her throat, but being held deep in her belly, like a ball of thick cement weighing her down with each attempt.

He was behind her.

She could feel it. She knew it. She had to run but she couldn't move. Each step was a moonwalk, flowing with impossibly heavy movement, like being underwater in the neighborhood pool at the crest of summertime.

He was coming.

She couldn't breathe. She could feel the heat of his hand reaching out–

> > > > >

The laptop jackknifed off her lap as Haylie woke to find her legs curled towards her chest, twisting into a knot in the leather chair. She sat up at full alert, eyes blinking, head turning left and right.

Where the hell am I?

She saw Benjamin asleep in the front left corner seat of the jet, his jacket and shoes neatly arranged on the bench across from him, legs crossed loosely on the table. Walter, a few seats over, looked back at Haylie with tired eyes.

"You were making some noise ... I thought it was best to let you sleep," he said in a soft tone. "You need it."

With her dream still heavy in her mind, she blinked repeatedly to come back online. She reached down to retrieve her computer, checking the corners and screen for any damage.

"I'm fine. Just a dream."

She stretched her arms up into the air and buttoned the zipper flap of her jacket up with a few snaps, sliding her blanket down and around her waist. Cracking the laptop back open, the jet's cabin was once again filled with the click-clack of rapid keystrokes.

"You've been under a lot of pressure, with Raven and everything," Walter said. "You should get more rest."

Ignoring him, Haylie checked newsfeeds and forums, finding comfort in her daily ritual. "You need sleep more than I do. You're old."

Walter chuckled, clicking off his light and pulling his blanket across his shoulder. He turned towards the window, bringing his knees up to his chest, and went silent.

Scrolling each forum, Haylie's brain slowly began to creep back to normal activity levels. She saw nothing new about the Raven puzzle from any of her sources or the public wires. *I guess no news is good news.*

She tabbed over to her outgoing chat messages, checking the collection of pings to Caesar that remained cold and unanswered.

I just want him to be all right.

As the world flew by below, Haylie tried her best to relax. The view wasn't much tonight, the white spider webs of a few illuminated small towns and highways littered the curves of the earth. The lights from inside the cabin reflected back across the glass, and Haylie caught herself staring at her own reflection for a few moments. *Write some code, analyze some data ... just do something that will put you back to sleep.*

She searched her desktop for inspiration, seeing a folder she had created just a few hours earlier labeled "`car_data`." *Hmm ... I forgot about this.*

When she had found herself stuck on the audio puzzle back in the car, she hadn't just quit and started searching pop culture websites or message boards. She had done what she always did when she hit a brick wall: challenged herself to solve a different problem to clear her head.

Once someone obtains—or in this case, is given—access to a wireless network, they can do all sorts of things. Haylie had decided to see if she could intercept all network traffic going to and from Walter's phone. Most of the information flowing over the network would be encrypted, but reading it wasn't really the point. She just wanted to see if she could get to the data, and she had done exactly that with a few lines of Python code. Now, all the text logs from Walter's incoming and outgoing communication from back in the car were sitting in a folder on her desktop, staring her back in the face.

Checking around the cabin to make sure all was clear, she loaded the data dump into her favorite packet analyzer tool. *Let's see if there's anything good in here.* Her mouth stretched into a deep yawn as she filtered the data down to show only outgoing transmissions, checking the log for any interesting web traffic.

She squinted at the HTTP results to see an unfamiliar messaging host; it was labeled 'Rubicon' and was responsible for a majority of Walter's traffic in the log. Doing a quick Internet search, Haylie saw reports of a new Brux chat application still in development with the same code name. *Interesting.* As she dove back into the logs, she realized that this early prototype didn't have encryption enabled; meaning that all text from every message should be right here in the data.

Gently placing her laptop on the table in front of her, Haylie shifted her weight to turn and face the brothers, still curled up and sleeping in opposite corners of the jet. As she slid from one side of the captain's chair to the other, she felt something wedged into her back pocket. *My souvenir from the Grove's archives.* She reached back to slip the papers out of her pocket, gently unfolding the pages to keep the crinkling paper quiet.

As she sifted the papers, she could feel a stark difference in weight and texture; the top two were older—much thinner, brittle and slick to the touch—and the second two pieces could have been fresh off a modern printer. She flipped the first of the newer pages and began to read.

Petition to Address the Leadership of the Bilderberg Group

Presented by: Benjamin and Walter Sterling, Bohemian Grove, Iron Ring camp

Our brothers in Bohemia, the Sterlings, prepared and delivered a petition to meet with the Bilderberg Group's inner leadership. Arguments included:

*Benjamin and Walter reminded the group that their service to the Bohemians over the past few years have been crucial to our organization's

recruiting efforts. **Their father, Andrew Sterling, also had a long and distinguished record with the Bohemian Club.**

*The Sterlings' access to capital and resources across banking, software, satellite technology, and other industries would prove to be useful for the success of The Project.**

The members in attendance heard all arguments and voted not to allow further meetings with the architects of The Project at this time.

Yours in Bohemia,

Brother Colorado

Haylie's face grew red as she re-read the document again and again, double and triple-checking each word to make sure the lack of sleep and altitude weren't causing her to hallucinate.

Walter and Benjamin are members of the Bohemian Club? That doesn't make any sense....

Her hands turned to fists as she stared down to the table, realizing that she was crunching the paper under the pressure between her trembling fingers.

They've been lying this whole time? Making a fool of me? And what the hell is The Project?

Looking back to her laptop, she opened Walter's chat logs and began to read. Combining the incoming and outgoing data streams, she sorted by timestamp to piece together the conversation between the brothers.

Walter:> need to keep her moving on the puzzle steps. clocks ticking.

Benjamin:> when do we cut her loose? we don't want her to know too much. as soon as we get to the leadership, she's gone.

Walter:> soon. but you need to stop being an ass, get her back on our side. make it seem legit. we need her to keep solving.

Benjamin:> I know. Will do.

156

Walter:> We should have just gone in the
Grove and found the clue ourselves. We
totally could have found it.

Benjamin:> And then what? We'd have to
crack the next code.

As she read each message, Haylie felt the rage building inside of her. Scrolling, her pulse quickened as she continued through their conversation.

Walter:> should never have paid Caesar
to solve this thing without staying with
him. babysitting this chick is a pain,
but at least she won't get away from us
like he did.

Benjamin:> lesson learned. we'll get it
right this time.

Her eyes shot daggers over at Walter, who lay unknowing, curled into a ball in the leather chair. He turned softly, pulling his blanket over his shoulder.

The anger grew as she read back through the logs, again and again. She could feel the heat flash across her cheeks as she planned the steps of what she had to do next.

She should have known better. She had fallen into their trap; she had become their pawn.

But that was all about to change.

CHAPTER TW3NTY FOUR

Titanhurst - London
March 9th, 12:12PM

"Martin, please come in. I only have a few minutes. I trust your flight was comfortable?"

Martin's footsteps clicked across solid, dark hardwoods as he took in the room; it was an architectural marvel. A collection of stitched leather furniture sat on islands of crisscrossed wooden slats, all bordered by pathways of slate gray tile and stone. The patterns guided Martin's eye around three different sitting areas and to the end of the room, where a battleship of a desk sat at the helm in firm command of the room. Dark wood wrapped around the walls and cabinets, highlighting the windows that only managed to show a dull glow of white behind their thick protective coverings. He could smell a mix of raw materials, epoxy, and sawdust fresh in the air.

Prime Minister John Crowne sat at the center of his formal leather couch with his laptop angled on the table, rising to his feet as his guest entered. Martin had always enjoyed their time together; it was difficult not to. Crowne had always been the type that reminded him of the best of times, even if Martin couldn't quite calculate whether the attitude was genuine or a means to an end. Either way, Martin tried his best to enjoy the attention without falling under its spell. It was difficult at times; Crowne was, after all, a politician.

"Thank you, sir," Martin said. "It's great to see you. Headquarters looks wonderful. Built to last a lifetime."

"Well, hopefully for the next few decades, at least. We've a lot of planning to do, lots of planning. A lot of that will happen right here within this office. I wanted it to be modern and classic all at the same ... oh, who am I kidding? Lucy designed it all. Don't tell anyone, just between us friends, okay Martin?" Crowne laughed out loud, grabbing Martin's shoulder playfully. *There was that charm again.*

"So listen, Martin, I just need a minute of your time. We're running final checks of all systems, safeguards, supplies, and personnel for the core group that will remain online during The Project; this is obviously an important time. All leaders and their families are getting prepped for the big day. Things are moving fast, but I think we're in top shape. In fact, I've received 'go' orders from all groups except for one: our technology leadership team. I've called you here to make sure we have our candidate for the lead position on board."

As Crowne gestured over to the couch, Martin gave a slight bow and took a seat.

"You must mean Caesar Black," Martin said. "He's our man that made it past the Raven 2309 tests. He's here at Titanhurst, staying in the apartment that would become his new residence. Assuming he accepts the position."

A confused expression shot across Crowne's face as he stared down into Martin's eyes. "Assuming? What do you mean, Martin, *assuming*? We're at three days until we flip the switch here. He hasn't signed on?"

"I've introduced our point-of-view to him. He needs some time to think about it."

"What's to decide? As of next week, he'll either be one of the most important computer scientists in Earth's history or he'll be reduced to ... a simple caveman. Doesn't he know that? Did you explain that to him?"

"Not in those terms, sir, no, but I've been pressing the upside of the opportunity. I believe he'll come around, he just needs a bit more time with some of the core concepts I've presented. I've left all the research with him," Martin replied, sinking back into the couch, still managing to keep his smile intact. "He seems quite sharp, I'm sure he'll come around."

"I'm sure he'll come around," Crowne repeated. "I see."

Pacing the length of the hardwood floor, one solid heel after another, Crowne stopped after reaching the desk at the end of the room. It was massive in stature, as if it had been carved out of a solid block of wood. The desk rested inset into a slight divot in the floor, like it had been dropped off a cliff to land solidly in this very office with a single room-shaking thud.

Only one item sat on the desk: a simple wooden box. It was just a bit larger than a cigar box, but lower in profile with intricate black, tan, and natural wood patterns curving up and down the routed edges. Crowne leaned over and cracked the lid.

"I've tried my best not to get greedy," Crowne said. "You and I, we know what's going to happen in a few days. So it's natural for there to be an urge, a temptation, to collect things. Once the power goes out, the looting will begin. We'll lose many of our treasures forever, they'll just disappear. Priceless paintings will end up in bonfires for warmth. Entire museums will be overrun with squatters and human waste. So why not save the things that we can, right?"

His voice grew softer as he flipped the lid back onto the front of the desk. Craning his neck slightly, Martin made a subtle effort to see his way inside.

Crowne continued. "But if we hoard the treasures—all the little things we want to keep close—it would set off warnings. Alarms. People would surely get suspicious that something was going on. We can't have that." Crowne nodded to himself as he continued to stare into the box. "So I was careful. But there was one thing that I wanted; one thing that I would hate to see lost to history."

Reaching in, Crowne retrieved a black and gray pistol from the center of the box. It was smaller than the handguns Martin was used to seeing in movies; it seemed like it would barely fit in a grown man's hand. Crowne stood back up straight, curling the gun into his palm, flipping it over and watching the light dance across the dull surfaces of the handle and the sheen of the stock.

"What is it?" Martin asked.

"Well, it's a pistol, Martin," Crowne said, deadpan.

"Yes sir, but…."

"I'm kidding. It's a Walther PPK. I had it retrieved from the basements of the British Museum. It had never been put on display ... never been officially entered into the system at all, in fact. Spending all this time sitting in the basement, tucked in behind the Head Curator's personal collection. It's been stored in the back corner of some rusty safe; hidden away from the world for the last few decades."

Flipping the gun's grip out of his hand and holding the relic by its barrel, Crowne extended the firearm in Martin's direction, gesturing for him to approach. Martin rose slowly, straightening the fabric on his suit pants with his palms, and walked carefully towards the Prime Minister. Martin slowly took the weapon with both hands and held it with care.

"But, why is it special?" Martin asked.

"It's the pistol Adolf Hitler used to kill himself."

Martin's face froze as he stared into the dark metal. His right leg began to flex and tremble as he concentrated to try and appear calm. Martin extended the pistol back to the Prime Minister and took a heavy breath. Crowne snatched it back, flipping the pistol comfortably into his palm.

"After they found him with Eva Braun in the bunker," Crowne said, "they burned the bodies. But a few of our guys got in there for intelligence. One of them, a nervous wreck of a Staff Sergeant, slipped the pistol under his helmet when no one was paying attention. Still had brains and blood all over it, ended up dripping down the back of his neck and making quite a mess. He made it all the way back to London with the thing—smuggled in suitcases, lunch boxes, that sort of nonsense—before finally having a panic attack and handing it over to his commanding officer. Isn't it something?"

"It is, sir," Martin replied, his eyes still locked on the pistol.

"Don't worry, Martin. I know what you're thinking. Hitler was a madman, no one's debating that. I didn't want the pistol as some sick tribute to him, that's not the point. We're not doing what he did. His goals were not our goals." Crowne tossed the pistol back into the box from a few feet away. The gun landed with a loud thud, causing Martin to jump on impact.

"I wanted the pistol to remind us of what we're up against. If we succeed, we'll be heroes. We'll have saved the human race. Technology and society will advance at rates like we've never seen before. Nature will heal itself and welcome us back into her arms. We'll be responsible for that next phase of humanity. We'll be the booster rocket for all generations to come. That's how we'll be remembered if we do this the right way."

Closing the top of the box, Crowne placed his palms firmly on the desk, leaning in across the table top and directly at Martin. "But if we fail, we'll look like the others. We'll be madmen in the eyes of history, even though we know that's not the case. They'll twist our thinking into their agendas; they'll rewrite our purpose."

Martin swallowed a dry gulp down his throat.

"We can't lose at this, Martin. We only have three days to get it right. Everything has to be perfect; we need all of the logistics around The Project to be ready to go. Technology is the key for our success, you know that. Technology will be the manner in which we soar or we fail."

Crowne's tone grew with anger as he crossed his arms firmly and stood tall. "The group needs a leader, and we need Caesar to be that leader. We need him on board, and we needed him to start *yesterday*. You have to do better."

His voice fell to a whisper. "Now, given what we're up against, I think we can both agree that 'I'm sure he'll come around' isn't good enough right now. Don't you think?"

Martin stepped back, exhaling and nodding. His pocket buzzed and he retrieved his phone, checking the fresh message.

"Don't worry, sir. I'll get him on board. I'm going to give our new friend Caesar something he can't resist," Martin said, regaining his composure. "I'm going to give him another puzzle to solve."

CHAPTER TWƎNTY FꞮVƎ

Titanhurst - London
March 9th, 2:37PM

The flowing gold and burgundy pattern of the hallway carpet began to cast a wicked optical illusion; in small doses, the ovals and surrounding ridges would have been fine, but the never-ending length of the hall mixed with Martin's rapid pace was causing Caesar's head to spin.

He reached out against the hard plaster wall, running his hand across the wainscoting for a moment, trying his best to right himself. He focused his eyes on the box-beamed wooden ceiling to grasp back a sense of direction.

"I'm not sure where you're taking me," Caesar said as he steadied his gait. "But I thought I was pretty clear. I'm not planning to help you."

Martin, walking a few steps ahead, simply looked back and flashed a smile towards Caesar.

"Yes, yes. I understood. You were quite clear," Martin responded, continuing his fast-paced march down the hallway. "I just want to show you something before you go. It won't take but a minute."

"Besides, your plan will never work," Caesar said. "People will never follow a single power across the globe, especially one that isn't elected."

Caesar lost sight of Martin momentarily as he turned a corner and sped down the connecting hall, picking up a slight jog to keep up with the pace.

"It won't be long now; we're almost there," Martin said, checking his phone with one eye as he kept his momentum.

Martin stopped at a door at the end of the hall and slapped his keycard up against a flat white security panel. "Here we are." There was a quick buzz-click-buzz and Martin pulled at the door, allowing Caesar to enter in front of him.

Taking a careful step across the threshold, Caesar craned his neck around the corner to check the room before fully committing. What he saw inside looked very familiar.

The room was enormous, almost like a self-contained, hyper-modern office building, all built inside a wing of Titanhurst. The layout, furnishings, and people scurrying about the room resembled a mid-stage startup company. About forty or fifty computer workstations, all manned by programmers, were arranged in three rows of plain desks lining one side of the complex. Large flat-screens littered the walls every few feet, but it was the structure on the south wall—an enormous stadium-seating pit—that drew Caesar's eye.

Fifteen engineers assembled in the pit facing a large array of screens, each displaying data from different parts of the globe. Grainy camera feeds of military bases, traffic patterns in Paris, and data from stock markets projecting the next morning's opening bell.

"What is all this?" Caesar whispered under his breath.

"Martin. What's up, man?" A young man with an American accent approached, reaching out to shake Martin's hand. He had a thin, scraggly beard, a t-shirt that read 'STARTUP OLYMPICS, BAY AREA, 2015,' and faded but stylish Adidas sneakers. He had the knowing eyes of a man that knew what he was doing.

"Sean. Good to see you. I just got into London earlier this morning. Oh, meet Caesar Black," Martin said with a smile. "Sean was the number two guy at LolliBook, but left a few years after the IPO. Designed their entire architecture from scratch and then scaled it as they grew, obviously. He designed and built the–"

"The NexBot open framework for rapid web deployment. I use that package on all my side projects. It's amazing," Caesar said, staring at Sean with awe.

"Yes, he sure did. Sean's been with us for a few months now," Martin continued.

The two men shook hands, and Sean quickly apologized for having to "bolt" before heading off towards his workstation.

"And Alexis...." Martin bellowed down into the pit. "Alexis, could you come up here, please? I'd love for you to meet someone." An older woman with graying hair and glasses looked up in his direction, skipping up the stairs with a smile.

"Caesar, do you remember the last mission to Mars?" Martin asked. "The one where NASA sent a rover wrapped in a collection of balloons that inflated on impact to cushion the blow? They said it would never work with the limited budget that they had ... Alexis was the lead engineer on that one. She's just joined us a few weeks ago but she's already been solving problems that left us scratching our heads for months."

Caesar shook her hand as they exchanged pleasantries and she returned back to her work. He surveyed the room.

This feeling—I know this feeling.

It's well-known in the startup world that to succeed, half the battle is finding a team with the right energy. Take a small space—a loft apartment, a warehouse, even the corner of a coffee shop—and get the right team of smart, independent, accomplished people together, and it will feel different; there will be a buzz, an electricity. Caesar knew that feeling well, and this operation had somehow tucked it into an English mansion.

"How ... how did you get all these people here? This is incredible," Caesar stuttered as the group continued to work all around them.

"This is my job, and I'm very good at it," Martin said. "I found them each in different ways. Nothing as elaborate as the Raven puzzle, I can assure you, but I discovered each one at the right time and the right place. And as for the NASA people, well, that wasn't that hard. They pay terribly over there."

"Do they all know what's going on here?" Caesar whispered to Martin. "About your plans?"

"Of course they do. You want to try keeping secrets from people that invented the email system used by half the world? Good luck with that. We've been up front and honest with everyone, and I'd be happy to tell you all the details as well, if you'll join us," Martin said. "Like I said back in the apartment, we're doing the right thing here; everyone understands the logic. And more importantly, they understand the opportunity. But while the people in this room are technical marvels, they aren't leaders—there's a difference, as you know. They need a man like you to lead them."

Caesar tried to wrap his brain around what he was seeing. Engineers white-boarding coding problems, schedules and timelines on paper taped to the walls, beer kegs and t-shirts. *I don't believe this.*

"Caesar, this is your team," Martin said. "No, sorry, they were *going* to be your team. Network operations, data science, artificial intelligence … designing systems to run the world over the next few hundred years. That's the goal, anyway."

Caesar exhaled, thinking about the possibilities.

"Listen, about that favor," Martin said. "I've got one last ask of you and then we'll get you on the next flight to New York; first class, of course. Come with me."

Martin led Caesar back over to the pit where he tapped an engineer and whispered in her ear. She dropped what she was doing and with a few keystrokes, commandeered two screens at the center of the main display. Live feeds appeared of the Main Lodge of the Bohemian Grove and Terminal A at JFK Airport.

"We've received another signal from the Raven puzzle," Martin said, gesturing towards the wall of screens. "Someone used the QR code from the Grove earlier this morning, London time. We believe that there's someone in your shadow, and to get this far, they must be pretty good."

Squinting to make out details on the screens, Caesar walked down into the pit for a closer vantage point. He focused on the view of the Bohemian Grove, showing a dozen or so security officers of all ranks mulling around the Main Lodge. A cut view showed the carcass of a charred boat being dragged to shore by an officer clumsily paddling a canoe, with a co-captain holding a small, black device in his hand.

"Wow," Caesar said. "They really did it."

"Indeed. Used a drone for surveillance, came in on foot. Very smart, must have taken weeks of planning. Unfortunately, they didn't realize there would be a mid-spring meeting for Bohemian Club members at the time, but still, they made it to the next clue while avoiding capture," Martin said. "As you know, if they are continuing on with the Raven steps, we have to assume they are now headed to New York."

Caesar nodded, side-stepping over to the video feed of JFK airport. He turned back to Martin and the rest of the team, who had now assembled around the pit. "So what do you want me to do?"

"Well, with your departure, we're still without a leader for our technology group," Martin said with a quick glance around the room. "Our timeline is of the essence; we'd like to intercept the hacker that is headed into the Morgan Library and bring them to London; offer them the lead position. Anyone under this kind of pressure, of course, is going to be a bit ... on edge, so we may need to get creative here."

Caesar stared back at Martin with a curious eye.

"We'd like you to catch your replacement, if you would be so kind."

CHAPTER TW3NTY S1X

The Kitano Hotel - NYC
March 10th, 8:15AM

"Is the audio coming across? Are you getting this?"

The jittered, pixelated voice cut in and out at high volume, piercing through the spacious hotel suite. Scents of coffee and eggs lingered as the sunlight poured through the east-facing windows and onto the caramel wood floors.

Haylie jacked in her headphones and toggled down the volume a few notches. She switched over to update the system settings, giving her Voice-Over-IP app the highest network priority.

"Hold on. I'm tweaking something over here," Haylie said. "I hear you, just wait a minute."

An hour earlier, Haylie had sent Vector a text asking him for an IRL voice conversation, which would be a first for them. He had shot back a link to his favorite VoIP client: open source, easy to set up, and most importantly, secure.

"Ok, try again," Haylie said. "Say something."

"No chance, Crash," a British voice sounded back. "You'll never get me to talk."

Haylie cracked a grin, the first she could remember in a long time. Vector's voice seemed kind, even refreshing, and that British accent, well that was a whole thing in itself. She exhaled with relief, as if a lifeline had been thrown her way after days adrift at sea.

"So what's going on over there?" Vector continued. "Why are you in New York?"

"I need your help," she sighed.

Haylie spent the next few minutes explaining everything—Caesar's disappearance, the Sterling brothers, and Raven 2309. As she described her journey, she felt a weight lifting off her sore shoulders with each story.

"Why not just go to the police?" Vector said. "That's an option, right?"

"The Sterlings know about my hacking history," Haylie said. "Not all of it, but a few of the big ones. No way I'm going to risk them turning me in. I think we can do this without the police."

"Where are the brothers right now?" Vector asked.

"I haven't seen them since we landed yesterday, but they should be at their cozy little corporate headquarters down in the Meatpacking District," Haylie said, wincing as she pictured the twins scheming behind her back. "They'll be busy for a few hours."

"The piece I don't get," Vector said, "is why do the Sterling brothers care so much about Raven in the first place?"

"It must be The Project—whatever that is—from the Grove document," Haylie said. "That has to be the connection, right? They were asking for a meeting with the leadership but no dice. Now, for some reason, they think that solving Raven is their only other chance to track down the group."

"What are they like?" Vector asked. "You know, in real life? I've read so many articles on them and their 'next big thing' approach."

"I'd say they're two guys that were born on third base and act like they just hit a triple," Haylie said in an annoyed tone.

"What...." Vector said. "What does that mean?"

"It's a baseball thing," she said. "An American thing. Sorry, I forgot. Never mind."

"Well, that's quite a week you've had," Vector said. "I wish you would have told me you were working on Raven; I could have helped."

"I couldn't ... I wish I could have," she said, "but there was no time to stop and chat."

"Sure, I get it, but really," Vector said, with starts and fits interrupting his speech. "I ... this is going to sound strange, especially with the week you've just had, but I know a thing or two about the Raven puzzles."

Haylie's brow furrowed as she stared at the blinking status indicator on the chat app. She nervously tapped her fingernails across the aluminum deck of her computer. *What does he mean, he knows a thing or two?* She waited for him to elaborate.

"Right, so a year back—no, must have been two—I got a gig from the MechChat forum boards. You know, those anonymous postings that you'll see on there each week? Small little coding projects for cash? Saving people's hard drives that have crashed, that sort of thing. Well, this one was from a bloke here in London that needed some custom work." Vector said. "It turned out to be a series of puzzles. If you did a good job building one, they'd send you another. Cryptography and image files, riddles, hiding objects around town. Any of this sound familiar?"

Haylie winced. *It sure does.*

"It was easy money," Vector continued. "Anyway, a few months later, I see a random post about Raven starting up again and I go to check it out. And bam, what do I find? One of the puzzles I had worked on was the starting point for Raven. Then it all made sense."

"Who are they?" Haylie said, as her heart beat faster. "Who were you working for?"

"No idea. It was dead drops for files and money from random bank accounts sending wire transfers in return. I never met anyone from their side, just a few other hackers that took the jobs like I did. I worked with one or two others on puzzles that included multiple forms of tech, stuff I wasn't good at. I can't even remember who they were."

"They have my brother," Haylie said, stopping herself as she felt her voice beginning to crack. *Keep your focus. Caesar will be fine. Everything will be fine.* She opened her Morgan research and checked the plan she had typed out on the jet.

"Here's the thing: the puzzle is getting harder with each step," Haylie said. "I'm going to need your help–"

"Taking down the Sterling brothers?" Vector asked.

"No, getting into the Morgan," Haylie said. "The brothers … I'll take care of them myself."

"Brilliant, let's get on with it. I've already called in sick for my shift tonight, just in case. Just let me know what I can do."

Haylie cut and pasted a block of text and sent it Vector's way via a burner email address. "I'm sending you what I need from you today, complete with timetable."

Vector clicked at his keyboard and Haylie heard a slight, nervous chuckle. "My goodness. This is really going to happen, isn't it?"

"You're damn right it is. I'm going to get in, grab this thing, and get the hell out of there before Walter and Benjamin even know what hit them. Afterwards, I need you to find those other programmers you worked with on the Raven puzzles. Dig them up; if they know something, I need to know it, too."

"What if the Sterlings figure out what's going on?"

"Then I'll make them wish they hadn't started this in the first place. I'll *ruin* them."

There was silence on the other end of the line, followed by the rapid clicking of keys.

"Right. Let's get on with it, then," Vector said.

She breathed in heavy and rose from the couch, looking out the window at the beams of morning sunlight. *They'll never see me coming.*

> > > > >

Brux Software HQ - NYC
March 10th, 8:31AM

Walter and Benjamin walked in step across the second floor lounge. The bright green walls of the bar and sitting area reflected like watercolors across the wood, contrasting with the white plastic chairs arranged here and there. Grown men sat in beanbag chairs as other employees wrote algorithm designs in fading blue and green marker on expanses of whiteboards and floor-to-ceiling glass partitions.

"So we're meeting up with Haylie at ten thirty, is that the plan?" Benjamin asked as he sipped his Americano. "Where did you decide on?"

"Right," Walter confirmed, checking his watch. "We'll be waiting in front of the Morgan Library in the SUV, and she'll meet us there when she's done. Nice and easy today."

"Was she able to get an appointment in the Reading Room at the Morgan?" Benjamin asked.

"Not exactly," Walter said. "Sounds like those things take months, sometimes years to schedule. But she texted me last night, said she was able to hack in and add her name to the system in someone else's place. Like I said: nice and easy. They'll never even know we were there."

A passing Brux employee gave the brothers a shy wave as she inched her messenger bag tighter and walked by. The brothers smiled back to her and waited for her to pass to resume their conversation.

"The people we talked to said that Raven should only be fifteen steps long," Walter said, keeping his voice low. "This one, the Morgan Library step, would be number twelve. We're getting close, but I'm still worried about the schedule. We only have a few days."

"We'll be fine," Walter said, as he stood. Benjamin followed and the brothers made their way down the hall. "You know, in a few days none of this will matter. The only thing left will be the people connected to The

Project. When we make our case, they'll understand what we have to offer. We just need the chance to explain."

The brothers turned the corner and ran full-force into Nancy, Benjamin's tiny executive assistant. Nervously laughing and holding her hands out as if to catch them if they fell, she stood back, pushing her glasses back up on the bridge of her nose.

"You guys … you're way too fast today," she said, catching her breath. "I've been looking all over for you. The board meeting has been moved up to the fourth floor executive conference room." She glanced down at the LCD screen on her watch. "You'd better get up there to do the meet-and-greet."

The brothers nodded in sync, checking their phones one last time.

"Oh, and the board meeting goes until ten," Nancy continued, "but then I see you both have your calendars blocked for the next few hours. Is there something in there that I can help with? I know you guys just got back from a trip."

Benjamin stepped forward, placing his phone back into his pocket. "Just shopping for Mom's birthday. We thought we'd do it ourselves this year. You know, get her something fun."

Nancy's head slid to an angle as she bent one knee, smiling and bobbing. "Aw, you guys. You're just too sweet." She patted Benjamin on the shoulder as they made their way to the elevator. "Such nice boys."

> > > > >

The Kitano Hotel - NYC
March 10th, 8:37AM

Haylie read her checklist one last time, sipping coffee as she memorized the run-through. The museum was a public place and would require a very different set of skills than the previous Raven steps. She would have to work her way past layers of security, gain access, grab what she needed, and leave everyone in the museum completely unaware. It was going to take careful planning, research, and coordination. Unfortunately, Haylie didn't have time for any of those things.

She had bought some wiggle room by laying out a plan to meet the brothers at ten thirty, which was the time she swore the Morgan Library's Reading Room began its first appointment. In reality, the Reading Room opened thirty minutes earlier.

It's amazing how some people are too lazy to Google stuff.

That wasn't the only lie she had told Walter yesterday. She hadn't actually hacked into the library's appointment calendar; getting into that system, it turned out, was impossible. After studying a collection of tourist photos scattered across the web, Haylie learned that the appointment list lived on a simple wooden clipboard hanging on a nail in the Reading Room. Their system was just pencil and paper. Old school.

That's not to say she still didn't have options on how to get into the room. The first option was to simply get access to the clipboard; just erase or white-out a name and pick your spot. But to do that, you need to get inside the building without anyone seeing you. The staff was probably already working this morning, preparing for the day, so that approach wouldn't work. The second option was pretending to be someone that had already made their way onto that list. Haylie didn't like that tactic, either.

Luckily, she had thought of a third way.

With all the valuable stuff in this place, there's going to be a ton of security: cameras, police, and guards. Just focus on solving the problem. Get what you need and get out.

She checked the timetable one more time and clicked her laptop shut. Ideally, she would have had two more weeks to design this type of exploit.

Checking her watch, she had about fifteen minutes.

> > > > >

Titanhurst - London
March 10h, 1:42PM

"Ok, this should be simple enough," Caesar called out, speaking to the group of fifteen engineers and security experts that had assembled around him. Each member of the team watched on as he paced before a giant whiteboard. The board was filled with all-caps writing, outlining the steps to catch the person trying to solve Raven as they entered the Morgan Library.

"You're all now familiar with the Raven steps," Caesar said. "The easiest way for us to stop the puzzle hunter would be to shut down the clue electronically, cancelling out any of the hosted files, QR codes, or other digital clues. Unfortunately, most of the remaining steps are physical, so that's not a viable option. But don't worry, we'll still get our guy. To begin with, we're monitoring all the major hacking chat rooms, boards, and groups where someone might be bragging about their progress to others or asking about specific systems. If they talk about Raven, we can identify them and intercept."

Members of the group nodded as others rolled office chairs over, apparently expecting this to take more than a few minutes.

"When I solved the Morgan Library step myself, I remember thinking about how well-designed it was," Caesar looked over to Martin, almost apologetically. "Most of the early puzzle steps could have been done by pretty much anyone. Hobbyists or thirteen-year-old script kiddies in their parent's basements. But the physical stuff really upped the ante. The Bohemian Grove required technical knowledge but also stealth and stamina. The Morgan required something else: a level of polish and sophistication. A kid in a black hoodie with a laptop isn't going to work his way into the Reading Room of this place, it's just not going to happen."

"Sure," Sean said from the crowd, "but what can we do from here in London, seeing as we're a few thousand miles away?"

"We already have a physical presence on the ground in New York. One of your agents has been assigned to this operation," Caesar said, checking a note on his phone before continuing. "We're just calling him Agent Blue. He's heading to the Morgan this morning. But in addition to boots on the ground, there's plenty we can do from here." Caesar pointed back to the whiteboard to a section reading '#1: VIDEO.'

"We'll start with video surveillance to monitor activity within the museum," Caesar said. "We don't have time to add our own cameras, so we'll just have to hack into the museum's security system. Sean, this should be easy for you. They have a relatively modern setup but they are a non-profit, which means they can't afford good full-time staff to maintain and secure everything they want to. I was able to find an online admin tool that we can hopefully still access. Check their IP range for anything that matches any of the default network settings across major video camera device IDs, or other markers."

> > > > >

The Kitano Hotel - NYC
March 10th, 8:55AM

Haylie pushed forward into a rush of wind, her hair flying straight behind her, as she stepped into the Kitano Hotel's back alley exit. She felt the steel fire door slam clumsily shut behind her, hearing the hearty scrape of metal on metal.

Hitching her backpack up on her shoulders, she slid her hands into her pockets. As her right hand found her new fake ID, she thumbed and flipped it, holding it for safe keeping. Twisting her new tweed skirt to what she thought was the right position, she made her way towards the gate. Her shopping trip last night had awarded her with some items that would help her fit in with the Morgan's academic crowd, even if it meant a bit of discomfort this morning.

She wrapped her scarf around her head, protecting her hair from the breeze, and adjusted her glasses. Her heels clicked as she made her way down the alley's bumpy trail of asphalt. The smells of steam and rotting garbage mixed and twisted all around as she made her way up a set of stairs. The gate squealed shut behind her and finished with a satisfying bang, signaling her arrival on the sidewalk of East 37th Street.

Just stick to the plan. Piece of cake.

> > > > >

Behind a dumpster with 'KITANO HOTEL' stenciled in white spray paint, a bellboy leaned in off the brick and wrapped his head around the side wall for a better view. He watched as Haylie made her way through the gate. A standstill line of cabs highlighted her silhouette as she turned right, whipping around the corner.

He tossed his cigarette at the nearest puddle, missing by a mile, and plucked his phone from his pocket. He typed out a text to a new number in his phone—the number of a man that had pulled him aside just that very morning.

"Easiest hundred bucks I ever made, man," he whispered to himself, hitting send on the text and pulling out another cigarette.

CHAPTER TWENTY SEVEN

Morgan Library - NYC
March 10th, 9:05AM

The border of grass and foliage circling the museum gave a refreshing few seconds of coolness to the city air, a welcome change to the hot steam pouring from manholes and the exhaust from the surrounding gridlock.

A single steel bench rested in front of the library's entrance, providing a full view of the Morgan complex: the old residence perched above the corner on the left; the office and old library on the right; and a new, modern museum that bridged the two. Haylie's pulse began to pound as she thought through her plan.

It's a public place. If anything starts happening that seems off, you bail. You run. Keep your head low when possible and away from the cameras.

Checking the time on her phone, Haylie stood and paced across the cobblestones towards the shining glass entryway. Walking into the front entrance of the Morgan Library felt like entering a day spa; the doors opened to reveal a modern, bright entrance filled with tanned wood and multi-colored glass paneling in the main atrium. She could smell the scents of brunch from the cafe just down the hall where well-dressed Manhattanites sat, drinking bubbly orange juice and sipping really, really good coffee.

Based on the maps she had studied online, Haylie knew the Reading Room was to the right and up the stairs, nestled at the end of its own dedicated hallway. She passed by the reception desk without giving the clerk a second look. *Act like you know where you're going.* Hooking a sharp right, she climbed up the small, deserted stairwell.

As she reached the top landing, Haylie saw two surveillance cameras: one pointing at the door, the other angled for a view of the hallway. She got underneath the hall camera and stretched up on her tiptoes to read the manufacturer's stamp; they were made by HexMark.

Excellent.

Any regular visitor on hacking message boards knew that the HexMark online administrator tool had a laundry list of open vulnerabilities, all of which would play in her favor today.

Under the lone hallway window, Haylie walked by a power outlet with a network plug-in beside it. Stopping and taking a knee on the cold marble floor, she retrieved a small, off-white device out of her bag and quickly plugged the two cords from the box into the power outlet and network jack.

The device, which looked remarkably like a typical power brick, was a refined version of what hackers call a "drop box." As soon as it was powered up, the box would run an array of scripts to gain network access using a predefined collection of network exploit tactics. Once the device succeeded in breaking the network's security, it would then simply call its owner and provide them with connection credentials to the system.

Haylie knew she still had a few minutes before the Reading Room opened. The first tour of the library started at nine o'clock each morning, so she might still be able to sneak into the tour group. Even with the extensive research as she had done online, she couldn't rule out the inside knowledge a museum tour guide could spill that might help her find what she came for.

She stole a glance at her phone, checking the note where she had copied the next Raven clue:

> **our secrets are our power.**
> **don't Panic.**
> **find Brother Libra's last meal.**
> **we'll see you there.**

Here I am. And I'm coming for you, Brother Libra.

She headed back downstairs, curving into the main hall and finding a tour group clustered together, working their way towards Morgan's private study. Haylie disappeared into the middle of the huddle, leaning in close to hear every last detail.

> > > > >

Morgan Library - NYC
March 10th, 9:12AM

William Morgan wore freshly ironed khakis paired with a blue blazer and waited in the cramped office space nestled into a corner of the third floor. William Morgan wasn't really his name, but it was today.

His real name was Jack Long, and inside The Project, he was known only as Agent Blue. The naming schemes had been confusing to him at first, but now after a few months of doing these types of ops, he could try on a new name and identity like a jacket in a dressing room; on and off with ease.

A slight mist of sweat glistened off his forehead, remnants from this morning's jog across Central Park. Checking his phone, he sat back and tried his best to relax.

William Morgan. William Morgan. Hi, my name is William Morgan.

He must have repeated today's false name a hundred times in his head, forcing it into the important places where he might need it today. Rubbing his eyes, he clutched his coffee cup, tired from a full night of research.

He had received the call detailing his assignment around ten o'clock last night, and spent the rest of the evening studying up on Raven 2309 and the details of this morning's operation, all in addition to learning the entire Morgan family history. He was tired but, hey, it wasn't everyday that he got the chance to act like American royalty, even if he was just pretending to be a distant, less-successful cousin of J.P. Morgan.

The Director burst in, ending a call on his phone and grinning from ear to ear. "William? Or is is Will? Great to meet you." The Director shook his hand vigorously, hovering over him with enthusiasm. "You know, we've had the occasion to meet so many different members of the family over the years, but this is the first time you've made it in."

"Yes, it's been on my list without a doubt. But with school and all, you know how it is; the time just flies by," William said.

"Well, I'd love to give you a tour of the residence, show you some of the rooms that we've preserved from their original state. I'm sure you'll find them fascinating," the Director said, beaming.

William smiled and checked his watch. "I'd love to do that at some point, but right now I'd really like to get started over in the Reading Room. I know it's due to open at ten and I'd like to get situated before things get too busy." He stood, buttoning his jacket. "The thing is—I'd love to start being useful, if that's all right with you."

A slow, knowing grin grew across the Director's face as he pointed towards William. "You! You've got your family's blood all right. Right to business. Let me get you over to the Reading Room and I'll introduce you to our Head Librarian."

The Director walked William out the door. "Right to business today, then."

> > > > >

Brux Software HQ - NYC
March 10th, 9:14AM

Walter studied the crowd, taking in the faces of each board member around the table, all giving his brother their full attention. Behind him, Benjamin stood at the head of the table, presenting the projected earnings for the quarter.

Folding his arms across his chest, Walter felt a buzz in his right breast jacket pocket. It was the phone he had purchased at one of those cheap, brightly-lit Times Square electronics vendors that preyed on tourists. Only one person had the number, and if they were texting, it meant Haylie was on the move.

Walter snuck a quick check of the time.

She just left the hotel. It's too early for her to be on the move. Something's going on.

> > > > >

Titanhurst - London
March 10th, 2:15PM

"Ok, let's talk about the guest list," Caesar said. "The Morgan only allows a few people each day into the private Reading Room where they are welcome to check out anything from the archives. All materials must be reviewed under strict supervision for security reasons; that means no laptops, phones, cameras ... not even pens or pencils are allowed in."

Caesar paced in front of the whiteboard. "These appointments are like gold to local academics. If the museum even allows you on the list, it's not uncommon to wait for more than a year for your scheduled appointment. And God help you if you forget to show up."

A woman sitting towards the front of the group spoke up. "When you were solving this step, did you try to break into the network and add your name to the list? That seems like the easiest way in."

"Sure, that's the first thing I tried. But didn't have any luck," Caesar said. "While many of their systems are online, the appointment system is not. Appointments are written on a clipboard inside the Reading Room. It hangs on the wall next to the desk behind the security door. It can't be changed over the network."

"So how did you end up getting in?" Sean asked. "How did you get an appointment?"

"I didn't," Caesar replied. "I went up to the Reading Room, pretending to be in the wrong place. The clerk let me in, and I started asking a bunch of questions about the inspection certificate on the elevators. She ran off to find the Head Librarian, and I was able to take a picture of the list on the board."

"So you didn't actually go into the Reading Room?" the woman in the front row asked.

"No. I researched the names on the list and called two of them—students at Columbia. I asked them to add the Zodiac materials to their own research during their appointments, threw a little cash at them." Caesar pulled over a desk chair and sat down. "One of them said 'no thanks,' but the other one agreed."

Sean laughed. "You got in without hacking a damn thing."

"Social engineering counts," Caesar replied. "Whatever gets you in the door counts. But we'll need to take that option away for our puzzle hunter. Agent Blue's first objective is to get his hands on that list, call the appointments one by one, and ask if they've been contacted. Scare anyone from helping some random person that comes knocking."

Caesar walked over to the video screens, now displaying a live feed of the library's interior. Tourists had begun to trickle in, roaming around inside the front entrance. "Whoever this guy is, we'll need to think two steps ahead."

> > > > >

Morgan Library - NYC
March 10th, 9:20AM

"In 1924, a great gift was given to the city and people of New York." The tour guide recited her words with a familiar tone, as if she had said them a thousand times before. "The financier J.P. Morgan, Jr. opened his father's entire home, library and study—as well as all items from the vast collections housed within them—to the public. Our journey today will take you into the history of iconic buildings, and J.P. Morgan's important legacy."

Entering Morgan's private study, the tour strolled into a strangely intimate setting. The room featured blood-red walls, a 16th-Century wooden ceiling, and a sitting area in front of an imposing fireplace. Across the room sat Morgan's original desk and a sturdy walk-in safe tunneled into the corner wall. Haylie ran her fingers across the thick steel bars that crisscrossed the back of the safe's door, peeking around the corner and into its belly. The safe no longer held secrets, just books and artifacts now on public display. *Boring.*

The tour guide threw out well-rehearsed facts and figures as she paced a familiar path, strolling backwards with confidence. It was in this room that during the Panic of 1907, Morgan had invited top bankers from around the city into his home, she explained. He told the men that they must find a way to save the U.S. economy that very night, even taking the extra step of locking the exterior doors and hiding the key. The bankers worked into the depth of the night to iron out their differences, emerging the next morning with a plan to save the U.S. financial system.

"Something fun to search for," the tour guide said with a smile, "are the exquisite details of the building. Mr. Morgan was a bit of an astrology buff, and has incorporated many elements of the Zodiac into the architecture." She paused, laughing mischievously. "He is, in fact, responsible for that famous quote: 'Millionaires don't use astrology, but billionaires do.'"

The tour group laughed politely, exchanging smiles and even a smattering of applause. Haylie felt like she was at a tennis match.

I need to check the rest of this place out before the Reading Room opens.

As the group meandered through the study's collection, Haylie tiptoed backwards towards the exit and slipped into the hallway. She snuck down into the Rotunda, making her way past the bright-white marble walls and gold molding. As she approached the huge, framed entrance into the next room—under a stone entryway reading 'Soli Deo

Honor Et Gloria'—Haylie felt the floor transition from cold marble to warm wood. The next moment, she was stepping into J.P. Morgan's private library.

The main library room was something straight out of a fairy tale; the first floor, plus two levels of walkways stacked high above, were filled to the brim with the rich, autumn colors of thousands of leather-bound books. A giant tapestry hung above the fireplace, covering most of the huge rear wall. On the floor, glass cases held ancient treasures of science and art—hand-written letters by J.D. Salinger and Galileo, and original musical scores by composers like Mahler and Ravel.

As she entered the chamber, she was startled by a loud boom to her right. Jumping back and spinning to face the bookshelves, she searched for the source of the noise. *What the hell was that?*

"Excuse me, miss." Haylie heard a familiar voice from over her left shoulder. She turned, knowing that the tour guide was standing right behind her.

"Hi, sorry, I just got a little ahead of the group," Haylie said, feigning a pinch of shyness.

"We're not allowed in here on the first tour of the morning," the tour guide said, nervously checking behind her to keep an eye on the rest of the group. "Security isn't even here yet. You can come back after nine thirty."

Haylie's eyes were drawn up to the elaborate painted ceiling, with too many colors, figures, and scenes to take in with one glance. The guide noticed her attention and cracked a slight grin.

"Come on, we need to get moving," the guide said, herding Haylie out the door with an extended arm.

As the tour continued down into the newer sections of the museum, Haylie quietly peeled off from the group. Taking a few reassuring breaths, she made her way back to the front entrance and headed for the stairs. At the top, she hooked a sharp right, walking towards the clerk's office of the Reading Room.

Time to see if this plan is going to work.

> > > > >

Brux Software HQ - NYC
9:25AM

"Great stuff today, Benjamin," the board member said along with a vigorous handshake. "Really excited about the next eighteen months and the product roadmap direction."

Benjamin enjoyed the moment, flashing a subtle smile. "Thanks, Calvin, we're really happy with our progress."

Another board member angled into the conversation to add his two cents. "Great talk track today. And efficient, as always. When I get five minutes back at the end of a meeting, I think I'll start calling it 'Sterling Time.'"

"Speaking of time," Benjamin said, "Walter and I have to get going. Lots still to do, as you've seen here today."

The brothers said a few loose goodbyes as they walked from the room, joining their pace together in lockstep as they made their way towards the elevator.

"I thought that went well," Benjamin said. "A few unexpected questions about the push to the cloud but other than that, a good meeting."

Walter shook his head as he picked up the pace. "I got a text from my guy at the hotel. Haylie left through the back exit a few minutes ago. She was headed towards the library. This wasn't the plan. She's up to something."

CHAPTER TW3NTY E1GH7

Titanhurst—London
March 10th, 2:32PM

"Appointments in the Reading Room start in just under thirty minutes," Caesar said, watching the live stream of security footage on the screens. "We should expect our guest to attempt access during either the first or the last appointments of the day; those are optimal times for entry— periods where the room might be short-staffed or attendants could be getting a bit lazy with security. Let's keep a wide view for now, test all cameras. I want to make sure we have good coverage across the building."

An engineer from the front row pointed up at a smaller screen in the corner. "Let's put camera sixteen in the big four." One of the four large LCDs flickered over to the view of the second floor landing directly outside of the Reading Room. "Okay, now camera fifteen. Okay, check twenty-two."

Caesar grabbed a fresh cup of coffee as the cameras flipped through different scenes of the museum. He caught a momentary glimpse of a woman heading up the stairs. She had a scarf wrapped around her head and a backpack on her shoulders, but the view quickly switched away.

It's early—she must be one of the desk workers.

"If I had to bet, I'd guess our guy will be here in about thirty minutes for the first appointment. He'll want to get it over with fast," Caesar said, turning to face the team. "It's pretty simple from here. If anyone shows up and asks to see any document related to the Zodiac Club, we'll grab them and call it a day."

> > > > >

Vector's Apartment - London
March 10th, 2:34PM

With a shriek of sirens flying by, Vector pulled the dark curtains from the edge of the window and peeked out. The police van traveled under his window, scooting down Charlotte Road as bicycles and cars curved out of its path. He slid his hands into his pockets, exhaling, feeling his heartbeat slide back down to normal levels.

Not for me. Not today.

A ping rang from across the room as Vector jogged over to his workstation. He looked down at his MacBook plugged into a three-monitor setup tucked neatly into the corner. He checked the notification and nodded to himself; Haylie's drop box hardware was calling out from its new home in the museum's hallway, and had just gained access to the network. The box was sending credentials Vector could use to access the Morgan Library's internal system. It had found the login of a junior admin who had chosen the weak phrase 'lovebooks' as his password.

Vector began running checks of the network and combing lists of file directories and user permissions. He found mostly administrative material; nothing to indicate that the archives' records were accessible from the VPN. He switched over to a browser and entered the HexMark default address to access the surveillance camera's admin panel. The screen lit up with a four-paned view of scenes from different rooms, hallways, and exhibits within the Morgan Library.

Bingo.

Pulling his phone from his pocket, Vector shot a quick text to Haylie.

> > > > >

Morgan Library Reading Room - NYC
9:40AM

As Haylie approached the Reading Room door, she caught a view of herself in the reflection of the glass; she saw an expressionless, stoic girl gazing back at her. Feeling a ping in her pocket, she checked the text and saw Vector's note, knowing that he was now watching her on the hallway camera above her.

She tested a quick, artificial smile, bending her grin into a few different shapes, trying to find the right expression for a desk clerk temp. Stopping at the glass, she saw a man inside, his head buried in the pages of a thick binder. She knocked lightly, barely making a sound.

The man's head rose. He stood from his chair, walking at a brisk pace towards the door while checking his watch. He cracked the door open and spoke through the slot. "I'm very sorry but appointments don't begin for another thirty minutes or so. You're welcome to wait downstairs in the lobby."

"Actually ... yes, I know. I'm not here for an appointment, I'm here to work the Reading Room desk." Haylie pulled out a crumpled piece of notepaper from her pocket and read the name she had scrawled across the center. "Kristen? Yes, Kristen ... called in sick this morning. I'm from the temp agency," Haylie said with a shy tone, and then quickly glanced around the hallway. "Am I ... is this the right place?"

"Of course it is. Come on in." The man pulled the door open and stood to the side to let Haylie pass. "I'm William, I'm new here today too. I was wondering who was going to be sitting across from me."

The smell of old books—hints of vanilla mixed with musty flowers and worn leather—hit Haylie as she glided into the small receiving room, her hands pulling nervously at the straps of her backpack. She saw two workstations positioned on either side of the room, with a path down the middle leading into the Reading Room. The room's corners held stacks of notebooks and multi-colored binders piled in a haphazard yet accessible fashion. She craned her neck subtly for a better view inside the next door as she followed William to one of the desks.

"Thanks. My name's Amber ... I'm with Star Staffing," Haylie said, plopping her backpack down on the desk. "It's nice to meet you."

It had only taken Haylie a few quick Google searches and phone calls last night to locate the name of the woman who was scheduled to be working the desk this morning. Kristen Morris was this month's clerk, a position that was apparently filled over the course of the year by a patchwork of volunteers and temps. As it turned out, Kristen required exactly $1,000 in cash from Haylie's emergency bank account that her parents had set up to be convinced that she didn't need to show up for work today.

"The Head Librarian was just in here, she's running around somewhere," William said with a smile. "I'm sure she'll be back soon."

Haylie slid into the desk's chair, practicing her fake smile.

"I hope so," Haylie said. "I'm really excited to get started."

> > > > >

Titanhurst - London
March 10th, 2:48PM

"Who's this?" Caesar muttered as he looked up to the view of the Reading Room's reception area. The camera clearly showed Agent Blue chatting with someone on the other side of the room: someone new. Caesar thought it might be the woman he had seen earlier, but from the camera's angle, he couldn't tell for sure.

"It must be the woman working the other desk this morning. Masters student or something," Sean said. He turned a few pages of his handwritten notes. "Kristen Morris? I think that's her name."

As the rest of the engineering team, now highly caffeinated and dialed in, began preparing their workstations, Caesar asked for the Alpha view to go up on the screens: feeds from the four cameras showing the main entrance, the second floor landing outside the door, the reception area of the Reading Room, and the main Reading Room camera. He kept his eyes on the woman across from Agent Blue, wringing his hands.

"Let's look alive. Twelve minutes."

> > > > >

West 23rd Street - NYC
March 10th, 9:52AM

"C'mon, c'mon, *c'mon!*" Benjamin shouted as the gridlock of taxis and trucks stood dead still all around them. Their driver's eyes flicked back towards the brothers in the rear-view mirror.

Walter shifted in his seat, craning his neck out the open window. His traffic app flashed red across the screen. "This isn't good—every route is blocked. Construction up at Madison." He turned to Benjamin. "And what the hell are we going to do when we get there?"

"We'll find her. Talk to her. Maybe it's nothing."

"She's up to something," Walter said. "We need to keep a low profile when we get there, we don't want to get recognized. Somebody's going to take a picture and Instagram it. We're taking a big risk."

Benjamin looked over to Walter, a bead of sweat running down the side of his jaw. "You don't think I know that? That was the whole reason for getting Haylie to do this in the first place, but I don't think we have a choice anymore. This was *your* plan. *You* screwed this up."

Walter took his phone from his pocket, scrolling nervously. "Her text from last night, let's check that again. Maybe we just misunderstood–"

Benjamin's hand flew across the back of the car, slapping the phone from Walter's hand. It fell to the floor, skipping end-over-end, finally resting at Walter's feet.

"We understood *just fine*," Benjamin said, tugging at his collar. "She's on to us. She figured it out. And if we don't find her before she finds the next clue, we're *done*."

> > > > >

Morgan Library Reading Room - NYC
March 10th, 9:55AM

Haylie held the five sheets of loose paper in her hands, the title 'READING ROOM DESK ASSIGNMENT PROCEDURES: VERY IMPORTANT' staring her back in the face. Trying with everything she had not to roll her eyes, she searched through the check-in procedures, book-handling tips, and coffee break rules for any login credentials to get her into the system, but there was nothing. Checking around the monitor's frame for Post-It notes with passwords, her focus drifted to William sitting across the room.

He sat at the desk, perched over his half-opened binder with his eyes fixed on the door. It was strange—he didn't have the dull daze of a man fighting his way through what was obviously a boring job. He was staring at the door with purpose. He was looking for something, or someone.

"Who are *you*?" a woman's voice boomed from behind Haylie, causing her to jump in her seat.

Haylie's hands shot forward as she turned, almost knocking the keyboard off her desk. She looked up to see an older woman perched above her, standing in the entrance to the Reading Room.

"I'm so sorry. I didn't mean to startle you; I'm the head librarian— my name's Ms. Lindon. I'm always excited to meet new desk assistants. My goodness, it seems like we get so many in here."

Haylie pushed her glasses up and inspected the woman. She was conservatively dressed in a lumpy forest green sweater complete with librarian's glasses, balancing a towering armful of bins and binders. "No, it's my fault. I should have been paying better attention." Haylie stood and introduced herself with her new fake name.

"Well, wonderful. Don't worry—I'm used to new people in here, we get a lot of that. Let's get you started," Ms. Lindon continued, placing the bins down on the table to shake hands with Haylie. "It's pretty simple, really. We've got the list of guest appointments over there on the wall. Most people that come in here know the rules in advance, so you shouldn't get much trouble from anyone. No cell phones, laptops, pens or pencils—anything that could record or take a picture—is allowed in the Reading Room. Now come with me for a quick minute."

Ms. Lindon led Haylie out of the receiving area and into the main Reading Room. Haylie spun a quick circle to get her bearings. She saw eight tables crafted from elegant, light-colored wood arranged across the room, each featuring two soft-white reading lamps. Surrounding them on all sides were volumes of books—rows and stacks filling the walls— behind locked cabinets, their spines visible through the security glass. Above her, a glass-encased second floor walkway framed the walls of the room from all sides and hung over the tables below. The room was deathly quiet and completely still of any life.

"When you're assisting guests, the volumes are organized based on the Dewey Decimal system, of course. We've mapped out the key locations in the room." Ms. Lindon pointed over to a small, printed map indicating the range of volumes that could be found in each row. "Now, most of the materials are actually located over in the original library, which is much larger. Have you been over there?"

Haylie nodded, recalling the Morgan's private library and its towering walls, the tapestry, and the three tiers of balconies.

"Good. Here's your key. This will give you access to any of the cases, and there's a swipe card attached for the doors." She handed Haylie the set of keys with a pale white card hanging from the ring. "There's a walkway to the top floors of the private library right up these stairs."

Ms. Lindon led Haylie back into the reception area. "You can search anything in the archives on the computer system here at your desk," Ms. Lindon said, "but I've asked William to take lead with assisting guests this morning. It would be great if you can help during the busier times and return the materials once our guests have completed their appointments." She handed Haylie a Post-It note with '25M0RG4N' scrawled across the bottom. "Here's the system password."

Finally. Haylie reached for the paper, showing her best poker face.

"You do...." Ms. Lindon asked with hesitation "You do know how to work a computer, right?"

Haylie shrugged her shoulders. "I'll do my best."

As the librarian trotted back into the main Reading Room, Haylie turned to her workstation. She scanned the main menu, trying with all her might to look like she didn't know what she was doing. She clicked on single buttons loudly and slowly, cursing occasionally at imaginary mistakes. Paging across the menu to the 'Search Archives' function, she typed in 'Zodiac,' executed the search, and read the results.

Her eyes flew from entry to entry:

`-> Libro di Sidrach, 1400`

`-> Cursus liborum philosophie naturals, 1494`

`-> Zodiake of life, 1543`

`-> Mercator map of the starry heavens, 1810`

`-> Treatise on the circular zodiac of Tentyra, Egypt 1824`

There was a sudden knock at the door, causing Haylie to jump in her seat once again. *Good lord, stop doing that.* She turned her head to see a man standing at the glass, clutching a faded blue backpack.

Haylie looked over to William, who just looked back and shrugged. *Don't worry about it, William, I guess I'll get that.* She tilted her monitor back to face the wall and walked over to the door.

"Josh Wood, here for my nine o'clock appointment," the man said as Haylie cracked the door open. He wore jeans, an out-of-style sweater, and an eager expression plastered to his face. "I'm right on time!"

He was, in fact, two minutes early, but Haylie didn't bother to correct him. "Sure, of course. Welcome," Haylie said, not knowing the correct way to greet someone at a billionaire's private museum, if there was a proper way at all. "Come on in."

As he waited for Haylie to open the door, the visitor bobbed up and down on his toes; a teakettle of excitement. He peered past her shoulders and into the waiting main Reading Room with hurried breath.

"You know … these appointments are not easy to get. We've been talking, that is, a group of us that talk all about the Morgan Library on our graduate studies online forum, about a better system that might allow you to get more people—qualified people, of course—in the room on any given day. It's—"

Haylie held up her hand signaling that he should stop talking, enjoying her new sense of power as the guardian to the gate. She was willing to play the part of a helpful clerk, but only up to a point.

As she turned back to face her desk, Haylie's face dropped. She felt her knees lose their hold and struggled to regain her breath. She held out her palm to the wall—it was now the only thing keeping her from falling onto the floor.

Across the room she saw William behind her desk, his eyes firmly locked on her search results. He stood with arms crossed, a crooked smile growing across his face, motionless.

Her pulse raced as she felt the panic crawl up her spine. *How could I have been so stupid?*

"Well, good morning, Josh," William said, his eyes locked on Haylie. "Welcome to the Morgan Library."

CHAPTER TW3NTY N1N3

Titanhurst - London
March 10th, 3:02PM

The engineering pit scurried with activity as the team scrambled to identify the man entering the Reading Room reception area.

"Okay, the guy at the door just said his name. Josh ... Wood," Sean shouted out as he ran a series of searches across various data sources.

"What do we know about him?" Caesar said, rolling over from his workstation.

"Google searches are coming up with a good amount of information. He's a graduate student at Columbia, doing his dissertation on *The Canterbury Tales*. He has a blog about it and everything," an engineer recited from the research summary. "He's single—shocker, there—and Instagram geolocation shows that he was in London a few months ago."

That got Caesar's attention. "Tell me more about why he was here."

"He did a study program at Westminster Abbey, where Chaucer spent a good amount of time back in the day," the engineer reported back. "It seems legit. Not seeing anything else on him that would point to any advanced computer knowledge or programming experience. He hasn't even locked down the privacy settings on social media, so he's not trying to hide anything, or even worse, he doesn't know how to."

"Okay," Caesar said. "He's still a researcher, which could fit the profile of someone trying to solve the Raven puzzle. I want to keep a close eye on him."

Sean laughed. "Everyone coming in the library is going to be a researcher, dude. That's what it's there for."

> > > > >

Morgan Library Reading Room - NYC
March 10th, 10:05AM

Haylie lifted one foot slowly towards the direction of her desk, but William didn't flinch. Checking quickly back at the exit, Haylie knew she wouldn't beat him in a footrace.

Stick with the plan. You're just a temp ... just a temp working the desk.

Haylie reached across William's shoulder and snatched the clipboard from the wall. She ran her finger down the schedule, reading names without giving him as much as a second glance.

"Josh Wood ... here you are." She scribbled her initials next to his name, trying her best to keep her hand from visibly shaking. "Let me walk you through–"

"Good morning," Ms. Lindon interrupted, standing with her arms stretched across both sides of the Reading Room entrance, excited to see her first researcher of the day. "Let's get you started, shall we? William, won't you be a dear and help this gentleman find the materials he's interested in?"

William's face fought a scowl as he looked over to Haylie, then back down to her screen. A rush of relief hit Haylie as she smirked back in his direction. *Yes, William, won't you please help the man?*

"Yes, of course," William said, stone-faced. "Mr. Wood, what are you looking for in the Reading Room this morning?"

"Oh, this is exciting," Josh said. "I'm doing my dissertation on *The Canterbury Tales*, and the original volume here in the Morgan is the last piece of the puzzle I need to fully document a good amount of the artwork. This is a very big day!"

William nodded with more than a hint of apathy. "Okay. Canterbury...." William typed as he spoke, with Josh leaning over the desk to watch his query.

"That's just one 'R' at the end there," Josh said, beaming and gazing into the Reading Room with awe.

"Right, one 'R.' Of course," William repeated back, writing the volume's location down on a slip of paper.

As Josh and William walked into the Reading Room, Ms. Lindon stopped their progress with an arm across the doorway and an audible "Tsk-tsk."

"Don't forget, gentlemen," she said. "No phones, no laptops, no cameras allowed. Please place them in these bins here. I'll lock them up nice and safe and you'll get them back when you exit the room." She gestured over to a small side table, which held two sliding cabinet drawers in its base.

William stared Haylie down as he tossed his phone into the bin with a clunk. She gave him a cheap smile in return. *Don't worry, William— we'll keep them nice and safe.* As the men made their way into the Reading Room, Haylie returned to her assigned desk. Ms. Lindon, speeding past with a fresh stack of folders, exited the room without giving Haylie a second look.

Haylie turned back to her search results, scanning faster now, paging down as her eyes scoured each entry for notes from the Zodiac Club. She scrambled for paper as a series of entries finally appeared:

> **-> Zodiac Club of New York, Meeting Minutes, December 1905**
>
> **-> Zodiac Club of New York, Meeting Notes, June, 1911**
>
> **-> Zodiac Club of New York, Meeting Notes and Menu, December, 1915**

"'Find Brother Libra's last meal,'" Haylie whispered, clicking on the final Zodiac listing. "This must be it." The listing's detail view showed her nothing more than a location number: 1024.544387. She penciled the number onto a scrap of paper, cleared her screen of search results with a few quick clicks, and grabbed her backpack.

Hustling out into the hallway, Haylie kept her head low as she passed under each security camera. She glided down the stairs and sped into the atrium, fighting her way through the initial trickle of visitors beginning to drift past the entrance. Making her way towards the old library, she eyed the uniformed security guards as she passed; each one slowly settling into their spot for the morning.

She reached the far corner of the atrium, pulling at the cold steel handle of the library's door with both hands. It gave way, sweeping open with slow, heavy movement. She sucked in the stale air as she jogged into the Rotunda and finally back into the private library. She walked to one side of the first floor's bookcases, checking the numbers labeling each section.

298.453778

298.453867

Nothing on that side was even close. She searched the opposite wall, kneeling in front of the center bookcase, running her fingers across the numbers.

412.435879

412.437890

She crinkled the paper in her hand, double-checking the number she was looking for. *I need to be in the 1000 section.* She looked up at the two levels of scaffolding hanging around the edge of each wall, holding thousands of volumes of books behind ornate metal gates.

It must be up there.

Faint chatter drifted down the hallway, followed by the distant boom of a door slamming shut. Checking around frantically for any hint of how to access the upper levels, she pushed the panic out of her mind as best she could.

Focus on the problem. Think. Think. Think.

> > > > >

W 30th St and 5th Ave - NYC
March 10th, 10:12AM

Walter stared helplessly out of the back window to see only a solid block of traffic at a standstill; they hadn't moved an inch in the past two minutes. Horns honked, engines idled.

"We need to get moving—why is this taking so damn long?" Benjamin yelled.

"We can still make it," Walter said.

Benjamin unbuckled his seatbelt and got in his brother's face. "You don't get it, Walter. If she finds the next clue and takes off, we're done. *Done*. We need to be there *now*!"

Checking out the window to read the nearest street sign, Walter did some quick math. "We're six blocks away. We can go on foot from here." He opened the door, and both men quickly slid across the leather seats and on to the pavement of West 30th St.

They jogged past a few taxis, making their way onto the crowded sidewalk. Pushing through a sea of shoulders and elbows—past tourists staring up at skyscrapers and young mothers holding their children's hands—Benjamin and Walter Sterling turned towards Madison Avenue.

They began to run.

> > > > >

Morgan Library Reading Room - NYC
March 10th, 10:14AM

William approached the Reading Room table holding an opaque plastic bin firmly in his hands. Placing the container on the table, he cracked the lid open to reveal a thick, leather-bound volume sitting on a bed of soft paper. Josh squealed in delight.

"The original 15th-Century manuscript," Josh beamed, standing from his chair to gain a bird's-eye view. "It's beautiful, it's wonderful."

William rolled his eyes as he reached into the bin.

"Whoa, whoa, whoa! Hold it. Don't move," Ms. Lindon yelled, waving her arms at William. "Gloves. You both need gloves."

William nodded apologetically as she snapped her fingers in his face.

"You need to pay better attention, William," she said, pointing down at the book. "This is important."

A grimace crept across his face as he slid the gloves onto his hands, snugging down one finger at a time.

> > > > >

Morgan Private Library - NYC
March 10th, 10:15AM

Haylie's pulse raced as she searched the library's stacks. There weren't any doors anywhere, just lines and lines of books locked behind a rolling lattice of metal, like a protective beehive keeping the volumes securely in place.

There has to be a door in here somewhere—a way to get upstairs. You're missing something. Think. Pacing back by the library's entrance, she stopped in her tracks.

That noise I heard when I was in here before ... the thud ... what was that?

Haylie remembered the noise sounding like a stack of books hitting a hardwood floor, but she hadn't seen anything out of place in the pristine room. It sounded almost like....

Turning, she backtracked her last few steps, searching the wall and bookshelves for any clues. She followed the polished wood baseboards into the corner where two vertical lines broke the surface of the wood. She knelt down, pressing her hand against one of the edges, and felt a cold rush of air.

No way.

Footsteps and conversation echoed down the hallway as Haylie heard the door to the Rotunda slam again. She stood and pressed her hands onto the bookshelf above the carved edges. She pushed with all her might, digging her heels into the carpet; the wall resisted at first, but finally gave way behind her force.

She tumbled through the hidden doorway and onto the floor of a grimy back room, the bookshelf quickly swinging shut behind her. Dusting herself off, she found herself at the base of a set of worn stairs, leading straight up. She caught her breath and began to climb with soft footsteps.

At the top of the staircase, Haylie found a much-needed map affixed to the wall of the second floor landing. Checking the index, she finally saw the location she had been searching for.

The 1000 range is on the upper deck, back in the Reading Room. The librarian said something about a doorway up here.

She jogged down the hall and used her keycard on the door marked 'READING ROOM, SECOND LEVEL.' As the door snapped open with an electronic pop, Haylie peeked through the crack.

She had made it back to the Reading Room, but now found herself on the landing that hung above the main floor. She was looking down from the narrow walkway that snaked around the edge of each wall and loomed over the tables below. The deck was only about four or five feet wide, anchored with a thin sheet of polished glass resting on a short wall of wood. Down in the center of the room and only about twenty feet away, she could see Josh and William sitting next to each other with their backs to her, inspecting *The Canterbury Tales.*

Ok, you can do this ... you can totally do this. No problemo, right?

Haylie dropped to her knees, dragging herself across the floor and over the threshold, having to release her backpack from the door's edge before making it clear through. She winced as she carefully released the door's weight, easing it closed with a quiet, precise click.

She pressed into the corner where the floor met the wood-paneled wall and crawled, arm over arm, staying low and hopefully hidden from the two men below. Slinking forward for what seemed like an hour, she looked up to realize that she had only made it halfway down the platform. She turned over on her back, looking up at the shelves above to gauge her progress, and saw '750.'

Keep going.

When she reached the shelf labeled '1000,' she stopped and rolled over to sit with her backpack pinned against the wall, staring up at the books and bins towering above her. The framework of elegant metalwork encased a series of thick volumes and white plastic bins.

She dug into her jacket pocket and retrieved the key, arranging it in her hand to fit the lock from her awkward angle. She slowly crept her hand up, scraping the metal cage lightly, tracing across the surface to help the key find its home. The key clicked into place and Haylie whispered a quick "Please" under her breath, turning her wrist clockwise. The bolt moved with it, and Haylie felt the door crack open against her arm.

She rested back against the wall to make way for the swinging cage door, searching the shelves above for her number. She saw the container labeled '1024.544387' eight bins up from the floor. Perched five long feet above her, the bin sat at the top of the stack.

Oh super, it's the top one. Of course it is.

She took a deep breath, slowly reaching up as high as her arm would stretch while staying low and out of sight.

> > > > >

Titanhurst - London
March 10th, 3:18PM

Pouring new coffee into old, Caesar contemplated adding sugar and cream this time, but passed. Stirring his new brackish mix of lukewarm caffeine, he heard a shout from the other side of the room.

"We've got a cage opening on the second level!" shouted an engineer, shifting the video surveillance camera of the Reading Room to the big screen. He stood and pointed to the black and white feed of a single cage door swinging, but without any hint of who or what might be opening it.

Engineers throughout the room shouted and pointed at the screen as they saw a single hand crawl up the wall, slowly snaking its way up towards the top bin.

"Get a message to Blue! Text him, call him, anything! This is happening!" Caesar shouted down to the team. "How did this guy get in?"

> > > > >

As Vector watched the cage slowly crack open, he shook his head in disbelief.

"She did it," he whispered. "Right, time to go dark."

Vector brought up the interface for the Morgan Library security system, quickly sending signals to the eight primary video cameras in and around the Reading Room to perform a full reboot. Each camera's system began the restart process, which would leave every lens dark and blind until completing its full startup sequence.

"You've ninety seconds, Crash," Vector said. "Go get it."

> > > > >

Titanhurst - London
March 10th, 3:19PM

The engineering pit erupted into chaos as the video feeds died out, each flickering to a flat black screen, one by one. The views of the Reading Room displayed only the status indicator 'offline: rebooting.' Caesar jumped down into the center of the pit and faced the team.

"What happened? The other feeds are active; what happened to the primary cameras?" Caesar screamed.

"We're not sure ... they're all restarting," Sean yelled, frantically switching between video feeds. "It'll be a few minutes before we get them back."

"This guy must have hacked into the security system," Caesar said. "Send in the backup agents. I don't know how this guy got in, but he's not getting out."

CHAPTER TH1RTY

Morgan Library - NYC
March 10th, 10:20AM

The Sterling brothers ran at full speed around the wrought-iron fence framing the outside of the Morgan Library, the frantic pounding of their shoes echoing off the sidewalk. Their breath turned to steam as they slowed their pace to a hurried walk in front of the entrance.

With quick swipes of their hands across their foreheads, tucking damp oxford shirts back into place, the brothers tried their best to compose themselves. They approached the front desk, and Walter asked for the Reading Room location with a polite yet forceful smile. The desk clerk pointed a finger across the hall as her face twisted, looking like she was trying to remember where she had seen the two flushed faces staring back at her. The brothers headed to the stairwell without even so much as a "thank you."

Flying up the stairs two at a time, the brothers rushed towards the door at the end of the hallway. Peering through the glass, they saw an empty room with a closed door on the other side. Walter began to knock, hopefully loud enough for someone beyond the receiving area to hear.

"Where is she?" Benjamin said between breaths. "She has to be here."

Benjamin pushed his face up to the glass and knocked, his taps growing to pounding, echoing down the marble hallway.

> > > > >

Morgan Library Reading Room - NYC
March 10th, 10:20AM

William jerked his head up from the musty volume of Chaucer and towards the door leading to the reception area. Over the whispers and periodic high-pitched exclamations of joy that Josh had been making during his research, William could swear he had been hearing something—a buzzing or rattle of some sort—for the past minute or so. But now it was accompanied by a muffled, methodical pounding sound. But he couldn't see anything past the closed door.

Turning back to his guest, William checked his watch. Only twenty-five more minutes with this guy, then the next appointment would walk in. He'd be able to head back to the desk and check on Amber, or whatever her real name was, grab his phone, ping the leadership in London, and figure out his next move.

He shuffled in his chair as Josh continued to flip page after page with delight.

> > > > >

Haylie took a long breath as she stretched her right hand higher and higher, slipping along the cool stainless-steel rail of the security cage. She extended as far as she could, placing the other hand across her mouth to keep any stray noises from making their way out, and finally felt a finger grasp onto the bottom edge of bin '1024.544387.' She exhaled and rose slowly, sliding her left hand up to meet the other side, feeling the slick plastic across her finger tips.

With two fingers from each hand now clutching both sides of the plastic container, she slowly slid the bin back in her direction along its rails. Inching the container and whatever rested inside its belly towards freedom, Haylie turned her head to catch a quick glance at the tables below. She got a clear view of the two men, sitting with their backs to her, heads down and not suspecting a thing. She nodded to herself.

You're actually going to pull this off.

As she twisted back to the cage, Haylie felt her foot slip across a bare patch on the deck's worn carpet. She fell backwards, fighting to regain her balance, as her grip on the bin went loose. The container suddenly gave way, sliding free from its home and flying into nothing as Haylie's fingers extended helplessly in the air.

With her feet twisted, Haylie hit the deck, cursing under her breath. As she landed, a sharp bolt of pain greeted her elbow. The bin continued its path through the air. Haylie could only watch, performing a quick, makeshift prayer for some sort of miracle.

The plastic container spun like a Frisbee, rocketing directly into the second floor's glass wall. It bounced back and fell at her feet as an ear-splitting shatter filled the air, the sound of an entire wall of glass exploding. The shards rained down into the Reading Room below, smashed into a million pieces.

Goddamnit.

The tranquility of the Reading Room was suddenly filled with a wave of mayhem as the room was showered with a tidal wave of glass, covering the floor and tables with daggers, slivers and dust. Josh went into a hunched position, startled, his hands over his ears and his head bowed.

Haylie grabbed the bin and looked over the wall of the second floor deck, feeling her expression drop as she watched William rise. Josh turned to check the damage, hovering over his beloved book, protecting it from certain doom.

"Is that … is that Amber?" she could hear Josh stutter.

William turned, shaking the glass from his head and peeling the gloves off his fingers. His eyes connected with Haylie's as he sprinted towards the stairs.

Haylie rose to her knees. Her heart pounded as she brushed the shards from the top of the bin. She yanked at the lid, flinging it down the walkway and looked inside. She found a single piece of parchment, decorated with intricate Zodiac symbols and calligraphy centered in the middle of the page. With no time to inspect it further, she quickly rolled the document, feeling the soft crunch of the delicate paper, and took off towards the door leading back to the old library. Skidding to a stop, she yanked at the door's handle. It resisted with a thud. *Locked.* She reached down to her pocket, scrambling, searching.

The cardkey. I forgot the damn cardkey.

Hearing William's footsteps racing up the stairwell, she bolted back to the opened rack, its door still swinging loosely at the hinge, and found the card dangling from the lock. Giving the key ring a quick pull, the metal slid free from the lock and into her hand. She sprinted at full speed back to the exit.

Slapping the card key across the faceplate, the door clicked open with a buzz. She slid into the passageway, fighting for breath, still clutching the parchment. She peered through the thick glass window, hoping he hadn't seen her go through.

A thump shook the door as William appeared in the window, only a few, short inches away. He paused to catch his breath, staring through the glass with rage filling his eyes. He reached down to fumble for his keycard, checking pocket after pocket.

Haylie didn't wait around for him to find it.

> > > > >

Titanhurst - London
March 10th, 3:21PM

The camera feeds of the Reading Room all sparked back to life within ten seconds of each other. Caesar saw Agent Blue running into a door on the second level, broken glass in every direction, a wide open cage with a missing box, and Josh Wood standing in the middle of the atrium, his head in his hands, clutching his precious book.

"Our suspect is on the run!" Caesar shouted. "Get our agents in there—*now*. And switch to camera fourteen, check the Reading Room reception area."

The screen flickered and showed a view of the two reception desks, both empty, with no one in sight. No one, that is, other than the two men banging on the outside of the doors.

"Wait a minute," Caesar asked. "Who are those guys?"

> > > > >

Morgan Library - NYC
March 10th, 10:21AM

Haylie raced down the narrow hallway, bumping off of stacked cardboard boxes and dented filing cabinets, and carved a quick right turn towards the staircase. She could hear footsteps echoing down the hall behind her, catching up fast. She tucked the parchment into the inside pocket of her jacket and sped up her pace.

She flew down the stairs, knees bobbing up and down like pistons as her lungs burned, both hands gripping her backpack straps to keep her balance. Through the darkness, she could barely make out the faint outline of a door at the base of the stairs. She paced her steps a bit to catch her breath, hit the landing, and pushed at the wall with all her might.

Crashing out onto the floor of the old Morgan Library, she found herself in the middle of a stunned tour group—half staring at her with concern, the other half looking through the newly-discovered secret passageway in the bookshelf. She straightened her glasses, pushing a smile onto her face past her exhaustion.

"You guys have to go up there. It's unbelievable," Haylie said between breaths, pacing backwards towards the Rotunda. "It's the coolest thing in the whole museum. Secret stuff!"

She waded into the crowd as the visitors herded into the narrow doorway, inspecting the edges of the bookshelf, marveling at the spectacle. By the time William had hit the wall of tourists, Haylie was nowhere to be found.

A grin crept across her face as she paced towards the exit. The adrenaline pulsed through her veins as she pushed forward, ready for whatever came next.

She knew she was supposed to feel afraid, but she didn't.

She felt powerful.

She felt indestructible.

She felt *alive*.

> > > > >

Titanhurst - London
March 10th, 3:27PM

"Ok, people. Where are we? Someone give me a status," Caesar said with a hint of despair, eyes closed, rubbing the bridge of his nose.

"We're scanning the crowds but we haven't found him yet," Sean replied. "Next we'll talk to this Josh Wood guy and figure out if he was involved. I'm pretty sure even *he* doesn't have any idea what just happened."

Pointing up to the screens, Caesar aimed his finger at the freeze-framed shot of the two men at the door of the Reading Room. "And what about them?"

"We have them in custody. Our backup agents came in dressed as NYPD," Sean replied. "They asked for their lawyer, which is just adorable. We're going to find out what they know."

"Bring them to London," Caesar said, pacing the room. "I'll need to let Martin know we didn't get our guy. Let's find out what Agent Blue knows. He better be able to help us piece this together."

Caesar looked down to his laptop, watching the river of tourists wander the museum hallways, all without a clue of what had just happened upstairs. As he checked scene after scene, he stopped in his tracks, focusing and clicking to take the view of Camera twenty-two to full-screen.

He saw a black and white scene of a woman gliding into the lobby and towards the exit. He leaned in for a closer look as she turned, only for a second, to look directly into the camera lens. Without even thinking, he hit a keystroke to grab a screenshot.

It can't be.

Caesar opened the image file and zoomed in. He jumped back, gripping the desk behind him to stay upright, as reality hit him like a sucker punch.

CHAPTER TH1RTY ON3

"Business or pleasure?" the passenger next to Haylie said with a nervous chuckle. He had angled himself towards her on their shared armrest to make conversation easier, but Haylie had already turned towards her window to discourage any attempts at small talk.

The cabin lights flickered off in a slow cascade of clicks, leaving only a pale blue tone across the ceiling. Haylie removed her glasses and rubbed her eyes, realizing she had been absorbed in her laptop for the past few hours as the plane cruised high and steady, pushing across the Atlantic Ocean.

"Have you spent a lot of time in London?" the neighboring passenger said, trying again.

"Sure," Haylie lied, grabbing for her earphones and slipping them in. "Who hasn't?" She shoved the final earpiece in, signaling the end of the conversation. *Why can't some people just shut the hell up?* She closed her eyes as her mind flashed back to scenes from the day, jumping in and out, replaying the ebb and flow of the last few hours. The memories blinked and cut out of order, racing forwards and backwards.

After exiting the Morgan Library and brushing the glass dust from her hair, Haylie had made her way northwest—three blocks up and one block over—to the New York Central Library. A nice, crowded public place with free Wi-Fi, the perfect temporary home to regroup and figure out her next step.

The main room of the Central Library held a football-field sized cathedral of a study area, with rows and rows of tables filling the floor and elaborate murals painted across the ceiling. Just entering the room had calmed her heart's pace and for the first time in a few days, she felt tiny and at peace.

She had found an empty seat and carefully retrieved the paper from her pocket, slowly unrolling the stiff parchment. It was an old Zodiac meeting dinner menu, listing a five-course meal complete with wine pairings and coffee. Rack of lamb. Boeuf Bourguignon. *No vegan options back then, I guess.* But as she scanned the paper, nothing had seemed out of the ordinary. That quickly changed when she flipped the menu over.

On the back, she found a square of machine-printed text, glued to the back of the parchment.

> **You've worked hard to get here.**
> **So let's just get to it, shall we?**
> **Head to the National Gallery.**
> **Figures set in stone.**
> **Find our father, our leader, our Principia.**
> **Más sabe el diablo por viejo que por diablo.**

She had done a few quick searches on the National Gallery, and had found plenty of results to work with. Poised at the top of Trafalgar Square in London, the museum housed a huge collection of priceless artwork from Van Gogh, Michelangelo, Monet; the list went on and on.

Haylie focused on the term "Principia," finding a collection of possible hits. There was the book *Philosophiæ Naturalis Principia Mathematica*, written by Isaac Newton, which she had bookmarked as she kept looking.

"Principia" was the Roman word for the center of a fort. *Could the National Gallery be the place where these guys hold their meetings?*

But Haylie had stopped in her tracks when she saw the next listing: a book titled *Principia Mathematica* by Bertrand Russell and Alfred North Whitehead. Over the years, Haylie had seen a series of threads on hacker message boards featuring homages to Bertrand Russell. Many hackers referred to him as "The Godfather," claiming Russell had laid the groundwork for modern computer science and artificial intelligence.

This has to be it.

As Haylie pored over Russell's background, she found plenty of material about his mathematical achievements. But what had pushed her over the edge were the series of articles about Russell's work after World War 2, detailing how he had become an outspoken supporter of a more centralized world government. One quote had stood out in particular:

> **Unification under a single government is probably necessary unless we are to acquiesce in either a return to barbarism or the extinction of the human race.**

With that, and with Walter's credit card that she had copied down earlier—just in case—Haylie had booked a ticket on the next flight to London.

She did a subtle check of the man to her left, who had now thankfully given up on Haylie and moved on to another passenger across the aisle. As the night flew by, Haylie stared out her window, welcoming the calm at thirty-five thousand feet.

She thought about Caesar, hoping for the love of God she would find him somewhere in London. He'd be fine; she just knew it. Somehow, somewhere, he was safe, and she was going to track him down. For once, *she* was going to help *him*, and not the other way around.

As sleep began to creep in, she remembered one last piece of the clue she had yet to figure out. She opened a browser window and typed the final line from the menu—'Más sabe el diablo por viejo que por diablo'—and selected the translate option from the search results. The literal translation came up with missing words, but additional search results identified the saying as an old Mexican proverb.

> **The devil knows more because he is old than because he is the devil.**

Haylie stared into the screen as the words pushed back at her, flying along with her quietly through the night.

> > > > >

Titanhurst - London
March 11th, 2:05AM

Fumbling with the remote, Martin cursed under his breath as he pressed the SELECT INPUT button again and again. The delayed response on the monitor—a two or three second lag each time—was almost as infuriating as how hard it was in the modern age to get a simple video call working properly. It had been six minutes and counting since trying to open a channel to Agent Blue in New York with no luck.

Selecting 'HDMI-3' from the input menu finally did the trick. After an awkward volley of "Can you hear me?" back-and-forths, Martin completely lost his patience.

"Stop," Martin said, sternly. "Agent Blue, talk."

"Yes. Of course, sir," Blue said. His eyes met the camera as he straightened his jacket. "The target worked her way around my visibility and into the old library. It was my understanding that the Reading Room was the only–"

"And the men we found at the doors? The Sterling brothers?"

Agent Blue looked down to the floor. "I never saw them, never met them. They arrived after I entered the Reading Room. I was focused on the woman at the desk."

"You knew she was a potential threat and you let her get in," Martin barked, leaning in to the camera. "And worse, you let her escape. Isn't that right?"

Agent Blue paused and composed himself before answering back to Martin. "We have video of her," he stammered, making his case. "We know where she's headed and what she looks like."

Martin pounded the keyboard with a solid fist and the video feed went dead. He began to pace the length of the room, interlacing his fingers behind the back of his neck, thinking.

His phone pinged with a message from Crowne.

Need status. Now.
Give me some good news, Martin.

Martin weighed his options, searching for his next step.

Worry grew to panic.

> > > > >

Titanhurst - London
March 11th, 6:29AM

As the morning sun poured in through windows, the team huddled around the coffee station for some much-needed caffeine. Caesar ran his hands through his hair, ratcheting his neck back and forth to shake off the few hours of sleep he had managed to scavenge. He stared at his laptop, zooming in with a few taps of the keyboard and studying the pixelated image on his screen.

Damn, she's good. I expected her to crack the code I sent, but not this fast—

"Caesar, what's up," said a voice from behind him. Caesar quickly minimized the image. He toggled over to the feeds from the Morgan Library, now showing police and security guards holding court in every available camera view. He turned to find Sean holding an extra cup of coffee extended his way.

"I'm due out on a flight later this morning," Caesar said, taking the coffee with a nod. "But I'm still trying to get my head around what went down yesterday. It's bugging me."

"Don't worry about it," Sean said. "We got those two guys at the door; they should be able to tell us something. The reports from Agent Blue are starting to trickle in. Sounds like it was a young woman that grabbed the document? Can't be anyone we had on our radar."

"Let me ask you something," Caesar said, lowering his voice. "Do you guys do operations like yesterday's all the time? Is that normal stuff around here?"

"It's a mix of different projects but that's what makes it interesting." Sean cocked his head slightly, with a glint of mischief in his eye. "Hey ... do you want to see something cool?"

Caesar, excited at the thought of thinking about anything but the Morgan for a few minutes, nodded back. Sean pulled his laptop from under his arm, laying it down on the table and cracking it open. He turned the screen in Caesar's direction, showing a document that held a photo of a man in his fifties, a line drawing of property lines, and a report titled 'Case 545: Harold Bussinger, Pri2, Status: CLOSED.'

"What's this?"

"This is Harold Bussinger," Sean said. "He's a dentist in Sydney, Nebraska. Not much there, really. Just a farming community and some small businesses in the downtown area. Anyway, he was targeted by a group of hackers a few weeks ago."

"A dentist?" Caesar asked. "What the hell are you talking about?"

"It's a project I've been working on; I finally wrapped it up a few weeks ago. A group of Ukrainian hackers have been targeting dentists and doctors in a series of small communities. The hackers take their computer systems hostage; their medical records, payment systems, vital equipment, scheduling systems."

"Hackers are targeting doctors?" Caesar asked. "What do they do once they have access?"

"Nothing. They hold it for ransom," Sean said. "Five-hundred dollars a piece. Small change for me and you, but not for someone trying to run a business in a small town. With payment, the doctors get a guarantee that they'll never be hacked again. For everyone that has paid, the hackers have kept their word to stay away."

"That's crazy. How many have paid?" Caesar asked.

"A lot. What else can they do? Doctors don't know anything about network security. They know so little that they are a bit embarrassed when this stuff happens, won't go public with it. The only people they tell are the other docs in their towns."

Caesar connected the dots in his head. "That's why they target multiple doctors in the same area. If the hackers keep their promise to stay away after being paid, the first wave of targets will advise the others to pay them and just get on with their lives."

"Exactly. Smart plan, but not smart enough. I tracked down the hacker cell where the attacks are coming from and took out their machines. And then I had their apartment buildings surrounded by local police. They're all done," Sean said, smiling and obviously proud of his work. "And that's a good thing."

With a look around the room, Caesar noted all the different projects live on each screen. He could make out maps of buildings, live feeds of ocean freighters, employment rate projections. He pointed to Sean's screen. "This … this is what you're doing here? I thought you were working on bigger stuff."

"This is a test case. Once The Project begins, we pretty much get to do whatever we want. I want to make people's lives better once the lights come back on, you know? I've got about thirty more projects lined up, each one better than this. Before The Project was formed, we couldn't touch groups like this. Wiretapping laws, privacy concerns, risk of pissing off a diplomat from whatever country," Sean said. "But once we're rolling, those restrictions will be history."

"That can be dangerous," Caesar said.

"In the wrong hands, sure," Sean replied. "But we're the good guys. People always paint a picture of big brother turning into an evil regime— abuse of power and hidden agendas—but that's not what we're doing here. In my last gig, I worked eighty hours a week trying to figure out how to get more people to click on ad banners, and now I get to change the world for the better. For real."

Caesar watched the room, not believing what he was hearing. *This is a chance to actually make a difference.*

"The people in this room, they're building the tech that's going to run the planet for the next few decades," Sean continued. "We get to hit the reboot button on the whole damn thing. Just think how great this world would be if the people with power were actually … good? If their agenda was just to make the whole thing better? People like *us*?"

As Sean turned to fist-bump a passing engineer, Caesar exhaled, his eyes blinking rapidly as he processed his options. Suddenly, everything clicked. He knew what he had to do.

"People like us," Caesar replied.

Feeling heat on his heels, Caesar turned to catch the sunlight stretching through the window and across the floor, lightly dusting his feet. The room buzzed around him as he paused and nodded his head.

"Tell me everything there is to know about The Project," Caesar said, his eyes back on the control room's monitors. "I'm in."

"You're just in time," Sean said with a smile. "Tonight is the night we flip the switch. Get ready to have some fun."

CHAPTER THIRTY TWO

Covent Garden - London
March 11th, 10:04AM

For the last three blocks, Haylie had been trying to figure out if she was lost.

She paused, nestling against the door of a corner shop. She toggled back to the Google Maps app on her phone and spun in a semicircle to follow its compass. *I think I'm headed in the right direction.* She worked her way back into the flow of foot traffic on St. Martin's Lane and pushed north into the crowds, her jet lag weighing on her steps like a sandbag tied to each foot.

The streets of London were laid out in a crisscross web of curving roads that seemed to only find the next intersection by blind luck. The arteries twisted through the city, sharp lefts and rights around ancient landmarks long disappeared. As Haylie tried to stay on track, she longed for the logical right angles of Austin. She traversed a five-way intersection, dodging a stew of taxis, bicycles and pedestrians, all politely nudging for right-of-way.

The city was foreign to Haylie, but she began to see patterns as she took in more information on each block. She could pick out the finance men easily; they wore gray suits, alternating white and blue shirts on every other chest. The older men still wore ties, but the younger ones left their collars loose. Black taxis on every corner. Dark colors on everyone: indigo jeans, short black topcoats with collars up, gray scarves. Crisp shirts and shined shoes. It was the only place Haylie had ever been where the men dressed better than the women.

Motorcycles and mopeds whipped past her as she cut through passing clouds of cigarette smoke that hung in the air. As she trekked up the sidewalk, languages from every corner of the globe drifted with the crowds. A French couple, arguing about God knows what. Chinese tourists, headed south with maps clutched in their hands.

Haylie squinted past the crowd to see St. Martin's Lane coming to a Y-intersection. *I must be getting close.* After a few more blocks, Haylie came across the dark facade of a corner coffee shop and stopped in front of the light wooden benches laid out under its windows.

Haylie walked in and ordered an Americano. Her nerves were on high alert for this morning's meeting, and the butterflies bounced off her guts as the barista sprayed and grinded out his remaining orders.

It'll be fine ... just be yourself.

She grabbed her drink and followed signs reading 'MORE SEATING DOWNSTAIRS,' pacing slowly down the steps and into the depths of the basement.

The underground seating area contained a network of tables with only a few patrons littered here and there. Almost everyone sat in pairs, chatting over closed laptops. But one man sat alone, far in the corner, staring Haylie directly in the eyes.

She carefully made her way towards his table, holding the coffee mug and saucer in both hands as she felt them begin to tremble. She studied the man on approach; he was dressed much nicer than she had anticipated—khaki pants, a tucked white oxford shirt, matching belt and expensive, shined shoes. His thick, sandy hair waved back, framing a slightly devilish smile.

No way. Vector is ... kind of cute?

He stood with a graceful swoop, grinning and gesturing to the chair across the table. They kept eye contact as she sat down, resting her coffee on the table to steady its shake. He tilted down his computer screen and they sat in silence for a few beats.

"Hi, Crash. It's nice to finally meet you ... in person," Vector whispered. "I feel like we have a lot to talk about."

"Yes, same here," Haylie said, pulling her hair back behind her ear. "And thanks for your help in New York."

"That was a close one," Vector said. "I'm pretty sure we just got lucky there. A few more seconds and ... well, you know."

Haylie checked each corner of the room. "Is this a place you come to a lot? Is it safe here?"

"The last time I was here was a few months back, and really just that once," Vector said. "But it should be safe for us to talk."

Smart—don't meet other hackers in places you go every day.

"I'd love to catch up at some point just to talk about ... everything," Haylie stammered, "but right now, I'd like to hear what you've found out about Raven—anything that can help me find my brother."

Vector looked up and snapped his head a bit, appearing to flip his brain over into work mode. "Right, yes, of course." He cracked his laptop back open. "I was able to locate the engineer I worked with on that Raven puzzle with a few years back. I pinged her and she—she calls herself Margo for projects she takes on—was able to tell me some very interesting tidbits."

"What kind of ... tidbits?"

"Right. Well, Margo said she was contacted by the same person that posted the Raven job for a follow-up job. It was consulting work for a think tank out of Italy. They do studies around population analysis, that sort of thing. But she quit the project about six months back after a few strange requests freaked her out."

"Like what?"

"They asked her to build out a model of global population growth," Vector said. "Basically, given a set of conditions—economic factors, disease, wars in certain regions—what different countries and territories would look like year over year. She built the model to forecast two hundred years into the future, based on conditions that might exist at that time."

"Okay, so what's weird about that?" Haylie asked. "Think tanks do stuff like that all the time, right?"

"The strange thing wasn't that they wanted a model, it was something else. It was the actual scenario they were trying to predict. Once she heard the details, she got spooked. She bailed." Vector hushed his voice back to a whisper. "They wanted her to model what would happen if the world lost all power and connectivity for six months."

Haylie, her coffee cup at her lips, paused. "The entire globe losing power?"

"Yes, everyone. And the 'for exactly six months' part, that's what freaked her out. She knew they weren't asking her to model some sort of random natural disaster; it was much more specific than that."

"So you said that this model went for hundreds of years? What year did they want to flip the switch?"

"I asked the same question. These models that data scientists build, they are very precise. So when there's an event they want to forecast, they don't just ask for a year. They plug in a date and time, down to the second. They asked her to model what would happen if the power went out on March eleventh of this year, at midnight."

Haylie heart raced. "That's tonight." She gazed down at the table and tried her best to find her composure. "So what if she's wrong? All we know is there's a group down in Italy doing doomsday projections ... that doesn't mean anything, right?"

Vector shook his head. "So that's the other thing—the guy asking for this model was pushing her timetable, needed it for a big meeting that started a few days ago. I did some checking and it turns out he was headed to Bilderberg."

The wheels spun in Haylie's mind for a minute. The word sounded familiar, but wasn't registering. She shrugged her shoulders back.

"Bilderberg is a meeting, a big meeting," Vector said. "The kind you wouldn't actually believe exists if it wasn't real, you know? It happens every year ... top secret stuff. The world's most powerful people. Even the list of attendees is kept under guard. This year it happened right here in England, just a few days ago."

"So you think this Bilderberg group ... they're the ones behind Raven?" Haylie said, leaning across the table. "You think they have Caesar?"

"What I think is that Caesar solved the Raven puzzle, and that he ended up finding a hell of a lot more than he thought he would. I think these guys are recruiting hackers to help them turn off the power to the rest of the world. All while millions of people die. No power, no anything for six months. You remember Iceland last week? Even the power going out in one country for a few hours caused a few hundred deaths."

Haylie's eyes grew wide as she hushed her voice. "Oh my God. *Iceland.* The power, the Internet routers, the phone networks were all taken out. That was a test. These guys were testing their code."

Her anger ratcheted up as she thought back to each Raven step. Cecil Rhodes—so certain that his money could bring the elite to Britain, and that he could reshape the world to a place of his design. The Bohemian Grove—all standing together in a tight circle, cloaked in secrecy, repeating the same words and chanting in unison. She pictured J.P. Morgan sitting comfortably at the Zodiac dinner table, laughing with the chosen few and chewing on a thick cigar, while butlers and maids rushed to bring fresh rounds of drinks.

Her eyes narrowed as she tried to imagine Caesar, wherever he was: in a room, or a cell, or a dark basement. Just waiting for his captors to throw him a piece of bread or slide him a cup of water, out of the goodness of their hearts. Being strong-armed. Being forced to make an unthinkable choice.

Everything makes sense now.

Raven wasn't created by outsiders trying to warn people about these men in power; it was created by the Bilderberg Group to *celebrate* these men. It was there to prepare hackers as they solved the puzzle. They were grooming Haylie, and people like her, to join a group so drunk with power they believed that they could rule the world. That they *deserved* to sit in that place. Raven was about a power that the world had never seen before.

Vector's face grew heavy. "This isn't about solving puzzles anymore, Haylie. This isn't even about finding your brother; this is bigger than all that. We can't let them get away with this."

"*We?*" Haylie said.

Vector smiled. "You're damn right."

> > > > >

Titanhurst - London
March 11th, 10:41AM

Walter Sterling walked a straight line, exactly as he had been instructed. The guard with a pistol stuck into Walter's lower back hovered directly behind, muttering directions as they moved through the depths of the mansion.

Through a whirlwind of activity over the past twenty minutes—transfers between guards, handoffs from room to room, in and out of elevators—Walter was having a difficult time figuring out how long he had been on the move. Sneaking a quick check to his wrist, he saw only empty flesh and quickly remembered that the guards had confiscated his phone, wallet, and watch hours earlier.

"We stop here," the guard said, nudging the barrel of the pistol into Walter's flesh to make his point clear.

"Sounds good," Walter replied, mimicking the man's accent back to him. "We stop here."

The guard cracked the door to Walter's left and let it swing open. Inside the office, Walter saw his brother huddled on a plush leather couch at the middle of the room. Walter stumbled towards him, seeing no one else in the room.

"You wait here. He come soon," the guard said, closing the door behind him.

The brothers took a quick inventory of each other without exchanging as much as a word. Getting his bearings, Walter's eyes fell on the impressive desk at the head of the room. He took one step in its direction when suddenly a voice boomed from behind him.

"Gentlemen. Let's talk about why you are here."

The brothers turned to face the voice and immediately recognized the man standing before. Prime Minister John Crowne looked both brothers up and down as a hidden door, flush to the wooden paneling of the wall, closed behind him. The PM sat down in the chair next to the couch, hinting with an extended palm that the brothers should sit as well.

"You were at the Morgan Library. At the door of the Reading Room, banging on the glass," Crowne said, slowly. "Tell me why."

Exchanging glances, the brothers both froze, each expecting the other to take lead. Benjamin sat up, drawing the lapels of his jacket in together, and spoke. "We have spent the past few months trying to locate you and your team, Mr. Prime Minister. We're interested in the value we can add to The Project."

Squinting with a hint of disdain, Crowne tried his best to keep his composure. "The Project. Which project? I'm sure I don't know what you're talking about."

Walter smiled and leaned in closer to Crowne. "I understand … *we* understand … how crucial secrecy is for a plan like this to succeed. That's why we haven't told anyone about you or your plans. *No one.* We're just interested in joining the effort. In helping."

"My plans?" Crowne asked. "I'm curious, who told you about these so-called plans, and what did they tell you?"

"Back in New York, at the Soho House," Benjamin said. "In one of the private rooms on the third floor. We were entertaining some guests but they had to run to the airport unexpectedly. We ended up meeting a Swedish prince, Prince Gudmund, who had a bit too much vodka to drink. He told us that he had been part of the operation, *your* operation, but had since been relieved of his duties."

"Gudmund is an idiot," Crowne said. "You shouldn't believe anything he tells you, drunk or sober."

Chuckling, Benjamin agreed. "That much we figured out on our own, but the details he shared were too rich to be made up out of thin air, and we decided to look into it further. We petitioned the committee at the Bohemian Grove with no luck. We sent Caesar Black to solve the Raven puzzle and lead us to you, but we believe he broke off on his own and made his way to the inner circle before we could catch up to him."

"And so now you've sent this girl?" Crowne asked.

"We made the decision to try it again with a new hacker," Walter said, jumping in to the conversation. "But she somehow discovered the truth after the Grove."

Crowne stood and walked over to the desk, eying the box. He flicked his fingers across the desktop, filling the office with the slight rhythmic tapping of nails on polished wood. "And this *value* you speak of. What is it that you can provide?"

"We are connectors and we have great resources," Benjamin replied. "We were born on the inside circle; we know how things *should* work. We know the pain of catering to the masses, watering down ideas to fit the lowest common denominator."

Shaking his head, Crowne didn't bother to turn to face the brothers. "I have all this already. We are a small and powerful team. There's a point with a group where adding another person, or two in this case, makes that group weaker instead of stronger," he said, placing both hands on the desk as he leaned over, staring back towards them. "You provide no value for me."

"The girl," Walter said. "In the short term, we can deliver the girl."

"The girl, it seems, is headed this way anyway," Crowne said. "I should have her in custody, just like you two, later today. Just in time."

"I ... we ... don't think so. She's too smart. She's not just an everyday puzzle hunter," Benjamin said. "And we think she knows about The Project."

Crowne's eyebrows raised as he cocked his head to the side. He walked back over to the couches and stood over the brothers. "Benjamin—you're Benjamin, right?—as it turns out, I'm not worried about some girl with a laptop."

"You should be," Benjamin said.

"Why is that?"

"Your people designed the Raven puzzle to find hackers, but now she's using it to find you."

Crowne flashed a smile. He sat back down in the chair, pausing for a few moments while staring down the brothers. Walter gulped loudly, waiting for Crown to say something. Finally, he spoke.

"So how is it that you, the newest members of the next world order, intend to help me find this girl?" Crowne said.

Walter exhaled, relieved. "That's simple. We'll start by having a chat with her brother."

CHAPTER THIRTY THREE

Timberyard Coffee House - London
March 11th, 11:13AM

The midday crowd had filtered out of the coffee shop's basement, trudging loudly up the wooden steps as they went, leaving Haylie and Vector to themselves. Haylie slid over to Vector's side of the table; twin laptops now edged side-to-side, screens pointed safely at the corner behind them. Their eyes flicked across each other's screens, checking the results of the tandem research from their past few minutes of work.

"We could always just go to the press," Vector said. "I know a few people over on that side. If we had some hard evidence, they'd run a story like this for sure."

"We don't have time," Haylie said. "Even if they believed us—which is a big 'if'—by the time they went live with the story it would be too late."

Vector thought it over and agreed. "You're right. Our best bet to find these guys is still Raven. Luckily, the National Gallery is just a quick walk from here. We're only a few minutes from Trafalgar Square."

Haylie tabbed over to her Google Map, showing a seven-minute walk straight down St. Martin's Lane and directly to the museum's entrance. "Is there a back way in? Something that's not as obvious? They're going to have people at the main entrance for sure."

"That's the problem," Vector replied, "there's only the one way. The Portico entrance that leads into the Central Hall."

"And we don't even know what we're trying to find yet," Haylie added, checking her search results. "There's a portrait of Russell in the

231

National Portrait Gallery, but that's a separate museum. It's not where the clue tells us to go, and the two museums don't even seem to be connected."

"The clue mentions something 'set in stone.' That doesn't sound like a painting to me. It has to be a sculpture, something physical," Vector said. "But who knows, maybe when you get in there, everything will make sense."

"Or...." Sitting back into her chair, Haylie looked over to Vector with a spark in her eye.

"What is it?" Vector asked.

"Here's the thing," Haylie said. "Thanks to the whole scene at the Morgan Library, these guys probably have photos of my face from the security feeds. We have to assume that there are going to be guards, agents, whatever all over this museum waiting for me to show up."

"But they won't be looking for *me*," Vector said with an annoyed glare.

"You're our best chance here."

As the concept soaked in, Vector shook his head in disbelief. "You want me to walk into a trap? Surrounded by guards that are watching me like a hawk? You're out of your mind."

"You need to decide what you're doing here," Haylie said, jabbing a finger in Vector's face. "You said it yourself: this is bigger than Caesar now. This is about a group of people that are trying to take control of the world. Do you want to help me stop them? Because if you don't, I don't need you around."

Vector thought for a moment, leaning over his laptop.

"So what are you thinking? How is this going to work?" he said.

"Don't worry," Haylie said. "I've got it all figured out."

He listened closely as Haylie walked through the plan. Shutting his computer, he stood from the table. "Wait here, I'll be back in half an hour. I've got something that can help."

> > > > >

A few minutes later, as Haylie treaded down the stairs with a fresh coffee cradled in her hands, her pocket buzzed. *That was quick, Vector.* She increased her pace to reach the table, setting down her cup and saucer before grabbing for her phone.

As she read the incoming message, she gasped.

CAESAR:> Are you there, Haylie?

Oh my god. Oh my god.

Sinking into her chair, she grasped her phone with two hands and typed back a message.

CRASH:> Yes, it's me. Where are you? Are you ok?

She gently placed her phone on the table, watching the glow of the screen for a response, anything, as she wiped tears from both eyes. *Please tell me you're all right. Please tell me something that makes this whole thing make sense.* Her phone vibrated across the table as Haylie snatched it up, bringing the screen close to her face.

CAESAR:> I'm ok. I know what you're doing. I know that you're trying to solve Raven to find me. I want you to stop.

Haylie's face scrunched into a question mark as she breathed an audible "What?" from her lips. She focused back on the screen.

If they are holding him against his will, they could be telling him what to say. Be careful.

CRASH:> I'll stop once I see you. Once I know you're safe.

The room filled with the pounding bass of two loud sets of footsteps on the stairs above her head. Haylie clutched the phone to her body and turned her back to the wall. She watched and waited as the steps grew louder, approaching the basement. As two young girls walked around the corner, giggling and whispering, Haylie felt another buzz from the phone against her chest. She checked the message.

CAESAR:> We should meet. Right now. I know you're in London, I'm here too. These guys I met after solving Raven, they are pretty great. They want to meet you. Where are you now?

Heart racing, Haylie clutched the phone with both hands and typed furiously with her thumbs. *He can't mean any of this ... none of this makes any sense.*

CRASH:> I know what they are trying to do. We can stop them.

Rubbing her eyes, Haylie reached for her coffee and took a long sip. She tried to calm herself, breathing in deep as the cup shook in her hands. She stared into the screen, waiting. A new message indicator lit up, and she scrambled to expand the message, bringing up the full text.

CAESAR:> It's not like that. It's more like a startup over here - hard to explain. They are working on some big things. You have to see it for yourself. It's not what you think.

Haylie scowled at the response. *A startup? Are you kidding me?* She typed a quick response and then tossed the phone down on the wooden table. It slid across the tabletop, spinning like a hockey puck, until it crashed into the wall.

On the screen, her final message was still highlighted:

CRASH:> I'm going to find you. And I'm going to get you out of there.

> > > > >

Titanhurst - London
March 11th, 12:03PM

Huddled at a table in a windowless room, deep in the bowels of the mansion, Caesar placed the phone down with a click. He closed his eyes and whispered a few words to himself. A voice from behind him broke the silence.

"That wasn't the script we had agreed on," Martin said.

"I didn't expect her to push back," Caesar said. "I had to improvise."

Martin picked up the phone, scrolling the conversation line by line, inspecting each word. "Tell me, did you mean what you said? About what we are doing here?"

Caesar looked up at Martin with a solemn face. "Of course I did. I meant every word of it."

Smiling, Martin sat down next to Caesar. "Don't worry, my friend. You did the right thing. We just want to bring her in to talk. She can help us, just like you are helping us, but we need to be able to talk to her. With all the upcoming events, she'll be safer in here, wouldn't you agree?"

Caesar nodded, saying nothing.

"I want to do something for you, Caesar," Martin continued. "I want you to meet our leader. He's very excited to meet you, that's for sure."

"I'd like that."

"There will be a few things that happen in the next few hours that may confuse you. I need you to know that no matter how things might appear in the short term, it's all for the greater good of The Project," Martin said. "We're running out of time. We're going to have to—how do you say it in Texas?—*up the ante.*"

CHAPTER TH1RTY FOUR

The National Gallery - London
March 11th, 3:52PM

The boats rolled dangerously to their starboard sides as they cut deep wakes in the sea; their sails plump and full of wind, pulling them towards the foam-tipped waves. The frantic sailors littered across both decks hung on for dear life with a front-row view of the black water awaiting them below. Storm clouds moved in above, dark and full of life, sending the two vessels on an unavoidable collision course.

A few minutes earlier, Vector had stopped to take a seat on the corner of a leather viewing bench, trying to blend in with the crowd of tourists all around him. But this painting, tucked in the corner behind a small chain fence, had pulled him in.

He stood, gave the painting one last look, and shuffled to the next gallery. Patting the side of his jacket, Vector checked to make sure the device in his interior pocket wasn't making too obvious of a bulge on his side. It was roughly the size of a brick, and felt about that heavy crammed in his pocket.

The small box in his possession was a hobby project he had finished last year, one he had found crammed in the corner of his apartment's hallway closet following a brief, frantic search. After Haylie had shared the plan back in the coffee shop, Vector was excited at the thought of finally having an excuse to use it.

It was a cell tower spoofing device called an IMSI catcher—otherwise known as a "stingray"—that allowed a hacker to connect to mobile phones in the immediate area. Once he flipped the power on, all devices in the museum would start connecting to his stingray instead of their regular cell tower, and he could access all data going to and from every phone within its range. That is, if the bloody thing actually worked. He had never used it beyond it's initial tests. It was something he had really just wanted to build, not use.

"You see anything yet?" Haylie's voice almost blew out his eardrum, causing Vector to flinch violently in the middle of the gallery. He retrieved his phone and edged down the volume to his Bluetooth earpiece by a few clicks.

"Nothing that we care about," he whispered back.

"Ok, well, you know … go find it," Haylie said into her headset. "And remember to blend in."

Vector shook his head, whispering "Cheers, I'll get right on that," under his breath.

He searched through rooms and alcoves adorned with paintings, sculptures, and other artifacts. He saw scenes of angels reaching down from the heavens to rain salvation upon the poor souls below, a painting of a man crawling on his knees to see the baby Jesus, and landscape scenes with smudges of burnt oranges and browns across the hillsides.

But nothing about Bertrand Russell, anywhere.

The hallways brought back memories of school field trips from Vector's youth. His class would return every few years to see the newest exhibit or explore a new wing. He remembered how each visit had grown more familiar, a few paintings had been changed out here and there, but the place stayed mostly the same. He remembered the lunches his mom would pack, eating apples in the cool sunlight, sitting on the stairs in the Square with his classmates all around.

"Give me a status," Haylie crackled over the channel. "Anything new?"

Pacing back towards the Central Hall, Vector shook his head in response. Realizing that wasn't very helpful, he whispered, "Nothing yet."

"Ok. Maybe try another wing?" Haylie said. "I'm going to run some tests on the stingray while you're looking."

Vector made his way back into the Portico entrance, searching for a map or signage, any guidance that might help him. "All the stuff I've seen has been too old for what we want. If there's a Bertrand Russell sculpture in here, it's going to look really out of place. I still think the clue is talking about the Portrait Gallery; this can't be right."

"No, all the clues up to this point have been dead on," Haylie replied. "It's got to be somewhere around you, you're just looking in the wrong place."

"Just make sure you're ready when I give you the word," he said. Vector could hear typing and frustrated sighs on the other side of the line. "What's going on over there?"

"Something's wrong, dude. Your Python script is throwing an import error. It says 'no module named config,'" Haylie said.

"That's impossible. I tested that code an hour ago. It works fine, try it again."

There were a few seconds of silence on the other end. "It really doesn't. It's your code. I'm going to have to rewrite this unless you can show me how it's running on your machine."

"Well, I'm kind of busy right now, could you just see if you can fix it?" Vector whispered, checking the corners of the room.

A few tourists formed silhouettes near the sunlit front doors. He raised a hand to shield his eyes from the glare, scanning the rest of the room. He stopped dead in his tracks when he spotted two figures down at the base of the stairs. Turning away, Vector bent his head down towards his chest.

"I'm seeing two men in the Portico. They don't seem like tourists. They are staring at me right now," he said.

"Like, *right* now?" Haylie asked. "Keep your head low and get out of there. Move to another area."

Vector began pacing towards the set of large, wooden double doors leading to the west wing of the museum. Keeping his head down, with his eyes focused on the mosaics decorating the floor, he moved across the gallery, breathing in and out, trying to blend in with the crowd. Each mosaic showed a scene, framed with lines of text: 'REST AND BE THANKFUL,' 'OPEN MIND,' 'LEISURE.'

He paced the floor, walking slowly. *You're just another tourist, just act normal and get to another room.* Suddenly, as a new image came into view under his feet, he stopped in his tracks. His felt his pulse race.

"We've got a problem," Vector breathed. He closed his eyes for a moment and made a silent wish, hoping that the two agents hadn't noticed him yet.

The mosaic at his feet stretched five feet across and outlined a caricature, in muted colored tiles, of a white-haired man. It looked exactly like the Wikipedia photo of Bertrand Russell, one Vector had studied earlier that afternoon. It showed Russell with an outstretched hand, peeling a mask off the eyes of a nude woman next to a set of scales; the classic image of Truth. A block of blood-red text, printed in a yellow ring around the circular scene, labeled the piece with its title, 'LUCIDITY.'

"What's up?" Haylie shouted over the radio. "Where are you?"

"I think I'm standing on it," Vector whispered back, trying to move his mouth as little as possible as he spoke. "Bertrand Russell is in a mosaic right here in the middle of the Portico."

Sweat began to form on the back of his neck as he felt the stare of the two agents behind him. He shuffled his feet, trying his best to seem uninterested about the patterns on the floor.

"Okay," Haylie said. "I'm trying to fix this code; I added a few things. But I'm still getting the import error."

"That seems like a pretty easy thing to fix."

"Wait a minute," Haylie stopped, typing away at the keyboard. "Are you using Python 2.7?"

"No," Vector said under his breath. "I upgraded to 3.0."

"When did you do that?" Haylie shouted back. "How have we not talked about that … that's kind of a big deal. You know that most of the big applications don't even support–"

"Can we please talk about this later?" Vector whispered, heart pounding. "I need to get moving, like, now."

"Okay, hold on. Let me update my version," she said, groaning. "This is going to screw up so many other things on my machine. Hold on."

Vector slowly retraced his steps back to the other side of the Portico. He caught a view of the two agents. They were on the move, beginning to make their way up the stairs, one on each side. *Damn.*

As Vector caught his breath, the double doors at the top of the landing swung open with a loud thump and a gaggle of Japanese tourists pushed their way out into the hall, filling the top landing. Seeing his opportunity, Vector made his way into the middle of the group and out the other side.

The agents reached the outer edge of the Japanese mob, and began to push their way in.

"Now would be a great time," he said, ducking behind a man with a map extended out with both hands. "Let's do this."

"Got it," Haylie said. "Incoming."

The Portico suddenly echoed with a collection of notification alerts. A screaming chorus of buzzes, chimes, bells, and ring tones sounded off and sent the crowd into a full-on panic. A woman at the center of the crowd shrieked, pushing the bodies all around her, screaming "Terrorists! It must be terrorists!"

A wave of fear spread across the crowd, with a steady row of bodies now flowing down the stairs and towards the exit. The two agents were shoved back down the stairs as more cries and screams echoed off the chamber's stone walls.

Vector dodged his way past the parade of fleeing tourists and sprinted across the landing, taking out his phone and snapping a few photos of the mosaic before disappearing back into the crowd.

"Did you get it?" Haylie shouted over the mic.

"I hope so," he replied over a collection of hurried breaths. "I'm getting out of here."

"Just go with the flow of the crowd; get out the front exit."

"I'm ... almost there," Vector said between pushes and shoves. "I'll make my way around a bit before heading over, lose anyone that might be tailing me."

Vector flew through the exit and into the crisp spring air, weaving into the crowds, past the fountain at the center of the square and into the gray ether of London.

CHAPTER TH1RTY FIVE

The Trafalgar Hotel - London
March 11th, 4:27PM

Throwing off flecks of water with a shake of his head, Vector entered the hotel room. Haylie stuck her head out into the hotel hallway to check for anyone else lingering about, but sank back in after seeing that everything was clear. Vector peeled his jacket off, tossing it onto the hook on the wall.

"You weren't followed?" Haylie asked.

"Nah," Vector replied. "I spent some time doing circles in the area around a few buildings and side streets, just in case. I think the two blokes in there were too busy trying to figure out what just happened to even notice me leaving."

Closing the door, Haylie hurried back to the desk where her laptop sat idling, the screen glowing with the colors of no less than five stacked application windows. She slid into the chair, rubbing her eyes, trying to remember where she had left off.

"It was a good plan," Vector said, peeling the curtain back to sneak a view of the shiny, rain-soaked street below. "The stingray and group text … I never would have thought of that."

"That's not the half of it. It wasn't just any regular text message that I sent," she said. "I added some Machina code to make things interesting."

Vector turned back from the window, his eyes wide. "You did *what*?"

Haylie had expected a cold response from Vector on Machina, which is why she hadn't brought it up earlier. She knew from years of back-and-forth with him that Vector tended to err on the more conservative side of hacking. The Machina exploit, in particular, was a lighting rod for attention in the hacking community. It was a bug in a popular mobile OS, granting free access to roughly nine hundred and fifty million phones around the globe if used in the right way.

"Where did you get the code from?" Vector asked.

"It's everywhere, Einstein. Things are easy to find if you know where to look."

"I can't believe you did that." Vector paced the room, nervously looking back at Haylie and down to her screen. "This is serious stuff."

"It's not that bad, chicken," Haylie said. "And now we can get full access to unpatched devices that were in the museum. I'm getting hundreds of results here. It might be the break we need to find these guys."

"You're going to get us thrown in jail; you know that, right?" Vector said, placing his hands on his head. "We're already in a load of trouble here. Bloody hell, this just digs the hole deeper."

"What do you think is happening here?" Haylie shot back. "If these guys succeed, everything's going to change. And it's not going to change *someday*, it's going to change tonight. *Tonight*. All this stuff we do." She pointed down to her computer and the other equipment now littering the hotel room. "It's all going to be completely worthless. And these people, the same powerful people that have always just done whatever they want, they'll have to answer to no one but themselves. The rest of us will be left out in the cold, begging them for our electricity back, which is exactly what they want."

Haylie scrolled the list of numbers, metadata, and messages from the stingray's log, eyes flying left and right as she searched for the line of text she had marked a few minutes earlier. She double-clicked on a listing, bringing up a detailed data dump from one of the devices that had been catalogued.

"Here," she said, jabbing a finger at the screen, "Check out this text message. It was sent right after you bolted out the door."

243

```
xx6789:> no sign of the girl. some
strange activity with phones in the
museum, we're keeping an eye for
anything else out of the ordinary
```

Vector mouthed an inaudible sound and then stood back up, smiling. "You just rooted one of the agent's phones?"

"I sure did," Haylie said. "I've got all the device information here. But check this out, it gets better." Scrolling down a few more lines, she selected a response to the same number.

```
xx8890:> understood. remain sharp. find
her, she'll be there.
```

"So what?" Vector said. "It's just a message back to the agent."

"I'm not interested in the message, I'm interested in the device information," she said. "This text is from their boss, and the response was caught by our stingray. We now have data from that phone as well."

"What about the photos of the mosaic I sent? Did you find anything?"

Haylie switched windows. "One of the tiles—over here, a black tile from the blindfold in the mosaic—there's a tiny little QR code. It must have been glued on there. You can see it better when I zoom." She hit a few COMMAND-+ keystrokes to resize the image. "This is the best angle out of the five you sent. I should be able to read the code from here." She brought up her QR code scanning app and snapped a picture of the screen.

Copying the URL over to her browser, she hit RETURN and waited for the page to load. The window flashed with a burst of white and loaded a black background with white shell text. The text read:

loading console...

"What is it?" Vector said, hovering over Haylie's shoulder.

"It's an interactive shell."

A cursor appeared. It blinked on and off like a traffic signal, waiting for input. *What does it want me to do?* She typed a quick "?" and hit RETURN. The console simply started a new line, the cursor continuing to blink, but nothing else.

"Check the page source," Vector said. "Maybe there's a clue in the HTML."

"Wait, look at this," Haylie stopped, pointing back to the screen as text began scrolling inside the shell. The output was being displayed one, two characters at a time in fits and starts. *This isn't a Raven clue. Someone is typing on the other end.*

> **ADMIN:>** Hello, Crash. It's good to
> finally meet you.

Haylie and Vector exchanged confused stares. Haylie rubbed her hands together to loosen her joints and rested her fingers on the slick, black keys.

> **GUEST:>** Who is this?

The two sat, waiting for a response.

> **ADMIN:>** My name is Martin - I'm a friend
> of Caesar's.

Anger clouded over Haylie's face as her rage became focused on a man, a name. *Martin. You're going to have a bad day today, Martin.* She took a deep breath and typed back.

> **GUEST:>** Tell me where I can find him and
> I won't tell anyone your plan. I just
> want him back.

"Get your phone out," Haylie yelled over to Vector. "Try to figure out who owns this URL. Maybe they got sloppy." Vector nodded and began typing at his phone with frantic thumbs.

> **ADMIN:>** It's a shame I had to shut down
> the rest of the Raven puzzle. You've
> been getting too close, I'm sure you
> understand. But the last puzzle—I just
> wish you could have seen it.

"Can they trace this back to us? Are you masking your IP?" Vector asked.

"I'm on the hotel's Wi-Fi but routing through the Tor network," Haylie responded. "They won't be able to figure out where we are."

> **ADMIN:>** I'd love to meet up, but maybe I
> should come to you? It's going to be

difficult for you out in public right
now.

Haylie glanced over to Vector, checking on his progress. He held up the results of the network lookup and shook his head, signaling no luck. She re-read his message, not understanding what Martin was trying to get at.

GUEST:> What are you talking about?

The console stayed static for a few seconds, only showing the blinking white cursor. Haylie drummed her fingers on the cheap wood desktop, waiting for the next message.

ADMIN:> Oh, poor thing. You haven't heard the news. Turn on your television.

Sitting back in her chair, Haylie looked over at Vector, who was already scrambling to find the remote. He pointed it at the screen and scrolled, finally finding a news channel, Haylie stared into the screen for a few moments, not believing what she saw.

> **"Scotland Yard, in connection with the FBI and Interpol, announced they have positively identified the hacker who is responsible for the catastrophic attack on Iceland just a few days ago, which left dozens dead. Her name is Haylie Black, a seventeen-year-old student from Texas, who also goes by the hacker name 'Crash.'**

> **She is now being connected to a number of exploits in the United States, including the Super Bowl power outage and gaining access to the head of the CIA's personal email.**

> **The joint task force has confirmed that she was seen in London as recently as yesterday. They are asking all residents to report any sightings, and to consider her armed and dangerous."**

Next to the anchorwoman was a large, pixelated picture. It was Haylie's own face, looking straight back into her eyes.

She crouched over in her chair, her head in her hands. *This can't be happening. This just can't....* Feeling Vector's hand on her shoulder, she sat up and feigned composure. She stared down at the screen and saw one last message.

> **ADMIN:>** Haylie, we're going to do such wonderful things together. You'll see. We'll have a man waiting on the third bench from the entrance to Paddington Station. We haven't much time. Chop chop.

As she reached up to type a response, the console went black.

CHAPTER THIRTY SIX

The Trafalgar Hotel - London
March 11th, 4:46PM

Rain pounded against the window as the two sat in silence. Vector had muted the TV, leaving only a silent slideshow of images: rotating pictures of Haylie, Iceland, and police officers at podiums. Bright blue banners scrolled across the bottom of the screen reading:

NOTORIOUS HACKER IDENTIFIED AND CONFIRMED IN LONDON.

Vector looked over to Haylie as she sat motionless, collapsed on the desk in a heap. He reached out to touch her shoulder. As soon as he made contact, her hand snapped around her body, swatting his arm like a nagging fly.

"Get away from me," she muttered.

"We can still fix this," Vector said, pulling his hand back. "We'll just meet them at the train station tonight. They'll cancel the alert; everything will be fine. You'll see."

"You don't know that," she said. "And even if it worked, they'll still force me to help them. I can't … you know that."

Thinking back to the events of the day, and considering the little time they had remaining, Vector shook his head. "I don't see that you have a choice."

Haylie stared back at Vector with daggers in her eyes. "I *always* have a choice."

Vector moved to the window, pulling back the curtain. He could make out the smudged white and red lights splashing along on the street below. He heard Haylie's voice, rising slowly, from behind him.

"You ... you helped them," Haylie said. "You helped them design Raven. You took their money."

"I didn't know!" he shot back. "How could I have any idea what they were doing? It was a job just like any job."

"No!" she yelled. "You should know better than that. You helped build this; you helped them get Caesar. And now they've got my face everywhere. All I ever wanted was to be left alone. I just want to be left alone."

"You're talking nonsense. You need to eat."

"Shut up," Haylie stood and slammed her laptop shut. "Don't talk to me like everyone else does, like I'm just some girl you get to boss around. I'm not just smarter than you, I'm *better* than you. Live with that."

Vector reached out with an extended hand—why, he wasn't quite sure—as Haylie threw her computer into her bag. Two seconds later, the door slammed shut behind her.

> > > > >

She'd felt alone her whole life, but the weight had never pushed down on her like tonight. Haylie paced down the crowded streets, just trying to get away from everything she knew. Hurried commuters brushed past her on both sides, surrounding her with a chorus of languages she couldn't understand. The passing grays and blacks of faceless trench coats swam by her on all sides, covered with beads of water dancing on dark shoulders.

Haylie had traced a figure-eight through the streets of London over the past half hour, blending into the thick flow of locals, and fighting the confused stops and starts of tourists covered in cheap plastic ponchos.

She kept her eyes on the soaked sidewalks below her, her hood tightly draped over her wet, knotted hair.

Passing umbrellas dripped cold water down as she twisted down the street, squinting to shield her eyes from the downpour as the rain flew in the sides of her glasses. She paused on a rounded street corner, feeling bump after bump of the passersby grazing against each shoulder. She checked up and all around to find her bearings, but had no idea where she was.

I just wanted to stay out of the spotlight ... I just wanted to help Caesar. But now we're both in this.

This is all my fault.

She looked up to see a CCTV camera hanging from the wall, pointed straight down at her. Snapping her head back down to her feet, she pulled the hood of her rain jacket farther down her face and moved on; heading somewhere and nowhere at the same time.

Pulling out her phone, she clicked the top button to power the device down, shoving it back deep into her pocket. *They're everywhere. They'll track me. They'll find me.* She looked around the street corner, searching for signs or landmarks. She coughed out a pathetic chuckle, spitting water from her lips as she exhaled; realizing that she didn't even know where she was trying to go.

Twisting around the iron poles at the sidewalk's edge, Haylie trudged down King Street and past a muted rainbow of storefronts. She slunk under purple then blue then white then red awnings and around construction pillars; the rain came and went with each makeshift roof. The puddles underneath her feet grew dark as the slosh of passing taxis on wet cobblestones filled her ears with a constant tide of white noise.

Turning onto a walkway with a sign reading 'COVENT GARDEN,' Haylie crouched, resisting the urge to plop down on the wet brick and just let the rain pour over her, wash away everything. Up ahead, she saw a large structure supported with four thick pillars. She slowly slunk under the shelter, falling into a sitting position between two pools of water on either side of an old doorway.

The rain fell steady as red and black umbrellas bobbed across the courtyard, floating into the darkness. She watched the traces of raindrops—smeared and pooling on her glasses—but couldn't muster the fight to wipe them clear.

> > > > >

Titanhurst - London
March 11th, 5:27PM

"Ok, let's run the system check one more time," Caesar said. "But make sure to keep all safeties on. We can't have any actual outbound network traffic until midnight."

Caesar looked down to his team of engineers from the top of the Control Room's pit. He had never worked with a group like this, and he guessed that no one ever had before. It was like sitting at the controls of the Space Shuttle, being handed the keys, and asking himself "Where should we go today?" It was a glorious feeling.

"All right," Sean said, reading a few pages of scripts. "You guys all know the drill. We start with Africa. Then shut down grids across the Pacific Rim. Move to South America, then North America. Finish up with Russia and Middle East, and finally to our own beloved European systems."

"I've got some updated numbers on timetable and cadence," a team member said as she pointed over to a whiteboard. "I've adjusted scripts four and seven to account for the regional bugs we found with the last test."

"And this progression," Caesar asked, "it matches our distributed server setup? We want to make sure we're not killing our own machines."

"Correct," Sean replied. "The pattern works. The only scripts being executed from London are for the final European shutdown." He looked back up to the whiteboard to double check the order. "By the time that anyone can tell this traffic is coming from us, they'll be dealing with local power outages."

"Caesar ... a moment?"

The room fell silent, turning towards the new voice coming from the back of the room. Caesar spun on his heels to see John Crowne standing by the door, observing the exercise with an air of pride.

"Sure, of course," Caesar said. "Sean, can you take the helm for a minute?"

Caesar jogged to the back of the room, taking a position next to Crowne and finding himself mimicking his stance; facing the pit, arms crossed, leaning back. The two men shook hands.

"It's impressive, isn't it?" Crowne beamed. "This team."

"I have to admit, it really is. The stuff we're building here, the impact we're going to have, I've never even dreamed–"

"Well, yes, the technology is top tier," Crowne interrupted. "But the teamwork ... I mean, just watch them. It takes other groups years to reach this type of flow."

Turning back towards the pit, Caesar watched the team members completing their tasks; code streaming in white text across black backgrounds, people handing off tasks and transferring data to each other. All like one continuous, well-oiled machine.

"They are working together," Crowne said. "No waste. No infighting. No salary demands, no scramble to impress their boss for their next quarterly review." Crowne took a step forward and faced Caesar. "This will be the way of the new world. Everyone working together for a better future."

"Sure, with the right goals," Caesar said. "This team has gelled, but a lot of that is thanks to the meaning behind the work. If you give people the right target to aim for, they will do amazing things."

"Leadership is about making things that are unimportant *seem* important," Crowne said. "We can't expect the entire world to function at the highest levels, or assume they'll be motivated by accomplishment. The ugly truth is that much of the world will continue to act like simple animals, and to a degree, will need to be treated as such."

Caesar snapped his head back towards Crowne. *Did he just say 'animals?'* He took a moment and tried to piece together some kind of response to the statement. "Did you just–"

"Tell me something. What do you think of Martin?" Crowne asked, cutting Caesar off.

Caesar chose his words carefully. "Well, he seems competent, precise; he's a great planner."

Shaking his head, Crowne exhaled with a sigh. "Honestly, Caesar, I think he's a buffoon. A man that wants only status and recognition. He's a liability."

Caesar looked back with surprise. "I thought you two were joined at the hip?"

"No, Caesar. I was actually hoping you might serve that role; you're obviously smart, but more importantly people follow you. This team would run off the side of the cliff if you told them to, no questions asked. You don't care about status; you care about results. That's what I need."

"What's going to happen to Martin?" Caesar asked.

"Stop worrying about Martin; he's a lap dog. He doesn't matter," Crowne said, extending his hand to Caesar. "He's made one mistake too many, don't you think? Martin is the past, let's focus on the future. You and I. Tell me Caesar … from up here, do you see what I see? Do you see the possibilities? The things we will do?"

Caesar's gaze traced back into the pit as the team continued to buzz with efficiency, a glowing map of the world hanging above them. Caesar extended his hand out to Crowne.

"Yes, sir," Caesar said. "I see what you see."

CHAPTER TH1RTY SE7EN

Covent Garden - London
March 11th, 9:21PM

Haylie watched the passing crowds with dull eyes. She blended into the world around her, mixing with the good and bad and all that came with it. For the past few hours, she had let it all soak in: she couldn't go to the police, and she couldn't beat Raven. It was less than three hours until the world went to hell, and she was all out of options. She was spent.

I give up.

The steady hiss of falling rain was suddenly cut by a sharp wail of sirens. Three police motorcycles splashed down the cobblestones with blue and red lights flashing, sending bystanders in their path scurrying. Haylie's head rose as the police formed a semicircle around her position, blocking each of her exit points. She stood and slowly raised her hands halfway up to her waist.

This is the end; they found me. She didn't know if she was headed to jail or to a locked room somewhere at the Bilderberg Group's headquarters, but it didn't matter any more.

Don't worry. I'm not going to run.

A fourth motorcycle pulled between the center two pillars, this one looked more like an old-style Harley-Davidson. The rider stepped off the cycle, walking slowly towards Haylie across the courtyard. As he pulled off his helmet and walked into the light, Haylie saw a familiar face.

"Vector?" she whispered.

> > > > >

Titanhurst - London
March 11th, 9:25PM

The knock was quickly followed by a slow turn of the brass doorknob. The Sterling brothers marched into the Prime Minister's office in single file, with Martin following just a few steps behind.

"Gentlemen," Crowne's voice boomed with enthusiasm, "good to see you again. Has Martin been getting you up to speed?"

"Absolutely," Benjamin replied, "but there's so much to learn about all aspects of The Project ... it's a bit like drinking from a fire hose. Your team seems ready; it's exciting, really, when you think about how tonight will change history."

"Truly impressive," Walter added. "A plan of this size and scope, but limited to so few people at the helm. I'm amazed that you–" He paused, checking to see if his statement had been taken as an insult. "That anyone, really, could think so big."

Crowne smiled. "Well, I can't take all the credit. The Bilderberg Group is filled with the right people—not only to make The Project a success, but more importantly, to serve as leaders when we recolonize in six months."

"Just let us know how we can help," Benjamin said.

"Yes, excellent," Crowne said. "I have something for you. As you know, time is of the essence. With power out shortly, all public-facing vital systems and transportation hubs will be down for quite some time. We're mobilizing our leadership to be embedded in key areas before that happens, just in case. I need you both to head to Rio."

Walter was the first to speak. "What's in Rio?"

"I've never had full confidence in our man that's currently placed down there, so he'll be reporting to you two now," Crowne said. "I'd like you to oversee South America for the next few years."

"South … America?" Benjamin said. "The whole thing?"

"Of course," Crowne said. "I mean, someone has to."

"But, Mr. Prime Minister," Walter responded, "we've never—we don't even speak Spanish."

With a brief flash of concern, Crowne paused. "People will speak whatever language we *tell* them to speak when the lights come back on. They'll line up in the streets to speak English when the time comes." He cocked his head to the side, thinking. "Is this a problem for you, gentlemen?"

The brothers stumbled over each other to respond. "No, sir," said Benjamin, the first to get words out of his mouth. "We're your men."

With a smile only a politician could get away with, Crowne slapped Benjamin on the shoulder, laughing heartily. "You lot are a crack up. We're going to have fun working together. Martin, please take these gentlemen to the airport and brief them on the way. Boys, The Project will be underway by the time you land, but our private airport will still retain full capabilities. We'll talk again soon."

"Martin," Crowne said. "A word on your way out?"

Each taking a turn to shake Crowne's hand, the brothers shuffled out of the room, still not sure what had hit them. Crowne motioned to the door as Martin walked over to shut it quietly.

"Drive them to Location Bravo. A team will be waiting," Crowne said, straightening his shirt's sleeves, and buttoning his jacket. "It was wonderful of them to point us to Crash—it really was. But I believe the brothers have added all the value we're going to get out of them. Wouldn't you agree?"

Martin leaned in close to Crowne's ear. "Absolutely, sir," he whispered.

"Try not to screw this one up, Martin," Crowne said. "Try very hard."

> > > > >

Covent Garden - London
March 11th, 9:32PM

Steam rose from Haylie's cup of coffee as the heat from the cheap Styrofoam warmed her chilled hands. She sat huddled on the back stoop of the police van, the Day-Glo orange and red stripes of the rear doors reflecting fire into the gray puddles below. As she went to take a sip, she was quickly reminded of her zip-tied wrists, fastened tight with white plastic and perfectly matching the bands on her ankles.

Vector stood twenty feet in front of her, whispering in hushed tones to a plainclothes officer and pointing over in her direction every now and then. Haylie caught them sneaking glances of her between exchanges, their bowed heads occasionally nodding in unison.

He was an informant all along, working for the police. Of course he was.

The heavy rain had pulled back to a fine mist; the headlights illuminating flecks of water into clouds of swirling movement like a school of fish, darting back and forth from any sign of danger, pushing away with each gust of wind whipping into the courtyard.

They'll never believe me—they'll think I'm making up the whole thing about Raven and the lights going out. They won't believe me until it's too late.

A second officer was called over to the huddle with Vector. After a discreet chat with the commanding officer, he turned, walking towards Haylie. The officer reached to his belt, slipping a stainless steel multi-tool out of its casing, and flipped it open with a flash of metal. He slowly clipped the zip-ties free from Haylie's wrists and feet without a word.

"What's happening?" Haylie asked as she squinted through the mist, fighting to see past the spotlights. "Are you guys taking me in or not?"

Vector approached, finding a seat next to her on the vehicle's rear deck. "You were never going in, Haylie. I asked them to restrain you so you wouldn't run; I didn't want you to freak out."

"So you're working with them, is that it?" Haylie asked, no longer holding back her anger. "You've been a mole this whole time we've been friends? I never should have trusted you."

"No, idiot," Vector replied. "I mean, yes, I've worked with them on occasion, but not usually like this. I've fed them some information, got in to systems they needed to crack—but that's it. I've never reported any hackers to them and I've certainly never told them anything *you've* done. Not that it matters anymore." He checked for any officers nearby before continuing, lowering his voice. "I do projects for them. Special stuff. Off-the-books stuff. If they need information about somebody, sometimes I can help."

"Any chance they don't know who I am?" Haylie asked, her eyes growing with hope. Whispering, she leaned in, "You know, that phone stuff we pulled off at the National Gallery is a *felony* back in the States."

"Yes, I'm well aware of that," Vector said. "And of course they know who you are. Everyone in the civilized world now knows who Crash is, now that your face is on every telly across the globe. And I had to give them some details about Raven; I needed them to take this seriously."

"So you outed me?" Haylie said, her head hung low.

"What—have you lost your mind?" Vector shot back. "Have you been listening? I outed *me*. And now that they know that I hang out with the likes of you, I'm pretty sure my police support services will no longer be required."

Haylie scoffed, pulling her hair back behind her head. "So I'm headed to jail?"

"No, listen," Vector said. "I explained what's going on, asked them to help us out. I think they believe me, but they are obviously suspicious. They need more proof about The Project. That's all they are interested in."

Haylie managed a muted smile as she tugged the police-issued blanket across her shoulders. She placed the coffee down on the wet cobblestone below her feet and leaned onto her elbows, thinking.

"You know, a lot of people would say 'thank you' at this point," Vector said, fishing for a response.

"Sorry, I'm…." Haylie stammered as she sat back up straight. "I'm not very good at this."

Flashing a grin, Vector reached his arm around Haylie's shoulders to try for a hug. She flinched back away from him, shooting him a look of death. He quickly jerked his arm back, his hands extended. "Right, not ready for hugs yet. Got it."

"We've got some time left," Haylie said. "Let's think about what we have. We know they want me at Paddington Station in about thirty minutes."

"We don't want to walk into a trap, but we don't have anything else to go on," Vector said, "They've shut down the Raven clues. We've no other leads. And what are we going to do when we find them?"

Haylie stood and began to pace, back and forth, as she thought. *If I can get into their headquarters, I'll be able to find all the evidence I need. I just need to find a way to keep them from putting a bullet in my head when they see me.*

Vector looked down to his phone's screen. "Google says it should take us fifteen minutes to get to Paddington," he said. "If that helps."

Her eyes focused on the glowing screen, shining light on the fine mist of raindrops falling down onto the glass. A smile worked its way across her lips.

"We have the device information for one of their phones," she said, walking back towards Vector. "From the stingray hack, remember? I need you to grab your laptop."

"Why?"

"Because I'm tired of this. We're going to track them down. We're going to find them, and I'm going to get Caesar out of there." Haylie craned her neck around the side of the police van. "I need to talk to whoever's in charge around here."

CHAPTER TH1RTY E1G4T

Covent Garden - London
March 11th, 9:48PM

"Ok, we've got it," the Inspector said after playing back the video on his phone. The rain-soaked splotches scattered across his topcoat were beginning to dry in the cool evening, fading out one by one. "You should be good to go." He waited for a response from Haylie but got nothing back; she had already turned, walking back towards the police van.

Vector sat on the rear bumper, reading news reports on his phone for any updates. He saw the image of Haylie's face again and again, but nothing else recent from the press. Noticing Haylie out of the corner of his eye, he quickly slid his phone back in his pocket and flashed half a smile her way.

"Are you sure about all this?" Vector asked.

"I'm sure," she shot back. "Besides, it's done. Let's focus on the next step. Let's find these guys."

"Have you changed your mind about Paddington?"

"No. I have a better idea," Haylie said. She pulled her MacBook from her backpack and placed it on the rear deck of the police van. Connecting to the network connection served from her phone, she brought up the stingray logs from the National Gallery. "This phone number—the one that sent a text to the agent—we're going to track down its location."

"How are we going to do that?" Vector asked. "You said yourself that we can't get location data from the information we have."

"You mentioned before that you've been working for the Department of Transport over here, right?" Haylie asked.

"Sure," Vector said.

"Great. I need you to use your access. Log in and bring up the system that tracks the roadside Bluetooth scanners," Haylie said, already on to the next task of installing a few new apps on her phone.

"Bluetooth scanners? That's not a project that I work on. How is that going to help us out?"

Haylie shot a 'c'mon' look at Vector, giving him a few seconds to put together the pieces. He stared back blankly.

"Okay." She put down her phone and faced Vector. "Years ago when cities wanted to track traffic patterns, they installed big magnetic loops underneath intersections. The loops would count the passing cars and it worked fine as a simple counter. But the problem was that it couldn't track where those cars were actually going; it had no idea which intersection the car would head to next. These days most cities in the US, and over here, have switched over to roadside Bluetooth scanners to track traffic patterns."

Vector rubbed his chin. "So, any Bluetooth device that's part of a vehicle is being tracked by the government?"

"No," Haylie continued. "Any device that's *in* a car gets tracked. Mostly phones. Each time a car passes one of these scanners, which are all over the place, the unique ID of that phone is recorded so that the city knows the traffic patterns for individual vehicles. It's a much better system for tracking congestion and traffic than the old magnetic loops, but it has obvious privacy concerns."

Vector chuckled, gesturing up to the CCTV camera angled down at their very conversation. "Privacy is something we've kind of given up on over here."

"The stingray gave us the Bluetooth MAC address for a phone," Haylie said. "That's the unique ID we need. We just need to throw that ID into the Department of Transport's database and do a lookup for its last known location."

Vector stared back at Haylie. "Bloody hell, that's going to work. I'm totally going to get sacked for this, but it's worth it."

With a few keystrokes, Haylie sent the phone's information over to Vector. He flipped open his MacBook and logged into the DOT's system with his credentials. He made his way to the list of available databases and connected his local MySQL database tool. With one or two queries, he now had a list of recent locations for the phone's Bluetooth ID. Sorting by date, he scrolled to the top to find the most recent.

"Give me those credentials," Haylie said. "I'm going to create a quick web service to pull fresh data down to my phone every few minutes."

"Why do you need to do that?" Vector asked.

"Because we're going after them," Haylie said. "Right now. And laptops don't do so well on motorcycles."

Vector checked the results and plugged the latitude and longitude into Google Maps. "Good lord," he said, "this phone was ten blocks away ... just three minutes ago."

"Let's go."

> > > > >

As the floating parade of boats made their way down the Thames, their choppy wakes broke the clear reflection of yellow light glistening off the water. The busy shoreline smeared into a mirror of gray and white, mixed and spackled together like a watercolor, all flowing in tandem down the waterway.

The Mercedes sped safely across the Waterloo Bridge, high above the cold waters below. The brothers sat comfortably in the back seat, each staring out his own window, planning their new empire.

"We need to execute this flawlessly," Benjamin said, running his fingers across the wooden accents on the car's door. "I want Crowne to understand that he made the right call."

"At this point, success is going to depend a lot on the team already assembled on the ground," Walter said. "We'll need to make sure we contain this guy—Santos—who's been leading the charge up until now. We can't have a coup on our hands."

Nodding, Benjamin turned to Walter, eyeing Martin in the front passenger seat. He lowered his voice. "Stability is key in the short term. But then we need to start testing some radical moves. Push forward. Bring in as many tech and strategy guys as we can find; we need plans that will get Crowne's attention. I want South America to be the brilliant gem that is admired by the rest of the globe. A model of success."

"Calm down for a second," Walter whispered back. "Think about where we are. *We've made it.* We're part of the leadership team for The Project. This was our goal. I think we should just enjoy it, while keeping the peace, of course. We don't need to start strutting now; we don't need to keep proving ourselves."

"There's always something else to push for, Walter. *Always.* Today, we're in charge of a continent, but we're still taking orders from someone. If we can grow South America faster than the other territories, we'll be calling more shots for the entire globe." Benjamin watched the passing lights in the night. "There's always another rung on the ladder."

As the Mercedes glided through backstreets, the driver took a quick left down a deserted city road. Walter rolled the window down to see rows of mixed dark and light gray garage doors, blue dumpsters, closed storefronts locked for the evening. The car rolled slowly, swerving around parked trucks and stray trash bins.

"This isn't the way to the airport," Walter said, loud enough for Martin to hear.

The brothers saw Martin shuffle in the passenger seat as Walter leaned forward to make his voice clearer. "Martin," he said, "where are we going?"

The interior lights clicked on, causing both brothers to shield their eyes from the sudden rush of white. As their vision adjusted, they saw what greeted them in the front seat: the barrel of a pistol pointed in their direction.

"We're going to make a pit stop," Martin said, turning to face them, a twisted smile creeping across his face. "We have a few things to take care of before the two of you decide to show the world how smart you are."

CHAPTER TH1RTY N1N3

Covent Garden - London
March 11th, 10:04PM

"Left turn coming up!" Haylie yelled into Vector's ear as they sped across the London night.

The motorcycle twisted through the narrow streets, slowing slightly at crossroads and roundabouts, heading southeast. Haylie hung off the back edge of the leather seat, her left arm wrapped around Vector's waist. She pressed her thumb on the 'REFRESH' button at the center of a makeshift web page, pinging the Department of Transport's database for the third time in the last few minutes. She whispered under her breath, hoping for a new result, but no new location appeared.

"Any new data?" Vector yelled over his shoulder, keeping his eyes on the road.

"Nothing yet. Based on the last two data points, they are headed south across the Waterloo Bridge," she yelled back, hitting the button again. "By the time we get there, we should have something new. Just keep going."

A taxi darted out in front of them, causing Vector to slam on his brakes. Haylie threw her other arm around his waist, throwing her full weight onto the center of the seat; her eyes flicked down, checking to make sure she still had a grip on her phone.

"We need to get moving," she yelled past heavy gasps of air. "C'mon, drive this thing."

Haylie was pulled backwards as the motorcycle accelerated, veering sharply around the taxi and flying down Wellington Street. They wove through a sea of cyclists, late-night theater crowds, and taxis as Haylie saw a dead end over Vector's shoulder. Fifty feet of sidewalk, framed by a cafe and bright red telephone booth, stood between them and the other side of the road. Across the sea of traffic, Haylie could see what looked like the on-ramp to a bridge in the distance.

"Hold on," Vector yelled. "I've always wanted to do this."

They swerved between the black iron poles which stood at attention like pawns on a chessboard, lining the sidewalk's edge. They skipped across the walkway and blindly shot straight through four lanes of traffic. With vehicles on every side, only missing bumpers and tires by inches, they flew past a mishmash of squealing brakes, honking horns, and shouting drivers. Gunning the motorcycle up the left side of the on-ramp, the cool breeze flowing off the river sent a shiver down Haylie's spine as she pulled her phone to her side to check for new data.

"Waterloo Bridge, just like you ordered," Vector yelled as they rode above the Thames.

Refreshing the web page with a quick flick of her thumb, Haylie squinted her eyes against the rushing air. She scanned the data, checking the embedded Google Map for new coordinates, and pulled the screen closer.

"Okay, new contact point," she yelled into Vector's ear. "The corner of Cornwell and Brad. It's on the other side of the river. They're making their way into the side streets."

"I don't know where that is. You're going to have to get me there," Vector yelled back.

"I got it," Haylie said, "but step on it. This contact point is just thirty seconds old. We can still catch up."

Haylie held on, tightening her grip around the seat with her knees, as Vector sped across the bridge, swinging left at a traffic circle and sailing around the building at the center, its dark glass window panes reflecting shards of light like a giant kaleidoscope in the London night. They cruised down Stamford Street as Haylie instructed Vector to take the next right. Pulling onto a one-lane side road, Vector slowed the bike.

"It's coming up on the left," Haylie said.

"Do you have any sort of plan for what we're going to do once we find them?" he asked, pausing at a T-intersection with a slow roll.

"We'll follow them," Haylie said, checking the phone again. "If we can stay out of sight, they should lead us right back to their headquarters."

They cruised down the quiet road as they approached a giant brick bridge blocking their way. Haylie saw a road sign affixed onto the corner reading 'BRAD STREET.'

"Okay, we're here," Haylie said. "Let's check for a car that would belong to our guys. Something nice, I'd guess."

Turning past a bakery perched on the corner, Haylie peered over Vector's shoulder as he rolled along at a low throaty idle. She focused her eyes down the long, deserted street. *There isn't anyone here.* Checking back down to the coordinates on her phone, she looked for any other signage or markers.

This should be the right place.

Gliding slowly across an intersection, they approached a white van parked on the right-hand side of the road. "Keep going, this doesn't look right," Haylie said. As they cruised past one last crossroad, Haylie could see a dead end two blocks down.

"I don't see anything. Maybe they're still moving?" Vector said.

"I don't know—there aren't as many Bluetooth sensors on the side roads," Haylie said. "They have to be back here somewhere."

Haylie looked down yet another side street as the rumble of a train rolled above them, the click-click-click of wheels sending thumps deep into the asphalt. She paused to watch the passing boxcars as her eyes slowly trailed down to the tunnel below. Nestled under the bridge was a Mercedes, the tail lights glowing red in the black night.

"Stop!" she whispered, grabbing Vector's head and tilting it to the right. He hit the brakes, killing the ignition and extinguishing the bike's headlight. Vector and Haylie watched the car for a few moments without saying a word.

He turned over his shoulder. "So now what?"

"We wait. I don't think they've spotted us," she whispered. "We'll sit here, nice and quiet, until they make a–"

Haylie was interrupted by the loud screech of squealing tires as the Mercedes took off in a straight line, disappearing into the night. After catching his breath, Vector rotated the motorcycle's ignition key.

"Okay. Time for plan B," Haylie shouted, holding on to Vector and flipping out her phone.

"What did you say?" Vector yelled as he accelerated, gaining on the Mercedes. Both vehicles passed under the bridge and down the narrow street. "Crash, what the hell is plan B?"

Racing past apartment buildings and into a short sprint down a one-lane alley, Vector squinted to see a T-shaped intersection ahead. The car fishtailed to the left, sliding across the slick pavement and nearly onto the opposite sidewalk, the assembled pub crowd frantically scattering out of its path. Gaining ground on the Mercedes, Vector cut the corner to the left, bumped across the curb, and followed in close pursuit.

While hanging on to Vector for dear life with her left hand, Haylie cycled through phone apps with her right, finding one with choppy graphic borders and a series of buttons each displaying a different alphanumeric code.

"Have you heard of Harlon and Mathers, those two hackers from Michigan?" Haylie yelled as they sped behind the car. "I've got an experimental version of their car hacking project. We're going to try it out."

"Experimental?" Vector yelled back. "What do you mean, *experimental*?"

"They've used it on a few different systems, but the commands aren't fully documented." Haylie flew through the list of auto makers. "Each car's wireless system is unique; different suppliers and manufacturers. We'll have to just do some trial and error here."

"Well you better start trying stuff; these guys aren't slowing down," Vector yelled back.

"Mercedes uses a cellular connection for its navigation system," Haylie yelled as her eyes flicked up from her screen. The car accelerated past a construction zone as Vector stayed in its wake. "Stay close; if I find the right combination, I should be able to shut down the engine."

"I'm trying!" Vector said, speeding across an intersection and back into another tunnel.

"Closer!" Haylie shouted. They flew past a graffiti-covered wall, feeling the motorcycle climb in altitude as they approached a bridge on-ramp, this one heading back across the Thames. The air grew thick with moisture as the motorcycle's engine buzzed near capacity. Vector increased their speed, almost ramming the car's rear bumper with his front tire.

Haylie tapped the app's CONNECT button a few extra times for good measure. The app's connection progress bar circled and spun, finally pinging Haylie with a mechanical ding and a slight vibration to the device.

"I'm connected," she yelled into Vector's ear. "Stay with them and I'll try to kill the engine." Looking down at the app's wireframe-like interface, she saw a mix of nonsensical buttons, all marked with different test labels. *What the hell, let's just start trying some.* With a shrug, she selected the topthe right button marked '4FR56X8' and pressed down. As she fixed her eyes on Mercedes, she waited for something dramatic to happen.

Nothing did.

"Are you trying it?" Vector yelled back. "I didn't see anything."

"Just stay close," Haylie shouted, looking through the list of remaining codes. "There's a lot of commands to work through." *This stupid thing isn't working.* She hovered her thumb over the next button, moving clockwise, and pressed.

Still nothing.

> > > > >

The brothers ducked down, their hands flying over their ears, as the car's radio blared at maximum volume.

"What are you doing, idiot?" Martin yelled at the driver. "Turn it off!"

"I didn't do anything, sir," the driver yelled back as he clicked the radio off. "It just came on by itself."

"Just like the windshield wipers just turned themselves on, too?" Martin yelled back. "Just drive the damn car!"

Walter turned to check the motorcycle, its headlight still weaving left and right about twenty feet behind. He swiveled back towards Martin, who was now frantically alternating his view between the front and rear windows, switching every few seconds, his pistol still aimed at the back seat. Walter could have sworn he saw Martin's hand trembling, but it was hard to tell with all the violent movement in the car.

"Lose them!" Martin yelled, spit flying from his mouth. "This wasn't part of the plan!"

> > > > >

"Are you sure you're using that thing the right way?" Vector yelled into the wind. They came down off of Blackfriars Bridge to the base of a traffic circle, hanging a tight corner around the left bank. Leaning into the curve, Vector stayed close on the Mercedes' tail.

"Shut up and keep your eyes on the car," she replied. *There are too many damn choices on this thing.* Scrolling to the last page of buttons, Haylie saw a screen with only two remaining. She exhaled and pressed the top left button.

A loud shriek filled the air as the tail of the Mercedes began to drift right, the front of the car sliding left. The car skid into a violent spin as Vector hit the motorcycle's brakes as hard as he could.

"That was the parking brake!" Vector yelled, yanking at the handlebars and steering just out of the car's path. He veered the motorcycle to the right, fishtailing slightly across the wet pavement and sliding the back tire towards a light pole standing in the center median. Haylie shifted to her left to try and regain her balance as the bike continued to drift out of control, but it was too late.

Damnit, this is going to hurt.

She pulled back her outstretched right hand as she fell backwards off the cycle. She landed on the pavement with a skidding thud, her phone and glasses flying off in two separate directions. She felt a rush of pain across her entire right side.

Stunned and dazed from the fall, she pushed herself up onto her elbow, the grit of the asphalt digging into her flesh. She rubbed the back of her aching head, checking for any blood, but finding none.

Looking back up and down the street, she saw that Vector had managed to maneuver the motorcycle to a full stop without crashing, but the momentum had pushed him halfway down the city block. She searched across the pavement to see her phone lying fifteen feet away, screen cracked with a spider web of glass, still glowing blue.

Just then, Haylie heard the roar of an engine. The Mercedes, now spun around and facing back in the direction of the river, had her directly in its path. The headlamps illuminated her fallen frame, casting long shadows down the black pavement.

Oh no.

The car spun its wheels, screeching down the road, aimed right at her. Haylie crawled on her hands and knees, pulling herself towards her phone, scraping her palms with glass and gravel as she made her way, arm over arm, trying to reach the light of the screen. She heard the humming of pistons as the driver shifted gears and accelerated at her. She could feel a rush of wind approaching as she continued to push forward.

I can make it.

Crawling faster, her elbows bloodied and knees scraping with every stretch, she rolled the final few feet. As the sound of the Mercedes' engine roared, she reached out as far as she could, pressing the last button she hadn't tried on the app.

She felt the grime and dirt from the road pressed between her finger and the phone's screen as the car's lights went black. She rolled towards the median as the roar of the car's engine cut out, replaced by the sound of tires rolling along wet pavement.

The ignition kill switch. Thank God.

The dark, dead car sailed just inches by her face, finally slamming into the corner of an adjacent building with a smash of glass and metal. The Mercedes found its final resting place halfway up the set of stone stairs that sat next to a red, white, and blue 'UNDERGROUND' signpost.

Haylie's heart pounded as she curled up into a sitting position and grabbed her glasses off the pavement, feeling a hand on her shoulder. She looked up to see a relieved Vector. She rose to her feet and ran towards the wreck, hobbling behind Vector as fast as she could manage.

She could see the airbags had deployed, knocking out the two men sitting in the front seats. They slumped over the deflating bags; she couldn't tell if they were dead or alive.

As she approached, the two rear doors of the car cracked open. The Sterling brothers emerged from their respective sides of the back seat, blood smeared across each of their faces. They looked at Haylie, Benjamin giving her a forced smile.

"You've got to be kidding me," she said.

CHAPTER FORTY

Blackfriars Bridge - London
March 11th, 10:18PM

"I should have known," Haylie yelled across the road in the rough direction of the Sterling brothers. "You two were behind this whole thing, weren't you?"

As Haylie spoke, Vector traced his way around the far side of the car, keeping an eye on Walter and Benjamin while checking for any movement from the two men in the front seat.

"Haylie," Walter stuttered as he took an awkward step towards her, stretching out a friendly arm. "It's so great to see you."

"Don't," she shouted back, "don't even try it with me. Was it you, Walter? Were you the one that sent the agents in the National Gallery? Were you trying to stop me from finding Caesar?"

"No, no, Haylie. You've got it all wrong," Benjamin interjected, bringing a hand to his forehead to check for injuries. "We were set up. The guys in there," gesturing to the front seat, "Martin, he tricked us. He had us at gunpoint until you showed up."

Haylie scowled. "Martin? So *that's* Martin? He put my face on every TV in the world." She walked slowly towards the car, trying to get an angle on the man's face.

"I think he's been taken care of," Benjamin said. "But there are more of them. And we can help."

"Here's the gun," Vector yelled, picking up the pistol that had been ejected onto the stone steps. He flipped it into his palm, turning it over and on its side to inspect the finish. "Never held a gun before." He raised his arm, pointing the pistol at the Sterling brothers.

"Who's *this* guy?" Benjamin asked, looking over at Vector.

Haylie just stared back, shaking her head. "I don't think you're in any place to ask questions," she said.

"Haylie," Walter said, "there's still time to stop this."

Both brothers slowly walked towards Haylie with their hands extended, the lights above showing the shards of glass and cuts littering their faces.

"I know how it looks," Walter continued. "Yes, we screwed you over, that was a mistake. But you have to understand, we're on the same team now. We've been double-crossed; we want to stop Crowne as much as you do."

"Crowne?" Haylie said. "Who's Crowne?"

"Crowne's behind this?" Vector said, looking over to Haylie. "He's our PM—Prime Minister." He shook his head in disbelief.

"He's the one that created The Project," Benjamin said. "It's been his plan to seize power and switch the globe over to a one-world government. Everything—the Raven puzzle, the Iceland tests, Caesar's disappearance—he's been calling the shots all along."

"And Caesar?" Haylie asked. "He's with Crowne?"

"Yes," Benjamin assured her. "The final step of the Raven puzzle led Caesar straight to their headquarters—they're still holding him there. Crowne thought whoever could solve the puzzles could help them with this new society—help design the technology that's going to be needed as they build out the next phase."

"Unbelievable. So rude of him," Vector said, looking down to the ground and chuckling. "Not very British of him at all, really."

Haylie thought for a moment. "When is Crowne planning to cut the power?" she asked.

"Midnight tonight," Benjamin said.

"But," Walter interjected, "we know where he is. We can find him … we can stop him. Just, please, put the gun down and we can–"

A gunshot rang out in the air.

The brothers dove to the ground. Haylie snapped down to her knees, her hands over her ears. She looked over to Vector, wondering why on earth he had just pulled the trigger.

Vector stood with the pistol still extended, his left hand now clutching his side as he dropped the weapon. It fell to pavement. Vector slumped down onto the street, the weight of his body crumpled over his legs, his right arm extended out and over the curb.

"A prepared ... man is a dangerous ... man," stuttered Martin, standing propped against the passenger-side car door with a small pistol pointed in Vector's direction. Martin's face, stained with trails of blood, contorted with rage as he moved the pistol's aim towards Haylie.

"Sometimes, one gun isn't enough," Martin slurred.

> > > > >

Titanhurst - London
March 11th, 10:20PM

Standing at the edge of the engineering pit with Caesar at his side, Crowne straightened the cuffs of his jacket as he took in the activity below. Clearing his throat, he called for the team's attention. The room fell silent as everyone turned from their work.

"We have less than two hours until the end of the world, everyone," Crowne said. "Then it will be time for a new direction, a better path. I have some tough news tonight; unfortunately, Martin has shown himself to be a man that is susceptible to ideas—ideas that are contrary to our main objectives. He's made poor decisions. It's truly unfortunate, really."

The room hummed as the monitors blinked with activity, unattended.

"Before Martin left, I had our security team install a remote detonation device in his vehicle," Crowne continued. "I asked him to take care of the Sterling brothers, who were also, sadly, a liability. But I wasn't fully confident that Martin would actually follow my orders. It seems my hunch was correct. They've been able to persuade him with the offer of finances or power, I'm not sure which. All I know is that I cannot have a high-functioning team with people I cannot trust."

The room sat waiting for what was coming next.

"Sean, let's get Martin's location up on the screen, shall we please?"

Sean gestured to a young engineer on the other side of the room who had just pulled his earphones down around his neck. The main screen in the pit flickered and switched over to a map of London, with a single red dot pulsing on the North side of Blackfriars Bridge. Sean turned back to Crowne with his full attention, saying nothing.

"Caesar, I would like to make this official," Crowne announced. "Martin has shown all of us tonight that he doesn't have what it takes. His interests lie only in his position in the world: being elite, being special. He thinks that by being part of The Project, he is somehow worth more than others."

Crowne placed his hand on Caesar's shoulder, and Caesar felt his skin jolt at the touch.

"But you're not a man like that," Crowne said. "I've learned that about you. You understand that what we're doing here is bigger than ourselves."

Scanning the room, Caesar saw a few faint smiles of approval mixed with questions in the eyes of others. He looked back to the screen hanging above the pit, the single red dot, pulsing. Blinking in binary—dead then alive then dead again—over and over and over, without a sound.

"In the new world, we do not have time for these types of agendas. These types of people," Crowne said. "Leadership takes sacrifice, and it takes hard decisions."

The past two weeks—*had it only been that long?*—flashed through Caesar's mind. *How has it come to this?* His heart pounded as the eyes of the room weighed down on him.

"Is...." Caesar struggled to get the words out. "Is Haylie with him?"

"No, she's not. But one of the last things Martin said to me," Crowne replied, "was that he was on his way to find your sister. He was going to stop her at all costs; he didn't want her reaching headquarters. Martin fears people like Haylie."

Caesar stared back at the screen, thinking. The dot blinked. And blinked. And blinked.

"Caesar," Crowne whispered, turning his back to the rest of the team. "I need you to give the order."

> > > > >

Blackfriars Bridge - London
March 11th, 10:22PM

"You thought … you thought you could walk in here at the last minute and ruin everything?" Martin screamed. "That you could stop what I've helped create?"

Haylie stood facing Vector, tears blurring her vision as she covered her face with her hands. She screamed his name, taking a step towards her only friend.

"Don't move!" Martin shouted. "Stay right there. And you two—the wonder twins—get over by her."

Benjamin and Walter paced backwards away from the car, hands elevated at their sides and palms facing Martin. They stopped next to Haylie by the center median. Haylie kept her eyes locked on Vector but couldn't tell anything about his condition; he lay silent and slumped over, still as a stone in the night.

"I've been doing everything, *everything*, that has been asked of me for years." Martin limped back towards the car, keeping the pistol locked on the group. His collar was stained a deep red, with blood flowing down from an open gash in his head.

Spit flew from his mouth as he screamed. "I gave up my life for this cause, for my mentor! Sacrifice. *That's* what shows people what you're made of. What have you ever sacrificed?"

He slumped back against the car and cocked the pistol. "The next step starts now. Too bad you won't get to see it."

As Martin raised a second hand to hold the gun steady, a loud click sounded from the Mercedes behind him. He turned just in time to see a fireball flowing from the undercarriage, igniting the gas tank with an ear-splitting explosion.

A wave of force sent the hood flying against the adjacent building as a push of hot air, glass, and metal shards sailed in all directions. Haylie and the brothers were thrown flat on their backs, lying in crumpled poses on the median. She spun away from the blast of heat that filled the air, as the night went dark once again.

A car door slammed to the ground directly next to Haylie's head, shooting sparks on contact as the twisting smells of burning metal and plastic filled her nostrils. She felt heat on her arm and looked down to the sleeve of her jacket to see a small patch of fabric on fire. She frantically padded it with her other hand, rolling away from the burning metal and scrambling in any direction where she didn't see flames.

Her ears rang and throbbed, overloaded from the shockwave that had hit the three of them. She tasted blood, and wiped at her mouth with her shoulder, seeing a small red smear soaking the olive tones of the fabric. She could make out Benjamin and Walter in the distance, both blown to the other side of the median, slowly rising to their feet, holding their ears with their hands.

Haylie raised her head from the asphalt to look back across the road, seeing Martin's burning body—cut into pieces and thrown twenty feet from the car —in a lifeless heap on the adjacent sidewalk. It lay still and splayed, like a burning rag doll.

She looked away, focusing instead on the fire as it danced around the skeleton of the car's frame, her eyes flicking along with the flames. She felt the heat rolling over the pavement, warming her face like a summer's day in Texas, back at home lying out in her backyard.

Vector. You have to check on Vector.

Pushing her body back upright, Haylie sprinted down the road, stopping and crouching down by Vector's side. Flipping him over, she placed her body between her friend and the heat of the burning car. His eyes were open, blinking, with a baseball-sized bloodstain soaking the shoulder of his jacket into a dark black pool.

"You'll be okay," she whispered, now almost able to hear herself as her hearing slowly returned. "You'll be okay."

Walter approached from the other side, dropping to his knees and reaching in to check Vector's pulse. He watched Vector's eyes as he felt for a heartbeat.

"He's alive," Walter said, out of breath. "He got lucky; it looks like the bullet hit his shoulder." He pulled out his phone. "I should be able to get an ambulance here in about two minutes."

"Okay, but seriously," Benjamin said from behind Haylie's shoulder. "Who is this guy?"

"None of your business," she shot back, not even giving him the courtesy of turning around.

She held Vector, looking out into the blackness of the London night. The chilled, wet air from the Thames rolled across her, sending her hair flying back across her shoulders, as she huddled closer to her best friend. Her only friend.

It's time to end this. It's time to find Caesar, stop this madness, and go home.

"Haylie," Benjamin said as he dusted himself off, "Crowne is dangerous. We need to stop him, and we need to go now, we don't have much time."

She rose from Vector's side, turning back to face the heat of the burning wreckage. A siren sounded in the distance.

She knew what she had to do.

"Just get me in the front door. I'll take care of the rest."

CHAPTER FORTY ON3

Titanhurst - London
March 11th, 11:52PM

My God, the time is almost here. Tomorrow will be a brand new day.

For such a key turning point in the history of the world, the halls of Titanhurst were surprisingly empty. Crowne had pictured the few moments before The Project's start as a frantic push to finish last-minute tasks or convince leaders on the right course of action. But it had all been taken care of. Things were running perfectly, according to plan.

And now, for the first time since he could remember, he had nothing to do.

Crowne strolled down the halls, winding his way slowly towards his office. He would stop there to grab a few things and then he'd work his way to the control room, where he was sure to receive a hero's welcome. And then, with Caesar's help, he'd make the world go dark.

And then we begin the real work.

His mind wandered with each footstep as he thought back to just a few minutes earlier, rolling through the final status checkpoints with a collection of leaders from across the globe. As Crowne had paced in front of the giant screens, back and forth like a tiger in a cage, he had examined the faces of each Bilderberg leader. Faces chosen from all over the world, from all cultures. That's when it finally hit him.

We're leading the globe to the place it needs to be, but not with guns or bombs or tanks. We're not doing it with tyranny; we're doing it with a new sense of global cooperation. It's a marvel.

Pacing leisurely through the halls, he dwelled on the one last loose end that hadn't been wrapped up. That hacker—*Crash, is that what she calls herself?*—was still running loose out in the streets, probably scared for her life, with her face plastered across every television screen in the civilized world. *She missed her chance ... in a few minutes, she'll just blend in with the rest of the darkness.*

Tracing his hand across the wallpaper's gritty surface, up and down and into figure-eights like his daughter would do on on a lazy Sunday morning, he drew a line towards his office as he glided towards the door. Crowne pulled his hand back into his pocket and eased his way in.

The echoing voices of the people—those poor, miserable, unknowing people—will finally stop ringing. I don't even know what the world will sound like without their pathetic, constant cries for–

Turning, Crowne froze as he focused on the figure that rose from the couch, standing in the middle of the room. A smile crept across his face as he looked down to her knees and saw his laptop splayed open on the coffee table in front of her.

He knew that face—the one that Martin had showed him from the Morgan Library footage. Caesar's sister.

It's so lovely to finally meet the mighty Crash in the flesh.

The girl stood firm, arms locked forward and legs at shoulder width, aiming Martin's pistol right at Crowne's head.

CHAPTER FORTY TWO

The pistol felt foreign in Haylie's soft hands, cold and heavy. As she adjusted her grip to something more like she had seen on TV, the metal bit into her palms. She brought one hand back to push her glasses up on her nose, quickly returning to a two-handed grip as they stared each other down.

"Hi," she said. "Been looking for me?"

Raising his hands in a move of mimicked surrender, Crowne laughed. "I believe I have. You must be the girl calling herself Crash, is that right? It's good to finally meet you; let's sit down and talk for a bit?"

"BEGINNING COUNTDOWN: FIVE MINUTES TO SCRIPT ACTIVATON," a digital voice echoed over the Titanhurst intercom speakers, causing both Haylie and Crowne to flinch.

"How did you get in here?" Crowne asked, taking on the unmistakable tone of an angry father.

"I'm not good at a lot of things," Haylie replied, holding the pistol steady. "But I can always find a way in."

"That's going to get you in trouble one of these days," Crowne said.

"Don't you have someplace to be?" she asked, with a quick nod at the door. "Armageddon won't just make itself, you know."

"No, no, I'm fine right here," Crowne said. "And Armageddon is such a loaded word. If you think about it ... if you *really* think about it, the civilized world got along without power for thousands of years." He lowered his hands slowly, the smile crawling back on his face. "A few more months shouldn't be a problem, right?"

"You're out of your mind," Haylie said, fixing her grip on the pistol as sweat began to form on her palms. "And somehow I'm the only person left to stop you."

"Out of my mind?" Crowne asked, beginning to slowly pace towards his desk, careful step over careful step. "Let me ask you this: who in their right mind would look at this world and think that we don't need help? More political divisions than ever before, terrorism runs rampant, and we're destroying our own earth while looking the other way. And *I'm* the madman that wants to fix things? The only one not saying '*everything's fine, please carry on?*' I don't think so."

"The world will always have problems," Haylie said. "But that doesn't justify what you're trying to do."

"There will always be problems, let's all get together and hug and talk about them," Crowne mimicked back, the anger growing in his voice. He'd finally reached his desk and leaned forward from its edge, one hand extended near the box at the center.

"But no one is *fixing* anything, Crash," Crowne continued. "It's still spinning in circles every day. Well, no more. *NO MORE.* If nothing else, history will say that I'm the man that said things have to change. I'm actually doing something to point our entire earth, our entire history, in the right direction. The world needs help. The world needs *this.*"

"There are better ways," Haylie said. "Better ways than killing people."

"I'm not killing anyone," Crowne demanded. "I couldn't do all this technical stuff—computer code and systems exploits—I couldn't do it if I tried. Your brother is the one who is seeing the final commands through."

"Don't lie to me," Haylie said, finding a tighter grip on the pistol.

"It's true, you can ask him yourself. But you'll have to put that silly gun down first. You Americans and your toys." Crowne drummed the fingers of his left hand across the desktop, next to the wooden box.

"Tell me where my brother is."

"He's right down the hall, in the control room with his team," Crowne said. "They've grown quite fond of him. He's a natural leader, your brother."

He's messing with you. Caesar would never join up with a group like this ... with a madman like Crowne.

"You're going to take me there right now," she said. "And I'm going to stop this whole thing."

"I'd love to, Crash," he said. "But I'm wondering if you're even as good as you think you are. Here with your brother, you could learn. How'd you like to stop hiding? Stop running? Start *leading*."

"FOUR MINUTES TO SCRIPT ACTIVATON," the intercom announced.

"No thanks," she said, gritting her teeth.

"I'm guessing you didn't have any luck getting into my laptop?" he said. "I had Caesar build out the security on that machine. My password was garbage, but he fixed it up for me, locked down some other technical bits. Must have made things difficult for you and whatever your plan is here to stop The Project?"

"You're right. I couldn't get into your machine," Haylie said, reaching with one hand into the pocket of her field jacket. She produced Crowne's phone, flashed it at him like a magician showing the missing card in a Vegas act, and tossed it his way. "But getting into *this* was a piece of cake."

The device flew across the room and hit Crowne in the stomach, clattering down to the hardwood floor. He let it lie there, his eyes still fixed on Haylie.

"I sent everything—a bunch of really interesting emails—over to the police," Haylie said. "Detailed plans for The Project, communication with the main leaders across the globe, and everything I could find about Iceland. Now they've got everything they need to lock you away. But you're right, I'm probably not very good at this stuff."

Laughing, Crowne looked down at the phone, shaking his head in pity. "I'm afraid you still don't get it," he said. "In just a few minutes, the police will be as powerless as you and every other person in the world. Besides, you're a felon—a dreg of society. They'll never believe you."

His eyes narrowed as he focused on her, pointing directly back into the mouth of the pistol. "Final offer—join us, or I'll make sure that your life and the lives of each and every one of your scrawny little high school friends is a living hell over the next few months. The darkness will be tough on the world, but, oh my goodness, I'll guarantee that it will be *unbearable* for you."

"Joke's on you, wanker," Haylie said, standing firm. "I don't have any high school friends."

Crowne looked over to the clock, and then down to the cigar box. "Very well, then."

As she tried her best to remain focused, her mind filled with a growing sound, a thumping bass rhythm—whump, whump, whump—that began to shake the floor under her feet. She saw Crowne freeze as he searched for the source of the noise. Then it dawned on her.

Looks like my backup is here.

"Before your project gets started, I wanted to give you a big sendoff," Haylie pointed to the remote on Crowne's desk. "It's your turn to flip on the TV. Any channel should do."

Crowne stared back at Haylie for a cautious moment before grabbing the remote. He faced the screen over his desk, turning his back to Haylie, and pointed the remote towards the monitor.

"THREE MINUTES TO SCRIPT ACTIVATON," rang across the intercom.

He clicked the power button.

> > > > >

The screen popped to life, showing a bright red 'BREAKING NEWS' banner scrolling across the bottom. A video of Crash played, showing her speaking into the camera while standing next to a police van. Crowne scowled, tapping at the volume button.

"....name is **Haylie Black**. I'm an American. You
know me better by the name that has been in the
press today: Crash.

I'm turning myself in to the authorities here in
London. I've done some things I'm not proud of, but
nothing to the extent of what has been reported."

Crowne stared deep into the screen, lost in the broadcast, as the
remote control dangled from his hand.

"I've uncovered a plot headed up by Prime Minister
Crowne to take control of the world with a handful
of other leaders. I know it sounds crazy, but it's
true. And I have proof.

His group plans to cut all power and
communications to the world as of midnight tonight.
What he tested on Iceland, he's about to unleash
across the globe.

I'm not going to run. I'm working with the police to
get all the information I can about Crowne's plan.
I'm done hiding."

His face glowing bright red, Crowne quickly slid his hand to the
cigar box, flipping the lid open.

"It doesn't matter," Crowne said calmly as he palmed the pistol,
slowly, into his hand. "The Project is just a minute away. The *new world*
is just a minute away. Just ask your brother...."

He turned, pointing the pistol into the center of the room. Crowne
searched for his target as he realized what had just happened, his lungs
fighting for air.

The door was open, still swinging loosely against the wall.

The girl was gone.

CHAPTER FORTY THR33

Titanhurst - London
March 11th, 11:57PM

Haylie raced down the hallway, her eyes darting between room markers as her heart pounded. *Turn right at the end of the hall, then left, two doors down on the right.* She kept repeating the instructions that Walter had given her as she ran. The plan was for Haylie to find Crowne's phone, send the evidence to the police, and meet back up with the Sterling brothers at the Control Room.

Is the next one a right or a left?

"TWO MINUTES TO SCRIPT ACTIVATON," the intercom sounded as Haylie increased her pace, fighting for oxygen. She hung a quick left and saw an open door just a few feet away. She ran in, seeing a room full of computer workstations and a team of engineers huddled over their keyboards, but her brother was nowhere to be found.

Where the hell is Caesar?

She paused in front of the engineering pit, looking up to the center screen looming high above the collection of workstations below. While the other monitors showed a combination of different data feeds, the main screen showed only a simple command line interface—bright green machine text on a dull, black background—running each line of a script, slowly scrolling the plain text as it progressed.

Haylie took a step forward, checking the code readout as it ended its initial test, now just displaying the name of the machine running the script next to a blinking cursor.

BlackBox:FinalPreCheck CBlack$

BlackBox? That's Caesar's MacBook. He's running the main script from his machine ... but where is he?

She darted out of the room and took a left—no, a right —as she tried her best to remember Walter's directions to Caesar's apartment. She flew down the staircase, her feet pounding on the marble, and turned the corner, sliding into the main floor hallway.

Room 76. Walter said Caesar's apartment was in Room 76. Across from a painting of a raven.

Haylie ran down a dark downstairs hallway, searching the room numbers hanging next to each door.

But if the script is running from his computer, then Crowne must be right. Caesar must be with them. Or maybe they just grabbed his laptop to frame him, set him up. My God, why would he–

She slowed, panting and doubled over, as she saw the painting: a raven, perched on a pitch black tree branch, its back huddled over and hackles extended, crying out, ready to strike. Looking to her left, she saw the room marker she had been looking for: 'ROOM 76.'

The door was open.

She crossed the threshold, shielding her eyes from the bright, white glow of the room. As her vision returned, her eyes fell on a man standing over a computer, typing away at the keyboard, with the familiar sound of keys clicking away.

"Caesar!" she screamed, running towards him and wrapping her arms around him.

"I can't believe you're here," he said, laughing and returning her hug with both arms. "You're okay, right?"

"I'm fine," Haylie said.

"I didn't know if you'd get here in time," Caesar said, turning back to his machine and resuming his frantic typing. "Just a few more edits to the script and we'll be good. I'm glad you're here ... you get to see this happen yourself. It's a big night."

"ONE MINUTE TO SCRIPT ACTIVATON," the intercom shouted.

Haylie angled herself between Caesar's line of sight and the screen. "What are you doing? You know what this will mean, right?" she yelled as Caesar dodged around her.

"Stop it, Haylie," Caesar said, pivoting his machine away from her. "You don't know what you're talking about. Just give me a minute, I'm going to finish what I started. You're safe here with me."

She welled with anger, grabbing for the computer as Caesar jerked it away. "I don't want to be SAFE," she yelled. "I'm all done sitting on the sidelines. We can stop this—pull the plug."

Ignoring her shouting, Caesar scanned the output of the test script.

Haylie took a few steps back as her eyes turned from relief, now heavy with worry as she watched him work, testing scripts and double-checking his code.

This can't be happening.

"You … you're actually doing this?" Haylie stammered, pointing at Caesar's laptop with a shaking finger. "You're … part of this? The Project?"

"It's not like that," Caesar said, absorbed in his code. "You don't understand."

"THIRTY SECONDS TO SCRIPT ACTIVATON," the intercom shouted.

"You sound just like Crowne!" Haylie screamed. "You need to stop this. You used to tell me its all about 'shades of gray'—well this isn't. This is black and white. This is *wrong*. You can't do this." She ran towards him, extending her hands in the direction of the keyboard.

"Stop!" Caesar yelled, pushing her back away from the machine. "You don't know what you're talking about!"

Haylie tripped backwards, falling to the floor, only able to look up as Caesar typed, flicking his eyes up to the clock in the corner of the screen as he added the final lines of code.

"I'm going to see this through," he said. "The script's already been set to run, you can't change that. I just need to make a few changes … so it's perfect. You'll see."

Watching in horror, Haylie thought back to everything that she had struggled through in the past week: Cecil Rhodes and hidden riddles and Mozart. She remembered the taste of dirt in her mouth from the Bohemian Grove; her heart raced all over again replaying the sight of a wall of glass, shattered and falling into the Morgan Library's Reading Room below her feet.

It was all for nothing.

The seconds ticked away as she drifted into a daze, getting lost in the dance of Caesar's fingers flying across the keyboard. The chorus of mechanical taps built into something more, something organic. A stream of sound that hypnotized her and took her back in time.

It transported her back to nights in her house past bedtime, after her Mom or Dad had said goodnight. Back to nights with the lights out and the door closed, drifting off to sleep to the sound of her brother working away down the hall, typing away at the keys. Those nights were filled with dreams of possibility—*What could he be building? And what could I be building?*—as she fell away to her dreams.

But now, that was all gone.

"Here we go," Caesar said, taking a step back from his laptop to admire his work.

"PROJECT INITIATION SEQUENCE COMPLETE," the intercom sounded, echoing in the halls, the apartment, and Haylie's mind.

She watched as Caesar stood, watching his work fire off command after command.

And then the lights went out.

CHAPTER FORTY FOUR

Titanhurst - London
March 12th, 12:00AM

Sprinting, flying down the halls of Titanhurst, Crowne made his way towards the control room.

No one can stop this. It's over. It's done. And I'm certainly not going to be stopped by some bird with a laptop. I'm guessing she's already been picked up by one of the guards.

Let's get on with it.

He took a few deep breaths to calm himself. He daydreamed his victory walk into the control room, filled with engineers finally seeing the fruits of their labor. Slapping each other on the back, cheers of joy, fist bumps. And for him—the architect, the mastermind—he would be the man of the hour for sure. For sure.

But suddenly, the hallway fell dark.

Crowne stopped, standing dead in his tracks. He waited and listened, hearing shouts from rooms down the hall, but no whirling of vents or computers or … anything. He waited for someone to flip the circuit breaker back on, or for the reserve power to kick in. But there was nothing.

Just calm, dead, ringing silence.

Something's gone wrong.

"Everyone to the Control Room!" Crowne screamed down the empty hallway. He pulled his phone from his pocket, illuminating the screen and using it to guide his way past doorways and corners, his eyes fighting to make out the details every few feet. Sudden bursts of shouting grew from outside the windows, mixed with the sounds of breaking glass.

I can't see a bloody thing.

Stumbling past stunned guards, Crowne bumped into an unknowing man from the side and spun haphazardly into the hard plaster corner. He sprinted forward, thumping step after step down the hall, pushing against each wall with his hands to aid his movement, struggling to keep his momentum.

"Get to your stations!" he yelled. "Somebody turn the lights back on!"

He took a sharp left into the Control Room. Stopping to catch his breath, he pushed off the door frame with his forearm to stand straight back up. His gaze falling down to his other hand, Crowne realized he was still clutching his pistol, pointed down at the floor.

He looked up to see the Control Room completely dark and unconnected to the rest of the world.

"Caesar!" Crowne yelled into the room. "Give me a status! How long until the fix is in place?"

As his pulse raced, he fought for gasps of breath, searching the darkness to find a small group of engineers huddled on the far side of the room. They all stared back at Crowne, past the glow of their screens, running on battery power. The monitors that adorned the walls, normally alive with data and video feeds from around the world, sat dark and dead.

"The network's down, sir … and Caesar's gone," said one of the engineers, taking a few careful steps back from Crowne. "Caesar and Sean—they grabbed some team members and their laptops; they all left together."

Crowne shook his head. "No, no—that's not possible, we need to get back online. The Project has begun … we need our systems back online RIGHT NOW!" He stomped along the rows of desks, pistol hanging from his hand, searching in the darkness.

Staring back into the eyes of the team, Crowne's face fell. He conjured the energy to take a few sluggish steps, stopping at the edge of the pit.

Outside the window, a wave of deep thudding beats filled the air as flecks of red and blue begin to appear against every glass surface in the room. Crowne once again heard the heavy bass thumps of helicopter rotors, this time much louder and clearer.

Turning to face the full wall of windows, Crowne saw two police helicopters, equipped with heavily-armored soldiers hanging out either side, tilting their pitch to land in the courtyard.

"Execute the D procedure," Crowne said to the team with an exhausted breath, looking back out past the windows, his face now lit with police lights.

"But sir," one of the engineers said, "that means...."

"Yes, I know what it means," Crowne said, "Burn it down. Burn the whole place down. Start with the server room."

The engineers exchanged looks and then sprinted towards the server room, grabbing a thick case from the wall marked 'D' on their way in the door. Crowne crumpled back against the wall at the pit's edge, unbuttoning his jacket and sinking onto the floor with a slump of his shoulders.

He looked down to the pistol in his hand. The dull shine of its barrel reflected the onslaught of lights now shining back into his eyes with hypnotizing beats of color.

As the room lit with the orange glow and heat of fire, Crowne lost himself in the dancing lights, highlighted by strobes of white, gliding and twisting and melting together like nothing else he had ever seen.

Like nothing he had ever dreamed of.

> > > > >

"What just happened?" Haylie asked as she rose to her feet. "We weren't supposed to go dark. What did you do?"

"I changed a couple of things," Caesar said, reading the final lines of the script's output.

Haylie took a few steps towards him. "You did?"

"The Project script was designed to take out the systems of every continent while keeping each Bilderberg Group location around the globe fully functional," Caesar said. "I just reversed the script. Now each headquarters for The Project has gone dark, while the rest of the world watches on, fully powered up."

"For a minute, I thought…." Haylie stopped herself before she could say the words out loud.

"What, with *these* guys?" Caesar said with a smile. "Please. These guys are assholes."

Walking over to check Caesar's screen, Haylie felt a wave of relief fall over her. She gave her brother a sideways hug.

"Let's get out of here," she said with a sigh of relief, peering through the window at the commotion outside. Two military helicopters sat in the courtyard, rotors still spinning, as soldiers forced their way into each wing of the mansion. "Let's go home."

Caesar shut his computer and plucked his messenger bag off the floor, sliding the computer in and zipping the bag shut. "I've got other plans."

"What?" she asked, spinning to face her brother. "What are you talking about?"

"Before I came here," he said, "I thought I was doing important stuff, that my work actually mattered. But now I know that I was wrong—there's this whole other world that I never knew existed. My eyes have been opened. The Project was a horrific concept, but the things they built along the way were actually pretty amazing. I've got their code … I erased it all from Crowne's servers, but I kept a copy. All of it. Access to every system in the world. Imagine the good we can do; this stuff can have a huge impact in the right hands."

"We need to hand that over to the police," Haylie said. "I don't trust that code with anyone, including us. What if someone else managed to get a copy? Just delete it, let's be done with all of this."

"You think the authorities—the police, the FBI, Interpol—they're going to forget what happened here tonight?" Caesar said. "They're going to lock us both up. We're dangerous to them now. That's what Raven taught me—didn't it teach you anything?"

"They'll understand," Haylie shot back.

"They never understand," Caesar said. "Listen, I pulled aside the best people from my team here—good people. They've already left, we're meeting up in East London tonight."

She stared back at him, silent.

"Haylie," Caesar said. "This whole thing—it's not our fault; but it still changes our lives. No matter which way we go, our worlds will be different tomorrow. You don't have to come with me, but you need to know that the feds will be looking for a scapegoat. You can trust the government, or you can trust me."

"I can't do this anymore," Haylie stammered with a shake of her head. "I need to go home. You can come home, too."

Suddenly, Haylie's nostrils filled with the smell of burning wood mixed with charred plastic. She saw smoke pouring through the open hallway door.

"There's no way that this works out for me," Caesar said. "We just saw the leaders of the free world try to seize complete power. And you don't think they'll come after us for what we know?"

"You need to trust them. You need to do the right thing," Haylie pleaded. "You've changed."

"We all change," Caesar said as he threw his bag over his shoulder, smiling. "You've changed, too. Change is good."

He walked over to her and gave her a hug. "I'll be in touch. I'll be fine. Don't worry about me. Watch out for yourself."

Haylie's eyes welled with tears as she hugged her brother, hoping to God that it wouldn't be for the last time. "Stay safe," she said.

"I will," Caesar said, looking up to the smoke hanging down from the ceiling. "Crowne must be burning all the evidence. Let's get you out of here."

They sprinted down the hallway and came to a T-intersection. Looking behind her, Haylie saw the growing orange glow of a wall of flames mixed with black smoke rolling in behind them.

"The courtyard is that way," Caesar said, pointing to the right and coughing, choking on smoke. "Just a few turns and you'll be there."

Giving Caesar one last hug, Haylie nodded, straightened her jacket and stood back. She gave him a quick wave, turned and ran.

She twisted down the hallways, fighting to bring her mind back from her brother's words and onto the task at hand. She worked her way into the smoke, feeling through the darkness with each step and searching for corners.

Finally, she saw two glowing, illuminated squares of the exterior door windows. She sprinted, pushing at the doors with both hands, running into the cool, fresh evening air and out of the mansion. Two figures stood at the middle of the courtyard, facing the fire and watching her approach.

She slid in next to them, taking in the scene. All three floors of the mansion, wrapped around them, fire spitting out of each window. Beams falling and smoke seeping out of every corner it could find.

"Not exactly how I thought this would all turn out," Benjamin said. She looked back at the brothers, their faces both smeared with black, their hair full of the falling ash that drifted down on the courtyard like snowflakes.

"Haylie," Walter added, leaning in towards her ear. "We should talk about what we're going to tell the police; get our story straight. I mean, you don't think we're like Crowne, right? We know that what we did was...."

"Shut up, Walter," she said staring into the fire. "Just shut up."

A pair of helicopters appeared over the mansion, blowing smoke and cinders into swirls and dust devils across the courtyard. Two spotlights shot down from above, lighting up Haylie as she stood and watched the mansion burn.

CHAPTER FORTY F1V3

The University of Texas
Austin, TX
September 30th, 1:32PM

"Wait up, dummy!"

Haylie turned as the familiar, British accent rang down the crowded hallway. She saw Vector pushing his way past the mob of students headed in the opposite direction.

"You look like one of those salmon swimming up stream," Haylie said. "We walk on the other side of the hall over here."

Huffing, but still managing a smile, Vector finally caught up to her. "Old habits die hard." He pulled out his phone, doing a quick check of email.

Reflexively reaching into her pocket for her device, and feeling an empty space where the phone was supposed to be, Haylie paused and shook her head.

You're right about that.

Haylie was still getting accustomed to each of the wonderful terms of her surrender that she had agreed to six months ago. Interpol and the FBI had shown her a good amount of mercy, mostly thanks to her help in taking down The Project.

Prime Minister John Crowne had taken himself out of the equation back at Titanhurst before the police reached him, but most of the other members of the Bilderberg Group, even with the evidence Haylie had found on Crowne's phone, had escaped prosecution in one way or the other. Some were still on the run, never to be heard from again; others were still in power, somehow implicating their staff or deputies while expressing regret for the situation, but not recognizing any knowledge of The Project. Powerful people tend to stay in power, it seems, and justice was not always a black and white result.

Haylie's deal had been negotiated over the course of a few weeks, with plenty of help from the Sterling brothers' high-priced legal team; she was allowed to remain out of prison, but would be heavily restricted in her access to anything connected to the Internet for the next few years.

She was now allowed to go online for only two reasons: one, as any core part of her computer science studies, and two, for any assistance the U.S. Government asked for with hacking-related research. The second piece of the agreement was one of the big bargaining chips for the government's legal team—they made it clear that they would be asking for Haylie's help frequently, and that she'd better pick up her landline when they called.

The only point of negotiation that Haylie had fought for was standing next to her; the government had agreed to pay for her college expenses, but she insisted that Vector be part of the deal as well. Having him attend school alongside her was non-negotiable, and as foreign as he felt in the middle of Texas, both of them knew that they could use a few calm years of college life after the events back in London. His gunshot wound had healed well and he barely even mentioned it, other than noting the occasional discomfort when his backpack was too heavy with textbooks.

As they made their way down the hall and towards their next class, students stared at them with mouths wide open, grabbing their friends, pointing fingers. Haylie was no longer that girl in your high school class that was quiet and smart and sitting in the back corner; her face had been on display across every newsstand in America over the past few months with headlines like "Crash: The Girl Next Door that Just Saved the World."

The government had gone public on almost every detail of The Project except for one: Caesar. Haylie still hadn't heard from her brother since that night at Titanhurst. He had fallen off the face of the earth, along with the team of eight engineers that went with him and all the code from

The Project. She wondered about where he was and what he was doing every day.

They passed a group of students working their way down the hall and Vector was suddenly nudged in closer to Haylie's side. As he brushed up against her arm, he gently grabbed her hand with his. She slapped it away, shooting him a nasty glance.

"Stop that."

Haylie squinted through the reflection in her glasses as she gazed past the hallway doors and into the warm sunlight pouring in from the quad. As she deflected the attention from the passing sea of students— some posing for quick selfies, others throwing up random high-fives and fist bumps to her or Vector—she felt the heat hit her as they escaped outside, the fresh fall breeze blowing her hair back across her shoulders.

They made their way across campus to their Computer Science 204 class, finding a space in the auditorium directly behind a group of four classmates.

"Hey, you made it," the girl on the left said as she spun to face Haylie with a wide smile. "We're still on for movie night tonight, right?"

The guy sitting next to her turned to face them as well. "We'd better be," he said, "I got a torrent of *WarGames*. It's some old movie that's supposed to be awesome."

"Um, you haven't seen *WarGames*?" Haylie shot back with a grin. "Don't even talk to me, loser."

"Please," the girl said, laughing. "You're the one who didn't know about *Firefly*. It's like, you're lucky to even be talking to me right now."

"Whatevs," Haylie said with a laugh. She looked up to the front of the classroom to find the agenda for the day's lecture projected on the screen. She broke a smile as she read the presentation's title slide.

It read:

```
Coding Beyond the Basics:
Now that you can do anything,
what will you do?
```

KERNS

****

About the Author

Christopher Kerns has spent more than twenty years advising top companies throughout the world on technology strategy. His thoughts and opinions on tech and data have been featured in *The New York Times*, *The Wall Street Journal*, *The Daily Mail*, CNBC, and *USA Today*. This is his first novel. He lives with his family in Austin, TX.

Contact

- Email: chris@chris-kerns.com
- Twitter: @chriskerns
- Facebook: facebook.com/ChristopherKerns.author
- Visit www.chris-kerns.com for more information on the technology and history referenced in Crash Alive. On my site, you can join my *Insiders List* email newsletter to be the first to know about upcoming books and news about Crash Alive and the Haylie Black series.

One Last Thing

Now that you've finished the book, please leave a review on Amazon—it's the best way to support independent authors and spread the word.

Thank you.